Un
Billi

NICOLA MARSH
ALLY BLAKE
TRISH WYLIE

MILLS
BOON

Published in Great Britain 2013
by Mills & Boon, an imprint of Harlequin (UK) Limited,
Eton House, 18-24 Paradise Road, Richmond, Surrey TW9 1SR

UNTAMED BILLIONAIRES © by Harlequin Enterprises II B.V./S.à.r.l 2013

Marriage: For Business or Pleasure?, *Getting Red-Hot with the Rogue* and *One Night with the Rebel Billionaire* were first published in Great Britain by Harlequin (UK) Limited.

Marriage: For Business or Pleasure? © Nicola Marsh 2009
Getting Red-Hot with the Rogue © Ally Blake 2009
One Night with the Rebel Billionaire © Trish Wylie 2009

ISBN: 978 0 263 90574 8
eBook ISBN: 978 1 472 00147 4

05-1213

Harlequin (UK) policy is to use papers that are natural, renewable and recyclable products and made from wood grown in sustainable forests. The logging and manufacturing processes conform to the legal environmental regulations of the country of origin.

Printed and bound in Spain
by Blackprint CPI, Barcelona

MARRIAGE: FOR BUSINESS OR PLEASURE?

BY
NICOLA MARSH

Nicola Marsh has always had a passion for writing and reading. As a youngster, she devoured books when she should have been sleeping and she later kept a diary that could be an epic in itself! These days, when she's not enjoying life with her husband and son in her home city of Melbourne, she's at her computer doing her dream job—creating the romances she loves. Visit Nicola's website at www.nicolamarsh.com for the latest news of her books.

With thanks to Laurie Schnebly, for being a great
teacher and for getting me to ask
my characters *why?*

CHAPTER ONE

THE rented SUV swerved on the dusty, potholed driveway of the Mancini place and Brittany Lloyd bit back a curse.

Her average driving skills had little to do with the state of the road or the unwelcome memories assailing her and everything to do with the naked man bent over a thresher.

Semi-naked, technically, as her gaze riveted to the tantalising expanse of bronze, broad back glistening in the scorching Queensland sun.

The muscles shifted, bunched, slid, as he straightened and thrust hands into back pockets of ripped, faded denim, and as her greedy gaze strayed to his butt she suddenly wished she hadn't stayed away so long.

Ten years in London had been a sane choice, a safe choice considering what she'd been running from, but seeing this hot guy on her first morning home reinforced no place on earth bred guys like Jacaranda.

She should know.

She'd fallen in love with one, had given him her heart, her virginity and her loyalty.

More fool her.

As she righted the car and approached, the guy half turned and this time the SUV sheered straight off the driveway and almost straight into a ditch.

The engine stalled, spluttered, died, as her white-knuckled hands gripped the steering wheel, shock and joy and mind-numbing lust slamming into her, leaving her powerless to do anything but watch *him* approach.

Not a flicker of emotion crossed Nick Mancini's face as he reached the car, leaned tanned, toned forearms on the open window and gave her a casual nod.

'Hey, Britt. Long time no see.'

A casual greeting, without rancour or bitterness; then again, she'd been the one left to pick up the pieces when he'd ended it.

The greeting and his lack of emotion didn't do justice to what they'd shared, what they'd given up and she'd be damned if she showed him anything other than the same lackadaisical nonchalance despite her jack-hammering heart and clammy hands.

'Ten years, give or take.'

She wanted him to acknowledge the time they'd spent apart, wanted him to ask how she'd been, wanted him to finally explain why he'd opted out.

Instead, he shrugged, her gaze drifting to those bunching muscles of their own volition, all too aware of how he'd filled out in the last ten years.

He'd been lean rather than muscular back then and now... She wrenched her gaze away from his impressive pecs and focused on his face.

Nick the teenager had been good-looking, cocky and a rebel.

Nick the man was drop-dead gorgeous in a rough-around-the-edges way, still cocky and, if she read him right, still out to prove to the world he didn't give a damn.

By the smug grin lifting the corners of an all too kissable mouth, she'd read him just right.

'What brings you by?'

'Business.'

Something solid, tangible and guaranteed to keep errant

emotions at bay no matter how much she wanted to ask him 'what the hell happened to us?'

She'd hoped to avoid him, had hoped to do business with his father but she'd been a fool. This place was in Nick's veins, of course he'd be here doing a hard day's work, working longer and tougher and harder than all his employees.

'Business, huh?'

His caramelised-toffee eyes narrowed and she wished he'd stop staring at her as if she had a dirt smudge on her nose. He'd always had the ability to see into her soul and right now that was the last thing she needed.

She needed to stay focused. Her promotion depended on it.

'I've got a proposition for you.'

He straightened, all six feet two of lean, hard muscle, and smiled that bad-boy smile she remembered so well, the smile that had haunted her for months when she'd first arrived in London, pining away for her first love—the same love who had turned down her offer to come with her, to build a life together.

'I just bet you have, Red.'

He opened the car door and she stepped out, wishing she could hide her blush, knowing it would do nothing for her freckles and hating herself for caring so damn much.

'No one's called me that in years,' she muttered, thankful her hair bore more coppery-blonde streaks these days than the fire-engine red she'd grown up with.

'That's a shame.'

He reached out, twisted a stray strand around his finger.

'They obviously don't know you as well as I do.'

She pulled away quickly before she did something stupid, such as stand there and let him twist her around his finger and not just by the hair. 'You don't know me at all.'

Ignoring the glint in his eyes, which seemed a richer, deeper toffee than she remembered, she glanced at her watch, hoping he'd get the hint.

'Is your father here? I need to discuss this with him.'

His eyes clouded, darkened, as pain twisted his mouth. 'Papa died. Guess the news didn't make it all the way to London.'

'I'm sorry,' she said, suddenly ashamed she hadn't kept in touch with news from home.

Not that the thought hadn't crossed her mind on occasion but then, he hadn't been the reason she'd fled Jacaranda.

'Are you really?'

She noticed the angry lines fanning from the corner of his mouth, the indentation between his brows, aging him beyond his twenty-eight years.

He'd never looked at her like this back then. Uh-uh. He might have been a rebel but he'd never been brooding or angry, far from it.

A decade earlier he'd only ever looked at her with adoration and desire, and for a brief moment she wished she could turn back time.

'Of course I'm sorry. Everyone around here loved Papa.'

'You're right.'

Swiping a hand across his face, he erased the tenseness. 'Though I'm surprised your old man didn't say something. You can't ride a Harley in this town without people lining the roads for a parade.'

His gaze flicked over her and she clenched her hands to stop from smoothing her Dolce and Gabbana suit. His eyes glowed with appreciation but she didn't miss the slight compression of his lips, as if her favourite designer suit didn't impress him one bit.

'Despite your fancy new clothes, surely you remember how it is around here?'

He was trying to bait her, just as he always did and, damn him, she wouldn't give him the satisfaction of knowing exactly how much she remembered, most of her memories centred on him.

'I've been busy the last ten years so forgive me if taking a stroll down memory lane hasn't been high on my list of priorities.'

'Busy, huh?'

She expected him to ask about her career, wanted to show him how far she'd come, how far they could've made it as a couple if he'd accompanied her.

Instead, he stood there, a semi-naked god totally at ease with his surroundings, the sheen of sweat and dust adding to his rugged appeal rather than diminishing it.

Clamping down on the mental image to run her hands over that glorious bare chest, she cleared her throat.

'I work twenty-four-seven. Being a senior exec at London's top advertising company takes up most of my time.'

'What, no time for play?'

His teasing smile slammed into her, the familiarity of it making her gasp.

She didn't play, not any more. Her play days had stopped when she'd hightailed it out of this town and never looked back.

Work helped her forget…everything.

Work proved how far she'd come.

Work gave her the hard-fought independence she'd clawed her way to the top for, an independence that guaranteed she'd never have to look back.

Biting back a pithy retort, she ducked into the car and grabbed the Manila folder from the passenger seat.

'What I do in my spare time isn't your concern. I'm here on business.'

'Whatever this business proposition of yours is about, you'll be dealing with me.'

He fixed her with a probing stare, a potent stare that sent a ripple of unease through her.

'And just so you know, I'm nothing like my father. I drive a hard bargain.'

She almost banged her head on the door jamb as his silky

voice slid over her. So much for a quick, clean presentation to Papa Mancini. The thought of doing business with Nick, let alone considering whatever bargain he might demand, had her flustered.

And she never got flustered, not any more. Some of the gang at work called her the Ice Princess behind her back and she liked it. Emotions got her nowhere and she'd learned to control her fiery temper along with the rest of her wayward emotions during the long, hard graft in the big city.

As she handed him the folder their fingertips touched and despite the length of time they'd been apart, her heart jack-knifed. Wretched organ. She shouldn't feel anything where Nick was concerned, especially not this strange déjà vu that had her dreaming of stepping closer and running a palm down his bare chest to see if it felt half as good as she remembered.

She took a steadying breath, ignoring the host of unwelcome feelings this man resurrected.

'There's a lot we need to discuss. Why don't we head inside so you can put on some clothes and we can do business?'

She'd made a fatal error in judgement, knew it the second his lips kicked up into a sexy, familiar grin that never failed to take her breath away.

She shouldn't have mentioned his state of undress, shouldn't have drawn attention to it, and as if of their own volition her eyes drifted south, riveted to that muscular expanse of temptation less than two feet away.

He was so bronze, so broad, so breathtaking and when she finally dragged her gaze away her knees shook.

'You sure you want me to get dressed?'

Damn him, he'd called her on her faux pas. A gentleman would've ignored her slip-up. Then again, since when had Nick been a gentleman?

Jacaranda's answer to James Dean had had girls swooning and fathers reaching for shotguns since he'd hit puberty and she was a fool for expecting anything other than bluntness from the guy who'd once rocked her world.

'Nick, don't.'

She held up a hand, about as effective as a cockatoo trying to ward off a charging emu.

'Don't what?'

He stared at her hand as if he wanted to grab it and she quickly let it drop.

'Don't remember the past? Don't admire the gorgeous woman you've become?'

The heat in his eyes scorched her, captivated her, held her spellbound.

'Or don't do something as crazy as this?'

Before she could blink, he hauled her into his arms and kissed her.

The kisses they'd shared as teenagers had been exploratory, tender and achingly poignant. Yet there was nothing remotely sweet or gentle about his mouth crushing hers now.

Their lips clashed in a frantic, hungry union, a fusion of tongues, a meshing of desire that left her reeling.

She should've been immune to him by now. She should've pushed him away and laughed it off as a quick reacquainting peck between friends for old times' sake.

Should've, should've, should've, as she stood on tiptoes, leaned into him and wrapped her arms around his neck, hanging on as if her life depended on it.

As he softened the kiss, plying her with a skilled precision he'd never had as a young man, her resolve to push him away melted, just as it had ten years earlier when she'd acted on all the bottled-up feelings she'd harboured for him for years.

She'd idolised him all through the endless teenage years and he hadn't glanced in her direction until she'd turned eighteen, thrown herself at him and been wonderfully surprised when the bad boy of Jacaranda had returned her interest.

They'd gone steady for exactly six months before things had come to a head at home and she'd been forced to flee.

She hadn't told Nick about her humiliation, wanting him to need her for who she was, not following her out of some warped sense of pity. So she'd tried to convince him to run away with her. And she'd failed. Not just failed, he'd pushed her away with a callousness that had shattered her heart.

So what the heck was she doing, kissing him like this?

As her common sense belatedly kicked in Nick broke the kiss, untangling her hands from behind his neck and setting them firmly at her side before glaring at her, as if she'd been the one to instigate their clinch in the first place.

'Don't expect me to be sorry for that,' he said, running a hand through his dark wavy hair, sending it in all directions.

'I gave up expecting anything from you a long time ago.'

She shrugged, aiming for nonchalant while her insides churned, and ran a finger along her bottom lip, wondering if it looked as bruised as it felt.

He'd kissed her…and she'd liked it!

So much for the Ice Princess. Looked as if her hard-fought emotion-free veneer had melted the minute he'd lip-locked her.

Nick muttered a curse and turned away from Brittany before he made another blunder and hauled her right back into his arms.

She felt good, better than he remembered and he had a damn good memory when it came to this woman.

She'd been the one for him.

And he'd sent her away.

He'd had no choice, but a day hadn't gone by when he hadn't replayed memories of the red-haired hellion who'd captured his heart without trying.

Here she was, just as incredible as he remembered.

And he was drawn to her as uncontrollably as ever. For the

spell she'd cast over him had never been simply caused by her blue eyes, porcelain skin and waist-length auburn hair that begged a guy to run his fingers through it. Nor did it have anything to do with her lithe body, with enough curves to turn a guy's head.

No, Brittany Lloyd possessed a more elusive charm, something that drew him surer than spicy tomato meatballs.

Class.

Something he'd craved his entire life, something he'd set about gaining the last few years but she'd been born with, and no amount of mixing in the right circles or business success could buy what she had, in spades.

'About this business proposition?' He turned back to face her, surprised by the vulnerability he glimpsed in her eyes. Hell, it was just a damn kiss, no big deal.

'All in there.'

She pointed at the Manila folder in his hands, stared at it as if it were a ticking bomb ready to detonate.

He weighed it in one hand, tapped it against his palm, gauging her reaction.

'Jeez, why don't you just open it?' She exploded, just as she used to in the good old days and he grinned.

'Good to see you've still got that fiery temper beneath all that polish.'

He looked her up and down, admiring the subtle changes to her appearance: the gold streaks in her now shoulder-length hair, the svelte body packed with more curves than a racetrack, the elegant wardrobe. As a teenager she'd been pretty. As a woman, she was stunning.

With a confident toss of that luscious hair, she fixed him with a newly acquired haughty grin.

'Actually, you're the only one who seems to bring it out in me. Now, back to business?'

Curiosity ate at him. To bring her back here, this precious

business deal of hers had to be important. In that case, he wanted to be one hundred per cent appraised of the situation before he started discussing anything with her.

He raised an eyebrow, rattled the folder and gestured at his bare torso. 'I don't do business like this. Where are you staying?'

To his delight, she blushed, her gaze lingering on his chest a few seconds too long. 'The Phant-A-Sea in Noosa.'

Oh, this just got better and better.

'But I don't expect you to drive all that way just to meet me. We can do this here—'

'I was heading into town after I'd finished up here anyway. Why don't I meet you there around five? We can discuss this over drinks.'

'That won't be necessary—'

'But it will.'

He leaned closer, her awareness of him evident in the widening of her pupils, the tip of her tongue darting out to moisten her bottom lip, and his gut clenched with how badly he still wanted her.

Maybe he should tell her the truth now and be done with it.

But then, where was the fun in that?

'Give me some time to clean up, take a look at your proposal and we can discuss it over a Shirley Temple.'

He scored another direct hit with reference to her favourite drink back then, her lips compressing into an unimpressed line.

'This isn't some trip down memory lane. This is business.'

His glance strayed to her lips, lush and pouting, before sweeping back to her eyes, registering the shock of arousal that made a mockery of their *business*.

'So you keep saying. Business. Ri-i-ight.'

To his surprise, she laughed. 'You haven't changed a bit. Still the charmer.'

She was wrong, dead wrong.

He'd changed and, come five o'clock, she'd discover exactly how much.

Propping on the bonnet, he crossed his ankles. 'Is it working?'

'Nope, I'm immune to rebel charmers these days.'

'Pity.'

His glance slid over her, taking in every delicious curve, earning another blush.

'How long are you in town for?'

'For as long as it takes.'

She'd gone cold again. Retreating back into the business at hand…

His glance swept the distant cane fields he loved so much, encompassing the sugar cane that was as much a part of him as his Italian heritage, wondering what she'd make of him once she discovered *his* real business these days.

Would she be impressed? Probably, though in all fairness what he did or where he came from had never been an issue with her.

They'd been friends before lovers in the old days, travelling on the same bus to school every day even though she'd attended the private grammar school and he'd gone to the local high school.

She'd pretended to ignore him at first so he'd done his best to rile her with constant taunts about everything from her shiny shoes to her long red pigtails. And when her fiery temper had sparked her into retaliating by ramming his bike with hers, their friendship had been cemented.

She'd never given a damn about the gaping hole in their social circles: the richest girl in the district hooking up with the Italian working-class farm boy.

But other people had. He'd heard the whispers, the innuendos, about her slumming it with him before she got married to a suitable man.

He'd let it taint what they had, had ended it for good

before things got out of control. But he'd never forgotten how dating her had made him feel. Simply, he'd wanted to be a better man for her.

All ancient history, and as he refocused he knew that impulsive kiss was a stupid move.

He didn't do impulsive any more. Every decision he made was carefully weighed, evaluated and executed with the utmost precision. He wasn't at the top of his game these days for nothing.

Pushing off the car, he tapped the bonnet.

'You better get going. Give me a chance to finish up here and meet you later.'

'Fine.'

He opened the car door for her and watched as she buckled up. Déjà vu hit and an irresistible impulse came over him in spite of all the resolutions he'd just made. He leaned in quickly through the open window.

'Hey, Red?'

'Yeah?'

He grinned and tweaked her nose just as he used to. 'You kiss even better than I remember.'

Before she could respond, he straightened, chuckling at the instant indignation sparking her beautiful eyes as he strode towards the farmhouse.

CHAPTER TWO

BRITTANY pressed her hands to her flushed cheeks as Nick strode away.

The man was a menace.

In less than ten minutes he'd managed to unbalance her, unhinge her and undermine her.

As for that kiss…she thunked her head on the steering wheel, twice, for good measure.

Not only had she stood there and let him do it, she'd responded! Like a woman who hadn't been kissed in a very long time.

Which in all honesty was probably true considering she'd been so focused on the managing director position coming up for grabs she hadn't dated in yonks.

But that didn't excuse her eager response, nor did the total and utter meltdown she'd experienced the second his lips had touched hers.

'Ice Princess my butt,' she muttered, releasing the brake and sending gravel flying before heading back down the drive.

Sneaking a peek in the rear-vision mirror, she wasn't surprised to see Nick staring over his shoulder with a grin as wide as the Sydney Harbour Bridge plastered across his smug face.

She clamped her lips shut on a host of expletives and headed for the main highway.

In a way, she was glad he'd suggested they meet at her hotel to discuss her proposal. She'd be much better prepared to face him again in the cool elegance of the Phant-A-Sea's front bar than inside the cosy farmhouse that held a host of memories.

Wonderful, heartfelt memories of sitting across from him at the handmade wooden dining table, tearing into steaming *ciabatta* hot from the oven, dipping it into olive oil and balsamic vinegar, licking the drips off each other's fingers…

Cuddling up on the worn chintz sofa, watching old black and white Laurel and Hardy movies and laughing themselves silly.

Clearing the family room of its mismatched lounge chairs and scarred coffee table stacked with newspapers and maga-zines so they could dance body to body to their favourite crooning country singer.

The memories were so real, so poignant that her eyes misted over and she blinked, caught up in the magic of the past when she should be focused on the future.

Her future as Managing Director of Sell depended on it.

Come five o'clock, she'd make sure Nick Mancini with his sexy smile and flashing dimples and hot body knew exactly the type of businesswoman he was dealing with.

Brittany sipped at her sugar-cane juice as she glanced around the Phant-A-Sea's bar.

She'd stayed in some gorgeous hotels around the world but this one was something else. From its sandstone-tiled entrance to its pristine whitewashed exterior, from its cascading water-falls to the stunning umbrella-shaped poincianas lush with flamboyant crimson flowers, it beckoned a weary traveller to come in and stay awhile.

As for her beautiful room with its king-size bed and six-hundred-thread-count sheets, double shower, Jacuzzi and locally made lavender toiletries, she could happily stay there for ever.

But this wasn't a pleasure trip, far from it.

She needed to seal this deal with Nick. It would give her confidence an added boost to face the other nemesis this journey: her father.

They hadn't spoken in ten years.

But she was here, he now lived in an exclusive special accommodation for the elderly and, as she wouldn't be back, she needed to put the past to rest, say a proper good-bye this time.

She'd taken up yoga in London, was a convert to karma, and wanted to ensure hers was good rather than being dogged the rest of her life for not doing the right thing when she had the opportunity.

Swirling the lime wedge in her juice around and around, she mulled over her dad's anger, his need to control, his escalating abuse before she'd left.

He'd always been domineering but when she'd turned eighteen he'd gone into overdrive. She'd escaped, hadn't looked back, but there wasn't a day went by when she hadn't wondered how different her life would've been if she'd stuck around.

Would she and Nick have married? Would they have a brood of gorgeous, curly dark-haired, dimpled kids?

Swallowing the lump of regret clogging her throat, she glanced up, and the lump expanded to Ayers Rock proportions.

Farm-boy Nick in faded, torn denim and sweat-glistening chest was hot.

Executive Nick in an ebony pinstriped designer suit, crisp white shirt accentuating his tan and a silk amethyst tie was something else entirely.

She froze as he strode towards her, all long legs and designer outfit and dimpled smile.

'Hope you haven't been waiting long.'

He ducked his head to plant a quick kiss on her cheek and

her senses reeled as she caught the faintest whiff of his familiar woody deodorant mingled with the sweetness of harvested cane.

Memories slammed into her: snuggling in the crook of his arm under *their* jacaranda tree, lying on top of him along the river bank, nuzzling his neck as they made love… She gulped a lungful of air, several, to ease her breathlessness.

His scent was so evocative, so rich in memories she struggled to remember what he'd just asked her.

Casting a curious glance her way, he sat opposite, his knees in close proximity to hers, and she surreptitiously sidled back to avoid accidental contact.

That was all she needed. As if she hadn't made enough of a fool of herself already.

'What do you think of the hotel?'

She managed to unglue her tongue from the roof of her mouth, take a quick sip of her juice before answering. 'It's gorgeous. There was nothing like it ten years ago.'

His proud grin baffled her as much as seeing him in a suit. 'Phant-A-Sea was built five years ago. Business is booming.'

Taking in the subtle lighting, the understated elegance, she nodded.

'I'm not surprised. I've travelled extensively for business the last six years or so, but haven't stayed in anything quite like this before.'

The mention of business cleared the sensual fog that had enveloped her the moment he'd strutted into the bar, and she glanced at his empty hands.

'Where's my proposal? Did you take a look at it?'

He shook his head, gestured to a waiter who scurried over as if the prime minister had beckoned.

'I prefer to hear this pitch from you first, then go over the details later.'

'Is that why you're in a suit?' she blurted, wishing she

hadn't asked when his gaze raked over her own change of clothes. The dove-grey skirt suit was another favourite, never failed to give her a confidence boost and with Nick's steamy stare sliding over her she needed every ounce of confidence she could get.

Before he could respond, the waiter said, 'The usual, Mr Mancini?'

'Yes, thanks, Kyoshi.'

Confused, she flicked her gaze between the two. Nick hadn't as much as glanced at the waiter's name tag, and along with 'the usual' it was obvious he frequented this place.

Strange, considering thriving, cosmopolitan Noosa was a good ninety-minute drive from the plantation and she hadn't pegged Nick for the bar-hopping type.

Then again, she'd been away a decade, people changed, so what did she know?

'You like?'

He glanced down at his suit, leaving her no option but to do the same, and she gulped at the way his chest filled out the shirt, how the fine material of the suit jacket hugged his shoulders.

'I've never seen you in one.'

His eyes glittered with a satisfaction she didn't understand as he pinned her with a stare that had her squirming.

'Times change.'

She gripped her glass so tight she wouldn't have been at all surprised if it cracked and she forced her hand to relax and place it on the table by her elbow.

'They do. So let's get down to business.'

Leaning back, he placed an outstretched arm on the back of his chair, the simple action pulling his shirt taut across the muscular chest she'd seen in all its glory earlier that day and she instantly wished for a drink refill to cool her down.

'I have to say I'm intrigued. This business must be pretty

damn special to drag you back here from the bright lights of London.'

Special? How could she begin to explain to him what this promotion meant? The long hours she'd put in over the years? The overnight jaunts to godforsaken places, going the extra yards to secure information, ensuring her pitches were bigger and better than everyone else's? The endless drive to prove her independence in every way that counted?

Nick wouldn't get it.

Papa Mancini had doted on him, not having a mum had bonded them like nothing else. Wish she could've said the same for her 'family'.

'I'll give you the short version.'

She leaned forward, clasped her hands in her lap and prepared to give the pitch of her life.

Securing the use of the Mancini plantation was paramount to her plans and would assure her that promotion. The current MD had virtually said so. Then why the nagging doubt convincing Nick wouldn't be as easy as she'd hoped?

'I work for Sell, London's biggest advertising company. We're doing a worldwide campaign for the sugar industry, driven by the mega-wealthy plantation owners in the States.'

A flicker of interest lit his eyes and she continued. 'I'll be honest with you, Nick. There's a big promotion in this for me, a huge one. If I nail this, I'm the new managing director.'

His eyebrows shot up. 'That's some title.'

Picking up the boutique beer the waiter had discreetly placed on the table in front of him, he took a healthy slug.

'So where do I fit into all this?'

She'd got this far. Taking a deep breath, she went for broke.

'Your place is the oldest sugar-cane plantation in Australia. If I could have exclusive access to it, shoot footage, use some of the history, I'm pretty sure the promotion is mine. That's it in a nutshell.'

She didn't like his silence, his controlled posture. She'd expected some kind of reaction, not this tense quiet that left her on edge and wondering what was going on behind those deep dark eyes.

'I've set out facts and figures in the written proposal. How much the company's willing to pay to use the farm, how many hours it will involve, that kind of thing.'

Her voice had taken on a fake, bubbly edge, as if she was trying too hard, and she eventually fell silent, waiting for him to say something.

When he didn't, she blurted, 'Well, what do you think?'

Something shifted in his eyes, a shrewdness she'd never seen before.

'All sounds very feasible.'

Elation swept through her, quickly tempered when he leaned forward and shook his head.

'There's just one problem. I'm about to sell the farm.'

'Sell it? But where will you live? Where will you work?'

His condescending grin sent a chill of foreboding through her.

'You still see me as some hick bumpkin farm boy, don't you?'

She fought a rising blush and lost. 'Of course not. I just meant that place has been in your family for generations. I don't get why you'd sell now.'

He gestured all around him. 'Because my place is here now.'

Confusion creased her brow as she followed his hand. His designer suit, his patronising smile, his cryptic comments, made her feel as if she was left out of some in-joke and the punchline was on her.

'You belong here?'

She shook her head, knowing if there was one place a guy like Nick belonged, it wasn't in this ultra-elegant hotel.

He'd always loved the farm, had been proud of his family's heritage, so what had changed? The Nick she'd known and loved thrived under the harsh Queensland sun, harvesting billets of sugar cane, getting his hands dirty with the machinery he'd loved tinkering with, riding down the highway on his beat-up Harley with the wind in his hair and the devil at his back.

He frowned, his shoulders rigid as he sat back. 'You find that so hard to believe?'

'It's just not you.'

'It is now,' he snapped, his control slipping as anger flashed like fire from those dark eyes she'd lost herself in too many times to count.

'Just because we had a teenage fling, don't presume you know me.'

That hurt, more than she could've thought possible after all this time.

'It was more than that and you know it.'

Understanding warred with passion before he blinked, obliterating the slightest sign he acknowledged what she'd said as true.

'Irrelevant to our business now.'

He glanced at his watch and stood up. 'Sorry, I have to cut this meeting short. I've got an interview scheduled.'

'You want to work here?'

He shrugged, the corners of his mouth twitching.

'I already do.'

'What?'

Thankfully, some of her old Ice Princess skills kicked in and prevented her jaw from hitting the floor.

'Though technically, that's not entirely right.'

Scanning his face, looking for a clue to what this was all about, she came up lacking.

'I don't understand.'

As he nodded to someone over her shoulder and held up a finger to indicate a minute he leaned down, his breath fanning her ear and sending ripples of heat through her. 'I don't just work here, I own the place.'

This time, as he strode away, she was sure her jaw did hit the floor.

Nick stared out of his office window on the fifth floor of the Phant-A-Sea, blind to the exquisite view of Noosa beach stretching into national park to the far right.

He'd loved this view when he'd first built the hotel, experienced a sense of immense satisfaction every time he'd sat behind this desk and stared out of the window.

Not today.

Today, whether his eyes were open or shut, all he could see was Britt's brilliant blue eyes wide with shock as he dropped his bombshell.

He'd expected to feel powerful, proud, even smug, when he told her the truth. So why the let-down, as if he should've come clean from the start?

What kind of game was he playing anyway? He didn't have time for them, not these days. On the verge of opening the fifth Phant-A-Sea hotel on Pink Sand Beach in the Bahamas and trying to build clientele here, he didn't have enough hours in the day.

That was why he was selling the farm. At least, that was his excuse and he was sticking to it.

He loved that place, had loved it from the first time Papa handed him a piece of sugar cane to gnaw on as a toddler, and it was as much a part of him as his love of the sea.

But that was part of the problem.

No one around these parts took him seriously as long as he was still connected to it, as long as every time they saw him they saw the rebel farm boy he used to be.

While the Phant-A-Sea was doing big business, he wanted

to expand, diversify, take his business to the next level and to
do so he needed investors.

If he didn't have the respect and backing of local investors
because of his heritage, what hope did he have with the
overseas moneymen?

Throw in the constant rumours about his reputation, label-
ling him as some Casanova playboy who couldn't possibly be
serious about business while playing the field, and he was
facing an uphill battle.

Not that it daunted him. He'd fought his way to where he
was today, had earned an MBA at night while slogging on the
farm trying to make a go of it during the days, had worked
damn hard to ensure a thriving cane plantation and the biggest,
brightest hotel Noosa had seen in years.

He'd fight now too, would show the investors he wasn't
some cocky upstart who'd lucked into the hotel business.

Yet the fact he had to part with a piece of his history, a piece
of his soul, to prove himself cut deep.

There had to be something else he could do…

Suddenly, he sat bolt upright, a ludicrous, crazy, just plain
loco idea shimmering at the edge of his consciousness.

He shoved it away, ignored it.

It didn't bear thinking about, wasn't worth entertaining for
one second.

Yet the more he tried to condemn the idea, the harder it
came, gnawing at him, demanding to be recognised as a valid
solution to his problem.

Slamming his silver ballpoint onto the desk, he pushed away
and strode to the window, planting his palms on the sill and
dropping his head forward until it hit the glass with a dull thud.

Questo è pazzia.

Papa had used the phrase often and it now echoed in his
head, 'this is crazy, this is crazy', making him feel the same
way when he'd been caught sneaking a smoke at ten, stealing

a kiss from a worker's wife at twelve and losing his virginity to a farmhand's sister at fourteen.

Hell, there'd be no way he'd be contemplating something as crazy as this if Papa were alive. The old man had been his conscience in more ways than one.

But Papa wasn't around any more and he owed it to him, to himself, to make the Mancini name one to be reckoned with, to bring recognition for a lifetime's hard work.

Contraccambio. Quid pro quo.

Britt wanted something from him, he wanted something in return.

But would she go for his proposal?

A simple business proposition, something she understood only too well if she'd travelled all this way for the sake of a promotion.

Yet what he had in mind was so…so…

Brilliant.

The businessman in him couldn't fault his proposition, whereas the carefree guy who'd fallen for a red-headed vixen the second he'd first laid eyes on her all those years ago knew that executing his plan wouldn't be simple at all.

CHAPTER THREE

BRITTANY gritted her teeth and rapped at Nick's door.

She'd been summoned.

Of all the nerve…if her promotion weren't so important she would've told him exactly where he could shove his summons.

But the promotion was all that mattered, why she was here, determined to keep a smile on her face and a lid on her curiosity no matter how much she wanted to know how Nick the bad boy had become Nick the billionaire.

The way he'd toyed with her, had dropped the information he was now a hotelier, rankled too, as if it had been one big game to him.

Well, screw him. And his four world-class hotels.

At least she'd come to this meeting prepared. After he'd dropped his little bombshell in the hotel bar she'd hightailed it back to her room and done a quick Internet search on the Phant-A-Sea chain.

What she'd discovered had blown her away.

Nick's hotels were luxury all the way, five-star elegance and beyond. Their breathtaking bedrooms were a signature feature, but all the reviews out there agreed that these classy hotels delivered on their promise—they were a fantasy experience all the way.

She'd been intrigued by the mention of a Caesar room, a

Casino Royale room and a Cinderella room, wishing there were pictures to go with the tempting descriptions.

Then again, if she played her cards right, maybe she'd get a first hand look at some of the rooms?

The thought of stepping inside the Jungle Safari room with Nick acting as tour guide brought a scorching blush to her cheeks and she pressed her hands against them, desperately trying to cool them before he opened the door and caught her on the back foot again.

The door swung open and she immediately squared her shoulders, ready for battle.

She'd left home at eighteen, travelled to the other side of the world, lived in a strange city and made a success of her life without using a penny of her father's money.

Making this deal happen with Nick should be a walk in Hyde Park, regardless of the games he seemed determined to play.

'Right on time.'

He stepped aside and gestured her into the room, a huge suite converted into an office, complete with monstrous mahogany desk, leather director's chair and a matching black leather lounge suite designed to make whoever set foot in the giant room at home.

She ignored the comfy-looking sofa and settled for the solitary chair opposite his desk, her back ramrod straight. She wasn't here to get cosy and comfortable, she was here to seal this deal.

Clasping her hands in her lap, she fixed him with a businesslike stare.

'Let's get down to it, shall we? You know what I want. You've had time to study the figures in my presentation. What's your answer?'

To her chagrin he grinned, a wide, self-assured grin of a fat cat toying with a baby mouse.

'It's killing you, isn't it?'

In an instant she knew what he was referring to. He used to tease her about being a nosy busybody all the time, so he'd know how much his bombshell was burning her up with curiosity.

As if she'd give him the satisfaction of knowing it.

Keeping her expression carefully blank, she shrugged. 'You're not the only one who's changed. What you've done in the last ten years, why you chose not to tell me the truth out at the farm, that's your business.'

She leaned forward, tapped her presentation folder sitting in prime position in the middle of his desk.

'And this is mine, so let's cut to the chase. Are you willing to make this deal or not?'

'That depends on you.'

He sat, leaned back and clasped his hands behind his head, stretching the fine cotton of his business shirt tight against his chest, drawing her attention, tempting her to stare, to linger, to envision what he looked like without it.

Not that she had to try too hard. She'd had an up close and personal look earlier that day and a glimpse of that entire bronze, hard chest was burned into her memory bank no matter how many times she hit the mental delete button.

She shook her head to clear it. 'Of course I want this deal to happen. It's why I'm here.'

The only reason I'm here, hung unsaid between them as she matched his steady stare, not blinking, not moving a muscle.

To her surprise he broke the deadlock first by reaching for the folder and pushing it towards her with one finger.

'I'm not interested in your money.'

That got her attention.

'Pardon?'

He tapped the folder. 'What your company's offering in here, the remuneration for use of the farm. I'm not interested.'

Her hopes sank faster than her first attempt at rowing on the

Thames as she struggled to come up with a new twist on her pitch, something, anything, to convince him to agree to this deal.

'But I do have something else in mind.'

She didn't like the hint of subterfuge in his smoother-than-caramel tone, the gleam of devilry in his toffee eyes.

'Like what?'

He pushed away from the desk, came around and squatted down next to her, way too close, way too overpowering, way too much.

'I'll agree to your precious deal if you agree to mine.'

His silky smooth tone sent a shiver of dread creeping across the nape of her neck, for she had no doubt whatever demands he made she'd be forced to agree.

Hanging onto her cool by a thread, she tossed her hair over her right shoulder and fixed him with her best intimidating glare.

'Go on, then. State your terms.'

Placing a finger under her chin, he tipped it up, his slight touch sending unexpected heat spiralling through her and slashing a serious hole in her concentration.

'It's quite simple. I hold onto the farm for now, give you complete access for however long you need it, on one condition.'

She leaned forward, drawn towards him against her will, his finger less of a guide than her own stupid attraction when it came to this man.

'Spit it out.'

With his lips a hair's breadth from hers, he murmured, 'You become my wife.'

With their lips so close, so tantalisingly close, and the ever-present heat shimmering between them like an invisible thread binding them despite time apart, it took a few seconds for his words to penetrate.

When they did, she jerked back, shock rendering her speechless.

Her mouth opened, closed, as her mind spun with confusion. She could've sworn he'd just proposed…

'You heard me.'

He straightened, and while half of her wanted to clobber him for the ludicrous statement he'd just made, the other half irrationally missed his proximity.

He perched on the desk, towering over her.

'Marry me. That's my condition.'

'Are you out of your mind?'

She leaped to her feet, stood toe to toe with him. 'What sort of stupid condition is that? Like I'd ever marry you, like I'd agree to—'

'The idea didn't seem so distasteful ten years ago. As I recall, you used to love talking about marrying me.'

Heat flooded her cheeks and she clenched her hands to stop from reaching out and strangling him.

'Come off it, I was young and stupid then.'

'So you're old and wise now?'

His mouth twitched and the itch to strangle him intensified tenfold.

'In that case, you'll see how much sense this makes.'

'None of this makes sense!'

Her temper, which she'd learned to control over the years, exploded like a tinder-dry bush touched by a match. 'You're insane! You've been playing some warped game ever since I saw you this morning and I have no idea why. You pretend you're still working on the farm, you hide your new job from me, then you come out with this ridiculous proposal.'

She paused, dragged in several breaths and released her hands before her nails sliced into her palms.

'I came to you in good faith, to try and put a simple deal forward, and what do I get in return? A bunch of patooey!'

'Patooey?'

This time, his mouth creased into a wide grin and she almost committed murder on the spot.

'Is that London speak for bullsh—'

'It sure is and you're full of it.'

Hands on hips, she leaned into him, shoving her face in his. 'When did you become such a jerk, Mancini?'

While Nick's smile didn't slip, his cool composure cracked a little. The woman he once loved thought he was a jerk and while it shouldn't matter, it did.

But he wouldn't dwell on that. The old Britt was still there, under the fancy business suit and blonde-streaked hair; she'd just shown him with that magnificent temper bursting like a tropical thunderstorm.

The old Britt wouldn't agree to his proposal, while the career-focused woman in sky-high stilettos and a designer suit would if he presented it the right way.

'Consider this a business transaction, a win-win situation for us both. Nothing more, nothing less.'

He saw a flicker of interest flash across her face at his mention of business before her temper flared again.

'You're crazy! Stark raving mad!'

She raked her hands through her immaculately blow-dried hair, sending it into the frizz he remembered. 'What's that expression Papa used to say? *Sei pazzo*, you're crazy, that's what you are.'

His heart griped as it always did at the mention of his father.

'You remember that?'

All the fight drained out of her and she slumped back into the chair, deliciously defeated, and he yearned to sweep her into his arms and show her this deal was the perfect solution for them both.

Raising wide blue eyes to stare at him in capitulation, she nodded.

'I remember a lot of things.'

He waited, captured by the deepening blue, by the emotions shifting like jacaranda blossoms floating on a spring breeze.

He didn't want to feel, certainly didn't want to feel like this, damn it, but when she looked at him with remembrance clouding her eyes and a softening around her lush mouth all he could think about was how incredible she used to feel in his arms.

He didn't want to rehash the past, to taint this deal with emotion, but he couldn't resist asking, 'What do you remember?'

Her tongue darted out to moisten her bottom lip, a simple, unaffected gesture that shot straight to his groin, nothing unaffected about his visceral reaction.

'Like how we used to lie under that jacaranda tree down by the creek and stare up at the clouds and see who could make the craziest shape.'

Her mouth softened some more and he stiffened, shocked by how much he wanted to ravage those lips.

'Like the times you took me into Noosa on the back of your Harley and how we'd choose to picnic down in Noosaville rather than mix with the hobknobs on Hasting Street.'

She gave up moistening her bottom lip in favour of worrying it and he clamped down on a groan.

'Like how you'd look at me with stars in your eyes, as if I was the only woman for you.'

She didn't glance away as he expected her to, didn't push him away when he swept her into his arms and crushed his mouth on hers.

She tasted of lime and sugar, tart and sweet, and he knew she'd been guzzling sugar-cane juice as she used to. She'd been addicted to the stuff back then, just as he'd been addicted to her.

He could never get enough of her and it looked as if nothing had changed as his tongue swept into her mouth, taunting, challenging, savouring her passionate response as she clung to him, her fingers tangling in his buttons as he pulled her flush against him.

This deal was supposed to be purely business but as their kiss deepened to the point of no return he knew he was kidding himself.

What he felt around Britt, how his blood fired when she was in his arms, had nothing to do with business and everything to do with earth-shattering pleasure.

The moment Nick eased off the pressure to kiss his way across her cheek, Brittany froze.

This was where taking a trip down memory lane got her: in the arms of the devil himself.

He'd proposed the most ludicrous deal she'd ever heard in her life and what had she done?

Let him kiss her. Again.

Had responded to him. Again.

She didn't get this, any of it. Business was business but what he'd proposed was…was…well, it was just plain nuts.

Marriage to Nick Mancini in exchange for her dream?

She couldn't entertain the thought for a second, let alone acknowledge the tiny voice that reminded her she'd do anything to achieve her goal.

Well, marriage to Nick didn't fall into the category of anything. It fell into the category of certifiable lunacy.

He set her away from him, his glib smile at odds with the surprising tenderness in his eyes.

'Well, I guess that proves being my wife wouldn't be all bad.'

She summoned her temper, needing it to anchor her threadbare control, that wavered the moment he mentioned the physical benefits to a possible marriage.

'If you think I'd ever agree to your proposal, you're mad.'

He shrugged, stepped away.

'Hey, I'm not the one who wants a promotion. Ball's in your court, Red.'

She hated hearing the nickname only he had ever called her trip from his tongue with familiarity. She hated the blunt truth of his casual statement even more.

She did need this promotion. It was the only way to get closure on a past she'd rather forget.

Studying him through narrowed eyes, she said, 'Not that I'd contemplate your crazy scheme for one second, but if I did, what's in it for you?'

Something furtive, mysterious, shifted behind his steady stare before he blinked, eradicating the enigmatic emotion in an instant.

'It's time I married.'

'Why?'

Why now? Why me? was what she really wanted to ask, but she clamped down on the urge to blurt her questions.

Why he was doing this? Why would he suggest something so outlandish when they shared nothing these days but a residual attraction based on old times' sake?

He shrugged and she hated his nonchalance in the face of something so important. She would've given everything she owned to be married to him once and now he'd reduced it to a cold, calculating business proposition that hurt way more than it should.

'I'm expanding the business, building more hotels in key cities around the world, but overseas investors won't take me seriously because of my age. They see a young, wealthy single guy and immediately think I'm a playboy dabbling in business for fun.'

He rolled his shoulders, tilted his head from side to side to stretch his neck and she stifled the urge to massage it as she used to. He'd always had tense muscles after a hard day's farm work, had relaxed under her soothing hands.

Her palms tingled with the urge to reach out, stroke his

tension away. So she balled her hands into fists and swallowed the unexpected lump in her throat. Damn memories.

He rubbed the back of his neck absent-mindedly, oblivious to her irrational craving to do the same. 'Marriage will give me respectability in their eyes, solidify my entry into wider business circles and open up a whole new investment pool.'

She stared at him, so cool, so confident, admiring the powerful businessman he'd become, lamenting the loss of the bad boy who hadn't given a toss what people thought of him.

'That's it?'

He nodded, showed her his hands palm up as if he wasn't hiding anything.

'That's it.'

'Why me?'

It had been bugging her since he'd first laid out his outlandish proposal, why a guy like him with charm to burn would choose her for his crazy scheme. 'Surely the legendary Nick Mancini would have a bevy of babes around here eager to tie you down?'

His eyes glittered as she inwardly cursed her choice of words and rushed on. 'I mean, why me in particular? What have I got to offer?'

'Do you really want me to answer that?'

Her breath hitched at the clear intent in his loaded stare and she took a step back. 'Yes.'

To her relief, he shrugged, the heat fading from his eyes. 'You're a motivated businesswoman. You wouldn't have flown halfway around the world to make your pitch the best if you weren't. And I need that. Someone with a clear vision in mind, a business goal.'

He pinned her with a firm glare. 'Someone who won't cloud the issue with emotion, which is exactly what would happen if I chose a local wife.'

His hand wavered between them. 'This marriage between

us is a straightforward business proposal, a win-win for us both. What do you think?'

She thought he was mad, but most of all she thought she was a fool for wishing his preposterous proposal held even the slightest hint of emotion she still meant something to him other than as a means to gaining *respectability*.

Summoning what was left of her dignity, she nodded. 'I'll get back to you.'

'You do that.'

His confident grin grated. He knew she was buying time to contemplate his marital equivalent of a pie chart.

With her mind spinning, she stalked across the room, head held high, his soft, taunting chuckles following her out of the door.

CHAPTER FOUR

'So, THE prodigal daughter returns.'

From the moment Brittany knew she'd be returning home she'd been bracing for this confrontation.

However, no matter that she told herself it was ridiculous, no amount of deep breathing, or steeling her nerves, or trying to remember how far in the past it all was could calm her in any way as she faced her father for the first time in ten years. She could feel her hands shaking.

She paused at the entrance to his apartment, one of the few in the exclusive Jacaranda special accommodation home for the elderly.

Not that Darby Lloyd would ever admit to his seventy-two years. He'd had work done on his face several times, had hair plugs to arrest a threatening bald patch and continued to wear designer clothes better suited to a man half his age.

But pots of money or cosmetic work or fancy clothes couldn't buy health and that was one thing he didn't have these days.

Five years ago, he'd tried to guilt her into quitting her job and returning to look after him as he grew older and more bitter. He'd nearly succeeded. However, some deep part of her had resisted his pressure. He had been a cruel tyrant who'd controlled her life until she'd come into a small inheritance from her mum when she'd turned eighteen and fled as far from him as she could get. She simply couldn't go back to the hell she'd left behind.

In her heart, she desperately wanted to be anywhere but in front of the man who would have ruined her life if she'd let him, but her pride wouldn't let her pay a visit to her hometown and not see him. She was older and stronger—surely she could stand to face him now? She had come here today to prove to herself she'd finally set the past to rest. Working harder, longer, than everyone else might keep the memory demons at bay, but she knew if she stopped, slowed down her frenetic pace, the old fears could come crowding back to fling her right back to the dim, dark place ten years earlier.

And she'd be damned if she let that happen. In a way, she should thank dear old Dad for shaping her into the woman she was today: strong, capable and successful, everything he'd said she'd never be.

But there was more to this visit and she knew it, no matter all her self talk to the contrary.

She was here because of hope.

Hope that he might have changed. Hope that after all this time they might actually have a shot at some semblance of a normal father-daughter relationship.

And if not? Well, she was different now: a woman on top of her career, a woman who depended on no one, a woman a far cry from the victim she'd once been.

She'd vowed back then never to be helpless again, had instigated huge steps to eradicate the confusion and fear, yet as she stood on the threshold to this room trepidation tripped across her skin as the anxiety she'd fought to conquer over the last decade clawed at her belly.

'How are you, Dad?'

'Much the same.'

He limped towards her, waving his cane at a seat for her.
'No thanks to you.'

Taking several deep breaths, she perched on the edge of the
chair, willing the dread to subside, hating the vulnerability
being this close to him elicited.

She needed to do this, needed to see if there was the slightest chance for them before she returned to London.

'You look good.'

He grunted in response, wouldn't meet her gaze, his surly
expression putting a serious dent in her hopes for some kind
of reconciliation.

'This place is lovely.'

Another monosyllabic grunt as his frown deepened and her
patience wore a little thinner.

'Dad, I really think it's time to—'

'What the hell are you doing here?'

His snarl caught her off guard despite his churlishness, yet
it wasn't his response that saddened her as much as the
contempt in his truculent glare.

She'd been a fool to hope for anything other than what she
got: more of the same from a boorish man who didn't give a
hoot about her.

'I'm here on business.'

He showed no interest, seemed bored more than anything
else. Faced with his silence she could not help asking him:

'Don't you want to know how I am? What I've been doing?
What I've achieved?'

His withering stare clued her into his response before he
spoke.

'I don't give a damn any more.'

Pain sliced her heart in two, the old familiar questions reverberating through her head: *What did I do wrong? Why did
you stop loving me? Could I have done anything differently?*

But she wasn't the same scared teenager any more.

She had her career skyrocketing all the way to the top and she'd be damned if she sat here and took any of his crap.

Resisting the urge to jab her finger at him to ram home her point, she sat back, folded her arms and looked him straight in the eye.

'Maybe you should give a damn. That way, you'd know I'm a senior executive at a top London ad firm, that I'm good at what I do and I've done it all on my own, no thanks to you.'

She'd come here with some semblance of the idealistic girl she'd once been, but that girl vanished beneath his lack of caring and she wanted to rub his nose in her independence, in her success, in the proof she'd survived despite what he'd put her through.

If she'd thought her outburst would gain a reaction, gain recognition for her achievements, she should've known better.

He glowered, drew himself up, resembling the towering giant of a man she remembered as he rammed his cane against the floor.

'You're a fool if you think I care about any of that.'

Her heart ached as she stared at the man who was her father biologically but didn't know the meaning of the word.

She could rant and rave and fling past hurts or present triumphs in his face but what would be the point? Darby listened to no one but himself, which was why he now found himself in this place. No amount of money on offer had induced anyone locally to play nursemaid and she couldn't blame them.

Slinging her bag higher on her shoulder, she kept her face devoid of pity for the father she'd never had.

'Sorry you feel that way. I thought…'

What? That the old despot might've changed, might've mellowed with time and illness? Not likely. If anything, his belligerence had worsened and she'd been crazy to come here, setting the past to rest while hoping for a miracle.

'Thought what? I'd welcome you with open arms after all this time?'

He snorted, waved his good hand towards the door. 'Just leave the way you came in.'

She'd cried rivers of wasted tears when she was a teenager for all this man had put her through and there was no way she'd stand here now and allow him to reduce her to tears again.

With a shake of her head, she turned away, ready to walk out and never look back.

'That's it, run away again. Though this time, you won't have a penny of mine to cushion you when you fall.'

Icy foreboding trickled down her spine as she slowly swung back to face him.

'What did you just say?'

His malevolent grin raised goose bumps on her skin. 'You heard. That money from your mother? It was a crock. She never left you a cent. That was my money you squandered on your little trip, my money that made sure you didn't end up in the gutter.'

She staggered, leaned against the doorway for support, her gut twisting with the painful truth.

'So, daughter dearest, looks like you owe me after all.'

With his words ringing in her ears, she stumbled from the apartment, from the accommodation and made it to her car before she collapsed, slumping over the steering wheel.

She'd thought she'd escaped his stranglehold ten years earlier, had fought hard for her independence, had found safety and confidence in her career.

She'd been wrong.

Right then, she vowed to do whatever it took to pay off her debt.

You owe me…

With the hateful truth ringing in her ears, her head snapped up as she straightened, knowing what she had to do.

There was only one thing that would clear a debt of that magnitude and, right now, gaining her promotion was a necessity.

In choosing between owing her dad a huge amount of money and agreeing to Nick's outlandish proposal, marrying Nick would be the lesser of two evils.

She'd come.

Nick squinted at Brittany between the spokes of his Harley, trying to read her expression and coming up empty.

She'd left a message for him at the hotel desk requesting a meeting and he had suggested to meet at the farm, hoping that the memories might throw her off balance—make her vulnerable, more easily manipulated. He hadn't anticipated that those very same memories might unsettle him as well, but with Britt standing there, dressed in a short white skirt and pink vest-top, gnawing at her full bottom lip, an action he remembered all too well, attending to his bike was the last thing on his mind.

He waited for her to speak, continued polishing the chrome, an action he found soothing. He rarely got time to lavish on his bike these days and this was the first opportunity he'd had to work on his baby in months.

Even with her forget-me-not eyes clouded with worry, tendrils of hair escaping her ponytail and draping her face in golden copper and that worried action which drew attention to her lush mouth like it always had, she looked incredible, like his greatest fantasy come to life.

Which she was, not that he'd ever told her. He'd had his chance ten years earlier and she'd made it more than clear what she'd thought of his rebuff back then.

'You blow this chance, Mancini, you'll never get another one. This is it, you and me, together. So what will it be?'

His answer had been pretty clear. He'd given her one last kiss, a bruising, harsh kiss to say goodbye to the best thing that could've happened to him, pushed her away and said, 'There is no us, Red. And there never will be.'

She hadn't cried and he'd admired her for it. She hadn't clung or tried to change his mind. She'd sent him a pitying look, shook her long red mane, held her head high and walked out on him, leaving him with an ache in the vicinity of his heart. An ache that had returned tenfold despite all his self talk what they'd shared back then was nothing more than a teenage fling.

Slamming a door on pointless memories, he stood, tucked the polishing cloth in his back pocket and leaned against the bike.

'You made it.'

For a second, he wished he hadn't sounded so flippant as her eyes clouded with wariness.

'Yeah, thanks for agreeing to meet me.'

The hint of vulnerability in her voice, in her expression, stunned him. The Brittany Lloyd he knew would never show weakness in front of anybody, least of all him.

'Let's pull up a seat.' He pointed to the outer perimeter of the machinery shed, where a few old-fashioned plastic garden chairs lay scattered. 'Have you given any more thought to my proposal?'

Stupid question. As if she would've thought of anything else since she'd stormed out of his office yesterday.

She ignored his question and said, 'I want to talk about my father.'

No way.

If there was one topic of conversation off-limits, that was it.

Darby Lloyd was an out and out bastard. He'd controlled everything and everyone in this district, had set out to ruin Papa. Until Nick had given him what he wanted.

Rubbing the back of his neck, he said, 'I don't have much to say on that topic.'

'Not many people do. But I want to know something. Did

he ever approach you about me back when we were dating?
Did he try to interfere?'

His blood chilled. There was no way he'd ever tell her the
truth about her father. Besides, it wasn't as if Darby were the
cause of their break-up. It'd been much easier to blame their
disintegrated relationship on her wanting to escape Jacaranda
for the bright lights of a big city. That way, he could live with
himself and what he'd done.

To help justify their break-up he'd told himself women were
fickle. His aunt had run off to Melbourne with a salesman, his
godmother had absconded with the butcher to Bunbury, his
mum had abandoned her family and Britt had followed suit,
hightailing it to London as soon as she hit eighteen.

Britt might have invited him along for the ride but he'd
known that was due to the teenage fantasy she'd built in her
head, the one where she saw him as some fancy Prince
Charming riding his white horse to save her.

The problem with fantasies was they weren't true and he'd
been forced to burst her bubble before he did something
silly—such as trust her as he'd trusted his mother.

'What did he do? Tell me.'

She clicked her fingers in front of his face and as he looked
into her luminous blue eyes a small part of him wished he'd
indulged her fantasy.

Where would they be today if he had? Happily married
with a brood of ruffians? Sharing confidences and dreams?
Spending every night wrapped in each other's arms, recreat-
ing the magic, the passion, that haunted him to this day? He
could've had one hell of a life.

But he'd made his choices, his sacrifices, and, considering
the successful hotelier he'd become, life wasn't all bad.

'Just thinking of the good old days,' he said, trying to distract
her. He didn't want to talk about her father, not now, not ever.

'Good old days?'

She gaped at him and he clamped down on a grin. 'Which ones? The ones where you tied my plaits to the bus seat, or the ones where you plucked my lunch right out of my hands, or the ones where you threw my pet rock collection into the river?'

He smiled at the memories, remembering how he'd used to tease her mercilessly and how she'd given as good as she'd got. She'd been a little firebrand back then, her red hair a definite symbol of a quick-fire temper. And a symbol of a simmering passion he'd been lucky enough to unleash.

Man, had she pushed his buttons back then and he hoped to God he'd grown out of it, whatever *it* was.

He didn't have time for emotions in this marriage. It was business, pure and simple. He had more important matters to consider, such as building his profile with investors, expanding into new cities and upping profit margins.

'You loved every minute of it. Remember that time I put a toad in your bag?'

She rolled her eyes, a smile twitching at the corners of her glossed lips. 'Oh yeah, I really loved that. Not!'

'How about the garlic I rubbed into your Spandau Ballet T-shirt?'

Her lips twitched more. 'You were a jerk.'

'What about the shed incident?'

'Which one?'

Her lips curved into a small, secretive smile and he clenched his hands into fists and thrust them into his pockets to prevent them reaching for her.

'The time you had me shovelling manure or the time you opened your mouth and poured the verbal variety on me so I'd fall into your arms?'

'Ouch!' He clutched at his heart. 'You haven't changed a bit, Red. That hurt.'

'And you haven't changed a bit either, still shovelling it in

the hope to distract me. Now, can we get back to the topic of
my father?'

She was onto him. Always had been, seeing right through
his tough-guy act, reducing him to a love-struck schmuck
around her.

Correction, lust-struck schmuck.

Big difference there. He'd never loved Brittany. Liked her,
lusted after her but he'd never dared love her.

He didn't do love.

Love equalled loss and loneliness and pain, emotions he
could do without.

Folding his arms, he leaned back in the rickety chair. If he
couldn't deflect her attention, he'd have to give her some
snippet of the truth to placate her before they tackled more important matters, like the question of their impending nuptials.

'You know how much your dad hated any guy who came
near you. Why dredge all this up now?'

She gnawed at her bottom lip, fiddled with the edge of her
short skirt. He'd never seen her this nervous before.

Well, maybe on one other occasion, the night she'd asked
him to go away with her, the night he'd made the final break.

Until yesterday, he'd convinced himself he'd made the
right decision. Women were unpredictable, erratic creatures
who couldn't be depended on. Then Brittany Lloyd walked
back into his life, making him re-evaluate his choice and think
a whole lot of 'what-ifs'.

What if he'd gone away with her?

What if they'd made a life together?

What if they fell in love and lived happily ever after?

Yeah, like happy-ever-afters ever happened in the real world.

'Because I visited him yesterday.' She raised stricken
eyes to his and it took every ounce of will power not to reach
out, bundle her into his arms and comfort her. 'He hasn't
changed a bit.'

He swallowed the bitterness that rose at the thought of Darby Lloyd and his far-reaching tentacles poisoning everything and everyone around him, including this remarkably special woman.

He hadn't blamed her for running away. He'd wondered what took her so long.

Unable to resist, he reached out and took hold of her hand, surprised and more than a little grateful when she let him. 'Want to know what I think?'

She nodded, her eyes wide with pain.

'You've moved on. From what you've told me, you're a successful businesswoman with one hell of a career so don't let the past suck you back in.'

He squeezed her hand, trailed his thumb across the back of it. 'It's not worth it.'

Brittany couldn't meet his gaze; it was far too kind. Far too full of memories.

'Thanks,' she muttered, and made an angry swipe at her eyes, dashing away the tears pooled there. She'd done nothing but make a fool of herself since she'd arrived in Jacaranda: making assumptions about Nick, letting him kiss her, hoping her father had changed. She didn't need to start blubbering like a two-year-old to top it off.

Teasing Nick she could handle. Compassionate Nick, holding her hand and staring at her with unquestionable warmth in his eyes, had the potential to undo her completely.

'Hey, don't cry.'

He leaned over and brushed away the tears that had spilled over and run down her cheeks.

Great. Just her luck she hadn't worn waterproof mascara today.

'Jet lag catching up with me,' she muttered, blinking rapidly only to find a veritable flood seeping out of her eyes.

'Come here, you.'

Before she could protest, Nick hauled her into his arms and cradled her close, smoothing her hair, making small crooning noises. Being enveloped in his strong arms, her face pressed against hard chest wall, surrounded by his familiar scent of sugar and spice and all things nice, should've soothed her.

It didn't. Being held by Nick dammed her tears but it resurrected a host of feelings that had nothing to do with comfort.

Desire seeped through her body as he continued stroking her hair, rendering her powerless to move. She couldn't have pulled away if she wanted to. And, God help her, she didn't want to.

She inhaled deeply, allowing the heady combination of sugar-cane sweetness, metal polish and tropical sunshine to flood her lungs, enjoying the momentary lapse in reason as she wished he could hold her like this for ever.

Sliding her arms around his waist, she allowed her hands the luxury of smoothing across hard muscle, revelling in the heat radiating through his cotton T-shirt.

Closing her eyes, she sighed, knowing there was no place in the world she'd rather be than right here.

London was her life now, the vibrant city a part of her new persona but even with her career shooting into the stratosphere, at times like this, in the warm embrace of an incredible man, it wasn't enough.

She'd tried to forget Nick, had rarely succeeded: wondering what he was doing, who he was doing it with, where they would be if he'd said yes to her all those years ago.

'You okay now?'

He pulled back with such swiftness she almost fell off her chair.

'Yeah, thanks.'

She scanned his face for an indication of what he was thinking, but true to form the Mancini mask had slipped into place, leaving her wondering what was going on behind those enigmatic dark eyes. She'd seen it their last night together ten years ago, the night he'd broken her heart.

'We have other business to discuss.'

Her heart sank.

For those all too brief moments when he'd held her, she'd forgotten the reason she'd requested this meeting. But the thought of her father, as poisonous as a puffer fish, leaped to mind and she knew she had to do this.

It was the only way.

She needed this promotion now more than ever, needed the money to clear a debt she'd never known existed and the sooner that was done, the better. Then she'd finally be free.

'You're right, we do need to talk.'

She twisted a strand of hair around her finger, a habit she'd long conquered, before belatedly releasing it. What was it about this guy that obliterated the last ten years as if they'd never happened and thrust her back to a time she'd rather forget?

'I have an answer to your proposal.'

'And?'

He propped against the bike, looking every bit the bad boy rebel he'd once been: dark, devastating, delicious.

She swallowed, her throat clenching with how much she still wanted him after all this time.

He might've proposed a marriage for business purposes but deep down she knew there wasn't a chance in hell she'd be able to keep her hands off him. And considering he'd kissed her, twice, she had an inkling the feeling was mutual.

So where did that leave them? What would the boundaries of their marriage be? Monogamous? Casual?

He straightened, stepped closer to her.

'Stop over-analysing this. Give me your answer and we'll go from there.'

With her heart pounding and heat from his proximity prickling her skin, she wrenched her gaze from his chest within tantalising touching distance and slowly raised it until wavering blue locked with questioning brown.

Her voice barely above a whisper, she nodded.

'My answer is yes.'

CHAPTER FIVE

NICK snuck in the side entrance of the conference room, not wanting to intrude but driven by curiosity.

Since Britt had agreed to his proposal, she'd morphed into a businesswoman dervish, throwing herself into work at a speed that made him, a confirmed workaholic, seem like a snail.

She'd commandeered the business centre of the hotel, had turned this room into a hive of activity.

In less than a day.

He shook his head, beyond impressed at her work ethic. He'd never seen her like this: focused, determined, driven, issuing orders and delegating to the team she'd assembled in record time.

Watching her in a power suit the colour of ripe plums, her hair twisted in a fancy topknot and her brow creased in concentration while she tapped on a keyboard with one hand and shuffled documents with the other, he understood why she'd said yes to his proposal.

Her job meant everything to her and, while he empathised with her ambition, he couldn't help but wish some of her agreement stemmed from the sexual tension strumming between them.

A surge of heat at the memory of kissing her had him sliding a finger between his neck and suddenly too tight collar.

Their marriage might be motivated by business, but who said they couldn't have a real honeymoon?

Her head snapped up and their gazes locked, as if he'd inadvertently telepathised his thoughts and he grinned, sent her a half-salute, not surprised when she frowned and gestured towards the stack of paperwork in front of her.

She didn't want him here.

His cue to saunter across the room and drop into the vacant chair next to her.

'How's it going?'

Frowning, she barely glanced at him. 'Busy.'

'So I see.'

'Don't you have work of your own to do?'

Leaning back, he linked his fingers and stretched. 'I'm taking a break.'

He smothered an outright laugh as she glared. 'Anything I can do to help?'

'No, all under control.'

Her laptop screen flickered and she swore, making a mockery of her previous statement.

'I've got the latest technology in my office if you need it.'

'I said I was fine,' she snapped, rubbing the bridge of her nose before mustering an apologetic smile. 'Sorry. I'm used to having my team around me in London. It's harder trying to get a cohesive unit together so quickly here.'

'Why the rush?'

He knew she'd see right through his innocuous question, knew she'd understand what he was really asking was 'how long are you sticking around?'

With her gaze firmly fixed on her laptop screen, she said, 'Deadlines. I'm sure you understand.'

Placing a hand on her arm, he leaned across to murmur in her ear. 'How long, Red?'

She stared at his hand as if it were a tiger snake before finally raising her eyes to his.

'I don't know. This pitch is big. Huge. The MD didn't set an exact timeline but he knows I'm a fast worker. As long as I deliver, it's up to me.'

He wanted to push the issue, wanted to discuss how long they'd have to make this marriage as real as it could get, but now wasn't the time or place.

Squeezing her arm, he released her and glanced at his watch. 'I do have an appointment, but we should get together later to discuss our *other business*.'

Her eyes widened as the pen in her right hand started rapping a frenetic rhythm against the Manila folder in front of her.

Amazing how the mention of their pending marriage could change her from uber-cool career-woman to nervous Nelly.

'I'm not sure how long I'll be here. I have loads to do, then I need to head out to the farm—'

'Perfect. We can discuss our plans over dinner.'

She opened her mouth to refuse and he raised an eyebrow, daring her to disagree.

'Not having second thoughts, are you? Because if you are, I might have to expedite the sale of the farm and—'

'Fine, I'll see you there.'

The coolness in her tone belied the angry flush creeping up her neck as he marvelled again at how damn important this promotion must be for her to go through with this.

Marrying for convenience occurred a fair bit in the business world, but never in his wildest dreams had he thought he'd do it, let alone to the only woman he would've ever contemplated walking down the aisle with once upon a time.

'Glad that's settled.'

He stood, looked down at her elaborate hairdo, his fingers itching to tug the pins out and send the whole thing tumbling around her shoulders.

As if sensing his thoughts again, she tilted back on the chair, glared at him. 'Was there anything else, because you're hovering?'

With a smile designed to provoke a response, he ducked down to murmur in her ear. 'I'll cook, but I hope you remember how much I love dessert.'

As the pen picked up tempo again he chuckled, snatched a hairpin and laid it on the stack of paperwork in front of her, before heading for the door.

'I brought dessert.'

Brittany held out the store-bought lemon meringue pie, wishing Nick would take the damn thing before it tumbled from her shaking hands.

This dinner was supposed to set her mind at rest, a pre-wedding get-together to discuss plans and take the edge off her nerves.

So far, it wasn't working.

'Thanks, looks delicious.'

His gaze flicked over her, appreciation lighting his eyes, and she had no doubt he wasn't talking about the pie.

She'd spent an hour deciding what to wear, aiming for casual yet wanting to make him look twice. After five changes she'd finally decided on caramel suede trousers sitting low on her hips and a chocolate rib top that fitted like a second skin. The warm tones highlighted her hair and skin to perfection, or so some stylist had told her at Harrods.

In London, she'd taken her appearance for granted, spending a small fortune on clothes and accessories to fit the image of a top marketing consultant. She dressed to impress, was used to it. That was her excuse for wanting to look her best tonight. Yeah, right.

'What's for dinner?'

She headed for the stove in an attempt to escape Nick's intense stare.

'Antipasto for starters, home-made ravioli filled with asparagus and leeks, smothered in a four-cheese herb sauce for main.'

He picked up a ladle, lifted a pot lid and stirred, the delicious aroma of melted cheese and garlic filling the kitchen and making her mouth water.

'You make your own pasta?'

She raised an eyebrow, beyond impressed. How did the guy find time to run a hotel, do stuff around the farm and be a whiz in the kitchen?

He cocked a hip and shrugged, deliciously smug and modest at the same time.

'What can I say? I'm a regular Neil Perry.'

'Who?'

'Australia's equivalent to Jamie Oliver,' he said, sprinkling fresh chopped parsley into the pot, sending her a cheeky grin that notched up the heat in the kitchen.

Either that or she was taking a lot longer to acclimatise to the Jacaranda humidity than expected.

'I'm impressed. Is there anything you can't do?'

'No, though I guess I'm better at some things than others.'

He winked and turned back to the stove, his attention riveted to the pot bubbling away while an embarrassing blush crept into her cheeks.

Oh, yeah, she remembered exactly how good he was at some things, which was why she grabbed the cutlery off the sideboard, trying to remember the difference between left and right as she struggled to place knives, forks and spoons in their right place.

She'd been insane to agree to his marriage proposal, absolutely stark, raving mad to think she could remain businesslike for the length of their marriage—yet another thing they had to decide tonight. For she was in little doubt this platonic union would have a time limit.

He'd asked as much earlier and she'd had no idea how to respond, didn't want to think beyond this pitch and what she had to do to secure her promotion.

Marriage to Nick, a business deal. And business deals had set time frames, both parties aware of how long the proposed business would take right from the start.

So why the sudden pang in the vicinity of her heart?

Once the table was set, she picked up the pasta bowls and took them to the stove.

'We've got a lot to talk about tonight.'

He held up a hand. 'Not on an empty stomach. Let's eat first.'

'Fine with me.'

But it wasn't fine, none of this was, and while they made polite small talk over his fabulous pasta she couldn't forget the real reason she was here: to set the boundaries of their marriage.

An event she'd dreamed of ten years ago, had planned in her head to the nth degree: strolling towards her incredible groom under the shade of their favourite jacaranda tree down by the river, him in a casual suit with his shirt collar open, the wind ruffling his too-long-to-be-neat hair, her in a flowing ivory silk minidress made for strolling down by the river after she'd married the man of her dreams.

Somehow, the quick, impersonal ceremony in front of a minister they would now go through didn't have the same ring to it.

There went her heart again, squeezing tight, hurting enough to show, no matter how much she pretended this was all business, she knew, deep down, she was selling her soul.

Nick tried not to stare at Brittany, he really did, but it was like trying not to look at the sun glistening on Jacaranda River first thing in the morning or the moon rising over a glittering Noosa at night.

Perfectly natural occurrences where a person's gaze was riveted by beauty, unable to do otherwise and that was exactly how he felt now, taking in her slight frown, pursed lips and thoughtful expression as she tapped a pen against the pad in her hands.

'We're forgetting something,' she said, screwing her eyes up as if trying to see the missing info.

From where he sat, the only thing forgotten was how damn good it felt to be with her like this.

'Want me to take a look?'

'Uh-huh,' she answered absent-mindedly, not looking up from the pad. 'I was sure we'd covered everything but…'

He perched on the couch next to her, grateful for the opportunity to get closer to the woman who was driving him slowly insane with every flutter of her mascaraed eyelashes, with every teasing smile.

Dinner had been a quiet affair and her genuine appreciation for his culinary skills made him feel like a god, yet the underlying tension with every glance, every smile, stretched taut between them.

While she looked amazing tonight, her fancy top and figure-hugging trousers outlining her body to perfection, a body that beckoned him to trace its contours, to feel every gorgeous line, it was more than that.

They'd slipped back into the comfortable camaraderie they used to share and he was thrilled. While he had no illusions about this marriage being anything other than what it was— a convenient business arrangement—it would be so much easier to be friends.

Or more than friends, if he was lucky. He wanted her just as badly now as he ever had, the driving hunger startling and ferocious and capable of sending him bonkers.

'Are you going to help me or just sit there with that goofy look on your face?'

She waved the pen under his nose and he managed a rueful grin. He'd settle for goofy when, the way his thoughts had been heading, she would've been more accurate in describing him as drooling.

'Let me take a look.'

He leaned towards her, a swift stab of longing shooting straight to his groin as a waft of her vanilla perfume hit him.

Vanilla: warm, sweet, tempting.

Exactly how he saw her. The same tantalising scent she'd worn that fateful night ten years ago, the night he'd told her there would never be anything between them.

He just wished he had the same self-control now, but with her inches away, looking like his living, breathing fantasy, a guy could only take so much.

'This list has stuff for you to do and the stuff I can help with.'

She tapped her pen against the paper in a sharp staccato sound, an action fast becoming a nervous habit, and he struggled to focus on her writing, more intrigued by the streaks of blonde through her copper hair and the way they highlighted her beautiful face.

'What's missing?'

'This.'

He tipped her chin up, drinking in her slightly flushed cheeks, her sparkling blue eyes, her glossed lips. Man, she was a stunner, and as a spark of desire flared in her eyes he knew this time he wouldn't be satisfied with a few kisses.

As he moved towards her she stiffened and pulled away.

'We need to concentrate. The sooner we get married, the sooner I can really get started on my work around here and the sooner I get my promotion. Capish?'

She sent him a nervous smile before waving the pad in his

face and, though he'd love nothing better than to see if her desire matched his, he relented.

The mention of her promotion did it. She was doing this for her career, as he was, with no place for emotions to cloud the issue.

Scanning the extensive list she'd made, he pointed to the last few asterisks.

'The licence, the legalities, all taken care of.'

When she quirked an eyebrow, he shrugged. 'Things get done when you have money.'

A shadow passed over her face and he silently cursed his choice of words. If anyone knew the cause and effect of money, she did. Her father threw enough of the green stuff around to buy whatever and whoever he wanted.

He should know.

'So the venue's all taken care of?'

For the first time since she'd arrived tonight, his confidence wavered.

'I thought the hotel garden would be a good spot? Beneath that poinciana tree near the pool?'

It was a perfect spot for a wedding, or so he'd been told by many guests: the towering umbrella-shaped tree laden with bright red flowers, Noosa beach in the background, clear blue ocean as far as the eye could see.

Britt had made him all too aware this marriage was a business merger, nothing more, yet he remembered how sentimental she'd get over the slightest thing and, while she appeared aloof with the planning, he'd bet his last dollar she'd want something a tad special.

'That's fine.'

Her pen picked up tempo as she focused on the list, obviously eager to get this over and done with so she could escape. Accepting this marriage was business was one thing, having to pretend to like it another.

Why did that rankle so much? It wasn't as if this were remotely romantic yet somehow, ever since she'd returned— and returned his kisses—he'd been having strange pains in his chest, the type of pain he used to have when she was around all those years ago.

She intrigued him, infuriated him, inflamed him and, though he tried to dismiss this marriage as a means to a goal, deep down he knew better.

He'd always wanted a family, the type of family he'd never had, and the only woman he'd ever let get close was sitting less than a foot away with fiddling fingers and a wary gleam in her blue eyes.

'Anything else?'

'What about a notice in the newspaper for an authentic touch?'

'That's it.' She jotted it down. 'I'd call you a genius but it'd just go to your head.'

'Try me.'

He leaned towards her with the sole intention of brushing a stray tendril of hair from her forehead. He never got the chance as their gazes locked for a heated moment before she leaped off the couch.

'Right, we're all done here. Thanks for dinner, it was great.'

She shoved the notebook into her bag, slung it over her shoulder. 'I'm pretty tired, so I'll head off now. Big day Friday.'

With an overly bright smile, she practically ran around the room. 'I'll get a copy of this list to you tomorrow. We don't have much time to get everything organised, so the sooner we get it done, the better. I'll—'

'Red?'

'Yeah?'

She paused mid-flight and took a deep breath, the simple action drawing his attention to her breasts and the way they filled out her ribbed top.

'For a city girl, you're sure behaving like a country virgin.'

He expected a host of retorts, or at least one decent smart-ass remark.

Instead, she glared at him, flushed a deep crimson and bolted out of the door.

Brittany wriggled her toes in her favourite Garfield slippers, pulled her fluffy tangerine robe tighter and cradled a hot chocolate while scanning her emails.

Not that she needed the extra calories after the mountain of food she'd consumed at Nick's, but chocolate didn't count, especially of the liquid variety. Besides, the way she was feeling right now, she needed comfort food, and this was it.

Nick had been right, damn him.

She *had* behaved like a country virgin, the exact way she used to act around him ten years earlier, jumping like a cane toad whenever he glanced her way; which had been often, though that hadn't been the hard part.

The hard part had come when he'd looked at her as if he wanted to gobble her up and come back for more. Several times.

As for that almost-kiss…yikes! She'd deflected it with some pathetic line about needing to concentrate, but he hadn't been fooled. She'd seen it by the knowing glint in his toffee eyes, by the smirk that had played around his kissable lips. And they were definitely kissable.

She'd wanted that kiss so badly she'd almost tasted it yet had done the smart thing and fobbed him off.

Smart for whom?

For both of them. She wasn't interested in making this marriage real. She had a successful career waiting for her in London, a fabulous promotion, good friends, a great apartment. Everything a girl could want.

But what if she wanted more?

If she did, Nick Mancini sure wasn't the guy to give it to her. His life was poles apart from hers.

His business was here, hers was in London.

His heritage was here, she'd always craved to escape family here.

He didn't want a real marriage, a small part of her did.

Huh?

Where had that last bit come from?

Sighing, she took a comforting sip of the creamy hot chocolate, savouring the mini marshmallows melting on her tongue.

Unfortunately, as fabulous as her life in London was, there was one thing lacking and that was a real, steady relationship. Not some casual fling, not some short-term dating and not some modern equivalent of 'being involved'—meeting once a week for a regular meal and sex. She'd tried these options and found them infinitely depressing.

No man had come close to matching what she'd felt for Nick, had once had with Nick.

And therein lay her problem.

'Just great,' she muttered, hitting the delete key on several joke emails and wishing she could erase her feelings for Nick as easily.

She'd been back a few days and had already reverted to her old ways: thinking about him constantly, wondering what he thought of her, hoping he felt half of what she did.

Pathetic.

The last email in her inbox effectively distracted her from the Nick problem. Her boss had given her leeway to complete this job, so why send her an email with 'Tight Timeline' in the subject header?

Clicking on the email, she quickly scanned the contents.

TO: BrittanyLloyd@Sell.London.com
FROM: DavidWaterson@Sell.London.com

SUBJECT: Tight Timeline

Hi Brittany,

How's my number one marketing guru enjoying her trip Down Under? Working hard, I hope.

I know we left your timeline fairly open for this pitch, but there's a change in plans.

Looks like Sell is expanding the NY office sooner than we thought and they want me to head it up ASAP, which means my job here needs to be filled within three months.

To be fair to all prospective candidates, we'd need your pitch presented in eight weeks.

Hope this is viable. If not, contact me.

We're expecting big things from you, don't let us down.

David

Brittany rubbed a weary hand across her eyes and quickly reread the email.

Eight weeks.

Two brief months to collate information, take pictures and perfect her pitch. Oh, and throw in a snap wedding.

What was she thinking?

But if the wedding didn't happen, she wouldn't have access to the farm, and no access meant no chance at the promotion anyway.

Her hands were tied. So why did it feel as if her insides were following suit?

Off the record, David had virtually assured her the MD role if she presented a killer pitch. She should be doing cartwheels.

Instead, the longer she stared at her boss's email, the more aware she became of exactly how far away London was from Noosa…and her soon-to-be husband who resided there.

CHAPTER SIX

'THIS place has changed so much.'

Brittany's head swivelled from side to side as she strolled up Hastings Street, Noosa's main thoroughfare, with Nick.

'Boutiques, cafés, restaurants, five-star hotels. We almost rival London in the trendy stakes, huh?'

'Almost.'

London had a vibe all of its own and she loved it, and coming home to find Noosa had turned hip and cosmopolitan was a nice surprise.

Nick laid a hand on her arm and she stopped, more startled by his touch than the mini-city's transformation. 'There is one thing we didn't discuss the other night.'

Just one? She could think of several, including how platonic this marriage would be, where they would live, how long they'd keep up the pretence. And that was just for starters.

'What's that?'

'How long you're sticking around for.'

She had to tell him the truth, had to tell him they had eight weeks to make it look as if they had a pretend marriage for real.

Shrugging, she pointed to the tapas bar they'd stopped outside.

'All depends on how long the job takes. Fancy a snack? I'm starving.'

'Okay.'

He led her into the bar, to a cosy table in the furthest corner, and ordered for them before turning that penetrating dark gaze back on her.

'So are we talking two months? Four? Longer?'

'You're really hung up on this timeline thing, aren't you?'

He raised an eyebrow. 'I wouldn't call it a hang-up. An honest answer will do.'

Hating the little white lie she had to tell, she said, 'As long as it takes. I have the workers in place, so once we're married I can really get stuck in.'

She picked at an olive from a tray that had been placed in front of them. 'I guess you want to know what happens after I'm done.'

To her surprise, he shook his head. 'Not really. I'm more concerned with the here and now, and solidifying my reputation with investors.'

She could leave well enough alone. In fact, she'd rather be discussing anything than their cold, calculating marriage scheduled for the morning. But if she left in two months as planned, where would that leave Nick and his precious reputation?

'So when I leave…'

She trailed off, not wanting to voice her doubts out loud. The way she saw it, she was getting the better end of this deal: full access to the farm to nail her promotion then she walked, back to her old life, leaving Nick to fend off curiosity about why his marriage fell apart so quickly and the possible financial fallout from his investors.

'When you leave, I act like nothing is wrong. We'll have a modern marriage, where we spend several months of the year together and have highly successful careers on different continents. Business people understand that.'

'But—'

'It's nobody's concern but ours,' he said, his tone cool and confident, at odds with the banked heat in his enigmatic gaze. 'This is going to work. Trust me.'

He placed a hand over hers before she could blink and rather than pulling away, the sane thing to do, she turned hers over and curled her fingers through his.

With a squeeze, he smiled and her heart flip-flopped in predictable fashion.

'That's my girl. So, you ready for tomorrow?'

'Ready as I'll ever be.'

She'd found a dress in a high-end boutique, shoes to match and had booked a hairdresser appointment.

Did a simple outfit constitute ready? A smart up-do? In reality, she'd never be ready to walk down the aisle with the only guy she'd ever really loved, knowing their marriage was fake.

'About the honeymoon…'

She snapped her gaze to his, not liking the naughty twinkle in his one little bit. 'A honeymoon isn't part of the deal.'

She all but yanked her hand out of his on the pretext of reaching for her water glass. He shrugged, a roguish smile playing about his mouth, and in that moment she wished she could take it back.

She'd always been a sucker for that smile, from the first moment he'd squatted to pick up her books strewn in the dirt when she'd tumbled off the bus the day they'd met.

He'd smiled his way into her life, her heart, and she'd be damned if she sat here and let him do it all over again.

'Okay, no honeymoon.'

'Good.'

She folded her arms, glared at him. With little effect if his growing grin was any indication.

'But we do need to have a wedding night.'

'No way—'

'This marriage has to look real. I'm a prominent business-man in the area and if we don't go away, we'd have to do something special for our wedding night, otherwise people would talk.'

He had a point, damn him.

No biggie. They could share a room; didn't mean they'd have to do anything in it.

'Fine,' she gritted out, her admission as painful as the time she'd had to admit she'd sent him that secret admirer Valentine's card in eighth grade.

Leaning forward, he whispered in her ear. 'You won't be disappointed.'

Hating the surge of lust that made her knees shake beneath the table, she managed a mute nod while sending a silent prayer heavenward for strength.

She had a feeling she'd need it to resist what the reformed bad boy had in mind come tomorrow.

Brittany's hand shook as she waved the mascara wand over her lashes and she blinked several times, grateful she'd chosen the waterproof kind.

She'd already been near tears twice, first when she'd opened the door to a gorgeous bouquet of frangipanis and then when she'd carefully hung her wedding dress encased in plastic on the back of the door.

Nick had sent the flowers. His note had been brief.

For my bride

Nick, x

While the flowers were breathtaking, that one little x had her clutching them and burying her nose in their heady fragrance, her eyes filling to the brim.

She wanted his kisses, wanted him, and, no matter how many times she told herself this wedding was a necessity to be free of her past, she knew when she walked up the aisle shortly she'd want him more than ever.

As for her dress…

She'd wanted to buy something understated, practical, a dress she could wear again, for why spend money on a real dress when this marriage would be far from real?

That was before she laid eyes on the strapless, sweetheart gown in ruched ivory silk chiffon and her neglected romantic soul demanded she buy it.

And she had, for when she touched the dress she imagined magic.

A magical marriage filled with light and laughter and love.

A magical mirage of a handsome groom with stars in his eyes and a bride who believed in the happily ever after she'd always dreamed about.

A magical mystery, that despite their motivations for this marriage they were embarking on something truly wonderful today.

Taking one last look in the mirror, satisfied she hadn't streaked her make-up in a fit of misplaced sentimentality, she shook her head.

Magic wasn't real and she was foolish to dream of anything other than what this marriage was: a business arrangement.

She slipped off her robe and padded across the room to the wardrobe, her fingers trembling as she slid the zip open on the dress's carrier bag.

Every metallic slide, every crinkle of the thick plastic, every rustle of silk chiffon brought her closer to her wedding and her tummy twisted as she reverently lifted the dress out.

Emotion clogged her throat and she swallowed several times as the soft flowing skirt cascaded to the floor in a silken ripple.

The dress was a dream, and her breath whooshed out as she steeled her nerve and slowly, carefully stepped into it, wishing she could channel some of that magic.

Closing her eyes, she tugged at the bodice, smoothed the skirt, ignoring the sick churning of nerves gone awry as the reality of marrying Nick hit home, and hard.

Almost faint from anxiety, she took a deep breath, another, before opening her eyes…and gasping.

She looked like a bride.

But it wasn't the divine dress or the fancy hairdo or the immaculate make-up that made all of this real.

It was the starry-eyed expression in her frightened gaze that said it all.

In spite of every sensible thing she kept trying to tell herself, she looked like a bride on the brink of marrying the man of her dreams.

Brittany's breath caught as she stepped out of the portico and got her first glimpse of her husband-to-be.

Nick stood under a beautiful poinciana lush with vivid crimson blossoms, his black tux framed against the vibrant colour. With the sun setting behind him, casting a golden glow over everything, and the fairy lights strung around the trees in the garden just twinkling to life, the entire scene was surreal.

It shouldn't be this romantic, this enticing, this special. This wedding was all business.

Tell that to my heart, she thought as she took a tentative step, her stiletto sandals skidding as they hit the sandstone pavers.

She couldn't see Nick's expression from this distance but as she walked towards him the shadows cast from the blossoms cleared and what she saw took her breath away all over again.

Honest to goodness, undiluted happiness.

Why would he look like that?

He was the one who'd proposed this ridiculous arrangement in the first place, had made it more than clear what they'd both get out of it.

So why the ecstatic, proud expression of a man who'd just glimpsed his real bride for the first time?

Her heart hammered in time with her steps, beating a rapid

rhythm as she all but tripped towards him, eager to get this over and done with.

While the setting might be picture perfect and her groom beyond handsome, this wasn't how she'd envisioned her wedding ceremony.

Sure, the groom might be the same guy she'd imagined, but that was a lifetime ago. So much had happened, so much had changed, and she was a fool if she thought for one second that anything about this marriage resembled her dreams of years gone by.

The closer she got, the louder her heart roared until she could barely hear by the time she pulled up next to him, a nervous, trembling mess.

'You're a beautiful bride,' Nick murmured in her ear, so close his warm breath raised a trail of tiny goose bumps along her neck and she knew while this marriage might be all business on paper, she wondered how on earth she'd manage to keep it platonic in the bedroom.

'Thanks.'

She cast a nervous glance at the civilian minister in a crass white suit, and a pair of bored witnesses in hotel uniforms. Her eyes squeezed shut as she dragged air into her lungs.

How had it come to this?

A quickie wedding, empty and meaningless, to a man she'd once loved with all her heart yet who hadn't loved her enough in return, when all she'd wanted to do when she'd come home was gather enough information to secure a promotion.

'Hey, it's going to be okay.'

Nick squeezed her hand and she opened her eyes, captured by the kindness in his, kindness underlined by happiness she'd glimpsed earlier.

'Trust me.'

Trust him?

She'd trusted him with her heart.

She'd trusted him with her virginity.

And he'd sent her away anyway.

So excuse her if she was a little light in the trust stakes these days.

Taking a deep breath, she forced a smile. 'Let's get this done.'

Shadows gathered in his eyes, obliterating his joy, and she mentally kicked herself for sounding so abrupt.

He wasn't forcing her into this. She was a big girl, she'd made her own decision, and now the moment of truth had arrived she had to suck it up.

Nick gestured to the minister to start and the next fifteen minutes flew by in a blur of meaningless vows, empty promises and pretend smiles.

Her heart ached so much she almost cried, twice, but one look into Nick's determined dark eyes gave her the strength to get through it.

Until the kiss.

'You may now kiss the bride.'

The minister beamed as if he'd just bestowed the greatest gift on them, but all Brittany could think was how she'd hold it together when Nick's lips touched hers.

Her eyelids slammed shut against the threatening tears, against the determination on his face as his head descended, slowly, agonisingly slowly, when all she wanted was for this to be done with.

She wanted a quick, seal-the-deal kiss.

What she got was something else entirely as his lips brushed hers, so soft, so gentle, so tantalising, drawing her towards him like an invisible gossamer thread being gently tugged.

She couldn't break the hold, break the spell, as he bundled her in his arms and kissed her, really kissed her, with every ounce of pent-up emotion bubbling between them.

The tears started falling then, swift, coursing, raining

down her cheeks and splattering his lapels as he dabbed them away with his thumbs, his smile too warm, too tender, too understanding.

'Damn you, Mancini,' she muttered, her gaze firmly fixed on the second button of his dress shirt as she blinked rapidly.

'I feel this too, Red.'

He tilted her chin up, giving her no option but to meet his scrutinising gaze. 'Don't fight it.' She had as much chance of fighting this as receiving a welcome-home hug from her father! But she knew she mustn't give in entirely to this attraction simmering between them, couldn't give into the insane dream to make this marriage real.

She had a life in London, a promotion to nail. Then why the renewed rush of tears at the thought of leaving all this, leaving Nick, behind?

'Come on, almost done, then we can relax.'

He held her hand the entire time through the signing of the certificates, through the forced pleasantries from the minister and the false congratulations from the witnesses she didn't know, and the trip in the elevator to the fifth floor.

'Where are we going?'

Stupid question, for she knew, and every cell in her body was on high alert.

They had to have a fake wedding night for people to believe this marriage was real, she got that. The part she was having trouble with was reminding herself of the *fake* part.

'Our suite.'

Two little words that sent a tremor of longing through her as she wished she were being whisked away to a fabulous room with her husband for real.

But this wasn't real, none of it was, and she needed to keep telling herself that as he held onto her hand as if he'd never let go.

'It's one of the hotel's best. The type of room that allows

the occupants to step into a different world and lets all their fantasies come true.'

Her head snapped up at his husky tone, her skin prickling in alarm at the basest desire glittering in his eyes.

Oh, heck, why did he have to go and mention fantasies? It would've been hard enough resisting him without the added pressure of envisioning all sorts of inventive ways she could share a room with the hottest guy to walk the earth, possibly seeing him naked, his hair ruffled by sleep first thing in the morning, that sexy smile playing about his mouth…

'I'm sure the room will be fine.'

Could she sound any lamer?

'Oh, it's better than fine.'

She inhaled sharply, Nick's subtle woody aftershave that had teased her for the last hours warping her senses when she had a precarious enough hold on them as it was.

'It's the French suite. Hope you like it.'

The French suite?

Suddenly, her magnanimous decision to share a room for a faux wedding night with Nick took on a whole new meaning.

A basic, boring, run-of-the-mill room she could've handled. Something like the French suite sounded way too seductive for comfort. Though right now, with Nick palming a key card out of his pocket as they stopped outside an elaborate ivory and gold door, she had more important things to worry about.

Such as how she could keep the guy she'd loved all those years ago at arm's length.

More importantly, did she really want to?

CHAPTER SEVEN

NICK gripped Brittany's hand as he slid their room card into the slot and waited for the tiny green light to flash.

Their room.

They'd be sharing a room, tonight, their wedding night.

He could barely think of anything else as he pushed the door open and gestured to her to step inside.

'Oh, my.'

Her gasp of surprise had him standing taller. Every inch of this hotel was his idea, from the boutique-styled foyer with its casual elegance to the extensive range of 'fantasy' suites designed to please the most discerning traveller.

Having the woman he'd married, the woman whose opinion he'd always valued, admire this room filled him with pride.

'You like it?'

She nodded, her eyes wide as they swept the room, alighting on the massive four-poster king-size bed covered in gold and ivory cushions and draped in yards of filmy chiffon—he'd labelled it 'some fancy thin material' and stood corrected by the aghast interior designer who'd taken him through the hotel suite by suite when he'd first dreamed up the idea.

The memory brought a smile to his face, a smile that quickly broadened when Britt turned her wide eyes, now filled with mischief, towards him.

'Knowing your sense of humour, for a second there when you mentioned French suite I had visions of a maid's outfit hanging in the wardrobes rather than fluffy robes and baskets of…'

She trailed off, bit her tongue and he raised an eyebrow.

'Of?'

With crimson cheeks, she said, 'French letters.'

He chuckled, urged her into the room with a gentle push in the small of her back.

'I haven't heard condoms called those in years.'

She waved her hand at him. 'Forget I said anything. Speaking before I think.'

She looked adorable with her flaming cheeks and wobbly smile, in stark contrast to her wedding gown and upswept hair.

He shouldn't tease her, he really shouldn't, but he didn't have her on the back foot very often and he couldn't resist.

'If this suite is too boring, we could always change to another. The Roman room, complete with marble columns around a central spa bath right in the bedroom, is pretty nifty. Or there's the Scottish room with its lavish faux fireplace and fur rug in front of it, or if you're feeling really adventurous there's always the Tack room, complete with whips, for those who need a little added excitement in their lives.'

'Whips?'

Her voice came out a squeak and he laughed.

'Okay, so I've just invented the Tack room, but hey, what the hell, it might draw a few customers.'

'What sort of hotel are you running here?'

'I resent what you're implying, lady.'

To his surprise, the mischief had returned to her eyes as she quirked an eyebrow. 'It's wifey to you now.'

Just like that, it hit him all over again.

They were married.

It was their wedding night.

And no amount of kidding around or playing the fool would douse his driving need to consummate this marriage.

Business might be the motivator behind their nuptials but his unquenchable need to have Britt in his arms again was a definite bonus.

Taking a step closer, he ran a fingertip down her arm, delighting in the slight tremor, proving she wasn't as immune to him as she'd like him to believe.

'Wife…I like the sound of that.'

'In name only, of course.'

Her biting response might have been edgy, but she didn't move when his finger continued its leisurely exploration, reaching her shoulder, skimming along her collarbone, resting in the hollow just above where her pulse beat frantically.

'Of course,' he said, ducking his head to replace his finger with his lips, turned on by her low moan and the way her head fell back to give him better access.

Her skin tasted better than he remembered, deliciously soft with a hint of vanilla, and it took every inch of his rapidly dwindling will power not to devour her on the spot.

'This isn't supposed to happen,' she murmured as his lips trailed slowly upwards, nuzzling behind her ear, nipping the lobe before swooping on her mouth in a fiery kiss that branded her his.

Raging need exploded in him as her tongue touched his, the same overpowering, overwhelming need that had driven him to possess her years earlier.

Nothing had changed, absolutely nothing. He was still the same star-struck guy helplessly under her spell.

The realisation should've angered him, for he was nothing like the blue-collar farm boy he'd once been. But he didn't give a damn, didn't care two hoots she now had him as ready and raring for her as he'd been as a horny eighteen-year-old.

Wrenching his mouth from hers and dragging in a breath,

he captured her face in his hands, noting the swollen lips, the rosy cheeks, the eyes midnight-blue with passion, his libido roaring in response.

'You know something? This was meant to happen from the first moment you came back.'

To her credit, she didn't look away, didn't take a step back.

'You're wrong. Nothing has gone to plan since I returned.'

The flicker of pain in her eyes hit him hard and he dropped his hands, gave her space and she took it, putting enough distance between them for him to feel the loss.

'Tell me you don't want to consummate this marriage as much as I do.'

There, he threw it out, knowing the firebrand she used to be would never back down from a challenge.

However, the forlorn bride in a fancy dress staring wistfully out of the window was a far cry from the feisty girl he'd known, and the thought he'd made her this unhappy was a kick in the guts. And the wake-up call he needed.

'Forget it. I'm going out for a while. I'll be back later.'

Failure didn't sit well with him, never had, and, hating how he'd botched this, he wrenched open the door.

'Nick, wait!'

But he didn't.

He walked out on his bride and slammed the door shut on his dreams of a memorable wedding night.

Brittany kicked off her sandals, ripped off the wedding dress and tore the frangipani from her hair, crushing it in her palm in the process.

She stared at the furrowed flower, limp, lifeless, and sank onto the bed, letting the petals drift from her fingertips to the floor.

She was like that flower: all pristine and showy on the outside, a crumpled mess on the inside.

As if getting through the ceremony hadn't been hard enough, pretending she didn't want a real wedding night had almost driven her insane.

Nick wanted her.

She wanted Nick.

Where was the problem?

A sharp pain shot through her chest as a timely reminder of exactly what the problem was: her heart. Her stupid, impressionable, just-break-me-now heart that jumped up and said 'pick me, pick me' every time Nick Mancini looked her way.

It'd been the same ten years ago and nothing had changed. She'd been home just over a week, long enough to realise singing the 'I'm only doing this for business' tune wouldn't cut it with Nick.

Not this time.

He'd let her walk away back then, he'd let her do it now, so why was she falling for him regardless?

With a frustrated groan, she headed for the bathroom. A good, long soak might ease her tension.

Yeah, right, just as trying to date other guys had eradicated Nick from her memory banks. Not a chance in hell.

While the bath filled she paced the bathroom, fiddling with the fancy toiletries, picking them up, putting them down, trying not to stare at her reflection as she did so.

The odd times she caught a glimpse in the disastrously monstrous mirrors, she didn't like what she saw.

A woman in sexy lingerie with thoroughly kissed lips, shining eyes and a glow no amount of blush could induce.

A woman who'd subconsciously bought the sheer ivory lace demi-cup bra and matching knickers edged in rosebuds in the hope the man she still fancied might get to see it.

A woman who was kidding herself.

That stung most of all, the fact she was a smart, astute businesswoman yet here she was playing silly games with herself.

She wanted Nick.

It all came back to that.

Her job and the promotion might be the reason she was here but right now, this very second, Nick was her motivation for staying in this suite when she could've quite as easily escaped.

She hated manipulation, hated lies: dear old Dad had seen to that. So why was she wasting time lying to herself now? She'd be gone in a few months, back to her orderly life. Why not make the most of the time they had?

For if she slept with Nick or not, spending the next eight weeks with him would break her heart regardless. At least this way she'd have some fun.

After closing off the gold taps, she carefully slipped out of the lingerie—she had high hopes for the stuff now—and dipped under the lavender-scented bubbles to her neck, resting her head against the giant Jacuzzi and sighing with pleasure.

Closing her eyes, she savoured the lavender scent infusing her senses, soothing, relaxing, helping her mind wander. And wander it did, taking a stroll down memory lane, to the first time Nick had made love to her.

Inviting her to dinner at the plantation when Papa had taken a business trip to Brisbane, the lukewarm pizza they'd fed each other while sitting on the frayed love seat on the back veranda, the icy cola fizzing up out of the can and dousing her in stickiness, Nick's tongue licking it off her…

He'd made her first time beyond special. He'd been caring and gentle and amazing, treating her virginity like a precious gift she'd given him.

She'd never forgotten it, never forgotten him and it was high time she stopped pretending she didn't want to recreate the magic they'd once shared between the sheets.

Sinking under water to sluice away her memories, she thought she'd done a fair job by the time she resurfaced.

Until she opened her eyes and saw Nick leaning against the bathroom door, staring at her with barely disguised lust in his incredible dark eyes, looking like a man in definite need of a bath.

CHAPTER EIGHT

NICK took several surreptitious breaths, willing his pulse to slow and his heart to stop pounding. At this rate, he'd collapse on the spot if it kept thumping with such ferocity.

'You came back.'

Her tentative smile had him gripping the door jamb to stop from striding across the bathroom, sweeping her out of the bath and holding her close.

Thankfully, only her head was visible, the rest of her delectable body submerged under a bubble cover that threatened to spill out onto the black-and-white-tiled floor. Not that the bubbles hampered his imagination. He could picture exactly what delights were hidden beneath those bubbles and the images weren't helping his heart rate.

'Yeah, couldn't stay away.'

'I'm glad.'

Her tongue flicked out to moisten her bottom lip in a totally innocuous gesture that slammed into his conscious like a bull ramming a gate in mating season.

'Are you?'

He was too old to play guessing games, too wound up to figure out why the turnaround.

He'd come back because this was his wedding night and, while lust might have temporarily blinded him to the real reason behind this marriage, the sight of more international guests checking into the hotel had alerted him to the fact he needed to make this marriage look real for investors to accept him as one of their own.

It was the reason he'd come up with this crazy scheme in the first place but somewhere along the line—probably around the time he'd first set eyes on his beautiful bride—his motivation had blurred until all he could see was Britt.

She nodded, gathering more bubbles with her hands on the surface and bringing them towards her chest. Damn, what he'd give for a fan now.

'Uh-huh. I didn't like how things ended before. Why don't you let me finish up in here and we can talk?'

Talk? She wanted to *talk*?

With that small smile curving her lips, droplets clinging to her eyelashes and her hair falling in tendrils around her face—he wasn't even going near those damn bubbles—talk was the furthest thing from his mind.

The corners of her mouth twitched as if she knew exactly what he was thinking and he quickly thrust his hands in his pockets and back-pedalled a few steps.

'Fine.'

'Give me five minutes and I'll be out.'

Her smile could've fogged up the mirror a lot more than the fragrant steam rising from the water and he managed a terse nod before backing out and closing the door.

Damn it, why hadn't she closed the door in the first place? Didn't she know the effect she had on him?

Of course she did. Then why the nasty thought that suddenly insinuated its way into his lust-hazed brain, making him see sense in her behaviour.

Since she'd arrived, she hadn't shown much interest in him as a man. Sure, she'd teased him, but that was nothing new, she'd always done that. The teasing often included flirting but that came naturally too.

He'd been the one to kiss her when she'd first arrived home.

He'd wanted to kiss her after dinner at his place and she'd pulled away.

He'd wanted to share a room tonight; by her reaction earlier it was pretty obvious she didn't.

Sure, she'd responded to his kisses, but maybe that had been for old times' sake? Giving in to him not to antagonise him, not to jeopardise their deal and her precious promotion? Made sense.

In reality, how far did he want to take this?

She'd be gone once her business here was finished, back to her high life in London, and he'd be left behind again, pretending he had a modern marriage where two busy business people lived on opposite sides of the planet.

He'd let her walk away last time, didn't tell her the truth; what would be different now?

Shaking his head, he took off his tux, pulled a T-shirt over his head, stepped into jeans, ran a comb through his hair and added a splash of aftershave. He would've loved a shower but the thought of using the bathroom so soon after Britt had vacated it, her scent lingering everywhere, evidence of her presence all over, would be too much.

She wanted to talk.

That was a sure-fire libido-killer. In his experience, when women wanted to 'talk' they wanted to lay down the law.

Well, whatever she had to say, he'd deal with it. Just as he'd deal with this crazy, one-sided obsession to make their marriage real.

After brushing her teeth, Brittany took a final look in the mirror: without make-up, the freckles on her nose stood out like sprinkles on a cupcake, her loose hair had turned frizzy courtesy of the humidity and her plain cotton PJs wouldn't win any Victoria's Secret competitions.

Just the look she'd aimed for…before she'd taken a bath and had that little revelation to make the most of the next two months with the sexiest guy to walk the planet.

Her bad boy.

Who was doing his best to appear good but she knew better, knew the underlying rebellious streak that lent him a dangerous edge she found infinitely appealing.

Most girls went through a bad-boy phase, lusting after guys they shouldn't and couldn't have, guys with attitude, guys you wouldn't dare bring home to meet the folks.

Nick had been her James Dean, Marlon Brando and Sean Penn all rolled into one and, while the designer suits and air of success had softened the edges, she just knew he was the same sexy rebel underneath.

But it was more than that, so much more, and the fact her heart had squeezed every time he'd entered a room these last few days was proof enough she'd developed a monstrous crush on her rebel with a cause all over again.

A crush she finally planned to fully indulge. However, there was one main problem. The pyjamas she'd brought were a deeply unsexy pair she'd bought especially to appear as unappealing as possible. Her body, humming with the heat of the bath and anticipation, informed her point-blank that fuchsia stripes wouldn't do the job.

As for the lingerie she'd intended on using to prove her point tonight, it had taken a tumble into the sink while she'd been brushing her teeth and there was no way she was walking into their bedroom wearing wet, see-through, ivory lace. That left only one viable option.

Wrapping the oversized bathrobe around her damp, overexcited body, she took a deep breath and prepared to leave the safe haven of the gloriously tiled bathroom.

Only a robe between her and Nick. As if she weren't nervous enough.

Nick had his back to her and she was darn grateful for that extra shot of oxygen a second ago, for the moment she caught sight of him her lungs seized.

Soft black cotton moulded to his broad shoulders, hugging the muscular contours of his back before tapering to a narrow waist, tucked into faded denim...

That was all he used to wear ten years ago, black T-shirts and denim, somewhat of a clichéd bad-boy outfit, but she'd never cared. He'd always looked delectable and nothing had changed.

With her eyes fixed on his butt, she must've made some terribly embarrassing sound akin to a groan for he turned, his gaze zeroing in on her damp, bare skin, what little there was on show. His eyes turned very dark brown and he swallowed.

Brittany smiled wickedly at him, his reaction fuelling her faltering courage.

He shook his head as if to break himself out of a trance, cleared his throat, and finally spoke in a low, dangerous tone.

'Just so you know—if you're planning on avoiding being seduced, you'll definitely need more than a robe. Maybe an entire wardrobe.' His voice sounded strained.

Brittany could see the bad boy inside was only barely contained. Just the thought of what might happen when he broke out added further to her inner tremblings. In a voice that sounded higher than her own, she said, 'Well, I wanted to talk about that—'

'Yes?'

His response was so fast it interrupted her mid-sentence, and she gaped at him like an idiot for a moment, her train of thought derailed.

'You were saying? Something about seducing me?'

His wide grin broke the tension as she remembered how much she liked this man and she grinned back.

'You wish.'

'You have no idea how much.'

His intense tone caused her belly to drop in a frightening free fall as liquid heat pooled in places long ignored, every inch of her hungry body on high alert as the bed dipped when he sat next to her.

While her scrambled brains tried to reform the words she was having such a hard time articulating, he sighed.

'But I thought about it, and you were right.'

What? No! She opened her mouth but he continued before she could speak.

'Let me guess. You're not interested in changing the status quo between us. You don't want to ruin a good working relationship. You don't want to risk wrecking our deal by letting sex get in the way of the sound business decision we've made, right?'

Wrong. Wrong, wrong, wrong!

Logically, he made perfect sense and he'd reiterated the arguments she'd been having with herself ever since she'd said yes to his ridiculous proposal.

Emotionally, she wanted to rant and scream and kick her Garfield slippers into the Great Barrier Reef, for now she'd made up her mind to alleviate some of this growing tension between them she didn't want to take the safe, sensible option any more.

But what could she say?

Backing down from her previous stance would make her seem fickle and indecisive and decidedly stupid, not to mention shooting down any credibility in convincing him her acceptance of his proposal was one hundred per cent business.

For him, having sex would be satisfying his lust factor. For her, it was so much more and he'd know it. She'd told him so ten years earlier and knowing Nick he wouldn't have forgotten.

'Just business, right?'

With a sinking heart, she nodded.

'Right.'

'Okay, then, glad we got that settled.'

He didn't move and when she raised her eyes to his she knew nothing was settled, far from it, for while Nick might be spouting the business tune his eyes were gobbling her up and coming back for seconds.

'Britt?'

She gulped, knowing her voice would come out squeaky if she didn't, for the longer he looked at her like that, the harder it was to breathe.

'Yeah?'

'You made a breathtaking bride.'

It wasn't his compliment that made her blush as much as the memory of how she'd envisioned him taking her wedding dress off.

'The dress was pretty special—'

'I wasn't talking about the dress.'

His hand snaked across the bed and rested on hers, the simple touch setting her body alight as her gaze flew to his, connected, locked, unable to look away even if she wanted to.

Tension crackled between them as she wavered between yanking her hand out from under his to re-establish equilibrium and closing the short distance between them and straddling his lap.

'You're still the most beautiful woman I've ever seen.'

A soft, wistful sigh escaped her lips, a sigh filled with hope and fear and wishes that things could be different for them, that this could be a real wedding night in every sense of the word.

Mustering a smile, she said, 'And you're still the charmer.'

He winked. 'Is it working?'

'Depends why you're trying to charm me.'

'Ah…the million-dollar question…'

Rather than releasing her hand, his thumb traced slow circles on the back of it, grazing her knuckles, dipping into the grooves, sending heat spiralling through her body.

Her eyes drifted shut, as if she could block out his touch and what it was doing to her body, but if anything the sensations increased tenfold.

Every nerve ending snapped to attention with every minute caress, every muscle liquefied with the barest brush of his thumb, and when he stroked her fingers from knuckle to tip the tension strumming her body coalesced into a fiery yearning that had her leaping off the bed like he'd prodded her.

'I'm really tired.'

His knowing gaze told her he knew exactly why she'd retreated, yet thankfully he didn't push it.

'Okay then. Do you want to have supper? I can get Room Service to bring us up something, or would you prefer bed?'

To her endless embarrassment, she blushed and scooted around to the other side of the bed, the very mention of which made her feel like a schoolgirl jilted by the high-school jock.

'I'm not hungry.'

She slid under the six-hundred-thread-count sheets. The sooner she feigned sleep, the sooner she could avoid looking at his delicious body and wishing he were supper.

'You sure?'

His deep, husky tone had her imagining warmed honey drizzled across his torso and strawberries dipped in chocolate nestled in his navel and she swallowed, at serious risk of drooling.

'I'm sure. Now, if you don't mind, I need some rest. So scoot.'

'Huh?'

'The couch? You know, that thing next to the table over there?'

He shook his head and sent her his best puppy-dog look, the one he'd perfected back in high school, the same one that melted her heart.

'I can't sleep on that. It doesn't convert into a sofa bed, it's two feet too short and has rocks under the cushions.'

'Well, you can't expect me to sleep there!'

And she'd be a fool to consider letting him share the bed. By the longing look he cast at the bed, she wouldn't have much choice.

'Red, as attractive as you look in the contraception-on-legs robe, this bed is big enough to fit four people. I'm sure we can share without getting into too much trouble.'

She almost would have believed him, if the last few tension-filled minutes hadn't happened. They might've agreed to a sex-free wedding night but, with her belly tumbling with nerves, her skin prickling with heat and the rest of her buzzing from repressed need, she knew trouble was only a tumble in the sack away.

But what choice did she have? She couldn't subject him to a sleepless night, it just wouldn't be fair. Or mature.

She could do this. Sharing a bed with Nick would be like having a friend over for a slumber party. And guaranteed she'd be the one spending a sleepless night!

'We can put pillows down the middle if you think that'll help.'

He grinned, a fully-fledged teasing grin that mocked her, and she briefly wondered what had happened to her bath pep talk. Lying in the giant bed with the sheets almost pulled up to her neck like a blushing virgin screamed prude and not the sassy city girl she liked to think herself.

Why couldn't she share a bed with Nick and consider it in a non-sexual way?

Because she wanted him! Bad.

That was when it hit her.

If she couldn't tell him what she wanted, what if she showed him by giving him a little bit of that teasing he was so good at?

She sat up straighter, allowing the sheet to dip, revealing the robe's gaping neckline, and sent him a smile that could've tempted a eunuch.

'No pillows needed. I'll keep my hands to myself, promise.'

To her surprise, his cocky grin slipped, as if he hadn't expected her to agree with him, let alone flirt right back.

Oh, yeah, this could be fun!

'You better not grope me in my sleep,' he muttered, sending her an almost hopeful look she'd do exactly that.

'Hands off, remember?'

'In that case, move over.'

Okay, so they'd settled the sleeping arrangements fairly painlessly. Good. This wouldn't be too difficult.

Think slumber party. Think friends. Think harmless fun. Easy.

However, the instant she dropped her guard, Nick did something to shock her all over again.

'What are you doing?' she shrieked as he undid the zip on his jeans and shucked out of them, standing next to the bed wearing the sexiest, briefest pair of black silk boxers she'd ever seen.

'I'm getting ready for bed. You don't expect me to sleep in jeans, do you?'

'N-no, but don't you own PJs?'

He shook his head, looking proud of the fact as she struggled to keep her gaze averted from those boxers and the lean, muscled legs beneath them. Sheesh, he looked good enough to eat—and she definitely wouldn't go there!

'Too hot. Besides, you should be grateful. I usually sleep nude.'

That shut her up as she closed her eyes and prayed for a miracle.

Her slumber-party theory wasn't working, not with Nick standing there in his underwear. His very sexy underwear.

'Trying to imagine what I'd look like, huh? Well, if you open your eyes, I can give you a demo—'

'No!' she yelled, her eyes flying open against her will in the faint hope he'd go through with his threat. 'Just get under the damn sheets and keep your underwear on.'

'Your loss.'

He had the audacity to shrug out of his T, toss it on a chair and slide in next to her, sending a dazzling smile in the process. Cocky, brash and totally shameless.

The next ten hours were going to be hell. Or heaven, depending how she looked at it, and right now, with an amazing expanse of broad, tanned chest on display, heaven seemed uncomfortably closer to the mark. ''Night, Red. Pleasant dreams.'

As if.

Pleasant would be the last word she'd use to describe what she knew would be an erotic kaleidoscope of images that would plague her all night long.

She turned off the lamp, grateful she couldn't see him any more. Not that she needed to. The image of Nick standing next to the bed wearing nothing but those black boxers and a smile would be a memory to treasure for years to come.

'Can I ask you something?'

She sighed and rolled over to face him, her eyes adjusting to the darkness slowly and just able to make out his reclining form at a safe distance across the bed.

Though were a few feet really safe? This was Nick Mancini she was sharing a bed with, *the* Nick Mancini she'd loved as a teenager and missed for years.

'You will anyway, so go ahead.'

'Why did you run away?'

'I didn't.'

The defensive words popped out before she thought about it, an instant response to a subject she'd rather avoid.

'Yeah, you did.'

His whisper floated on the darkness, a mixture of accusation and regret, and she wondered how he'd felt at the time.

When she'd first arrived in London, she'd been too busy coping with her own hurt to think about anything else. The people she loved in her life kept hurting her: her dad, then

Nick, and she'd struggled to hold together while trying to build a new life.

Part of her coping strategy had been to paint Nick in a bad light: he wasn't worthy of her; he didn't care; he wasn't capable of emotions.

But what if she'd been wrong?

What if he had cared and there was another reason behind his refusal to accompany her? After all, she'd hidden her real reason for fleeing.

'I just needed a new start.'

Which was partially true. She just couldn't tell him the reason behind her desperate yearning for a new start.

'But why London? You hung around Brisbane for a month before you left—you could've stayed there. Even Sydney or Melbourne at a pinch, places where we could've kept in contact, tried to maintain a re…' He trailed off and she resisted the urge to sit bolt upright and flick the light on.

Had she heard right? Was he saying they could've had a relationship if she hadn't wanted to get as far away from her father as possible?

'Maintain a what?' she prompted, eager to hear the words but almost wishing he wouldn't say them.

What was the point of bringing all this up now? She couldn't change the past, couldn't change what she'd done, and knowing she could've had a future with Nick even outside Jacaranda would hurt her all over again.

'A really strong friendship,' he finished, and disappointment pierced her.

So what? Wasn't that better than hearing he might've loved her back then as much as she'd loved him?

'I know I acted like a jerk before you left, I know we had our share of troubles, but we were really good friends. I missed that after you left.'

Wow, he'd missed her. And actually admitted it!

Time to lighten the mood before she lost her head completely, blurted out the truth and sought comfort in his strong arms.

'Aw, shucks. I didn't think you cared.'

'I cared.'

His two little words hung in the growing silence between them, laden with untold truths and forgotten dreams. 'But, hey, life happens.'

This time, he broke the tension with a forced chuckle. 'We've both come a long way. And however many times I tied your hair to a chair or put frogs in your bag, I still care. Goodnight.'

Nick's admission filled her with a slow, delicious warmth that seeped through her body, leaving her cocooned in a delightful haze.

How could she maintain her immunity when he said stuff like that? Better yet, did she want to?

'Don't let the bed bugs bite,' she murmured, snuggling under the sheets and closing her eyes, hoping for sleep and knowing it was useless.

She had too much to think about, starting with her re-awakening feelings for a man best left in her past.

CHAPTER NINE

NICK stirred some time around midnight, his dreamless sleep disturbed by a puff of air somewhere in the vicinity of his ear lobe.

His eyelids cranked open a fraction, half-heartedly investigating the source of air, only to snap open as he registered a luscious woman draped over his upper torso, her arm flung proprietorially across his chest and a leg nudging the vicinity of his boxers.

Not just any woman.

Britt.

His wife.

Whom he wanted to make love to something fierce.

Considering the chaste way they'd fallen asleep he should gently slip out from under her and try not to wake her.

But his good intentions evaporated when she snuggled closer, her knee edging towards a fast-growing hard-on, and he froze, gritting his teeth to stop from groaning out loud.

He could play the gentleman, but where would be the fun in that? Britt had always called him her bad boy and, while a small part of him had thought she only hung around him because she was tempted to slum it for a while, he'd liked the reputation.

And it had grown, fuelled by idle gossip of small-town inhabitants and the fact he smoked, rode a motorbike and lived in denim.

He'd heard the rumours, from his fictitious tattoo of skull-and-crossbones on his butt to riding bare-chested all the way to Sydney.

He'd laughed, silently appalled at how reputations could be made or broken by hearsay. Considering he'd been working his ass off trying to make the plantation stay afloat at the time, he hadn't much cared.

Another puff of air, another small moan in her sleep had him easing away before he did something she'd regret. Make no mistake, she'd been about to give him the 'don't think you can seduce me' talk last night before he'd cut her off. As if he wouldn't have got the message from seeing her in that libido-killing bulky robe.

She'd made her point earlier and he'd be damned if he sat through it again, rehashing stuff he didn't agree with. Especially when she was half naked, with all the distraction that would have entailed. The way he saw it, they could keep this marriage business focused while having fun too but there was no way, no how, he'd be pushing the issue now.

Britt had made her feelings more than clear.

'Nick?'

Her sleepy whisper slammed into his consciousness, beckoning him to stay right where he was. But he couldn't, he wouldn't take advantage of the situation no matter how turned on he was or how badly he wanted his wife.

'Shh, go back to sleep.'

He stroked her hair, a small part of him melting as she snuggled deeper and, rather than pull away, he cuddled her closer with his arm.

Her hair tickled his shoulder, her cheek, so soft and warm, pressed against his chest and the faintest scent of lavender and vanilla lulled him into believing that, for now, this was enough.

* * *

If Nick was a bad boy, Brittany was a bad girl.

A very bad girl.

When she'd woken in Nick's arms that first morning, she'd felt him pulling away, sensed him trying to disengage. And while winding up with her head resting on his chest and the rest of her draped over him hadn't been planned, she'd taken full advantage of the situation.

Maybe not *full* advantage, as that would've entailed doing a lot more than cuddling, but she'd pretended to sleep while savouring the hard chest cushioning her cheek, the warm, toned body beneath her hands and his intensely male scent, which set off her pheromones in a big way and always had.

She could've stopped there but, no, she'd been a really, really bad girl.

And proceeded to do the same thing every morning.

For the next two weeks.

The tension was killing her. If only it were doing the same to her husband.

'How's business coming along?'

Her head snapped up from where she'd been resting her chin in her hands, staring out of the window and daydreaming of exactly how bad she'd like to be, to find the object of her wicked fantasies staring at her with cool detachment.

It had to be a ruse. After all, wasn't he the one who'd been hot to trot on their wedding night? Surely he couldn't have turned off just like that?

By his compressed lips and grim expression, apparently so.

Feigning nonchalance she didn't feel, she waved her hand towards the stack of paperwork on the table in front of her.

'The photographer's been out to the plantation every day this week and taken loads of shots. The cameraman's due out there tomorrow, and I'm collating some of the historical info

I got from your grandfather's ledgers. So everything's coming along nicely.'

He crossed the room, perched on the edge of the table, her eyes now level with his crotch, and she quickly stood, not needing to look *there* considering she'd been having bad thoughts a few moments ago.

'You've been busy.'

'Loads to do. I've got a task list a mile long today, including heading out to the plantation to scout more locations, checking the ones I've already chosen, making sure they match the information I'm in the process of adding to the pitch—'

'Hang on.'

His hand shot out, gripping hers and preventing her from putting some much-needed distance between them.

Trying not to show how much his simple touch affected her, she raised an eyebrow.

'What's up?'

Shaking his head, he squeezed her hand before releasing it. 'I'm no good at this.'

'At what?'

'This whole fake marriage thing.'

'Oh, thaaat.'

Well, well, well, maybe the tension was getting to him after all.

'Not used to sharing a suite, huh?'

He must've heard her teasing tone but rather than smile, he fixed her with a piercing stare.

'Not used to sharing a suite with you.'

Right then she knew, no matter how cool Nick was playing it, how busy he was, he was just as rattled by their underlying attraction as she was.

'Oh? I thought it'd be a breeze.'

She waltzed around the room, picking up floral skirts and summer dresses and the odd piece of lingerie or two.

Okay, so she wasn't playing fair with the lingerie but, hey, she wanted to get a reaction out of him, and if the tortured look that flickered across his face as she twirled an ebony satin bra on the end of her finger before tossing it into a drawer was any indication, her plan was working.

'A breeze? More like a damn tropical cyclone,' he muttered, shoving off the table and heading for the wide window affording a glorious view of Noosa beach.

'I'm getting to you, aren't I?'

She snuck up behind him, just stopping short of sliding her arms around his waist and laying her head against his back.

He didn't turn, keeping his gaze fixed on the stunning view.

'I guess this business arrangement of ours isn't quite what I expected.'

'That's because we share a past, you dufus.'

Oops. Had she really said that out loud?

By the speed at which he turned to face her, she had.

An endearing smile curled his lips. 'Dufus?'

'I've called you worse.'

His eyes darkened as they hovered on her mouth, as if he was remembering everything she'd ever called him and more.

'Yeah, I remember.'

She'd come this far, might as well go for broke.

'What else do you remember?'

Silence stretched between them, surprising her. Nick might be many things, but chicken wasn't one of them. She'd called his bluff, expecting some kind of answer even if it was a dismissive smart-ass remark.

Just when she'd given up, he finally reached out and twirled a strand of her hair around his finger.

'I remember you wore your hair long, to your waist. I

remember how you used to squeal on the back of my bike as I rounded the bends.'

He tugged on her hair, bringing her closer…and closer… and closer until there was a whisper between them.

'But most of all, I remember how you made me feel back then.'

Unexpected emotion clogged her throat, effectively clouding her sweep-me-into-your-arms fantasy.

She'd wanted to prove the sizzle existed between them, wanted to tease him, wanted to get a reaction out of him. The last thing she'd expected was this serious trip down memory lane from a guy who acted as if they didn't have a past most of the time.

'How did I make you feel?'

He was so close his breath feathered her lips, sending a ripple of longing so intense through her it took her breath away.

'Like I could make all our dreams come true.'

She sighed, wishing he hadn't pushed her away, wishing he'd said yes when she'd asked him to move away with her all those years ago, wishing he had made her dreams come true.

He was all she'd ever wanted, until her freedom became all important.

She'd thought she'd had it all, convinced he'd move to London and they'd have the life they wanted. Until he'd withdrawn from her, shutting her out emotionally, physically, citing work and study and family as a means not to see her.

She'd persisted, convinced they were meant to be together, captivated by the occasional glimpse of the guy she'd fallen in love with, wary of what he'd become the harder she pushed for them to leave town.

Her dreams had been big, had been big enough for both of them. But Nick wasn't the dream-maker she'd been foolish once to believe he was.

Acknowledging their attraction was one thing, opening

her heart another, and while she wanted him now more than ever she knew nothing had changed.

He still wouldn't follow her to London even if she were crazy enough to ask.

'Nick, I don't think—'

'Then don't. Think, that is,' he murmured, a second before his lips locked on hers in the softest heartbreaking kiss that reached all the way down to her soul.

It lasted less than a few seconds, a fleeting glimpse of tenderness rarely seen from this passionate man, and when he raised his head, brushed her bottom lip with a fingertip and walked away, she was left reeling.

Reeling with the knowledge she still believed in dreams.

And his ability to make all hers come true.

Nick entered the marquee, his gaze immediately drawn to the stunning woman in a white dress chatting to the richest guy in the State.

Brittany looked incredible, a soft, clingy Grecian-style dress fastened on one shoulder with a silver clip, leaving her other deliciously bare, her hair piled up with soft golden streaks falling softly around her face and just enough make-up to enhance her beauty.

Hell. Just looking at her from a distance was making him crazy; what hope did he have up close?

Sure, she looked like a supermodel tonight but he still couldn't erase the image of her clad in that supersized robe on their wedding night.

He'd lied about the robe being contraception on legs. The minute he'd caught his first glimpse of her, framed in the bathroom doorway with vulnerability written all over her face, he'd wanted to cross the room, haul her into his arms and never let go.

That had been one hell of a night.

Not for the reason he might've anticipated, considering she fired his libido as no other woman ever had or probably ever would.

He'd lain awake for hours, listening to the soft sounds of her breathing, wishing things could've turned out differently between them, silently chastising himself for being a bloody fool.

He'd thought by getting her to talk about the past, she might relax, learn to trust him again. Instead, she'd fed him some lame excuse about why she'd run away and he'd been the stupid one to blurt out he still cared. Go figure?

Thankfully, the last fortnight had passed in a frenetic blur with finalising details for the new Caribbean hotel and, apart from that slight aberration yesterday when he'd almost made a pathetic declaration of how much he liked having her around, they'd managed to maintain a polite distance.

All business, which was exactly why she'd agreed to accompany him to the Bachelor and Spinsters Ball tonight. A ball the Phant-A-Sea chain was sponsoring, a ball where every billionaire in Australasia would be in attendance, a ball where he'd learn how far his plan to marry Britt had got him.

Hotel occupancy was up fifty per cent, phone calls from potential investors tripling since he'd married. Maybe the old-school tycoons had finally recognised him as a successful, wealthy businessman with one thing on his mind: making his hotels the best in the world.

Tonight would prove how far he'd come, for calling him was one thing, accepting him as one of their own in public another.

Britt glanced up at that moment and their gazes locked, hot, intense, and he strode across the harvesting shed, which looked like a cross between a country-and-western saloon and a high-school disco.

It would be the plantation's final hurrah, for once Britt had completed her work here he'd sell the place, sever ties to his past once and for all.

He'd prevaricated for the last twelve months, plagued by guilt. This place had been Papa's pride and joy, built from the ground up with grit, sweat and determination. It had been the only place he'd ever called home but, more than that, it had been a refuge after his mum had abandoned them.

The old farmhouse should've repulsed him, should've been a constant reminder of what happened when he loved a woman too much.

But he'd deliberately blocked out the few memories of his mum, had filled his head and his heart with new ones, mostly centred on a wizened Italian man with a penchant for ripe tomatoes, coarse wine and sugar in his veins.

Papa had been more than a parent, he'd been his idol. The thought of bringing shame to the family name had stopped him from taking his rebel image too far, Papa's steadfast support a constant reminder that he could be anybody he chose to be.

But that was the problem.

As long as he held onto the plantation, people would be reminded of his humble beginnings, would still harbour doubts about his ability to mix it with the big boys.

It would kill him to sell, would tear him clean in two, but nothing could take away memories of a father who'd helped mould him into the man he was today.

Papa would've understood, would've encouraged him to move forward, and that was exactly what he would do, despite the nagging gut feeling he was turning his back on family.

'Well, if it isn't the man of the moment. Glad you finally showed up at your own shindig, Mancini.'

To his amazement, Bram Rutger stuck his hand out, something he'd never done despite the many times they'd crossed paths at similar functions in Sydney or Singapore the last few years.

He shook it, vindicated his plan had worked yet despising himself for caring what this pompous old fool thought of him.

'Business, you know how it is.'

'That I do, my boy. Something we'll discuss more of when you return my phone calls. I'm looking to expand my investment portfolio and I think we should talk.'

Bram's announcement reinforced he'd made a sound business decision in marrying Britt, but his satisfaction evaporated when the old fool slipped an arm around Britt's waist.

'And I hear congratulations are in order. You've picked a fine woman here.'

Bram squeezed Britt's waist as Nick's hands squeezed into fists. 'I've known young Brittany since she was in the cradle, so make sure you take good care of her, you hear?'

Oh, he'd take good care of her, starting with punching the supercilious coot in the nose, but he forced a smile and nodded.

'Shall do. Now, if you'll excuse us?'

He held out a hand, biting back a grin when Britt all but bolted out of Bram's hold. 'Nice seeing you again, Bram.'

She wiggled her fingers in a teasing wave and Nick growled under his breath as they walked away.

'You shouldn't tease the old goat. Might give him a heart attack.'

Her cheeky smile lit up her face. 'Well, then, his kids will thank me. Apparently he's worth billions these days.'

'You're incorrigible.'

She quirked an eyebrow. 'This, coming from the guy who used to do very poor impersonations of Bram and his cronies?'

She shook her head. 'You've changed. Become a snob like them.'

'This, coming from the girl who wouldn't sit down by Jacaranda River unless I'd spread out a blanket first? From the girl who wouldn't hop on the back of my bike unless I made sure there wasn't a dot of grease on the seat? From the girl who—'

'Okay, okay, I get your point. Sheesh.'

She reached out, smoothed a lapel, her innocuous touch enough to fire his blood and set his heart pounding.

'Nice tux, by the way. Very debonair.'

'Glad you noticed.'

Their gazes locked again and this time he didn't look away.

He'd already got what he came for tonight: vindication he'd made it into the big league, recognition he was more than the blue-collar farm boy he'd once been.

Time to get this party really started.

'Come with me.'

'Where?'

'Does it matter?'

She shook her head, the tendrils framing her face swaying gently and beckoning him to reach out and twist one around his finger, draw her close and hold her all night. But there was plenty of time for that. For now, he'd settle for getting her alone and kissing her senseless.

'Come on.'

He grabbed her hand and they fought their way through the crowd. He was surprised by the turnout, hundreds of well-dressed revellers who had descended on his property, bringing their own supplies, including tents for camping overnight.

Singles balls were all the rage these days and, while he liked seeing people having fun, a huge part of him was relieved he was no longer a bachelor.

It wasn't everything it was cracked up to be, especially now he had a fortune behind him, with the women who'd once shunned him for having grease on his hands and dust in his hair clambering for a date—or, worse, a relationship.

Britt had never been like that; she'd liked him regardless

and the thought sent a burst of warmth through him, urging him to pick up the pace.

'Great turnout, huh?'

With her blue eyes glittering with excitement, she looked like a society hostess basking in the success of an event. 'And the film crew are getting loads of footage I can use in my pitch.'

'That's great, though personally I can't believe there are so many desperadoes out there.'

'Most people are here to party, not pick up.'

They caught sight of a couple kissing in the back of a ute at the same time and Britt chuckled. 'Well, most of them.'

'Get a room,' he muttered, suddenly annoyed by the sight of the amorous couple doing exactly what he'd like to be doing with the gorgeous woman by his side.

'What for? If they're anything like us, a room won't sweeten the mood.'

He risked a quick glance at her face, wondering if she were serious but, by the cheeky smile tugging at the corners of her glossed mouth, she wasn't.

'The room doesn't matter to us because we have an arrangement. And we're friends.'

More the pity. Though he planned to change all that, starting tonight.

'So are those two, by the look of it. *Good* friends.' She chuckled and slipped her hand around his elbow, a casual gesture that shouldn't have sent the blood rushing to his groin. But it did and he could barely focus on anything other than the way she smelt and how she felt tucked in to his side.

Having her stand so close to him, her signature vanilla enveloping him in seductive sweetness, was hard enough to tolerate without her smoky midnight eyes sending him signals he knew were all in his own head.

'So what did you want to show me?'

'It's in here.'

He all but dragged her through the back door into the dimly lit kitchen, knowing this was crazy but unable to stop.

Her soft laughter echoed in the empty room, his favourite in the house. He had a lifetime of family memories here: making ravioli from scratch while his dad pored over the Sunday newspapers, Britt poking her tongue out at him from across the table as she lobbed a bread roll and feigned innocence.

Yeah, this room was a definite favourite and he was about to add another treasured memory.

'Okay, apart from this place needing some light, what's the prob—?'

Nick covered her mouth with his, cutting off her words and sliding his arms around her waist, marvelling at how right this felt.

Rather than protest and try to shove him off, she groaned and wrapped her arms around his neck, opening her lips beneath his, teasing him to pleasure her, to taste her and come back for more.

He was more than willing to comply, deepening the kiss to the point where he couldn't breathe, couldn't think, couldn't feel anything beyond this incredible woman in this unforgettable moment.

She hung on tight, her hands stroking his neck, tugging him closer until he could feel the heat of her skin through his dress shirt, the sizzling, wicked heat urging him to back her up against the table and do what he'd wanted to do for weeks now.

Make sweet love to his beautiful bride.

He must've moved a fraction for she groaned, brushing her breasts against his chest, and he slid his hands around her ribcage, filling them with her full breasts, caressing them, skimming the peaks with his palms until she murmured incoherently, almost making him explode on the spot.

Alarm bells clamoured in his head—what happened to just business? What happened to getting her to make the first move this time? And he happily ignored them, allowing himself this one brief taste of pleasure before sanity returned and he'd be forced to apologise for making a complete jackass of himself.

She sensed his hesitation, for she broke the kiss, only to snuggle into his neck and playfully nip the sensitive skin there.

'I can see your problem.'

'What's that?'

His hands glided over the slinky material of her dress to caress her butt, the heat of her scorching his palms through the thin silk of her dress.

'You've got the hots for me.'

She chuckled, the small sexy laugh of a confident woman who knew exactly what sort of a schmuck she was dealing with.

'It's your fault. You're irresistible.'

He kissed her again, softly, lingering, wondering how he'd ever had the will power to turn this amazing woman down all those years ago and wondering what the hell he was going to do when she walked out of his life this time around.

She had his libido firing on all cylinders but it was more than that. They'd reconnected on so many levels, their special friendship a thing to be treasured.

But what had changed?

Career-driven Brittany Lloyd would hightail it out of Noosa without a backward glance, leaving him cursing the day he'd been foolish enough to let her back into his heart, a heart he'd deliberately closed off from ever loving any woman too much.

He might've obliterated memories of his mum but he'd never forgotten the pain of abandonment, the intense loss that had clawed at his insides, the doubts that had plagued him for years that he wasn't good enough to be loved for ever.

'How irresistible?'

Now wasn't a time for doubts or deliberating or questioning as he kissed her again, deepened the kiss, craving intimacy as the parched outback craved water to sustain life. The thought of losing her did it, prompting him to do all manner of crazy things like back her up against the table, wishing he'd had the sense to lock the back door.

Her hands dived into his hair, angling his head for better access to his mouth as she wrapped a leg around his waist, bringing him into delicious contact with her heat, and blind, raging need slammed through him to the point of no return.

He was out of his mind with need for her but he'd be damned if he took her standing up against a kitchen wall after all this time.

She deserved more.

She deserved the universe and then some.

Wrenching his mouth from hers with effort, he exhaled on a long, ragged breath as he broke the full-length body contact he'd been relishing so much.

'Nick?'

'Not now, not here, not like this,' he said through gritted teeth, desperate to rein in his libido as he tried not to focus on her swollen mouth, on the lips he'd tasted, lips he'd savoured, lips he'd kiss all night long if he had his way.

'Then when?'

Confusion clouded her eyes as he balled his hands to stop from hauling her back into his arms, silently cursed making a hash of this.

Desire pounded through his veins, untamed and undisciplined and uncontrollable, but he'd subdue his ferocious need for now, bide his time, for when they gave into this tempestuous passion he would stop at nothing less than making love to her all night long.

With great restraint he settled for trailing a fingertip down her cheek, along her jaw, enjoying the instant flare of heat in her sparkling eyes, the soft little smile playing about her lips.

He cupped her chin, his gaze not leaving hers. 'Soon, Red. Very soon.'

Something fierce, something wild and something altogether terrifying flashed across her face before she nodded, slowly.

'Good,' she breathed on a sigh, setting his heart pumping with wild anticipation as he grabbed her hand and almost dragged her out of the door before he changed his mind.

Brittany hadn't had this much fun in ages.

Sure, she attended swank parties in London and rubbed shoulders with the rich and famous thanks to her brilliant job, but those events were filled with pretentious flakes who spoke to you depending on which designer dressed you or how many millions you made a year.

She hated the way money talked, hated the way it divided people into classes and, while she understood Nick's drive to gain acceptance into the privileged world she'd been born into for the sake of his business, she couldn't help but wish he'd wanted to marry her for her all those years ago.

They'd both changed so much, yet when he touched her, when he kissed her, the last decade vanished on a wistful sigh.

They'd been too young back then; she could see it now. She'd romanticised what they had, had mistaken the throes of first love as being something to build a lifetime commitment on.

But Nick hadn't been ready and, while his deliberate sabotaging of their relationship at the end had hurt, she understood.

His father had meant everything to him while she hadn't been able to wait to escape hers. They'd had different dreams at the time, different goals.

So where did that leave them now?

Could two successful, career-driven people take a chance on love?

She collapsed onto a portable chair in a corner of the harvesting shed, her gaze homing in on Nick surrounded by a bunch of investors while images of the scintillating kiss they'd shared in the kitchen a few hours earlier replayed over and over, making her shiver anew.

That had been some kiss. Passionate, mind-blowing and way too intense, the type of kiss to pin hopes on, the type of kiss to give a girl ideas of how he felt. And on the heels of his admission on their wedding night, when he'd said he cared about her, way too baffling.

She'd been trying to tempt him, trying to seduce him, but he'd had nerves of steel.

Until tonight.

That kiss in the kitchen had changed everything.

He wanted her as much as she wanted him, so why had he stopped? Pulled away?

Damn, the man was infuriating and confusing the heck out of her.

Every time he touched her, she lost it. But that didn't mean she had to lose her head completely.

Having fun and walking away was one thing.

Having fun and falling for him another.

No. This time, she'd be smarter than that. She'd come too far from the scared, confused teenager who'd bolted like a fugitive into the night to regress.

She didn't need anyone. She'd been doing fine on her own for the last ten years, thank you very much, and getting involved emotionally with Nick would only lead to heartache for them both.

'Hey, what's with the look?' Frida Rutger, Bram's much younger trophy wife, flopped into a chair next to her and fanned her face. 'Is it hot in here or what?'

'Sure is.'

Brittany deliberately ignored Frida's first question, glad for the interruption; anything to distract from her thoughts of Nick.

However, she should've known the astute young woman who'd hosted parties for world dignitaries wouldn't let her off that easily.

'So, why the glum look? Has that dishy new husband of yours done something to upset you?'

'No.'

Unless she counted upsetting her equilibrium. 'Just tired, I guess.'

Frida's gaze bordered on jealous as it zeroed in on Nick. 'I'm not surprised, married to someone like that.'

Uncomfortable with the woman's frank admiration—and shocked by the urge to scratch her eyes out—Brittany aimed for distraction.

'Your dress is gorgeous. Local designer?'

Thankfully, Frida's greedy gaze abandoned Nick and focused on her stunning ochre and crimson layered chiffon dress, the bodice hugging her fake boobs until it reached her waist, where it cascaded in a fiery waterfall of riotous colour to her ankles.

'I designed it myself.'

The thought of the wife of Queensland's richest man making her own dress almost shocked her as much as Nick's unexpected kiss earlier.

'Wow, you're a talented designer.'

To her horror, Frida's bottom lip wobbled as she blinked frantically. 'Pity Bram doesn't think so.' She sniffed, plucked at a chiffon layer in her lap. 'He said it looked like a bottle of orange soda exploded all over me.'

Brittany watched Bram, paunchy and balding and florid-faced, slap Nick on the back, while his beautiful wife fought tears.

Searching for a diplomatic answer, she finally said,

'Bram's a great businessman, but maybe his fashion sense isn't up to par?'

Frida dashed her tears away with an angry swipe, a smile twitching at her mouth.

'He also said I need liposuction and another facelift.'

Outraged, she abandoned all sense of politeness. 'Guys are jerks.'

However, when her gaze returned to Nick, drawn by the magnetic power he exuded by just being in a room, she knew her statement wasn't entirely true. Not all guys...

'You can say that again.'

'Guys are jerks.'

Frida chuckled and she joined in, wondering how an attractive young woman could hook up with an overbearing ass like Bram.

It all came down to money and, once again, she thanked her lucky stars she'd escaped that world and all it stood for.

'Aren't you the lucky one? Here comes your delicious husband.' Frida jumped up and smoothed her dress, tears forgotten as she batted her eyelashes at Nick. 'Nice to see you, Nick.'

Nick nodded, his gaze fixed on Brittany rather than the eye-catching figure sashaying away in a fiery dress, earning him more Brownie points than she could count.

He sat beside her, his aftershave teasing her to lean closer, to fill her senses with it, as she had earlier when she'd lost herself in the wonder of his kiss.

'I don't like it when women natter in corners. They're usually planning trouble for us mere males.'

His frown didn't work when accompanied by a slow, sexy smile that notched up the heat between them in a second.

'Safety in numbers, I guess.'

Leaning towards her, he crooked his finger. 'Looks to me like numbers are dwindling, and you know what that means?'

'What?'

He sent her an exaggerated wink. 'It means we'll have to spike the band's drinks so we get rid of the rest of the revellers pronto.'

She laughed while her heart stopped its jumping around and settled with a resounding thud.

For at that moment, she knew.

His promised 'soon' had arrived and with his bow tie askew, his dark hair rumpled and light brown eyes blazing with an emotion she daredn't analyse, she had as much chance of not falling in love with Nick again as flying solo back to London.

And the knowledge he still held that kind of power over her scared her beyond belief.

'How much longer?'

She needed him to hold her, to erase her thoughts, to banish the yearning to be with him for ever. Surely they would make love tonight, would assuage the tension strumming between them? 'Soon' couldn't come quick enough as far as she was concerned.

Sensing her eagerness, he slid an arm around her waist and cuddled her close.

'I'll get the band to announce this is the final number. How's that?'

'Perfect.'

'Don't move. I'll be right back.'

Feathering a kiss across her lips, he strode away, leaving her to deal with her newly awakened feelings and how much they terrified her.

The time would come shortly for her to sort them out and she wasn't looking forward to the wake-up call she knew was inevitable when she had to leave, not one bit.

CHAPTER TEN

BRITTANY paced the kitchen, waiting for Nick to see the last reveller off the property.

She shouldn't be this nervous.

It wasn't as if she'd never made love to him before.

Though as she watched him stride towards the house, broad shoulders squared, long legs eating up the distance, a full moon casting shadows across his face and glinting in his dark hair, she knew the man he was today was a far cry from the boy he'd been ten years earlier.

If she'd loved that Nick unreservedly, unashamedly and unabashedly, what hope did she have of holding back her emotions this time around?

As he neared the door she quickly dropped into the nearest chair and picked up a magazine from a messy stack in the corner, pretending to flip through it without a care in the world.

When he entered, she took a peek over the top of the magazine, confused by his wide grin.

'Everyone gone?'

So much for casual. Her voice came out a high-pitched squeak and she cleared her throat, rustling the magazine, ready to duck behind it.

'Uh-huh.'

He stalked towards her and she gulped, wanting to be in his arms so much it hurt, yet petrified once she was there she'd never want to leave.

'A bit of light reading?'

'Mmm.'

His muffled guffaw said he hadn't bought her ruse for a second. 'That's interesting. I'd never have pegged you for a girl interested in cattle mating seasons.'

Heat swept her cheeks as she slapped the pages shut, flung the magazine back on the pile and folded her arms.

'Because if you are, you can have those magazines. They were Papa's and I'm in the process of doing a major clean-out before the sale, so be my guest.'

Seeing the funny side of it, she shook her head. 'Thanks, but I'll pass. Leave the cows and bulls to it.'

The twinkle in his eyes intensified as he held out a hand to her and gently pulled her to her feet. 'You know, you don't have to be nervous around me.'

'I'm not.'

A quick rebuttal easily belied by her tumbling belly and wobbly knees and hands that shook ever so slightly.

He sent a pointed glance at the magazine and raised an eyebrow. 'Really?'

She sighed, placed her palms on his chest to anchor her before she wobbled any more and embarrassed herself further.

'Okay, okay, I'm a tad nervous. Aren't you?'

'No.'

He slid his arms around her waist, creating a welcoming cocoon she could quite happily snuggle in for ever.

'We're not strangers. This is you and me, Red.'

'But—'

'No buts. Unless it involves this one.'

He gave her backside a playful pinch and she laughed, her nerves dissipating as he'd intended.

'Tonight is about you and me. No second guessing. No overanalysing. No regrets. Okay?'

It all sounded very logical when he put it like that, but she knew come morning she'd be analysing every single second.

She'd always been this way around him, off course and off kilter, and now the moment she'd been anticipating had arrived she couldn't quell the bundle of nerves knotting her resolve.

She wanted him. It should be simple, right?

But nothing was simple about her relationship with this dynamic, enigmatic man and the moment she started underestimating the power of his hold over her was the moment she'd lose control.

Not a bad thing entirely, but she was scared, terrified in fact, by the depth of emotion for a bad-boy rebel who still cradled her heart in his powerful hands.

'You're thinking too much.'

She nodded, her mouth kicking up in a wry grin. He knew her so well, knew she'd be analysing every angle of this momentous step.

'Well, I'm done thinking.'

Before she could blink he covered her mouth with his, his commanding kiss obliterating every doubt, every thought, she'd just had.

As his tongue duelled with hers she lost herself in the mindless passion instantly ignited between them, the frantic flurry of eager hands and low moans and hot, bare skin.

'I didn't want it to be like this, not here—'

'Don't stop,' she panted, arching into him, her pelvis melding to his, so hard and ready. 'Please, Nick, now.'

His low, guttural groan raised goose bumps along her skin as his hands bunched her skirt up around her thighs while he plundered her mouth again.

Sensation after sensation bombarded her, from his mouth

ravaging hers with fierce intent to his hands stroking her thighs and brushing against her mound.

Endless, mindless pleasure, which built and receded and built again until she could barely stand any more and when his fingers finally delved beneath the elastic of her thong and circled her clitoris she came apart on a long, drawn-out cry.

'Nick, that was—'

'Just the beginning.'

His wicked grin sent a tremor of excitement through her sated body and she gasped when he spun her around, his arm pinning her waist, her back in delicious contact with his front. His very aroused front.

'Let me please you—'

'You already have, sweetheart, by hearing you come,' he whispered in her ear, his teeth grazing the lobe, nipping, nuzzling until she could do little but sag against him, boneless with longing and pleasure. 'But just so you know, I'm calling the shots now.'

'Ah…my forceful bad boy is back.'

With a faux growl, he hugged her tighter. 'Then it's time I showed you just how bad I can be.'

Her body shuddered as he slid his hands up her ribcage to cradle her breasts, his thumbs teasing her nipples until a veritable flood of mind-numbing need drenched her.

He didn't stop there, oh, no, making good on his promise of being 'bad' as one hand braced the wall over her shoulder while the other played over her wet core.

Desire tightened within her, her hips rocking of their own volition as her inner muscles spasmed again and again as she threw back her head in absolute abandonment.

'Nick…'

She cried out his name as a part-plea, part-warning; she couldn't take much more of this, needed him inside her now.

'I'm right here.'

With a swift rip of unzipping metal and a rustle of tearing foil, he was back, pushing against her, holding her hips and angling them forward as he nudged against her entrance.

'Nick, please…'

He drove into her, hard and fast and heart-stoppingly long, the exquisite pressure filling her, tantalising her.

She'd waited so long for this, had dreamed about it, and when he started to pull out and thrust back into her, again and again and again, the sheer intense beauty of it robbed her of breath, of reason.

'Britt, my Britt.'

His possessiveness thrilled her as much as his hands gripping her hips, tilting them to increase the tempting friction as he plunged into her repeatedly, his rhythm driving them both towards a shattering climax.

'Wow,' she breathed on a sigh, her entire body humming and thrumming and sated as she sagged against him, her head lolling against his shoulder.

His barely audible oath had her head jerking up as she spun around to face him. 'What's wrong?'

'This. Here.'

He gestured around the kitchen before dropping his gaze to her bunched skirt and thong around her knees, shaking his head. 'You deserve more than this.'

Mustering what little dignity a woman with her knickers around her knees could have, she wriggled back into her thong before jabbing him in the chest.

'Don't you dare apologise for the best sex I've ever had. It was perfect. Better than perfect, it was stupendous.'

The corners of his wickedly sexy mouth kicked up. 'The best, huh?'

She nodded emphatically. 'The best.'

His grin widened. 'So you like a guy so out of control he can't make it to the bedroom?'

Grabbing his lapels, she hauled him close until their noses almost touched.

'Not just any guy, I like you, Nick Mancini. Every delicious bad-boy inch of you.'

'I love it when you talk dirty to me.'

'I didn't mean—'

'I know.'

He chuckled, rubbed noses with her as he stroked her back, long, languid strokes that relaxed her, and she rested her cheek on his chest, inhaling his seductive scent.

'Do you think it's ironic we're back here where it all started?'

She pulled away, glanced up at him. 'You mean my first time?'

He nodded, caressed her cheek with a tenderness that stole her breath and warmed her heart.

'I wanted to make it special for you then too. So what happened? The oven was on the blink so the pizza was cold, the dessert wouldn't defrost and I sprayed cola all over you.'

She smiled at the memories. 'That night was special, and it was all because of you.'

Her fingertips skimmed his jaw, savouring the faint prickle of stubble before hovering over his lips, tracing their outline. 'You were incredible, and I've never forgotten that night.'

Or the few months after it, when they'd sneak down to the river to make love underneath the towering eucalypts or beneath the beautiful jacarandas.

To this day, she couldn't walk past a jacaranda without blushing, its unique fragrance a poignant reminder of Nick laying her on a carpet of purple blossoms and taking her to the heavens and back.

'I say we recreate the magic. Though this time, we might even make it to the bedroom. You in?'

Excitement trickled through her body, fast becoming a raging torrent as she nodded and he swept her into his arms and headed for his old bedroom.

'I'm definitely in,' she said, laughing out loud when he twirled her around a few times before bumping the door open with his hip.

'Good, because if you'd said no I would've dropped you.'

Nipping the skin beneath his jaw, she nuzzled him. 'You wouldn't dare.'

'Never dare a rebel,' he said, dumping her on the bed before joining her, their laughter surrounding them in lovely warmth.

'Oh, wow.'

She glanced around the room, at the wooden shelves stacked high with trophies, several motorbike helmets in one corner, old leather jackets in the other.

'This room hasn't changed.'

He shrugged, somewhat embarrassed. 'I never stay out here. My life's in Noosa now. I guess Papa was too busy running the place when he was alive to worry about changing the bedrooms.'

Did he know his voice changed when he spoke of his father? Deepened? Softened? As if caught up in good times.

She envied him that, had always envied him the easy, close relationship he'd shared with his dad. It was one of the reasons she'd liked hanging out here so much; that and the mean lasagne Papa used to cook.

'I love this place. Do you really need to sell?'

A momentary shadow clouded his eyes before he blinked and it vanished.

'It's not fair to let it run down. And I just don't have the time to do much out here.'

'Why don't you hire a manager? Farm hands? Get the plantation up and running again?'

He shook his head, the tiny indentation between his brows a sign she was butting into business that was no concern of hers.

'You know what this place meant to Papa.'

He didn't have to add 'and to me'. She could see his reluctance to sell in his clenched jaw, in his rigid neck muscles, could hear it in his tense tone.

'All the more reason to keep it, bring it back to life—'

'It's time to let the place go. You of all people should understand the power of memories and the need to move on from the past.'

Oh, yeah, she understood the need to move on all too well. As for memories, her good ones were all focused on Nick and, rather than push the issue about the farm, she needed to start creating new ones.

'Yeah, I get it.' Her gaze caught a flash of silver hanging off the mirror. 'Hey, is that the medallion I gave you?'

He followed her line of vision, the slight pink staining his tanned cheeks a dead giveaway he'd rather forget the fact he'd kept a girly trinket.

'Maybe.'

She rolled off the bed, evading his arms as he made a lunge for her.

'It is! I can't believe you kept it all this time.'

'Like I said, this room has been untouched since I left it.'

Her heart expanded as she slung the delicate chain on her finger, tracing the outline of the star on the medallion with her finger.

'You know why I chose a star, don't you?'

He shook his head and she dangled the chain on her finger a second longer before rehanging it on the mirror.

'Because you hung the stars and moon for me back then.'

He came up behind her, slid his arms around her waist and held her close.

'And now?'

'Let's find out.'

She turned in the circle of his embrace, ready for his kiss, every cell in her body crying out for him, only him.

His mouth moved over hers, hot, challenging, and she matched him, their kisses deep and long and luscious, the type of kisses to melt a body and sear a soul.

If they'd kissed like this all night long she would've been happy, but she didn't want to settle. Not tonight.

Tonight she wanted those stars and that moon.

'I want you so much,' he murmured, trailing his lips down her neck as his thumbs nudged the underside of her breasts, toying with her, teasing her, before drifting upwards to circle her tight nipples through the silk.

Her head fell back on a moan as he deftly flicked the clasp on her shoulder and the Grecian dress slithered down her body in a rustle of silk, its caress almost as erotic as Nick's hands.

'Jeez,' he muttered, his gaze raking her from head to foot before resting on her breasts, the naked need in his eyes sending a tremor of unbridled lust shooting through her. 'You're even more gorgeous now, if that's possible.'

Smiling, she tugged on his jacket. 'Still the sweet talker.'

He shook his head, his dazed expression vindication he found her mature body just as appealing as the lithe teenager she'd once been.

Sliding the jacket off his shoulders, she started working on his bow tie. 'But for now, less talk, more action.'

'You want to see some action?'

His scorching kiss had her grateful for the edge of the bed bumping the backs of her knees as she collapsed onto it, happily watching as he shucked off the rest of his clothes in record time.

'I like those,' she said, pointing to the black boxers that had been haunting her dreams ever since she'd glimpsed them on their wedding night.

'And I like those.'

He toyed with the top of her white lace thong, sending a river of heat straight to her core.

'But not enough to keep them on.'

He whipped them off and tossed them over his shoulder, his eyes glazing as his gaze roamed her.

'Come here.'

She held her arms out to him and he entered her embrace in a second, the touch of his bare skin against hers sizzling hot.

He kissed her, laved her, delved his fingers into her until she was panting for release, clutching at him, crying out his name, sobbing her need when the mind-numbing tension climbed and spiralled and shattered into a million shooting stars.

She couldn't think, couldn't speak, and she whimpered when he left her for a moment to rip off his boxers and roll a condom on.

'I'm right here, sweetheart.'

'Where you belong,' she said, a second before his mouth claimed hers and he lay on top of her, sliding inside with a smooth, powerful thrust that made her gasp.

He filled her, completed her and she wrapped her legs around him, tilting her hips to encourage deeper contact.

Then he moved, sliding in and out, every move sending shards of exquisite pleasure firing through her, making every nerve ending sit up and cry for more.

And he gave her more.

He drove into her, his chest rasping her sensitised nipples, his tongue mating with hers, his rhythm taking them higher and higher until he stiffened and cried out her name, shuddering into her.

Brittany had no idea how long they stayed locked together, their heart rates slowly calming, their breathing soft and ragged.

She didn't mind his weight, didn't mind the slick of sweat between their bodies.

She'd asked for the stars and the moon.

Nick had delivered the whole damn solar system.

CHAPTER ELEVEN

SLEEPING with Britt had been a bad idea.

Not that there'd been much sleeping involved.

Their cataclysmic night had changed everything.

'This place hasn't changed a bit,' she said, tugging his hand as she ran towards the river's edge, leaving Nick no option but to follow.

And follow he would, to the ends of the earth if she asked, for last night had shattered any illusions he had about this marriage being all business.

With every kiss, with every caress, with every gut-wrenching moan, she'd stripped away the years, catapulting him straight back to a time he was so crazy for her he couldn't see straight.

Nothing had changed, absolutely nothing.

Even that was a lie.

Ten years ago, he'd been a fool, kidding himself all he felt for Britt was lust.

Now he knew the truth.

What they'd shared had never just been about lust; it was more than that, so much more.

And their night of passion had hurtled him back a decade, to a time he couldn't get enough of her, to a time where his heart clamoured towards her while his head reeled back with the implications of trusting a woman.

'Do you miss Jacaranda?'

She stopped, alerted to the seriousness of his question by something in his voice as he waved towards the river, trying to distract her.

It didn't work, for she reached up, cupped his cheek, her simple touch as catastrophic as if she'd reached into his chest and squeezed his heart.

'I tried not to. I tried to forget.'

Her fingertips trailed down his cheek, lingered on his jaw, before dropping lower where she placed her palm flat against his chest, directly over his heart. Claiming ownership. It was hers, had always been hers, he just never admitted it.

'But I couldn't. This place is in my blood. I never forgot it.'

She paused, massaged his chest gently as if soothing his soul. 'I never forgot you.'

'Same here.'

He settled his mouth over hers, needing this kiss, aching for it. Nothing like the ache of how he'd wanted her last night, when he'd been blinded by lust and passion.

Uh-uh, this ache settled right over his heart, exactly where her hand was, the kind of ache that scared the hell out of him.

Her lips parted, so soft, so moist, and he groaned as his tongue touched hers, going a little crazy as he backed her up against the nearest tree, their bodies melding perfectly, his hands sliding under her top, cupping her breasts.

'Nick…'

Her wanton plea made his hard-on throb as he lifted her top, ducked his head, and captured an erect nipple between his teeth, plucking at the lace covering it, her low moans firing him to flick the clasp and allow the tempting lushness to fall into his hands.

But the Jacaranda fauna had other ideas as a raucous cackle of a nearby kookaburra pierced the silence and reminded him of where they were.

In the good old days this river bed was deserted but now the worn track along the bank showed exactly how popular this spot was with bushwalkers and tourists and he had no intention of providing an X-rated show for any of them.

Reluctantly tugging her top down, he brushed a soft kiss against her lips.

'You used to love those damn birds. Too bad this one has shocking timing.'

She laughed, a clear, joyous sound that had him chuckling right along with her. 'Remember the time we made out down here and—?'

'Can we change the subject?' He sent a pointed look at his groin. 'You're killing me, in case you hadn't noticed.'

As she ground her pelvis against his her smile was pure evil. 'Oh, I noticed.'

She slid her hands around his neck, bringing her breasts flush against his chest. 'Why don't we continue this *discussion* back at the farm?'

'You're one wicked woman,' he said, smoothing stray tendrils of copper gold away from her face, his heart bucking at the adoration in her eyes.

He wanted her to look at him like this, wanted her. Then why the faintest doubt he was deluding himself, about everything?

One night and he'd been blinded to the transient nature of their marriage: her job, her promotion, their deal.

Last night changed everything, but they hadn't discussed it, any of it, and while now wasn't ideal there would come a time soon, very soon, where they'd both need to lay it all on the line.

'Come on, let's head back.'

He didn't need to be asked twice and as they sprinted back to the farmhouse, laughing and falling over their flying feet, he banished his doubts and decided to live in the moment.

For now.

* * *

Brittany paced from one end of their suite to the other, casting malevolent glances at her laptop on each circuit and the incriminating email on the screen.

The promotion was hers.

David had seen the preliminary pitch she'd emailed, blown away by the video footage, pictures of the plantation and the accompanying spread, had evaluated it and made his decision.

She was the new managing director of Sell.

She'd done it.

Which meant her work here was done.

So where did that leave her and Nick?

She should be ecstatic, her dream finally a reality with the added bonus of clearing her debt to Daddy dearest and finally being free of her past.

Instead, dread warred with terror as she mentally rehearsed her spiel.

She had to tell Nick the truth.

She was leaving, heading back to her job, back to a dream she'd worked incredibly hard for, had strived for, had given up a heck of a lot for.

But what if the dream had changed?

What if the dream had evolved to include a sexy billionaire, a pristine beach and a very real marriage?

At the sound of the door opening she stopped, lunged at the laptop and slammed it shut.

She was nowhere near ready for this.

'Hey, how's the most beautiful girl in Noosa doing?'

'Great.'

She forced a smile, quelling the urge to blurt the truth the instant he stepped through the door.

He opened his arms. 'Come here. Rough day at the office and I need a welcome kiss from my wife.'

She flew into his arms, crushing her lips to his in an urgent, validating kiss before burrowing into his chest, seeking comfort, seeking warmth, seeking a solution to her terrible dilemma.

She wanted the promotion.

She wanted him.

And never the twain should meet.

'What's up?'

He pulled away, his hands spanning her waist, anchoring her in a world spinning dangerously out of control.

'We need to discuss our arrangement.'

Frowning, he dropped his hands and stepped away, leaving her cursing her choice of words and wishing there were a simple solution to this.

But there wasn't and she needed to face the truth: she'd fallen for Nick all over again, had blown her 'have fun for a short time not a long time' motto and, in doing so, had the potential to blow her dream job too.

'By arrangement I assume you mean our marriage?'

She nodded, biting her bottom lip as his face wiped of all expression, his cool indifference a frightening reminder of the emotional barriers he'd slammed up the weeks leading up to the night he'd dashed her dreams of a future ten years earlier.

'I got the promotion.'

'Congratulations.'

He thrust his hands in his pockets, his calculating gaze not leaving hers, as if daring her to continue, daring her to speak her mind and put an end to this.

'It's all happened rather soon—'

'When do you leave?'

No begging her to stay, no declaration of undying love.

But then, what did she expect?

Ever since their marriage had turned physical they'd slipped into old ways; comfortable with each other, teasing, joking, making up for lost time in the bedroom.

Yet they'd skirted around the issue of a future, never

chatting beyond the day-to-day events, making love with frantic abandon as if each time could be their last.

It reminded her of the past, of the fragile nature of their relationship back then. But Nick wasn't the bad-ass rebel any more and she wasn't the wide-eyed romantic dreaming of happily ever after.

She hadn't got as far as she had in her career without being practical and there was no way she'd give up on them without a fight.

There had to be a solution to this, there just had to be.

Grabbing her hair and twisting it into a loose knot at the base of her neck, she sank onto the edge of the bed and patted it.

'My leaving depends on you.'

He eyed her warily, his rigid posture at odds with the fleeting yearning in his eyes as his gaze strayed to the spot next to her.

'Come on, take a seat. We need to sort this out.'

'Fine.'

With a terse nod, he flung himself into an armchair opposite, his inflexible expression not giving an inch.

'Don't trust me?'

'Don't trust myself.'

A glimmer of a smile tugged at the corners of his mouth, giving her hope. 'You know what happens any time I get near you on a bed.'

'Not just a bed, from memory.'

His eyes darkened to burnt caramel and she swallowed. It was so easy slipping into old ways with him; teasing, flirting. But flirting wouldn't solve this, nothing but a good dose of honesty would, and she steadied her resolve to confront this rather than tumble into bed with him and forget everything.

She shook her head, breaking eye contact, and when she met his gaze again he'd cooled, slipping those darn barriers firmly back in place.

'What do you want?'

The million-dollar question: if only she had a priceless answer.

'Honestly? I want it all. My job, the promotion, you…'

She trailed off, hoping he'd fill the void, say something, anything, to give her some indication he wanted this marriage to work as much as she did.

But he didn't move, didn't speak, his lips clamped shut in tight disapproval, leaving her floundering for her next words when she was usually brilliantly articulate at work.

With her job, she knew what she wanted and knew what to say to get it. She'd nailed pitches other companies craved, had climbed to the top with sheer determination.

Those skills weren't exclusive to advertising and right now she knew what she wanted, and he was staring at her with studied apathy she knew had to be a front.

'I know this marriage was a business arrangement at first, but the boundaries have changed.'

Taking a deep breath, she made the pitch of her life. 'I want this marriage to work, and not just because of our deal at the start. We've got something special, something that time apart hasn't erased, and I know if we give this a chance it can be the best thing to happen to us.'

His expression thawed, his shoulders relaxing as he swiped a hand over his face and she went for broke.

'Whatever it takes to make this marriage work, I'll do it. If it means giving up my job in London and moving here…'

She shrugged, shocked by the words coming out of her mouth, yet strangely relieved.

She'd voiced a solution, a terrifying, monstrous, life-changing solution, and rather than being overwhelmed by the enormity of it her heart expanded, filled with a surprising peace.

Shock darkened his eyes to chocolate as he leaned forward, bracing his elbows on his knees.

'You'd do that for me?'

'For us.'

Padding over to join him, she plopped onto his lap, leaving him no option but to hold her.

'Hell, Red, I don't know what to say.'

'Then don't say anything for now.'

She placed a finger against his lips, yearning to trace the contours but knowing this wasn't the time. Despite his shell-shocked expression he hadn't lost the wariness and she knew he needed time: time to think, to assimilate, to decide.

She knew what she wanted; it looked as if her husband needed to figure out the same.

'Think about it. We'll talk later.'

Brushing a kiss across his lips, she slipped from his arms, saddened he let her go but determined to give him the time he needed.

She'd done her bit to save their marriage.

The rest was up to him.

CHAPTER TWELVE

NICK did the one thing guaranteed to blow away the cobwebs of confusion threading his thoughts into a muddled jumble.

He hit the road.

Slamming his visor down, he glanced over his shoulder, let out the throttle and savoured the roar of the motorbike as he pulled out onto the open highway.

It had been way too long since he'd done this.

Putting his past behind him came at a price and, while slaving his guts out to make a success of his business had worked, he missed the simple things in life. Like making pasta from scratch, cooking the rich, creamy sauces Papa had shown him, growing the herbs to complete any good Italian meal, taking off on a whim and riding as far as a tank of petrol lasted.

And Britt.

He'd missed her more than he'd ever imagined, hadn't known how much until she'd strutted back into his life with her fancy suits and stellar career.

The simple life…he'd had it once but had moved on. For what? Fame? Fortune? To impress a bunch of rich phoneys who hadn't given him the time of day until he'd proven he could be responsible by marrying?

He'd been a fool.

None of it mattered, not any more.

Britt wanted him.

At what cost? He couldn't let her give up her dream for him and, as much as he appreciated how far she was willing to go to give them a chance, it scared the hell out of him.

They'd barely been married six weeks and she was willing to lay it all on the line? For him?

Old doubts crept under his guard, crawled under his skin until he itched to pull over and scratch them away.

What if he wasn't good enough for her?

What if he couldn't be the man she deserved?

What if she didn't need him as much as he needed her?

Yeah, the same old doubts, undermining the confident, successful man he'd become.

Crazy. But then, so was their unrelenting passion that hadn't waned in ten long years.

But were they making up for lost time? Fulfilling an affair they never really had first time around? Confusing a sizzling attraction for a deeper emotion they'd need as a solid foundation to build a real marriage on?

The wind filled his ears, not loud enough to obliterate the questions whirling through his head, and he glanced down at the speedometer, muttering a curse as he realised he'd momentarily lost concentration.

All this mulling was pointless anyway. Until he cleared the past, he couldn't make way for the future.

If they were to have any future, he had to tell Britt the truth. All of it.

Making an impulsive decision that had landed him in more scrapes as a youngster than he cared to admit, he slowed, checked for traffic and made a U-turn.

Time to pay his past a visit.

Nick rang the reception bell, glancing around as he waited. He'd assumed the local special accommodation for the elderly

would be shabby, run-down, with the cloying smell of disin-
fectant and overcooked stew in the air.

Surprisingly, this place could pass for a hotel with its manicured lawns, new whitewash, elegant furniture and sweeping
veranda, with floor-to-ceiling windows highlighting a breathtaking vista. Then again, would he expect Darby Lloyd to live
in anything less?

'Can I help you?'

A middle-aged woman in a nurse's uniform bustled out from
a back room and leaned over the desk with a beaming smile.

'I hope so. I'd like to see Darby Lloyd?'

To her credit, the nurse's smile didn't slip, but he saw the
fleeting surprise in her twinkling eyes.

'Certainly. Darby doesn't get many visitors so I'm sure
he'll be thrilled to see you.'

He bit back a grin. The last thing good old Darby would
be was thrilled.

'Follow me.'

If the outside had been impressive, the inside of the place
knocked him for six as he followed the nurse down a series
of corridors. Paintings of every size and description covered
the walls, antiques tastefully arranged on every available inch
of furniture and the rich, polished Tasmanian Oak floorboards
gleamed in the late afternoon light pouring through the
atrium-like ceilings.

The nurse came to an abrupt halt outside a mahogany door
and gestured him forward. 'Just knock and head on in. Though
please keep your visit brief. Darby's blood pressure's elevated
and he has a tendency to overdo things.'

'You have my word.'

His wink was rewarded with a blush and a smile as she
bustled away, leaving him with lead in his boots.

He shouldn't have come here, unannounced, especially if
the old man was having a bad day. He hadn't seen Darby in

ten years, hadn't wanted to after what he'd done, but that was the past and if he wanted to move forward he had to lay it to rest, once and for all.

He took a deep breath, knocked twice and pushed the door open.

'Mr Lloyd, it's Nick Mancini.'

He'd hated this man for years, had mentally prepared himself to face his nemesis. What he hadn't prepared for was the swift rush of compassion for the pale, frail old man sitting in a recliner, propped up by a mountain of pillows, his eyes closed.

He'd never seen Darby anything but overbearing, arrogant and mean, lording his wealth over everyone foolish enough to get close to him and anyone else who crossed his path. But that man had disappeared beneath a plethora of wrinkles and a greyish pallor that suggested a long-standing illness.

Anxious to get this over and done with, Nick cleared his throat and stepped into the room.

'What the hell are you doing here?'

Darby's eyes flew open, their feverish glint a startling contrast to the pallor of his pasty skin.

'We need to talk, clear the air.'

'I've got nothing to say to you, so get out.'

Still the same cantankerous fool, but there was no way he was leaving without saying his piece.

'I will, but before I go you need to listen.'

Nick kept his voice devoid of emotion, not wanting to agitate the old guy further considering he'd now flushed an ugly crimson.

'About you marrying my daughter? About bringing disgrace on this family? Dragging our name through the mud?' Darby sat bolt upright, shook a fist at him. 'I don't want to hear it. You've won, damn you. Isn't that enough?'

Clenching his fists, Nick shoved them deep into his jacket

pockets, not willing to show the slightest indication he felt anything other than indifference for Darby's poisonous barbs.

Before he could utter a word, Darby pushed up from his chair, his neck muscles rigid, his expression thunderous, his eyes gleaming with a maniacal edge.

'Just because I'm stuck in this godforsaken place don't think I'm stupid, boy. I know what you're up to, marrying Brittany out of spite, taking your revenge on me.' He stabbed his finger in the air, tottering slightly. 'That stupid girl deserves everything she gets for running around with the likes of you. She won't get another penny out of me now. I've given her more than enough to pad her new life in London. So if you were hoping for a silver lining to your marriage, too bad. You can both go to the devil.'

Nick silently swore and took a step back, not wanting to believe what he was hearing but, like onlookers at an accident, drawn to the horrifying carnage.

The extent of Darby Lloyd's hatred didn't shock him half as much as his total disregard for his only child, and if the old guy didn't look as if he had one foot in the grave, Nick would willingly give him a shove in that direction for his callousness towards Britt.

Instilling a calm he knew would drive the old coot mad, he said, 'You're wrong. Our marriage has nothing to do with you or what happened in the past. She's your daughter. Don't you care enough about her to at least maintain civilities with me?'

Darby flushed puce, staggered and flopped back in his chair while Nick shook his head.

He'd been wrong to come here.

Time hadn't soothed the old man's rampant prejudice; it had festered and grown until he couldn't see reason.

'Get out, Mancini, and don't come back.'

Shaking his head, Nick opened the door. By the old guy's shallow breaths and mottled red cheeks, he should probably send the nurse in before he left.

'One more thing, Mancini.'

He paused on the threshold, turned, eager to get out of this place and back to Britt. He could tell her all of it now, for nothing either of them could say or do would make an ounce of difference where Darby was concerned.

'Yeah?'

'I hope you rot in hell for going near my daughter in the first place.'

Without a word, Nick walked out and didn't look back.

Brittany reread the same paragraph for the fifth time before leaping up from the keyboard.

Work had succeeded in distracting her from losing Nick a decade earlier, but it wasn't doing a thing for her now. She'd scanned her emails, managed to form coherent replies for the important ones, read the documentation David had forwarded from Human Resources and toyed with an idea to grab the lucrative advertising contract for a World Cup soccer team.

All perfectly stimulating stuff she would normally thrive on, but today she couldn't concentrate for more than a few seconds at a time, her mind constantly drifting to Nick.

Where was he?

What was he thinking?

Why had he run out on her when they needed to discuss this like two normal people?

He needed time, she understood. But the fact he'd barely spoken more than two syllables since she'd dropped her bombshell didn't bode well.

Bombshell? She'd detonated their relationship clean out of the water; first, with the news she was leaving, then with her follow-up declaration she'd give up her dream job to be with her dream man.

Was she crazy?

Yeah, crazy about a bad-boy billionaire with molten-toffee eyes and a smile that made her belly clench with desire.

Heading for the window where she could waste another half-hour or so staring at the killer view without really seeing it, she stopped as she heard the door open and swung around in time to see Nick burst into the suite, his hair dishevelled, his expression wild.

'Are you okay?'

His eyes lit up as they fixed on her. 'I am now.'

'What's all this about—?'

He crossed the room in two seconds flat, swept her into his arms and crushed his mouth to hers, effectively silencing her, annihilating the need to talk with a frantic, hungry kiss that wiped every sane thought from her mind, let alone the questions that had plagued her for the last few hours.

After an exquisite eternity, they came up for air and she clung to him, needing a steady anchor for her boneless legs.

He'd always had the ability to do this, turn her into a quivering, love-struck girl, but she wasn't a naïve young woman any more.

She needed more than a ride on the back of his bike and a roll in the plantation's hay. She needed a guy willing to accept her for who she was. She needed him.

'I've been doing some thinking.'

'I figured that, considering you tore out of here like a cane burnout was sparking at your heels.'

He grimaced, released her to run a hand through his hair. 'Sorry about that. I needed space. You know I need time out when things get tough.'

'Tough? You ain't seen nothing yet.'

She smiled, while her belly twisted in an agony of nerves. Now he was here, she wanted to shake the truth out of him, wanted him to tell her exactly what he was thinking and put her out of her misery once and for all.

'You should take the job.'

'Oh.'

Disappointment ripped through her, the pain of losing him again cleaving her heart in two.

She'd made the pitch of her life—and failed.

'But only if we work out a way to spend at least six months of the year together. It's going to be hard enough letting my wife out of my sight for that long as it is.'

Her gaze flew to his, seeking some hidden meaning behind his words, not daring to believe her dream could still become a reality.

'Are you saying—?'

'I'm saying this marriage is as real as it gets, Red.'

She let out an ear-splitting squeal as he picked her up and swung her around until she was breathless and laughing and crying all at the same time.

'Hey, don't do that.'

His tenderness in swiping her tears away only made them fall faster and he bundled her into his arms, stroking her hair as she burrowed into her favourite place in the world, inhaling the pure ambrosia of fresh air and ocean and Nick.

She couldn't get enough of him and the thought they had a lifetime together ahead made her light-headed with joy.

'About this marriage—'

The funky tune of her mobile vibrated against her thigh and she fumbled for the phone, switching the darn thing off with a flick.

'You were saying?'

He grinned. 'That could've been important.'

'Nothing's as important as hearing you talk about *our* marriage.'

'Well, then, let's—'

She let a curse slip as the suite's phone rang, loud and jarring, and she laid a hand on his arm as he reached for it.

'Leave it.'

Sweeping a swift kiss across her lips, still tingling from his recent sensual assault, he said, 'Maybe someone's trying to get hold of you? First the mobile, now here? Just answer it, fob them off so we can get to the good stuff.'

He nuzzled her neck and she moaned, trying to block out the incessant jangling of the phone before giving in with a reluctant curse and snatching it up.

'Hello?'

'Ms Lloyd? It's Nurse Peters from the Jacaranda special accommodation facility. I'm sorry to say your father has had another stroke. It's best you come as soon as possible.'

'I'll be right there.'

An instinctive response, a response she might not have given if she'd had time to think, but once it had slipped out and she'd hung up she knew she had no other choice but to go, regardless of her ambivalent feelings towards her dad.

'What's wrong?'

Twisting her hair into a knot at her nape before letting it fall, she said, 'It's my father. He's had another stroke.'

'Hell.'

Nick turned away, but not before she'd glimpsed a flicker of guilt she didn't understand.

'I have to go.'

'Of course. Want me to come with you?'

She shook her head, laid a hand on his arm. 'No, I'll be fine.'

Her hand drifted upwards, stroked his cheek, her heart swelling with love for her husband. *Her husband*. She had the right to really call him that now and she couldn't be happier.

'You stay here, I'll be back as soon as I can and we can talk some more.'

He pulled her in for one last, hungry kiss before releasing her and she hurried out the door.

The faster she paid her father an obligatory visit he'd done nothing to deserve, the faster she could start the rest of her life.

CHAPTER THIRTEEN

BRITTANY paused on the threshold of her father's room, focusing on the man that had made her life a living hell propped up in bed.

He didn't deserve this, no one deserved to suffer like this, mind and body wasting away, sapped of dignity, no matter what their sins.

She'd rushed here out of what? Obligation? Caring? It certainly wasn't love. He'd wiped any semblance of that emotion the first time he'd raised his hand to her.

Taking a deep breath, she stepped into the room.

Whatever sense of familial duty had made her come, she didn't want to stay. If he hadn't wanted to broach the gap between them a few weeks earlier, there was no way things would've changed now. If anything, being incapacitated would sour his mood further and she had no intention of bearing the brunt of his temper. Never again.

'Dad?'

She tiptoed to the bed, reaching a hand out to touch his arm before letting it fall to her side when he turned his head slightly, saw her, then rolled towards the wall.

'Go away. Leave me to die in peace.'

The words came out on a croak rather than his usual grunt, shout or bark and for a second a sliver of remorse prompted her to touch him on the shoulder.

He stiffened, allowing her fingertips to linger before shrugging them off.

'You're not dying, Dad. The doctor said you've had another minor stroke with no residual effects.'

He made a sudden move, rolling towards her, and she hated her first reaction was to take a step back.

When was the last time she wasn't afraid of this man, afraid of what he was capable of?

The last time they'd had a normal conversation without his latent temper threatening to explode, she'd been sixteen years old and he'd been teasing her about taking French as an elective at school. It had been the day before her mum had left and the memory stood out as a particularly poignant one as the last time she'd ever connected with him, the last time she'd ever felt safe in his presence.

'What do those old fools know? Pumping me full of heart tablets and blood thinners and goodness knows what. Quacks, the lot of them.'

She hadn't come here to argue, hadn't come to listen to his moaning.

From what the doc said, Darby wasn't going to die any time soon and she could leave him to harass the highly paid staff here and walk away, safe in the knowledge she'd done the right thing no matter how much it stung he didn't give a damn.

'You'll be fine—'

'What are you doing here anyway? Had a fight with that no-good husband of yours?'

His malice-filled eyes narrowed, a nasty grimace twisting his lips as he lifted a trembling arm to jab a finger in her direction before letting it fall uselessly on the bed, and she determinedly quashed a surge of pity.

'Nick and I are happy. We—'

'Happy? More fool you. The only reason that lousy son of

a gun married you was for revenge. Even came around here earlier to gloat.'

Unease gnawed at her, insidious and malignant. She had no intention of listening to the hateful ramblings of a vile old man hell-bent on poisoning everyone around him with his vitriol, but something in his smug grin made her skin crawl with apprehension.

'Hates my guts, always has, ever since we made our little bargain.'

She clamped her jaw shut, determined not to ask what he meant, but her curiosity must've shown for he struggled into a half-sitting position, his expression positively gloating.

'Bet he didn't tell you about our pact. He stopped sniffing around you, I let his stupid old man keep that pathetic excuse for a plantation.'

A faint buzzing filled her head and she took several quick breaths, desperate for air, desperate for anything to wipe the last few moments.

'How does it feel, to come in last in a two-horse race?'

His bitter laugh raised her hackles and she backed towards the door, shocked she'd once loved this man, horrified at what he'd become.

'Yep, revenge, pure and sweet. Mancini must be real happy with your *marriage*.'

He spat the last word and she turned and bolted, clutching a stomach that roiled with the sickening truth.

Nick didn't love her.

Their marriage wasn't real.

This had all been a sick, twisted game to him.

Her feet flew down the corridor and as she stumbled into the fresh air and doubled over with the pain of his deception she promised herself she'd never get taken in by Nick Mancini ever again.

* * *

By the time Brittany arrived back at the hotel, the legendary temper attributed to her hair colour had hit boiling point.

She wanted to pack her bags and jump on the first flight back to London, but not before she'd told Nick a few home truths.

She might have been the good little girl ten years earlier who'd gone quietly after letting him walk all over her, but not any more. This time, she'd go out with a bang.

She could kill him for making her love him again, for causing the incessant ache gripping her heart until she could barely breathe.

All she needed was a reason, and that reason glanced up from his desk and fixed his melted toffee gaze on her as she stalked into their room.

'How's your dad?'

'You tell me.'

She slammed the door, leaned against it when his gaze turned compassionate. She didn't need his compassion, damn it, she needed the truth, all of it.

'Apparently you're so chummy you visited him.'

She snapped her fingers. 'Oh, wait, that wasn't about being friendly. You just wanted to gloat about finally getting your revenge.'

His expression wary, he stood, moved around the desk towards her.

'What are you talking about?'

'Don't patronise me!'

Her tenuous control on her temper snapped as she pushed off the door, met him halfway, placing both hands squarely in the middle of his chest and pushing, hard.

'He told me about your pact, about you choosing Papa over me. I get that family is important to you, but you could've told me, damn you. Do you know how long it took me to get over you? Do you?'

She pushed again, softer this time, a feeble attempt as her anger gave way to anguish.

'Let me explain—'

'Don't bother. I get it. You didn't love me enough then and you sure as hell don't love me now.'

To her mortification, she ended on a sob, knuckling her eyes to complete the pathetic picture with tears.

'Hey, you've got this all wrong.'

He manacled her wrists and she let him, all the fight drained out of her as she slumped onto the back of a chair.

Thumping him wasn't an option, not any more, with concern and tenderness and God-honest sincerity blazing from those unforgettable eyes.

'Have I? Because what my father said made sense.'

Releasing her wrists, he stepped back and ran a hand through his hair, his expression thunderous.

'Remember when you went to Brisbane for a month before leaving for London? Darby didn't know it wasn't a holiday, he thought you were coming back. So he warned me off you, threatened to take the plantation off Papa if I didn't back off.'

Anger tightened his voice, tensed his shoulders as he stalked to the window and braced against it.

'After Mum left, it was the only thing keeping Papa going and I couldn't let your father ruin him, so I did what I thought was right at the time, letting him believe he'd succeeded in ending things between us.'

Damn her dad.

Damn Nick for being right.

She couldn't blame him for his loyalty to Papa, couldn't fault his logic, but she didn't want logic or rationale right now, she needed to vent.

Snapping her fingers, she glared at him. 'Moot point, considering you'd already ended things between us.'

'I didn't want to let you go, Red.'

The sorrow in his tone had her head snapping up to scan his face for proof he was hurting as much as she was.

'Then why? Why did you shut me out those last few weeks? Push me away at the end?'

'You had your dreams, I had mine. We weren't in the right place back then to sustain a relationship.'

His sincerity twanged on her heartstrings, hard, and she gulped as a fresh wave of tears swamped her.

'And now? Our marriage—'

'Was never about revenge, not for one damn minute.'

He strode across the room, dropped to his knees and grabbed her hand. 'Do you honestly think I'd use you like that?'

'I don't know what to think—'

'Then don't.'

He hauled her into his arms and plastered his mouth to hers, obliterating the need to talk, to discuss, to rationalise, obliterating the need to do anything other than lose herself in the magic of his kiss.

But no matter how many times he kissed her, held her, made love to her, there would always be the nagging doubt he'd done this out of spite.

Sensing her wandering thoughts, he broke the kiss, gripped her arms as if he sensed she'd bolt.

'Our marriage was purely business at the start. That was the only reason I married you.'

'And now?'

'Now I want it all.'

She'd wanted to hear those words when she'd first come to him, had first poured her heart out to him.

She'd wanted him to sweep her into his arms and tell her he felt the same way.

But now…

'You still want the same thing, right?'

His desperate gaze searched hers and all she could manage was a slight nod.

But her game plan had changed.

Words were cheap. She'd learned the hard way: the first time her father had called her a filthy name and apologised with empty words, the first time he'd shoved her against the wall followed by more of those meaningless words, the first time he'd raised a hand to her, his pointless words not enough to bridge the yawning gap that had opened up between them.

She'd fled to London, had started a new life. Ironic, as she'd never felt as safe here as she had the last few weeks, only to have it ripped away by doubts planted by the one man she'd never believe and sending her fleeing to London all over again.

'I'm leaving for London.'

His face drained of colour. 'When?'

'Tomorrow.'

'But what about all that stuff you said? About wanting a real marriage? Surely you don't believe Darby—'

'I believe you, Nick, but I have a job to do. I can't just walk away from that. You're a businessman, you understand.'

She played the business card, knowing he'd buy it. Considering the success he'd made of himself, how far he'd gone to cement his reputation, it was the one argument guaranteed to sway him.

Ironic, she would've given away her precious MD job in a second if he'd professed his love a few hours earlier, but what did those three little words actually add up to? Actions spoke louder than ever and right now Nick could say anything and it would be tinged with the doubts her father had raised.

Reaching out to her, he slid his arms around her waist, tugged her close, and she let him.

'I love you, Red. You know that, right?'

The inner girl head over heels for this guy leaped up and punched the air while her mature, sensible counterpart patted her on the head, shoved her down and said, 'Hang on a minute.'

'It's the first time you've ever said it. How would I know?'

He flinched, the hurt in his eyes driving a stake through her heart.

'By my actions.'

'Which one? Where you chose to lie to me rather than tell me the truth ten years ago? Where you married me to get ahead in business?'

He laid a hand on her cheek, brushed her bottom lip with his thumb. 'Every night of our marriage has been real, every single moment I've held you in my arms. You can't fake what we have. And you can't walk away from it.'

'I'm not.'

She dropped her gaze, focused on a tiny thread working loose from his top buttonhole.

'Like hell you're not.'

He released her, stepped away, the tension between them palpable.

'I have to do this, Nick. It's important to me. As to what happens with us, we can work it out—'

'Give me tonight.'

She'd give him the next fifty years of her life if she could trust him, but right now she couldn't get past the doubt, couldn't trust herself around him, let alone anything he said.

She needed time, space. Yeah, as if that would help ease Nick Mancini out of her soul.

He held up a finger. 'One night, our last together for a while. Can you give me that?'

Words bubbled to her lips, empty, meaningless refusals about packing and winding up the local contractors Sell had used and saying goodbyes, but none of them spilled as she found herself nodding.

'Okay.'

Pulling her in for a swift kiss that left her head spinning and her heart a pounding mass of riotous confusion, he said, 'You won't regret it.'

She already did as he strode out of the door.

CHAPTER FOURTEEN

NICK could've wasted time and energy cursing Darby Lloyd but, instead, he put his plan into action.

When he'd initially heard what Britt had said he'd wanted the old man dead, Darby's hatred obliterating the temporary guilt his visit might have caused another stroke.

The old man was vile, determined to ruin his own daughter's happiness. What sort of a father did that to his only child, try to wreck her relationship?

Nick had never been Darby's favourite, especially when he'd started making it big in the district, but what about Britt? Didn't the old guy love her at all?

Something niggled at his conscience, wedged like a spur, digging and needling…something about Britt not knowing about Papa's death.

He'd put it down to Darby not giving a damn about Papa, not bothering to inform Britt about something so trivial in his high-and-mighty world, but what if there was another reason behind her lack of knowledge?

For a woman hell-bent on gaining a promotion she'd travelled halfway around the world to do it, why hadn't she spent more time with her father? A father who was ailing?

He hadn't given it a second thought, happily taking up

every spare moment of Britt's time when she wasn't working, but now he thought about it…

Yeah, something wasn't right and when he'd asked her about it, had mentioned what Darby had said about not giving her any more money because she'd married him, she'd paled before swiftly changing the subject. He could've pushed the issue but didn't want tonight to be about anything other than them.

Staring around the room, he hoped he was doing the right thing.

Would she remember?

Would it mean anything to her?

He'd told her he loved her but it wasn't enough. He'd seen it in every reluctant cell of her body.

Well, he was through talking.

Time to prove their marriage was real in every way.

He had no intention of letting her walk away thinking otherwise.

Unwelcome déjà vu washed over Brittany as she stood outside her father's room.

She'd been a fool to come here, especially after everything that had happened, but something Nick had said about her father niggled.

They'd been discussing Darby and she'd clammed up, not interested in rehashing anything her father had done or said when Nick had visited him.

That was when Nick had dropped his little gem: even though Darby was a nasty old coot, he must love her enough to give her money to start a new life in London.

Just like that, the emotional blinkers blinding her eyes lifted a fraction.

Considering why she'd fled home, headed for the opposite side of the world to escape, when he'd told her she'd instantly assumed Darby's reason for giving her the money had been about control as always.

Never once had she contemplated any other reason.

But the more she thought about it, the more it didn't make sense.

If he'd truly hated her back then as she believed, why would he cushion her? Why not see her fail and hope she'd come running home rather than give her money to prop her up?

She had to know why he'd done it.

Clenching and unclenching her hands, she rolled her shoulders, stretched her neck from side to side like a prize fighter about to take on the champ.

With her muscles as relaxed as they were going to get, she knocked and entered, striding across the room to the bed, where her father lay. He looked so old and tired that she felt a sudden rush of pity, until he looked up and sent her a ferocious glare.

'Thought I told you to—'

'Why did you do it, Dad?'

His upper lip curled. 'Trust Mancini to tell you about our bargain—'

'Not that. The money. Why did you give me that money and pretend it was Mum's?'

She'd never seen her dad anything but aloof, cold, angry after her mum left, hadn't seen him blink when the news of her death had reached them, and for the first time in for ever she saw uncertainty cloud his eyes, contort his expression into that of a confused old man.

He didn't respond, his gnarled hands wringing beneath the bedcovers.

'Dad? Tell me. You owe me that much.'

She expected him to say 'I owe you nothing' in a classic gruff Darby response, so she almost keeled over when he pushed into sitting and beckoned her closer.

'The only reason I let you go to Brisbane for that holiday is because I couldn't stand the sight of you cowering any more.'

He stared at the coverlet, his frown deepening. 'Then when you didn't come back and sent that email you were in London and weren't coming back, I was worried.'

'You'd have to care to worry,' she said, hating the flare of hope she'd finally get some answers to questions that had plagued her for years.

'I cared.'

His shocking declaration came out a whisper and she almost slapped her ears to ensure she'd heard right.

'You call abusing me caring? All those put-downs and shoves and—' She inhaled sharply, breathed deeply, trying to relax. A futile effort, as years of resentment bubbled up. 'You were my dad, you should've loved me! What did I do wrong? Why did you treat me like that? Tell me, damn you!'

To her amazement, tears squeezed from the corners of his eyes and trickled down his wrinkled cheeks unchecked, the sorrow in his gaze wrenching a soul-deep response she didn't want to acknowledge.

He opened his mouth, closed it, before shaking his head.

'None of it was your fault, none of it.'

His low groan of pain had her darting an anxious glance at the heart-monitor machine but the blood-pressure numbers weren't rising and the spiky lines were unchanged.

'I was a monster. What I did was unforgivable.'

'Then why?'

He took a deep breath, knuckled his eyes before fixing them on her. 'Because looking at you was like looking at the young version of your mother I fell in love with. Because seeing you every day reminded me of what she'd been like and what she'd become when she ran out and got herself killed. Because it hurt right here—' he thumped his heart and this time the machine gave an alarming beep '—every time I looked at you and wished you were her.'

She had her answers but they did little to erase the years of bitterness as she belatedly realised nothing he could say or do would make up for what he'd put her through.

Then it happened.

His trembling hand snaked towards her, palm up, begging. She stared at it, expecting to feel repulsed or, worse, fearful, remembering the last time he'd extended the same hand had been to hit her.

None of those feelings materialised as pity trickled through her, pity for the weakened, frightened man he'd have to be to extend the hand of friendship to her after all these years, after all he'd done.

Sadness clogged her throat as she placed her hand in his briefly, squeezing once before snatching it back.

Maybe it was more than he deserved, but in that one, fleeting touch some of her residual anger receded, faded, eased.

'I'm so sorry,' he said, flexing the fingers on the hand she'd clasped as if not quite believing she'd done it.

Needing to escape before she broke down, she managed a brisk nod.

'So am I, Dad, so am I.'

Brittany stepped into the Crusoe Suite, the air whooshing from her lungs as she clutched at her chest, rubbing the sudden ache centring over her heart.

Every detail of the incredible room, from the sheer ivory chiffon draping the open-air French doors leading to a crystal horizon pool to the raised alabaster king-size bed, from the countless tea-lights shimmering in the dusk to the heady scent of frangipani lingering in the air, all screamed he remembered.

He remembered.

Her gaze lingered on the picnic blanket spread in the middle of the spacious room, on the feast of chocolate-dipped strawberries and double-roasted almonds and petit fours, a bottle of chilled Muscato in an ice bucket.

All her favourites, in her ultimate fantasy room.

When had she told him? Their first date? Their second? Their tenth?

Irrelevant, considering he'd remembered her island fantasy and recreated it to perfection in this breathtaking suite.

'I'm glad you came.'

What little breath she had left stuck in her throat as Nick stepped into view, brushing chiffon aside to enter the suite.

If the room was gorgeous, the view sublime, Nick was out of this world. Wearing formal black trousers and a crisp white shirt open at the neck, his hair ruffled by the ocean breeze, he padded barefoot towards her, every step accelerating her heart rate towards cardiac arrest.

'I had to say goodbye,' she managed on a squeak as he swept her into his arms, strode to the picnic blanket and gently deposited her, nuzzling her neck in the process.

'Shh…'

He brushed a soft kiss against her lips, a kiss to fuel dreams, a kiss laden with promise.

'No talk of goodbyes. We have the whole night and I intend to make every second count.'

If his kiss rendered her speechless, the clear intent in his eyes clammed her up good and proper, for there was little doubt that once they'd eaten he'd be feasting on her.

'Here, drink this.'

He handed her a wine glass, his knowing smile telling her he knew exactly how flummoxed she was.

After several unladylike gulps, she cleared her throat and finally managed to speak. 'This must be the most popular suite in the hotel.'

His eyes glittered as he shook his head. 'It's never been booked.'

'I don't understand.'

'This room is never available. It's never been used.'

'But—'

'Tonight's the first.'

Raising his glass in her direction, he said, 'Rather fitting.'

He couldn't possibly mean…he wasn't implying…

'Are you saying—?'

Swooping in for another stolen kiss, he whispered against her lips, 'This is your room, Red. Your fantasy. Surely you know I could never share it with anyone else?'

Her heart swelled with love for this amazing man.

She loved him with everything she had but she couldn't silence the doubt demons perched on her shoulder, whispering in her ears what she'd be giving up, what she'd be risking if she stayed now.

While she'd taken the first tentative step towards forgiving her father, everything she'd been through with him had moulded her into the woman she'd become today: a strong, independent woman too scared to rely on anyone else, a woman wary of loving too much and giving too much.

This room was a fantasy, her fantasy. Was her marriage the same? Started on pretence, built on shaky foundations, something transient, intangible, that could vanish as easily as any dreams she once had for the two of them?

'Why did you build a room like this when you had no idea I'd ever see it?'

He shrugged, his expression delightfully bashful. 'I've built my dreams from nothing. And when you have nothing, hope is a powerful motivator.'

She shook her head, confused. 'You hoped I'd come back?'

'Counted on it.'

His confident smile set her pulse racing.

'I used to come up here for time out.' He pushed to his feet, gestured to the room. 'Did some of my best thinking here.'

'But I only came back for work and we only married out of mutual benefit for our businesses. How could you have known I'd ever get to see this?'

'You would've come back, Red. It's fate.'

'Don't believe in it.'

She made her own luck, had ever since she'd had the sense to flee home and relocate to London. Fate had dealt her a bum hand in the paternal stakes and she'd lost faith in it a long time ago.

Smiling, he held out his hand to her. 'It's the Italian in me. We believe in higher powers.'

So did she at that moment as she placed her hand in his and he tugged her to her feet, where she landed flush against his body.

'I also believe in us.'

She wanted to lose herself in the moment, lose herself in the fantasy, but logic wouldn't be denied. She was leaving tomorrow, wanted to make sure he knew where things stood with their marriage.

'You didn't ten years ago. Not enough to make us work.'

He swore under his breath, hugged her tighter. 'I was young, idealistic—a fool. Let me prove to you how much you mean to me.'

'You don't have to—'

He crushed his mouth to hers, eradicating her protests, her rationale, her reason.

She shuddered as he deepened the kiss, his tongue slipping inside to touch hers, his hands tugging on the sash holding her tie-around dress together.

It slithered to the floor in a hiss of silk, leaving her flesh bare to his exploring hands and explore they did, skimming her skin, his fingers trailing up her thighs, lingering at the edge of her panties before delving beneath.

'Oh…'

She melted against him, clung to him, her need for Nick astonishing in its all-consuming power.

She couldn't think when he grazed her clitoris, didn't want to think when he thumbed it, circled it, backing her slowly towards the bed without breaking tempo.

'Step up, sweetheart,' he murmured, guiding her like a maestro when they hit the dais, gently laying her on the bed, playing her body until she could've sung encore arias all night long.

He kept her on the edge, tormenting her with pleasure as she arched her back, thrust her hips up, desperate to feel his touch, begging for release.

'We have all night.'

He kissed her, swallowed her plea, toying with her until she was incoherent with mind-numbing need.

'Nick, please…'

Finally, he picked up the tempo, his thumb circling her clitoris with perfect pressure, and on the next stroke spasms rocked her body, wave after wave of intense, mindless pleasure drenching her.

Before she could catch her breath he'd whipped off his pants, sheathed himself and was inside her, hard, insistent, demanding more of her than she could give.

She was spent, listless with satisfaction, but as Nick drove into her, smooth and unrelenting, she reignited, tensed and exploded at the same time he did, their cries mingling on the night air before fading away to a contented silence.

She was gone.

He knew it the second he woke, not needing to open his eyes to know Britt had left.

She was a part of him, always had been. He hadn't been

kidding when he'd told her about this room, his hopes she'd come back.

Everyone returned home to their roots at some stage and he'd counted on it. She was the only woman for him and now she was his wife and they loved each other…well, nothing would stop them.

Then why was he lying here, alone, and she was winging her way to the other side of the world again?

He'd let her get away once. *Porca miseria!* Never again.

But he couldn't control her, couldn't hold her back any more than let her go. He understood her drive, her ambition, the same need for success pounding through his veins.

So why the crazy feeling she'd left for good?

They hadn't resolved anything last night. He'd planned to, had wanted to talk, but his good intentions had crashed and burned around the time he'd been unable to keep his hands off her. From there, all bets had been off as they'd pleasured each other repeatedly, all night long, finally falling asleep around five a.m.

He didn't need to glance at his watch to know it was around nine now, the brightness of a cloudless Noosa sky indicative of the late hour.

Pushing out of bed, he wrenched on his trousers, hopping and cursing alternately when his foot caught and he pitched off the dais.

Britt couldn't have got much of a head start on him and he needed to see her, needed to make sure she understood the depth of his feelings before she boarded that plane.

Shrugging into his shirt and caring little for the buttons, he strode to the door, his hand stilling on the knob as a glint of metal on the hallway table caught his eye.

The streaming sun reflected off the object, scattering shards of golden diamonds against the pristine walls, and as he moved a fraction to the left he saw what it was.

His heart stopped.

No, it couldn't be.

Sweeping the ring into his palm, he juggled it like a hot coal, fury warring with disbelief.

Britt had taken off her wedding band, had left it behind.

Which could only mean one thing: she wanted out.

Santo cielo!

Shoving the ring deep in his pocket to eradicate the painful reminder of how much she didn't want him no matter what they'd shared, he yanked the door open.

He wasn't losing her without a fight.

Not this time.

CHAPTER FIFTEEN

BRITTANY fiddled with her empty ring finger the entire twenty-four-hour flight to London.

Had she done the right thing?

With the skin rubbed raw where the wedding band had resided, she forced herself to stop tracing the faint tan line, folding her arms and tucking her hands safely out of fiddling reach.

A good thing too, for if she stopped touching the skin where the ring had been she might be tempted to rub her forehead to erase the big fat C branded there.

C for coward, for that was exactly what she was, a spineless, quivering coward for yanking the wedding band off in a fit of madness and bolting into the early-morning light while Nick slept soundly.

Last night had changed everything.

She didn't trust words, needed actions, and Nick had proved to her how much he wanted this marriage for real, how much he loved her. With every silken caress, with every murmured endearment, with every soul-reaching kiss, he'd shown her he loved her.

That was when she'd realised she had to run.

She couldn't have left if they'd woken together, if he'd asked her to stay. The realization terrified her. She, Brittany, poster-girl for the independent career woman, was so completely in love that she no longer had control over her own actions. She'd had a final window of escape and she'd taken it.

She had to flee. There was no other way.

Nick knew nothing of the truth about her father, about why that debt weighed so heavily upon her or about how much she knew of the way people who loved you could hurt you.

Telling him the truth would've been the brave thing to do, but just thinking about it made her tremble.

She didn't want his pity or his sympathy. She couldn't rely on that love because one day it would no longer be there. She'd nearly lost herself before—this time she knew that if she let herself fall, there'd be no coming back.

She didn't want him dragged into her sordid family life, didn't want to tell him the whole truth.

This was her past.

She needed it wiped clean before she could concentrate on her future.

Courtesy of a minor catastrophe with the new Phant-A-Sea project in the Bahamas, Nick spent three weeks stewing over his wife's disappearance.

He'd tried calling; she didn't return his calls.

He'd tried emailing; she'd sent him a brief response about how busy she was in her new position, how she didn't have a spare moment, how she'd get in touch soon, yada, yada, yada.

It was a crock, all of it.

How long did it take to tack on 'I love you' at the end of an email? A quick text message 'I miss you'?

While his wife was industriously breaking through the glass ceiling he'd had three long weeks to replay and rehash and remember every moment of their marriage, culminating in that last night together.

If she didn't get it after that night she never would and

he had a good mind to pack his bags, head back to Noosa, bury his nose in business and forget all about their short-lived marriage.

But Red wasn't the only one with a temper and twenty-one long days had served to fuel his fury.

He wanted answers.

He deserved answers.

And, by God, he'd get answers.

Picking up his mobile, he flipped it open, his thumb poised over the keypad.

If he called she probably wouldn't take it, so he'd send her a text of his impending arrival. But what good would that do? Considering the cold shoulder she'd been giving him, she'd probably take off on some piddly business trip just to avoid him.

Better to have the element of surprise on his side.

Knowing his stubborn wife as well as he did, he had a feeling he'd need all the help he could get.

Brittany checked the address on her BlackBerry and squinted at the faded number above the crumbling stone door.

Yep, this was the place.

Some conglomerate she'd never heard of wanted to turn this old Edwardian place in the middle of Chelsea into a boutique hotel. Doing a quick sweep, she noted the disintegrating brickwork, the fragmented window frames and the general dilapidated air of the once grand home; they had their work cut out for them.

But it wasn't her job to assess viability of the building. She needed to wow them with the potential advertising campaign she could produce for a project of this scale, needed a brand-spanking new, bright shiny project to absorb her focus and occupy her every waking hour. That way, she could stop dwelling on Nick and how much she missed him.

Missed? More like craved, an intense, unstoppable, uncontrollable craving that intensified rather than lessened with each passing day.

It had almost been a month and, while she was grateful he'd stopped calling her every day, had stopped emailing her, a small part of her curled up and howled every time she checked her messages or her inbox and found nothing from him.

She'd picked up the phone so many times, desperate to hear his voice, before slamming it down, knowing if she heard his dulcet tones professing his love she'd break down and blurt the truth.

And she couldn't afford to, figuratively and literally. Just a few more months and she'd be free...every cent paid back to her dad and, after that, who knew? Maybe her future had room for a husband and a renewed relationship with her father?

Her BlackBerry beeped, caller ID displayed the new client's number and she read the message.

MEET ME ON TOP FLOOR.
EAGER TO GET THIS MEETING UNDER WAY.

'Damn tycoons,' she muttered, shoving the BlackBerry in her handbag, hitching her portfolio higher and pushing through the front door, not surprised when the hinges groaned in protest.

Grateful the building was only three storeys high, she climbed the rickety stairs, admiring the soaring ceilings, the elaborate cornices and the chandeliers that would be magnificent once restored to former glory.

In fact, the crumbling façade of this grand old dame hadn't done justice to the treasure-trove inside and she could see why someone would want to turn this place into a hotel.

Reaching the top landing, she made for the one open door

at the end of a long corridor, drawn by the light spilling temptingly into the gloom.

Ideas had assaulted her from all angles as she'd climbed the staircase and she couldn't wait to put some of her enthusiasm to good use and wow her potential new client.

Smoothing her hair with one hand, she tightened her grip on her portfolio with the other, assuming her best professional smile as she stepped into the room.

Her client stood in front of the window, making it difficult for her to see, but as he turned and took a step towards her she saw too much.

Her smile slipped along with her portfolio, which crashed to the ground with her hopes of holding Nick Mancini at bay until her work was done.

Nick's first instinct was to rush to Britt, sweep her into his arms and forget the agony of the past month.

That was before he saw the stubborn set of her mouth, the angry sapphire glint as she fixed him with a haughty stare.

He'd flown around the world to be with the woman he loved and she was *angry*?

Thrusting his hands in his pockets, he leaned against the window sill.

'What? No welcome kiss for your husband?'

She picked up her bags, placed them on a nearby table, too cool and controlled for his liking. He wanted her off guard, nervous, so he could bully the truth out of her as to why she bolted, why she'd given back his ring. Instead, she smoothed a too-tight hound's-tooth skirt, tugged on the hem of a matching jacket and perched on the table's edge.

'What are you doing here, Nick?'

'Business.'

'Of course.'

Her slight nod annoyed him as much as her clipped response.

'Unfinished business.'

Unable to control himself, he crossed the room in four strides, hauled her into his arms and kissed her.

She struggled for all of two seconds before melting into him, a perfect fit as always, and he growled, a deep, possessive sound ripped from deep within.

'Don't.'

On the point of deepening the kiss, she shoved him away and if he hadn't seen the real fear in her eyes he would've pushed the issue.

He stepped back, gave her space while the old familiar need to have her clawed at him, demanding and uncontrollable as always.

'Don't what? Give you this?'

He reached into his breast pocket, pulled out her wedding band and, grabbing her hand, held her fingers open while he dropped it into her palm.

'You left it behind, though for the life of me I can't figure out why.'

Her mouth opened, closed, in a fair imitation of a goldfish, and he curled her fingers over the ring before releasing her, not trusting himself to touch her one moment longer without hauling her back into his arms.

'Last thing I knew, you wanted this marriage to work. Sure, you wanted to head back here, and I thought we'd figure out logistics.'

He ran a hand through his hair, rattled by her distant expression, as if she'd closed off emotionally. 'Instead, you bolt before we can say a proper goodbye, leaving your ring behind. Which begs the question. Do you want out of this marriage?'

A taut silence stretched, grew, before she finally raised her gaze to his and what he saw blew his mind: the shimmer of tears, the glimmer of defeat.

'Hell, Red, I didn't mean to—'

'It's okay, I should've told you…' Her words hitched on a sob and he folded her into his arms, powerless to do anything but hold her while the woman he'd seen defiant, sassy and brave cried.

Even when he'd callously shoved her away ten years earlier she hadn't shed a single tear, and he'd admired her for it. Now, as the floodgates opened and she clung to him, her tears drenching his shirt, the tiny crack in his heart that had opened the moment he'd found that wedding band lying forlornly on the hall table widened and he knew he could never repair it again.

Desperate to deflect her tears, he said, 'So are you going to help me transform this place into a Phant-A-Sea or what?'

Her sobs petered out as she sniffled and swiped at her eyes before raising her head.

'You're really going to convert this place to a hotel?'

'Uh-huh. But I'll need the undivided attention of Sell's MD to help me do it.'

'For how long?'

'A lifetime.'

Her eyes widened as she gnawed on her deliciously plump lower lip. 'Are you—?'

'I'm saying I love you and I want this marriage to work, Red. I would've been here sooner but I had to clear up urgent business so I can spend as long as it takes here in London. With you.'

He grabbed her hands, held them splayed against his chest, directly over his heart beating wildly for her, only her. 'It's what I wanted to say to you the morning you ran out. I'll do whatever it takes to make our marriage work, to show you how much I love you.'

Her lower lip wobbled and he shook his head. 'Oh, no, you don't.'

He kissed her, slowly, tenderly, infusing every ounce of his love for this incredible woman into it, hoping she could feel one tenth of his love for her.

To his horror, she broke the kiss, wrenched out of his embrace and backed away, her gaze firmly fixed on her shoes.

'Red?'

When she finally met his gaze, hers was anguished. 'There's so much I haven't told you.'

'Try me.'

Taking a step towards her before thinking better of it, he held his hands out to her, palm up. 'There's nothing you could tell me that would change how I feel about you.'

Brittany swallowed a sob.

She couldn't comprehend Nick was here, let alone absorb the impact of his words.

He loved her.

He was willing to spend however long it took to make their marriage work with her, here, in London.

He'd followed her here, had made the effort he hadn't made before—could it be that he really had changed? That he was offering her something entirely new?

But rather than blurt out the truth, as was her first instinct, she stalled, searching for the right words, humiliated at the thought of the man she loved seeing her anything less than capable.

'Why did you run? Leave the ring behind?'

'Because this job is everything to me.'

Nick glared at her, his toffee eyes turning icy in the wan light filtering through the tattered velvet drapes.

'I see.'

From his rigid posture to his clenched hands, tension radiated off her and she knew she'd have to tell him the truth to salvage their relationship.

'Actually, you don't.'

Weariness seeped through her body as she slumped into a

stuffy armchair, waving away the puff of dust that arose like a mushroom cloud.

'I need the money. Desperately.'

Realisation dawned as he sat opposite and leaned forward by bracing his elbows on his knees.

'But if you need cash I could—'

'That's exactly why I left.'

She shook her head, twisted her hair into a loose knot before releasing it. 'I need to do this on my own. It's my problem, I'll take care of it.'

'What problem?'

Wincing, she rubbed the bridge of her nose, a futile gesture to ward off the headache building between her eyes.

'My father.'

Nick stiffened as she'd known he would. 'What's he done now?'

She sighed, toying with the frayed edge of the chair's arm before folding her fingers to stop fiddling.

'You know about him giving me money when I left Australia to start here?'

'Yeah?'

She leapt from the chair, started pacing. 'He knew I didn't want a cent of his money. He knew I wanted nothing to do with him. I thought it was all about control. Even tried to flaunt it when I tried to make peace after ten years.'

Suspicion clouded his eyes. 'Why did you need to make peace? Haven't you kept in touch?'

She shook her head, hating the road their conversation had taken, for it could only lead to one destination: full disclosure.

'When I left, I severed all ties.'

'Why?'

'For freedom.'

Freedom from fear, from tyranny, from a father who'd morphed into a monster.

Nick frowned in confusion. 'You moved to London to be free of him and—'

'But I'm not free. I'll never be free until I've paid back every cent.'

Nick shook his head. 'You're not telling me everything.'

He stood, reached out to her, but she stubbornly backed away. 'Tell me.'

'I can't.'

Her whisper faded into silence, finally broken by his exasperated sigh.

'I'm your husband. I love you. I'm here for you, *always*.'

The concern, the sincerity, the honesty in that last word broke through her emotional barriers and she sagged against the window sill.

'He hit me.'

'That bastard! I'll kill him!'

She didn't know what she'd expected when she finally told someone the grimy truth after all these years, but seeing Nick furious, bristling with rage and ready to defend her, she suddenly knew she'd made a mistake bottling all this up.

If he hadn't told her the truth when she'd left, she'd done him the same discourtesy, and if they were to have a future she needed to tell him, everything.

'When I came to you ten years ago and asked you to leave, it wasn't out of some misguided romantic notion. I had to leave. His escalating violence left me no option.'

He swore, viciously and voraciously, clenching his hands as if he'd like to thump something, preferably Darby.

'He changed the moment Mum left. Then when we got news Mum died a year after she'd run off, the abuse escalated. A shove here, a bump there.'

She swiped a hand over her eyes, determined not to shed one more wasted tear over him. 'Then he hit me. That's when I knew I had to get out, as far away as I could get.'

'You should've told me. I would've protected you.'

His cold-as-steel voice sent a shiver down her spine.

'How? You had a farm to run, your dad to help. Besides, I asked you…'

'And I turned you down.'

He swore again, thumped his fist on a table. 'If I'd known—'

'We'd already drifted apart, you'd pulled away from me emotionally, so I guess it came as no surprise when you said no.'

Another curse ripped through the air as he rubbed his neck.

'I'm sorry, sweetheart, I was an insecure jerk who pushed you away before you woke up one day and realised you were slumming it.'

Her mouth dropped open, his rueful grin annoying her more than his ludicrous assumption.

'Since when did I ever give you the idea I was *slumming it*? That's the most ridiculous thing I've ever heard.'

She refrained from stamping her foot, just, as he laid his hands out to her, palm up, in surrender.

'People talked, I foolishly listened. Not that I needed a reason to sabotage us.'

'What does that mean?'

Shaking his head, he thrust his hands into his pockets, but not before she'd seen them clench so hard the knuckles stood out.

'It means I was so cut up about my mum running out on me, I didn't want to allow another woman to get close, really close, let alone love her. When we first got involved I thought you had the perfect family. Two parents, money, everything you could possibly want, while I had nothing to offer you.'

She held up her hand, stopped him. 'It was never about the money. Surely you knew me better than that?'

'I guess I knew it deep down but I didn't want to believe it. How could someone like you love a nobody like me?'

It was her turn to swear and he smiled. 'You can't reason

with a young Italian male, especially one trying to hide his insecurities behind a black leather jacket and a Harley. But I've grown up, wised up.'

He took a step towards her, another. 'I didn't come after you last time because I was too proud and too stupid to risk being hurt. But now it's different, I'm different, and it hurts too damn much being without you, so here I am.'

She'd wised up too, and if there was one thing she'd learned over the last decade it was to fight for what she wanted.

'It's good we've been honest if we're to—'

She faltered, swallowed.

Was she really doing this?

Giving them a chance, ignoring her doubts, ignoring the sterile way their marriage started, ignoring the fear that screamed she'd almost died the first time she'd lost Nick, losing him again if this didn't work would finish her off?

'What?'

'Have a future,' she murmured, her eyes not leaving his, her heart's choice vindicated by the explosion of elation in his unwavering stare.

His exuberant whoop echoed in the cavernous room as he picked her up and twirled her around until she was breathless from laughing.

When he finally stopped, she slid down his body, savouring the delicious contact, the spark of heat sizzling between them.

'Do you have any idea how much I've missed you?'

'Bet it's not half as much as I've missed you.'

She caressed his cheek, her fingertips scraping the stubble. 'I love London, but arriving back here and having to mend a broken heart courtesy of you for the second time sure as heck hasn't been fun.'

'Hey! You ran out on me!'

'Oh, yeah…'

Her rueful grin had him chuckling as he pulled her flush

against him, their hips moulding perfectly and exacerbating the slow build of heat as he traced lazy circles in the small of her back.

'You know I love you, right?'

He stopped tracing circles, his gaze locked onto hers. 'What did you just say?'

'Don't make me say it again, Mancini. Once a day is more than enough. A girl's got her pride, you know.'

'You're in love with me? I mean, I'd hoped, but you've never actually said it and—'

'Yeah, no accounting for taste.'

She shrugged, unable to keep a goofy grin from spreading across her face and her heart stopped as he captured her hand and raised it to his lips.

'I.'

He placed a soft kiss on her palm, his tongue lightly tracing her lifeline until she shivered.

'Love.'

He nibbled along her knuckles, grazing them with his tongue.

'You.'

He nipped at the fleshy base of her thumb, sucking it gently until she moaned.

'Good answer,' she gasped as his mouth covered hers, stealing her breath along with her heart.

His mind-blowing kiss ignited the store of hope, happiness and dreams she'd harboured for so long, sending a surge of longing through her body that took every ounce of strength she possessed not to ravish him on the spot.

Nick Mancini loved her.

Her husband loved her.

She'd finally found the 'something' that had eluded her for so long and she couldn't be happier.

'So you're serious about staying around?'

'Hell yeah.'

He kissed her to prove it, a delicious, desperate, devastating kiss packed with emotion and feeling and love, so much love.

When they finally came up for air, he smiled, the slow, sexy smile that set her pulse tripping as he reached to cup her face in his hands.

'I thought starting the Phant-A-Sea chain was the best thing I'd ever done, but I was wrong. You're my fantasy and there's no one I'd rather live my dreams with than you.'

'Keep that up and you'll have me blubbering again.'

'I love you, Red. Will you live the dream with me? For ever? As my wife?'

He kissed her, tenderly, softly, as if knowing she needed a moment to recover from the ecstasy of hearing the guy she'd loved for ever pledge his life to her.

'You bet I will,' she whispered against the side of his mouth, knowing that, as far as dreams went, this one was the stuff made of legends.

EPILOGUE

'YOU sure you wouldn't like to elope?' Nick asked, sitting on a suitcase while Brittany struggled with the zip. 'We've got the most romantic cities in the world on our doorstep. How about Paris? Or Venice? Wouldn't you like to renew our vows there?'

'We've had this conversation a hundred times. And the answer is still no.'

Brittany tugged on the zip, wondering how she always managed to pack way too much stuff considering she ended up only using half of it. 'Just move your butt a little to the left, if you don't mind.'

'Like this?'

Nick wiggled towards her with a sexy grin.

Biting back an answering grin, she slapped his butt playfully, letting her hand linger on his firm muscles. 'As impressive as I find this fine piece of anatomy, could you actually concentrate on the task at hand?'

'Hey, I'm not the one losing concentration here.'

He picked up her hand and returned it to the zip. 'Now, hurry up. The sooner you finish, the sooner you get to have dessert.'

Her mouth always watered at the prospect of Nick's cooking, and tonight she had a feeling he'd whipped up one of her favourites.

'Tiramisu?'

'Maybe.'

'You're a hard man, Nick Mancini.'

'Only around you, sweetheart,' he murmured, his double entendre sending an illicit thrill through her.

Heat seeped into her cheeks and she gave one, last hefty tug on the zip, grateful when it finally slid into place.

'You're wicked too. Now, where's my reward?'

Nick slid off the case and hauled her into his arms. 'Right here.'

She feigned indifference, a difficult job considering her favourite place in the world was right here in his arms. 'Dessert sounds more tempting.'

'I'll show you tempting,' he muttered, nuzzling her neck in the sensitive spot at the base, just above her collarbone, until she squealed.

'Okay, okay. You've made your point. Now can I have dessert?'

She slid her hands up his back, caressing the sinews, revelling in the hard muscles beneath her hands.

She'd lived with this man for one, incredible year and, rather than tiring of each other, their love grew stronger every day. How did she get so lucky?

Nick dropped a sweet, lingering kiss on her lips. 'You're insatiable.'

'For food too. Now, dessert!'

Chuckling, he held her hand and led her into the kitchen of her Chelsea apartment, sat her down and made a big show of unveiling dessert.

'I hope this is to your satisfaction, miss?'

He bowed low while placing a huge serving of tiramisu in front of her.

She licked her lips and patted his butt again. 'Oh, I'm very satisfied. Care to join me?'

'Now there's an offer I can't refuse,' he said, slipping onto the chair next to her and opening his mouth for the little piece of heaven on a fork she offered him.

Taking a healthy mouthful herself, she sighed in bliss as the blend of sweet ecstasy burst on her taste buds. 'You really are one heck of a catch. Master chef, billionaire hotelier, plantation owner. Which, by the way, was a master stroke of genius, hanging onto the farm so we can let our kids get their hands dirty when they tire of playing hide and seek in all those fantasy rooms at the hotel. Sure you want to be stuck with little ol' me?'

Every now and then, the fear of the past ten years—the endless, lonely years when she'd convinced herself Nick didn't care—raised its head. Thankfully, he quashed it in typical Nick fashion.

'You're the love of my life, Red. Where else would I be but by your side? Besides, I need to stick around if we're to make some of those kids you just mentioned...'

Her throat clogged with tears, she leaned forward and kissed him, licking a tiny glob of cream from the corner of his sexy mouth.

'Eloping sounds kind of neat, but I think we should head back to Jacaranda to renew our vows like we planned.'

He pulled back, searching her eyes for any sign of doubt.

'You sure? We've made our own memories here. Why not leave the past in the past?'

'The past can't hurt me any more. I made my peace with Dad before he died and nothing I feel now is going to change what happened. But Jacaranda means a lot to you and to me too. It's where we grew up, where we met, where we first fell in love...' She trailed off, blinking back the tears in earnest now.

'I can't believe you actually loved me all those years ago. I was convinced you were only interested in having me along for the ride to London because you were scared of being alone, being the uptight little princess you were.'

'And you'd be the expert to judge, being the troublemaking rebel you were.'

He laughed and cupped her cheek. 'You're gorgeous when you fire up. Always have been.'

'Yeah, well, you bring out the worst in me.'

'And the best.'

He inched towards her, his fingers feathering against her face, caressing with infinite skill and patience. 'I love you. Now and for ever.'

'Now and for ever,' she murmured, a second before their lips met in a burst of sweetness and light and untold promise.

* * * * *

GETTING RED-HOT
WITH THE ROGUE

BY
ALLY BLAKE

When **Ally Blake** was a little girl, she made a wish that when she turned twenty-six she would marry an Italian two years older than herself. After it actually came true, she realised she was on to something with these wish things. So, next she wished that she could make a living spending her days in her pyjamas, eating M&Ms and drinking scads of coffee while using her formative experiences of wallowing in teenage crushes and romantic movies to create love stories of her own. The fact that she is now able to spend her spare time searching the internet for pictures of handsome guys for research purposes is merely a bonus! Come along and visit her website at www.allyblake.com.

To beautiful, sunny Brisbane.
The city that gave me my first crush,
first kiss, and first love.

CHAPTER ONE

'MR KELLY?'

Dylan looked up from his corner office desk on the thirtieth floor of Kelly Tower to find his assistant, Eric, practically quivering in the doorway. 'Shoot.'

Eric's voice tremored as he tried to say, 'I… There's… I'm not sure I quite know how to…'

Whistling a breath through the smallest gap between his lips, Dylan pushed back his chair and leant his chin upon steepled fingers. 'Take a breath. Visualise your happy place. Count to ten. Whatever it takes. Just remember that I am a very busy, very important man and get to the point.'

Eric did as he was told, so quickly Dylan thought the kid might hyperventilate. But he managed to say, 'I have to get onto your computer for a sec.'

'Go for your life.' Dylan pushed his chair back to give the guy room.

Eric slid into place, his fingers flying over the keyboard with the speed of a kid born with a laptop attached to his thighs. 'A friend of mine works for an online news mag and he messaged me to say I had to see something. This address ought to give us a direct feed.'

Dylan's cheek twitched. 'Seriously, kid, if you've come in here all a fluster because some blog has footage of me feed-

ing spaghetti and meatballs to that nifty little Olympic diver
I met in Luxembourg last week…'

His next words froze on his tongue and he slid his chair
back beneath his desk with such speed Eric had to leap out
of the way.

The monitor was not in fact showing any footage of him.
Or the nifty little Olympian. Or meatballs, for that matter.

Dylan didn't even have the chance to be the slightest bit
ashamed of his own self-absorption as the crystal clear digital
footage brought his *raison d'être*, the family business he
championed day in day out, back to the forefront of his mind
with a wallop.

The half-acre forecourt keeping Kelly Tower clear of the
maddening CBD crowds that traversed Brisbane's hectic
George Street had in its north corner a twenty-foot-high,
silver, zigzag sculpture—symbolising the impressive escala-
tion of fortune that securing representation with the Kelly
Investment Group ensured.

The sculpture usually stood proud and alone bar a few
stray pigeons brave enough to cling to its slick diagonal bars.
Today it had been taken over by camera crews and reporters
with mini-sound recorders and logo-labelled mikes. That kind
of excitement had encouraged a crowd of ten times as many
interested onlookers.

No wonder.

From what he could make out through the sudden ache de-
scending upon his head, the excitement in the reporter's voice,
and Eric wheezing in the doorway, in some kind of crazy protest
a woman had handcuffed herself to the zig. Or was it the zag?

Dylan had nothing against handcuffs per se. They had their
place in the zeitgeist of the single man. Just not in the middle
of a busy workday, not in front of *his* building, and not when
as the head of Media Relations it was his job to make the fact
that a crazy person had picked that particular statue to attach
her daft self seem less interesting than it certainly was.

The crowd parted, and Eric's friend's camera slipped into the gap, giving Dylan a better look at the ruination of his afternoon.

She was fair skinned, dark-eyed, with dark wavy hair made all the more interesting by the fact she kept having to shake its wind-mussed length out of her face. A floral top cinched and flowed in all the right places, telling tales of the kinds of curves and hollows that could distract a weaker-willed man. Not to mention the white calf-length trousers into which her second-glance-worthy bottom had been poured, or the pair of the most insanely high-heeled hot pink sandals...

And, of course, handcuffs.

'What are we going to do?' Eric said in whispered awe.

Dylan jumped; he and the woman had been having such a moment he'd forgotten his assistant was even there.

The heel of his palm reared up over the mouse, ready to jab the webpage closed, when a sudden gust of breeze blew the woman's hair away from her face and she looked directly into Eric's mate's camera lens.

Dylan's hand went rigid a breath from touchdown leaving him staring into a pair of brown eyes. Bambi eyes, for Pete's sake. Big, beautiful, liquid brown with long, delicate eyelashes that made them appear wounded. Vulnerable. Repentant.

His gut twisted. His teeth clenched. A shaft of heat shot him upright, then filled him with adrenalin. Every masculine instinct reached out to him as the deep-seated urge to protect her clobbered him from the inside out. He felt himself rising from his seat, his wrists straightening as though preparing to slay whoever it was who had put that look in those eyes.

Then she licked her lips, shapely pink lips covering the sexiest kind of overbite, and blinked those big brown eyes. As her gaze shifted left she dropped her chin a fraction and she grinned flirtatiously at the person behind the camera.

The trance splintered like broken glass, ringing in his ears as it dislocated around him.

He swore beneath his breath, regained control over his

mouse hand, closed the damn webpage and gave his usually exceptionally discriminating protective instincts a good mental kick in the pants.

They knew better. Far better.

The only people he sheltered by way of his vociferous guard bore the name of Kelly. The blood of his blood. That was as wide as his circle of trust stretched.

His family *needed* to stick together. Tight together. For, no matter how sincere people might seem to be in courting amity, the downside of being richer than Midas and more recognisable than the prime minister was that they would always be considered Kellys first, everything else second.

He'd learnt that lesson nice and young. No matter how beguiling a woman might be, how well bred, how seemingly genuine, they all wanted something from him—his wealth, his connections, even his name.

Nowadays he only let himself play with those who wanted the heat of his body and nothing more. No history and no hereafter. It was a process that had worked beautifully for him for some time.

The fact that not a single one of the warm bodies had stoked the fire of his protective instincts like the one with the soft brown eyes was something he had neither the time nor inclination to ponder.

Feeling mighty fractious, he was out of the chair and through the door before Eric even realised he was moving.

'Sir!' Eric cried.

Dylan waved a hand over his shoulder, and all but ignored the wave of hellos and bowing and scraping that followed in his wake as he jogged down the hallway towards the elevators.

Eric was puffing, red-faced, and his hands were shaking by the time he caught up. 'Tell me what I can do!'

'Don't go anywhere,' Dylan said as the elevator doors closed so slowly he made a mental note to talk to his brother, Cameron—who, being an engineer, surely knew where to source faster-closing ones. 'And tell your mother you'll be late home. I have the feeling this will be a long day.'

Wynnie's wrists hurt.

That's what comes from not doing a trial run with new handcuffs, you duffer.

Ever the pro, she did her all not to let the discomfort show. She dug her fingernails into her palms, hoping it might take away her focus from the itchiness and scratchiness encircling her wrists. And she smiled at the bank of reporters, each of whom had no idea they were about to become her new best friends in this town.

'What's KInG ever done to you?' a voice from the back called out.

She looked down the barrel of the nearest camera, discreetly spat a clump of windswept hair from her lip gloss, and said, 'They've never once returned my phone calls. Typical, right?'

She rolled her eyes, and a few women in the crowd murmured in appreciation.

She made sure to look each and every one of them in the eye as she said, 'The past week I've met with top men and women in local and state government to talk about what we can all do together to help reduce the impact each individual person in this city is having on our environment. Those civil servants, good people with families at home and middle-income jobs, have been full of beans and ideas and enthusiasm. Yet the Kelly Investment Group, the largest company in town, a company with hundreds of employees and capital to burn, has time and again refused to even sit down with me, a new girl in town looking to make new friends, and have a chat over a cuppa.'

More twittering, this time with more volume.

'What does a company have to do to get a cuppa with a girl like you?' a deep voice called out from the back.

Wynnie bit her lip to stop from laughing as that question had come from her one plant at the event—Hannah, her close friend, and fellow Clean Footprint Coalition employee—who was currently hiding behind a cup of takeaway coffee and staring at a radio reporter as though he were the one who'd asked.

Wynnie waited until the crowd quieted. She leant forward, or as far as she could with her hands anchored behind her. 'Kids, today I'm gonna need you all to tap into your imaginations. Hark back to those powerful images of environmentalists in the eighties chaining themselves to bulldozers to stop them knocking down ecologically imperative forests. Fast-forward to the twenty-first century and the corporate giants, such as the Kelly Investment Group—'

Better to use their whole name, she thought, *rather than the cute moniker they'd picked up, or possibly even coined themselves.*

'—are the new bad guys. Collectives with power, and resources, and influence who choose to turn the other cheek while you and I do our bit. We take shorter showers to conserve water, we recycle our newspapers, we unplug our appliances when we're not using them. Right?'

Smiles all around. Lots of nods. If someone held a fist in the air she wouldn't be surprised. The wave of solidarity gripped her. Her heart thundered all the harder in her chest, her skin hummed, the ache in her wrists all but forgotten.

'Did you know,' she said, lowering her voice so they all had to move in closer, 'this sculpture is lit twenty-four hours a day? Yep. Even now, in the middle of a sunny Brisbane spring afternoon, it has thirty separate lights making sure it always looks as shiny as it can possibly be. Thirty!'

One by one the faces turned to glare at the shimmering silver edifice behind her. She could smell blood in the air. That was a triumph in itself considering the Goliath she was putting herself up against.

Her bosses had done their research, looking at popular fashion stores, television stations, national café chains when deciding who to lobby. But every lead had led back to the same destination. The Kellys.

They were the most famous, respected, fascinating family in town. Their reach was unmatched. Their influence priceless. If she got them on board as the first major corporate partner with the revamped Clean Footprint Coalition, the exposure would be unimaginable, and Brisbane would fall into her lap like a pack of cards.

'I am a concerned citizen,' she continued, 'as are you all, as are my colleagues, the band of environmental groups together known as the Clean Footprint Coalition. While the Kelly Investment Group, with the hundreds of ambivalent corporate clients they represent, is the biggest bulldozer you have ever seen.'

Hannah yelled out a mighty, 'Yeah,' and the crowd took up the cry until it all but reverberated around the square.

Wynnie bit back a grin of victory. God, did she love her work. These moments, when she had something to do with making people think about their place in the grand scheme of things, she really felt as if she could change the world.

The rush of pleasure was yummier than chocolate. It was more profound than a Piña Colada on an empty stomach. Hell, it was better than sex. Thank God for that. The hours above and beyond the call of duty that she dedicated to her work were such that she barely remembered what the latter was like.

A sudden ripple of noise from behind her mercifully pulled her from contemplating the extent of her accidental chastity. She turned, as well, and naturally got just far enough that her shoulder jarred, sapping every one of those lovely endorphins with it.

The pain had her sucking in a sharp breath, and hoping the trickle of sweat that had begun its journey down her neck and between her breasts wouldn't show up on camera.

She needn't have worried. Every camera panned left, microphones swerved in their wake, all pointing towards Kelly Tower.

And she knew why her audience had dared stray.

The saucy handcuffs and her subsequent introduction to the media of Brisbane as their new avenging angel had been mere foreplay. For any good show to be newsworthy every angel needed her very own personal devil. And she was about to meet hers.

Little spikes of energy skittered across her skin as she imagined who it might be. An overweight security guard with no authority and less of a clue? Some red-faced lackey sent to try to shoo her away?

'Kelly!' a radio guy called out.

'Mate, over here!' another followed suit.

Kelly? Could one of the gods have come down from the tower himself? She tried to find Hannah's face within the crowd to share the rush. Hannah had her hands on some guy's shoulders as she too tried to make out which bright, shiny Kelly it might be.

As she tried to see without causing a permanent injury Wynnie's mind backtracked over the Kelly family members she'd read about amongst the hundreds of local luminaries she'd been made aware of in the preceding days.

It wouldn't be Quinn Kelly, CEO, surely. The fellow had always been elusive to the mere masses, and of late had become as reclusive as Elvis. She was kind of glad. His ability to slay even the most steely backed opponent with a single glance was legendary.

Brendan Kelly? He was next in charge, the heir to KInG's throne, but not at all press-friendly from what she'd heard. If it was either of them she'd eat her shoes. Mmm. She liked her shoes. They were one of the only things she'd brought with her from Verona. Maybe she'd eat Brussels sprouts. She hated Brussel sprouts so that seemed a fair compromise.

So if it wasn't Quinn, and it wasn't Brendan, and since neither the younger brother Cameron, the engineer, or youngest sister, Meg, the seemingly professional ingénue, worked for KInG, then it had to be the one whose photo she had pulled from the file and stuck to the back of her office door with a great red pin through his forehead. The one she hoped she might *finally* get to after weeks of negotiating, pushing, prodding, making a nuisance of herself. The one she believed could help her make the Clean Footprint Coalition's dream a reality.

Dylan Kelly. Vice President, Media Relations. The spare to Brendan as heir. The public face of KInG, he could charm the heck out of any female with her own televisions, was constantly photographed wining and dining the city's most gorgeous women at benefits, sports events, and everywhere in between, and generally held the gossip-hungry city in thrall.

Wynnie was sure it helped that he appeared to be one of the more beautiful men ever to grace the planet. Her chin had practically hit the conference table when she'd first seen his photo. Heck, if he weren't a corporate bad guy she might have worked pro bono to have him declared a protected species.

'Ladies,' a deep voice rumbled from somewhere over her now throbbing right shoulder. 'Gentlemen. What a pleasure it is to see that you've all decided to come by on this fine sunny day. If I'd have known there was to be a party I would have ordered dim sum and wine coolers for all.'

A few cracks of laughter, several deeply feminine sighs, and the slow flopping of microphones told Wynnie she was losing her audience fast.

She took a deep breath, flicked her hair from her face, and prepared to win them back by beating Mr Slick to an ethical pulp. He might be infamously charming, but she had right on her side, and that had to count for something.

Finally the crowd cleared, and through the parted waters came a man. Standard light blue shirt. Discreetly striped tie. Dark suit. So far not so much the kind of devil she had in mind.

But the closer he got, the more the details came into focus. His suit was tailored precisely to highlight every hard plane of the kind of body that spoke of restrained power, and made walking through big cities at lunchtime a guilty pleasure. His clenched jaw was so sharp it looked to be chiselled from granite. His dark blond hair was short, but with just enough scruff to make a girl want to run her fingers through it. Tame it. Tame him.

But the thing that trapped her gaze and held it was a pair of hooded blue eyes. With all the other inducements he had on show, there was no other colour they'd dare be.

And it was then that she realised they were trained completely on her. Flat, piercing, bewitching baby blue.

And he wasn't merely looking at her, he was looking into her. As if he was searching for the answer to a question only he knew. Her throat tightened and her mouth felt unnaturally dry, and, whatever the question was, the only answer her mind formed was, 'Yes'.

She tried to stand straighter—her handcuffs bit, jerking her back. She found herself twisted in what suddenly felt like a wholly defenceless position—breasts pressed forward, neck exposed. For the first time since she'd snapped the handcuffs closed she wondered if this had been entirely the right move.

'So what's this all about, then?' he asked, his eyes skimming away from her and out into the crowd.

Someone actually had to point a thumb back her way. She rolled her eyes.

He took a moment before turning and spotting her again, using all the subtlety of a double take. She squared her shoulders, looked him in the eye and raised an eyebrow.

He took two slow steps. To an untrained eye he might have seemed as if he was out for a stroll, to her he was clearly a predator stalking his prey. Either way he was nowhere near as cool as he was making himself out to be.

'Well,' he drawled, 'what have we here?'

With the cameras whirring over his shoulder she found perspective. The man before her might be one hell of a kick start for a sorely undernourished libido, but she had to remember he was the devil—though one with enough influence to make a real difference, and she had every intention of making him renounce his bad ways.

She managed to gather a breezy smile. 'Good afternoon.'

He slid his hands into the pockets of his trousers, drawing his shirt tight across his chest, and drawing her eyes to his zipper region in one clever move. 'How's it going?'

'Peachy,' she said, dragging her eyes north. 'Some weather we're having, don't you think?'

His cheek twitched. And he ambled to a halt—close enough that she could all but feel the choleric steam rising from his broad shoulders, but far enough away that every camera on site had access to his captivating face.

He looked away for a moment, and she let go of a lungful of stale breath. He glanced briefly at her high heels, and she figured he planned to keep out of kicking distance. It was the move of a man who'd been in danger of being castrated before. Her confidence came back in a whoosh.

Until he moved closer still. Close enough she could see the rasp of stubble glinting on his cheeks, a loose thread poking out of one of his shirt buttons, the shadow of impressive muscle along his upper arms.

Her nostrils flared as she sucked in oxygen, and the immediate intense physical reaction stunned the hell out of her.

'You've got yourself quite a crowd here,' he said, loud enough everyone could hear.

The cameras and the desperate hush of a dozen journalists reminded her why that was. She gathered her straying wits, tilted her chin downward, batted her eyelashes for all she was worth and, with a cheery smile said, 'Haven't I just?'

The crowd murmured appreciatively. But that wasn't the thing that made her cheeks feel warm, her belly feel tumbly, and her knees feel as weak as if she'd been standing there for days. That was purely due to the fresh, devilish glint in Dylan Kelly's baby blues.

She stood straighter, accidentally jerking her arms and twinging her shoulder, which created a fresh batch of friction at her itchy wrists. Wynnie sucked in a breath to keep from wincing. She kept it all together admirably, promising herself an extra twenty minutes of meditation on the yoga mat when she got home, as she said, 'The handcuffs brought them out. But it's what I have to say that's keeping them here.'

'And what's that?'

Research and appearances backed up the notion that he wasn't a silly man, but he'd just made a silly move. The first rule in shaping public opinion was never to ask a question you didn't know the answer to.

Buoyed anew, she said, 'Since you asked, not a moment before you graced us with your presence, we all agreed that you have been acting terribly irresponsibly, and that it's time you pulled up your socks.'

Before she had the chance to provide some beautiful sound bites dripping with the kinds of statistics newspapers loved, Dylan Kelly grabbed a hunk of suit leg, lifted it high to show off a jet-black sock and enough tanned, muscular, manly calf to create a tidal wave of trembling through the predominantly female crowd.

Okay, so he wasn't at all silly. He was very, very good. Who knew naked male calf could trump handcuffs?

Dylan took the attention and ran with it, on the face of it focusing back on her, but she knew his words were for everyone else. 'You oughtn't to believe all you read in the glossy pages. I'm not all bad. My mother taught me always to wear clean socks, and the hideous memory of my father trying to teach me about the birds and the bees when I was twelve years old scared the bejesus out of me so much it made me the most…responsible man on the planet.'

He might as well have pulled a concertina row of condoms from his pocket as he said it, for the feminine trembling turned to almost feverish laughter as the lot of them got lost in thoughts of Dylan's underwear and what it might be like to be the one with whom he might one day act altogether irresponsibly.

The men in the crowd were no better. She could read them as easily as if they wore flashing signs on their foreheads. They wanted to buy him a beer, and live vicariously through him for as long as he'd let them near.

Unless she pulled a shoe-sale sign and a *Playboy* bunny from somewhere her hands could still reach she might lose them all for good. It was time *her* press conference was brought to a close.

'Mr Kelly,' she said, using her outside voice. 'I concede that your socks are indeed…up. And since my points have obviously fluttered over your head, perhaps I need to be clearer about what I want.'

The crowd quieted and Dylan Kelly slowly lowered the leg of his trousers. Again when he looked at her she felt as if he were looking deep inside her. Testing her mettle? Hoping the force of his gaze might make her explode into a pile of ashes? Or was he after something beyond her comprehension?

The ability to stick one's hands on one's hips was underrated. As was the ability to cross one's arms. She could only stand there, torso thrust in his direction, staring back.

His voice dropped until it was so low it felt vaguely threatening. 'Tell me, then, what it is that you want from me.'

'I want you to take the same duty of care with your business practices, in the example you set for your employees and clients with regards to your impact on the environment, as you do your choice of footwear. I want your company to do its part and reduce its prodigious impact on the environment.'

He slid his feet shoulder-width apart, his toes pointing directly at her. 'Honey, I'm not sure what you think we do in there but we sit at computers and wangle phones. Not so much rainforest felling as you might believe.'

'You might not be the ones swinging the axes, but, by not being as green as you can be, you may as well be.'

While he looked as though he was imagining ways in which he might surreptitiously have her removed from the face of the earth, she kept her eyes locked on his and was as earnest as she could be when she said, 'Just hear me out. I promise you'll sleep better at night.'

Dylan's eyes narrowed. For a moment she thought she might have pierced his hard shell, until his exquisitely carved cheek lifted into a smile. 'I sleep just fine.'

And she believed him, to the point of imagining a man splayed out on a king-sized bed, expensive sheets barely covering his naked body as he slept the sleep of the completely satiated. Okay, not *a* man. *This* man. *That* body right now unfairly confined by the convention that city financiers wear suits.

She blinked, and her lashes stuck to her hot cheeks reminding her she'd been standing in the sun for half an hour, strapped to a sharp, uncomfortable, metal statue. 'Come on. What do you say? Don't you want your family name to stand for something great?'

Finally, something she said worked. The chiselled jaw turned to rock. The blue eyes completely lost the roguish glint. His faint aura of exasperation evaporated. And right before her eyes the man grew into his suit.

Debonair and cheeky, he was mouth-watering. Focused and switched on he might, she feared and hoped, be the most exceptional devil this angel was yet to meet.

His blue eyes locked hard and fast onto hers, pinning her to the spot with more power than the manacles binding her hands ever could. Her skin flushed, her heart rate doubled, her stomach clenched and released as though readying her to fight or fly.

His voice was rough, but loud enough for every microphone to pick it up as he said, 'Both KInG and the Kelly family invest millions every year in environmental causes such as renewable energy research and reforestation. More than any other company in this state.'

'That's excellent. Truly. But money isn't everything,' she shot back, holding his gaze, feeling the cameras zoom in tight. 'Action is the marker of a man, and the actions within that building beside us in the last year have added up to the waste of more than forty thousand disposable paper cups a *month,* more water usage than the whole of the suburb I live in, and enough paper waste to fell hectares of old forest. What I want from you is the promise that you are going to become the solution rather than being the problem.'

When the devil in the dark suit didn't come back with an instant response her heart thundered with the thrill of a battle won, with the knowledge that the cameras had their sound bite. And if Dylan Kelly, VP Media Relations, was worth his salt he knew in that moment there was no way that he could just walk away.

'So what do ya say?' she said, bringing her voice back down to a more intimate level, loosening her grip, relaxing her stance and slipping on a warm, friendly and just a little bit flirty smile. 'Invite me in for a coffee and a chat and I'll spend tomorrow bugging someone else.'

She felt the whole forecourt hold its collective breath as they awaited his next move.

When it finally came, Wynnie was again glad of her shackles, uncomfortable as they had become, as this time when those blindingly blue eyes met hers they were filled with such self-possession, such provocation, such blatant reined-in heat her knees all but buckled beneath her.

'You want to come up to my place for coffee?' he asked, his voice like silk and melted dark chocolate and all things decadent and delectable and too slippery to hold on to. 'Now why didn't you just say so in the first place?'

CHAPTER TWO

AS THOUGH Dylan Kelly had a magic button in the pocket of his trousers, Security arrived at that moment to discreetly move the onlookers away. The city workers and tourists had had their free lunchtime show. The press had their story. Wynnie's awareness campaign was off to a flying start. Everyone was happy.

Everyone except Dylan, who was staring at her as if she were a piece of gum stuck to the bottom of his shoe.

'That was a cheap trick you just pulled,' he growled quietly enough that only she could hear.

Wynnie shook her hair out of her face. Now the crowd had dispersed, the breeze whipping up George Street was swirling around her like a maelstrom. 'I prefer fearless, indomitable and inventive.'

'In the end it will be they who decide one way or the other.' He motioned with a slight tilt of his head to the row of news vans on the sidewalk.

'Lucky for me,' she said with a smile.

'Mmm. Lucky for you.' He glanced at his watch, then back at her. 'So did you want to conduct your bogus meeting out here or were you planning on staying here for the night?'

Wynnie twisted to get her hands to the tight back pocket of her capri pants, which had been ideal for the Verona autumn she had left behind, but in the warm Brisbane spring sunshine they stuck to her like a wetsuit. 'Oh, no. I'm done. Horizontal is my much preferred method. Of sleeping,' she added far too late for comfort.

She glanced up to find him thankfully preoccupied enough to have missed her little Freudian slip. Unfortunately he was preoccupied with the twisting and turning of her hips.

His voice was deep, his jaw tight, when he said, 'I could have had you arrested, you know. This is private property.'

'Nah,' she said. 'The globe belongs to none of us.'

He'd moved closer, having seemingly reconciled himself to the fact that she wanted to get out of the handcuffs as much as he wanted her to, and that her shoes were made for looks and functionality, not for use as a secret weapon. Without the clamour of the crowd making the square smell like a fish-market, she caught a waft of his aftershave—clean, dark, expensive. Suddenly she felt very, very thirsty.

Despite his focus, she twisted some more. Her shoulder twinged but better that than have to keep trying to appear professional while cuffed to the statue, and while the touch of his eyes made her skin scorch beneath her clothes.

Her fingers made it to the bottom of the tight coin pocket to find it was empty. Her heart leapt into her throat until she remembered she'd put the tiny key inside the breast pocket of her shirt at the last minute.

Naturally when she tried to reach it, she couldn't. She stood on tiptoes, looking for Hannah, knowing it was a lost cause. She would have been back at the office the minute lunch hour was up.

Wynnie closed her eyes a moment, took a deep breath and said, 'Would you do me a favour?'

Dylan's deep voice rolled over her. 'You certainly aren't backwards about asking for what you want, I'll give you that.'

'I need you to get the key for my cuffs.'

After a long, slow pause he said, 'The key?'

She squeezed her eyes shut tighter. 'It's in my top right

breast pocket. I can't reach it. So unless you do want me to become a permanent fixture—'

The rest of her words dried up in her throat and her eyes sprang open.

It seemed she hadn't had to ask twice. Dylan's hand was already sliding into the pocket, his fingertips brushing against the soft cotton over her bra; just slowly enough to make a ripple of goose bumps leap up all over her body, and just fast enough she couldn't accuse him of taking advantage.

All too soon he held up the key. 'This the one you're after?'

She hoped to God it was. If he made another foray in there she didn't know what she might do.

She nodded and looked up into his eyes. Up close they were the colour of the sky back home, the unspoilt wilds of country Nimbin—the kind of wide-open blue found only in the most untouched places on earth. But the colour was the only virtuous thing about them. Barely checked exasperation boiled just below the surface.

She lifted her hand to take the key, was reminded why he had it in the first place, then gritted her teeth as she twisted so that she could expose her wrists, and her back view, to him instead.

This time he managed to have her unlocked without touching her at all. Not even a whisper, an accidental grope, a playful pat. She actually felt disappointed.

When God was handing out the mechanism for knowing who a girl could safely lean on, Wynnie had so-o-o missed out. If there was ever a man in her vicinity who was about to act against her own interests, that was the one she was drawn to.

She shook her head and vowed to ask Hannah to set her up on some sort of blind date and fast. Or maybe just a night out dancing at some dark, hazy club. Or she could take up running. Not as though she'd ever lifted a foot in purposeful exercise in her life, but there was no time like the present to begin! If she didn't manage to release some of the sexual tension this man had summoned, she was going to make a hash of everything.

She slid the cuffs from her right wrist, sucking in a short sharp breath as the pain of their release grew worse than the dull ache of the wearing of them.

'Are you okay?' he asked, and she looked up in surprise.

For the briefest moment she thought she saw actual concern flicker within his gaze. She blinked and it was gone. She hid the cuffs and her red wrists behind her. 'I'm fine. Now how about that coffee?'

'First things first,' he said, rocking forwards on his heels until her personal space became his personal space. His dark scent became her oxygen. His natural heat her reason for getting up that morning.

Her toes curled and her tongue darted out to wet her lips.

'I don't make a habit of having coffee with a woman without at the very least getting a name.' He held out a hand. 'Dylan Kelly.'

Wynnie blinked, mentally slapped herself across the back of her head for letting her imagination run rampant, then took his hand, doing her best to ignore the frisson of heat that scooted up her arm as his fingers curled around hers. 'Wynnie Devereaux.'

His eyebrows rose. 'French?'

'Australian.'

His eyebrows slowly flattened out, but the edge of his mouth kicked up into a half smile as he realised she had no intention of illuminating him further.

The truth was that Devereaux was the maiden name of a grandmother she'd never met, and her little brother, Felix, had never been able to pronounce her real name as a baby and had called her Wynnie from the time he could talk.

Felix. The whisper of his name in the back of her mind made her soul hurt, and reminded her how her patchy instinct on who to trust could go so terribly wrong.

Either way, she had no intention of talking to Dylan Kelly, or anyone else, about the existence of her brother. Or, for that matter, her real name.

'Next,' he said. *Before I inflict you upon my place of business*, he didn't need to say. 'Are you here on your own whim or as an ambassador for others like you?'

Wynnie raised an eyebrow at his snarky attitude. She then pulled a business card from the skinny travel purse looped beneath her shirt and hanging against her hip.

Her fingers brushed over the crystal and white-stone butterfly clip attached to the strap of her purse, and like the touchstone it was, it helped take the edge off her soaring adrenalin.

She handed her card over, a handcuff still dangling from that wrist.

The whisper of a half-smile tugged at Dylan's mouth, and her body reacted the same way it had every time that happened. It stretched and unfolded and purred.

Which was insane. He'd made no bones about how unenthusiastic he was about the prospect of spending time with her. And he was a target, not some anonymous hot guy in a club who might, if she was very lucky, turn out to be an undemanding friend with benefits. But she couldn't help herself. It was as though the laws of nature were having their way with her without her consent.

She whipped the cuffs behind her and unhooked them, shoving one end down the back of her trousers before they became more of a distraction. Or an apparent invitation.

He glanced at her for one long moment more before his eyes slid to her business card. His lip curled as he said, 'You're a *lobbyist*?'

'Is that better or worse than whatever it was you were thinking I was before you saw the card?'

He tipped her business card into the palm of his hand and out of sight. And if she'd thought he'd filled out his suit before, now he stood so erect he looked as if he'd been sewn into the thing. 'To tell you the truth,' he said, 'I'm not sure.'

But at least he waved an arm in front of her, herding her towards the formidable Kelly Tower.

As Wynnie's feet moved under her she realised she was kind of stunned. The spectacle had actually worked. Her employers, whose previous public persona was devout and dull, would come out of this appearing anything but. They would get prime-time news coverage, and she had gathered several leads with reporters who wanted follow-ups. She couldn't have asked for more.

The fact that she was now heading inside enemy camp meant she was a few steps ahead of the game.

So naturally she had none of the meticulously prepared, Kelly-centric pamphlets loaded with detailed cost projections and time frames on hand to back her up. There was no room in her purse for more than a credit card and house key. And nothing else was going to fit down those trousers.

Well, she'd be fine. She'd just have to wing it. Having grown up with hippy parents in Nimbin, the flower-child capital of Australia, spouting green was what she had been born to do.

She snuck a glance sideways at her silent new acquaintance to find his profile was even more daunting than front-on. His thick, dark blond hair was being lightly and sexily ruffled by the breeze shooting around the building. Those stunning blue eyes were hooded beneath strong brows so that they looked to be peering down at the world via his perfectly carved nose. And then there were those lips.

She wondered which lucky girl out there was allowed to kiss them whenever she pleased. Was able to run her finger across their planes whenever the fancy took her. Was able to lean her chin on her palm and watch them as they talked, and smiled and laughed. Her own lips tingled just looking at them.

His cheek dimpled and she knew she'd been caught staring. As he turned his head her chin shot skyward so that she might pretend to be taken with the facade of the skyscraper named after his equally daunting family.

She lifted her right hand to shield her eyes from the glare

shooting off the glass panels of the top floors when pain bit her shoulder. She crumpled in on herself and let out a shocked squeal.

He noticed. This time there was no mistaking the flicker of a supporting arm in her direction. 'Are you *sure* you're okay?'

She grabbed the handle of a glass door leading inside, using her left hand. 'Once you're standing beside me in front of a bank of cameras, telling the people of Brisbane the ways in which you and your company have helped reduce your impact on the planet thanks to the help of the Clean Footprint Coalition, and admitting how easy it will be for every individual sitting there on their couch at home to follow suit, then I'll be ecstatic. Until then, assume I'm about middling.'

She pulled open the door and, with her head held high, stalked through.

The thick glass wasn't thick enough to shield her from the surge of laughter tumbling from Dylan's beautiful lips. Or the ripple of awareness that lathered her entire body at the seriously sexy sound.

She frowned. He didn't need to be declared a protected species. He needed a warning label stapled to his head. *Beware: come within ten feet and your sexual appetite will exceed local limits.*

A few more steps inside and Wynnie's high heels clacked noisily to a halt as she tipped her head back, spun about and assimilated the Kelly Tower's entryway.

Acres of golden marble floors were only made more stunning by the most intricate black marble inlays. Two-storey-high columns acting as sentinels to a long hallway leading away from the front doors were lit by reproduction antique gas lamps. Numerous arched windows a floor above let in streams of natural light. And a massive clock, twice her height, ticked away the minutes until the banking day was closed.

It was the most stunning space she had ever seen. And that was just the lobby.

The CFC think tank had been spot on. This place, this *family* were the right choice. If the businesses of Brisbane didn't all secretly want to be them, if every single citizen didn't want to do behind closed doors exactly as they did, then she might as well have stayed in Verona.

That would have kept her from spending the past glorious month hanging with Hannah, her closest friend in the whole world. It would have kept her from working for an organisation that rang her bells like no other on earth. It would have kept her tens of thousands of miles from the beautiful place she grew up rather than a few hours' drive…

'You can buy a postcard with this exact view from the newsstand on the corner,' a deep voice rumbled from just behind her.

She turned to him, her legs twisted awkwardly and a hunk of hair caught in her eyelashes. As elegantly as humanly possible she disentangled herself. 'Not necessary.'

'Then would you care to accompany me upstairs?' he asked.

Right. Yes. She might be inside his lair but the hard work had barely begun.

It was game on. His job was easy—all he had to say was 'no', over and over again. Hers was nearby impossible—all she had to do was get him to say 'yes'.

She took a deep breath and followed Dylan into the large art-deco lift. Going with the catch-more-flies-with-honey theory of negotiation, she cocked a hip and smiled at his reflection. 'Why do I get the feeling I'm not the first girl you've invited into your office for coffee?'

Though the rest of him could have been cut from the same marble as that in the lobby, a flicker of heat ignited in his eyes. They were his tell. The one sign that she had that maybe one day his 'no' might turn into a 'yes'. Lucky for her, looking into them was no chore.

As long as she gave no tell of her own. She didn't need him knowing that her need to get this job done right was as important to her as anything she'd ever done. Or that her body was as attuned to his as a weathercock channelling a coming storm.

Dylan took a seat behind his one of a kind, polished-oak desk, and waited for Eric to lay out a chai latte for his unexpected two-o'clock appointment and a sweet black for him. He unbuttoned his cuffs and rolled up his sleeves in preparation for whatever the hell else would be thrown at him this afternoon.

Eric moved to the doorway, half terrified and half smitten with the creature ambling about the office. His eyes begged Dylan to let him back in. But this was one meeting he was doing all on his lonesome. Dylan shook his head once and the door closed with a pathetic click.

'What happened to Jerry?' Dylan asked as he waved a hand at the couch on the opposite side of his desk.

Wynnie remained standing as she picked up her mug and blew cool air across the top. 'Jerry who?'

He tried dragging his eyes away from the small round hole formed between her full lips, but then realised he might as well get his enjoyment from this unfortunate meeting where he could. 'Your predecessor at the CFC.'

'Oh. He doesn't work there anymore, and now I do.'

Dylan's cheek twitched, and not for the first time that day.

Meeting Wynnie Devereaux in the flesh had done nothing to temper the fact that at first glance she'd seemed just the kind of woman he would normally like to sink his teeth into after a long day at work—pocket-sized, hot-blooded, skin like fresh cream.

Half an hour in her presence had told him she was also just about the most infuriating creature he'd ever met. She was a lobbyist, of all the rotten things—a professional charmer who'd chosen his family to lure to her cause. She *had* to be new in town or she would have known better than to come gunning for him.

Still, for one tiny moment out there in the forecourt, something in those absorbing brown eyes had yet again charmed him. And as that chink in his usually rock-hard armour lay exposed she'd been able to confound him, twist his words and finally outfox him at his own game. All that with both hands strapped behind her back.

His gaze meandered away from her lips to her small hands. Both of her wrists were so pink and painfully chaffed that his own itched and stung in empathy. And the instinct to soothe the hurt, to make it his own, slammed him from nowhere once more. Only this time he managed to catch himself in time before, like a sucker, he asked her if she was okay.

He shifted on his seat. Every part of him uncomfortable, some for different reasons than others. 'If you're hoping to find where I keep the busts of the baby seal cubs I club for fun, they're in my home office.'

Her mouth curved into a smile. 'Right by the barrels of crude oil you spill into the river at night just for kicks.'

'You have done your research. So, where were you before the CFC?'

That had her eyes sliding back to his. Despite himself he searched their depths for the singular vulnerability that kept grabbing him through the middle. Now all he saw was the rush and fire of fierce intelligence. Unfortunately it didn't serve to squash the attraction nipping at his skin.

She said, 'Where I've come from is not important.'

'It is if you wish to finish that coffee before my burly security guards throw you out on your sweet backside.'

She gave him a blank stare, but she couldn't hide the rise and fall of her throat as she swallowed. She slowly took her seat, put her half-drunk chai latte on the edge of his desk, crossed her legs and dug in.

He hid his smile as he pretended to look for something in the top drawer of his desk. Poor old Jerry would have been quivering by now. And apologising. And practically offering to throw *himself* out.

Then again, he would never have accused Jerry of having a sweet backside. True, Jerry had never managed to be alone in a room with him before and he hadn't been as close to Jerry's backside as he had to Wynnie Devereaux's...

The few remaining bits of him that weren't coiled like springs coiled now, so tight they ached as he relived her turning her sweet backside his way so that he could set her free of her restraints.

Curves poured into tight white fabric, thick but not completely opaque, offering him the faint outline of a floral G-string. A flash of creamy skin peeking out from between her beltline and her shirt. His hand following the gentle curve but not touching. How did he manage to get so close without touching...?

Who was he kidding? The painful pleasure of those few moments of deliberate self-restraint were the highlight of his week.

He shut his drawer, sat back in his chair. Now he *really* wanted to know where the CFC had found her. And he made a mental note to get HR to headhunt their headhunter.

Her nostrils flared as she took in a breath. 'Mr Kelly, what I've done before is not nearly as important as why I am here. My method of getting the name Clean Footprint Coalition on everyone's lips may not have been typical by any means, but my mission is a deadly serious one. The CFC is a collective of respectable, hopeful, forward-thinking people. And it's clear to all of us that KInG needs to go green, and quick smart.'

She sat forward, shuffled her sweet backside to the very edge of her chair and gripped the perimeter of his desk.

'I need you,' she said.

Her breathy voice came to him on a plea. A vulnerable, naked, genuine supplication. His own ability to breathe seemed to have gone walkabout as all the blood in his body was suddenly needed elsewhere.

She was good. More than good. She was a siren with a mission. But then, right when she had him where surely she wanted him, she seemed to recognise exactly how she had affected him, and her fingers uncurled from the edge of his desk and she sat slowly back in her chair. Confounding woman.

'Our organisation,' she said with added emphasis, 'needs KInG. And KInG need us. Getting into bed together is win-win for all of us.'

He shifted on his seat again, knowing he was running out of positions in which he could sit upright and not hurt himself. At least he saw a chance to give her a taste of her own medicine.

'All of us, hey?' he said. 'For some reason I'm seeing futons involved and that's just not my style.'

She shook her head, and seemed to struggle to find her words, the siren lost within the skin of a delightfully befuddled mortal woman. 'Forget getting into bed.'

'But now you've brought it up, it's out there. I like big beds, not too firm, with plenty of room to move.'

She held out a steadying hand, as if willing him with every fibre of her being to shut up and let her finish. 'I meant it's a win-win situation for both companies. We are looking to make a difference, and just think of all the lovely, happy, warm, free PR that would come to KInG if you led the way on how to be an authentically green business.'

An electronic Post-it note blinked up onto Dylan's computer from Eric, telling him he had a client waiting. 'You have two more minutes. Give it to me straight up. What exactly do you want?'

'A partnership.'

Dylan couldn't help himself, he laughed. Her responding dark frown was adorable.

'With KInG?' he clarified.

'And the Clean Footprint Coalition.'

He leant forward. 'Honey, I'm not sure which hay cart you rolled in on, but somebody's been pulling your leg if they gave you any indication that this company had any desire, need or care to be in cahoots with anyone.'

She leant in towards him, too, recrossing her legs, and giving eye contact as good as she got. 'But you already are. Your largest corporate clients are in car manufacturing, oil production, shipping, some of the largest polluters on the planet. Is that something you'd rather we were focusing on in our press material?'

The skin beneath his left eye twitched. It was a timely reminder that no matter how adorable her frowns might be she had an agenda, and it involved targeting his family in her tree-hugging games. If she backed him any further into a corner he would have no choice but to claw his way back out, and if she was in his way so be it.

His voice was as sharp as cut glass as he asked, 'So why the hell didn't you chain yourself to a sculpture outside one of their businesses?'

Rather than sensing how close she was to grave danger, the minx smiled, her eyes gleaming like warm honey. 'I like yours better.'

Dylan growled. He actually growled, right out loud, and shook his fists beneath his desk. And right when his frustration reached its peak, her voice came to him like hot chocolate on a cold night. 'Mr Kelly, I told you a small fib when I promised to bother someone else tomorrow. You're it; the only company I even have on my radar. My every working hour has been and will be focused on bringing you home. So why not save us both some time, and a lot of aggravation and let my people come in here, strip you down to your bare essentials and build you back up again when it comes to energy consumption, consumables and waste? You'll barely notice the cost and you will go to bed knowing the planet is breathing better for your minimal efforts.'

'Why me?' he asked, questioning not only her but whichever god he'd annoyed enough that day to bring this woman to his doorstep.

'You are the company every other one in the country wants to emulate. Your success is legendary. Your influence off the chart. Where you lead others will follow, and we want them to follow. Turn off one light overnight, who'd notice? Turn off all the lights of Brisbane overnight, and it's a revolution.'

She took a breath, licked her lips, sent his body temperature up a notch in the process, then said, 'So what do you think?'

He leant back in his chair, but his eyes never once left hers. 'Here it is, hopefully clear enough none of it will flutter over *your* head. I do not respond well to threats. I do not respond well to having my business or my family singled out so publicly by upstarts with an agenda. I think the stunt you pulled out there might be a lucky winner for one news cycle, but in taking me on you have bitten off more than you can chew. I think you should shine your green light elsewhere before you find it's dimmed forever.'

She blinked up at him, those warm brown eyes somehow holding in whatever it was that *she* was thinking. Eventually she uncrossed her legs and she stood. She ran her hands down the sides of her thighs and he noticed they were shaking. His gut clenched. He pinched himself on the arm, hard.

She gave a small nod, and said, 'Okay, then. That sounds like my cue to thank you for your time and let you get on with your day.'

She made her way to the door of his office. He pushed himself from his chair and followed. Halfway there he laid a hand on her lower back to guide her. Guide her? It was a straight line to the office door. He held his hand as still as could be while the muscles of her back and hips slid against him in an erotic rhythm.

There was no professional reason to touch her. If she'd been Jerry he wouldn't have even left his chair. If she'd been Jerry she wouldn't have made it past the front door. He was touching her as a lightning rod, as a way to stop himself from doing anything more extreme.

When she reached the hallway and turned towards him, his hand slid around her waist. The twist of her shirt, the soft dip of warm skin… He pulled his hand away quick smart.

She looked at him as though she had no clue as to the commotion raging inside him. 'Thank you,' she said, 'for this afternoon. We appreciate your time.'

Suddenly he found himself not quite ready to have seen the last of her. He leant his shoulder against the doorframe of his office door. 'Thank *you* for this afternoon. It has to be the most eventful Tuesday we've seen around this place since Melbourne Cup Day.'

'Stock prices soar by triple figures, did they?'

His laughter carried out into the hall and several lackeys rushing past stopped to see why. He ignored them and explained, 'A bunch of guys and girls from the legal floor dressed up as horses and jockeys and replayed the race for our amusement.'

She raised an eyebrow. 'Well, I can only hope that when you tell the board about our meeting today you do so with as much verve and enthusiasm as you had for an inter-office lark.'

Her voice was pure sarcasm, yet she stayed where she was on the ocean of polished wood with its discreetly papered walls and sculpted cornices, and flurry of assistants keeping the place abuzz, and she clung to her small purse with both hands.

And it hit him like a three-foot fishhook through the guts. She wanted more than their two companies to work together. She wanted him. She was standing there acting as if she had ants in her pants as she was crushing on him big-time.

For the briefest moment he imagined sliding a hand into the back of her hair, pulling her to him and kissing the daylights out of her.

It rankled. He wasn't the kind of guy to get suckered in by the simple sweet tug of desire. Only those of a particularly cool and indifferent ilk warranted his time. And Wynnie Devereaux appeared neither cool nor indifferent. While she was outwardly vivacious and implacable, he had the sense that on the inside she was as fragile and beautiful as the jewelled butterfly her fingers were tracing on her purse.

She was also a lobbyist working the other side of the table.

He pushed his way back upright and looked into her eyes just long enough that he didn't feel the strange, warm, encouraging trap closing over him, and said, 'I'll plant a tree this weekend and think of you.'

Her full lips curved into a slow smile. 'Plant a dozen and think of your kids.'

'I don't have kids.' He added a wink. 'So far as I know. Goodbye, Wynnie.'

'Till next time, Mr Kelly.'

After one last long look, one he understood all too well, she turned and walked down the hallway.

He couldn't help but grin when he spotted one half of her handcuffs swaying and bouncing against her sweet backside until she rounded the corner, out of sight.

CHAPTER THREE

WYNNIE nudged her high heels off her feet, let them fall to the floor beneath her bar stool, and massaged one bare foot with the other. She then closed her eyes and pressed her fingers into the tops of her eyelids.

'What are you doing?' Hannah asked.

'Trying to permanently block out several particular moments of my day.'

Hannah laughed. 'Come off it. You did brilliantly! Better than we could ever have hoped. You've already made the four-thirty reports. You actually got inside the building. As far as the CFC is concerned you're a rainmaker.'

'Nevertheless I'm still of the opinion that threatening to start a campaign whereby I would blame the most influential business in town with single-handedly poisoning the planet on purpose was a real high point.'

Wynnie let her head thunk onto the shiny red bar of the funky Eagle St Pier beer garden. But the knock to the head did nothing to shift the images stuck fast to the outer curve of her skull.

Dylan Kelly's knee-weakening half-smiles when she flirted with him. His debilitating dark smiles when she pushed him a step too far. And most of all his delicious parting smile, which had made her think, for one brief shining moment, that maybe she wasn't the only one who'd spent the afternoon having a professional conversation on the outside and a very personal one on the inside.

'Nah,' Hannah said before downing the rest of her cocktail in one gulp and asking for another in one swift move. 'I'm going to have to vote for the nickel allergy as my favourite Wynnie moment.'

Wynnie lifted her head, flicked her fringe away from her face and ran gentle fingers over the bandages on her wrists. 'That's not funny.'

Hannah laughed so loud a dozen heads turned to see what they were missing. 'Right. You went from making a business contact no one at the CFC has ever managed to wangle, to having a just-out-of-med-school doctor diagnose you with being too cheap to buy quality handcuffs.'

Wynnie sat on her hands. 'No way was I going to use the funds of a non-profit organisation to spend as much as I could on top-of-the-line handcuffs.'

Hannah only laughed so hard she had to push her stool back so that she could clutch her stomach. Wynnie grabbed her so-called friend by the belt loops of her jeans and tugged her upright before she took out some passer-by.

As Hannah continued to giggle Wynnie took a deep breath, drinking in the aroma of beer and lemon-scented banksias filling big earthenware pots around the floor. It was a deeply Australian smell, and, after many years living abroad, it was unexpectedly comforting. As were the last vestiges of Brisbane spring sunshine pouring through massive skylights and floor-to-ceiling windows.

The labours of her day finally began to ease away.

Wynnie glanced down the bar. 'I'm not sure if a nickel overdose can make a person thirsty but I am dying for another drink.'

Problem was, since she was on cortisone for her red wrists, she had to stick with pineapple juice, which did nothing to help her forget Dylan Kelly's brawny forearms, the curve of short thick hair that turned from gold to brown just above his ears and those deep, glinting, hooded blue eyes.

When their drinks arrived, the nice barman had added a sugared strawberry to the edge of her glass, and an umbrella for good measure. He also gave her a long smile.

He was terribly cute. She was pathologically single. And obviously in need of some mollifying male company if her performance that afternoon was anything to go by.

But there was a kind of puppy-dog softness about the eyes that told her he was a boyfriend kind of guy. Girlfriends shared stories of family and past folly as pillow talk, something she'd never be able to do, which meant she'd never be a girlfriend kind of girl.

She gave him a short nod, then turned her body away from the bar and towards Hannah, who was grinning at her over her Fuzzy Navel.

'Wynnie has a new little friend,' Hannah sing-songed.

'Wynnie has no such thing.'

'Give him another five minutes and he'll be back with a rose between his teeth and a mandolin. Better yet, you order the next round of drinks and save us twenty bucks.'

'Don't be ridiculous.'

'And why not? A new man for a new town. After the hours you've put in this month you deserve to let your hair down some.'

Wynnie raised a hand to her hair, which she'd pinned up off her neck while at the doctor's surgery, sliding her butterfly clip above her ear to hold back her fringe. 'It was down today. And look where that got me.'

'Ah,' Hannah said, with way too much of an inflection.

'What does "ah" mean?'

'It means so that's why you're all down about the mouth when considering the success your day has been you should be as high as a kite.'

'I'm not high because I'm not the one on my fourth cock-tail,' she said out of the side of her mouth.

Hannah waggled a wobbly finger in her general direction. 'First my little recruit has proven herself professionally, making me look shiny and fabulous for insisting she be hired, and now she has gone and got herself a little crush on Mr Dylan Tall Blond and Handsome Kelly. I'm celebrating!'

Wynnie's naked feet pointed hard at the floor as some kind of strange physical response shot through her at the mere mention of Dylan Kelly's name.

She opened her mouth wide to deny everything, but suddenly she was too exhausted to bother. 'It might have been nice to have a heads up that he is that gorgeous.'

'I thought the fact that I had to wipe drool from my chin every time his name was mentioned in passing during strategy meetings was giveaway enough.'

'Not nearly enough. You do know he's stunning. Matinee-idol, suit-model, high-school-crush, knee-weakening, super-models-only-need-apply stunning.'

'Did your voice just crack a little?'

'It did not,' Wynnie shot back. Then for some unknown reason added, 'But it's not just his looks. He's sharp, and focused, and canny and funny when you don't expect it.'

'So I've heard. But I am a respected lawyer, you know. I must show some decorum. Did you? Show decorum?'

Wynnie's hands went straight to her eyes to rub them again. 'I might have become a tad tongue-tied on more than one occasion, and made inferences that I wanted to go to bed with him, but that's it.'

Hannah's laughter turned heads the whole way around the bar. 'So are you gonna ask him out or not?'

Her hot hands dropped to cup her blissfully cold glass. 'For what purpose?'

'Um, dinner, a movie, the horizontal tango?'

'Han! He's *the* only mark. The one who can make or break this deal.'

'And that's why you won't ask him out?'

'No. Yes! Well, that and the fact that he's probably got a line-up of women wiping drool from their chins.'

Hannah's answering smile was most unfriendly.

'My working hours are far too full on right now to even think about starting up any kind of anything with any man.'

'Anything else?'

'Yeah, he's just a huge flirt. He flirted with me, every female reporter within eyeshot, some of the men, and a pot plant on the way into his office. It's pathological.'

'Finally something I understand! Now this isn't the kind of thing you would have found in the stuff the researchers gave you, so here goes. The stories do circulate that he is… How do I put this?' Hannah tapped her chin and looked to the heavens. 'He's a man with a limited attention span.'

'Meaning?'

'Never appears to date the same girl twice. Though they are all beautiful. All fabulous. All about as warm as ice sculptures.'

Wynnie blinked. 'And you think I might be interested in being one of those girls of the week, and that I fit that description? I'm not sure which part of that I should be insulted by most.'

Hannah slapped her on the arm. 'Stop trying to be offended and think about it. You've found time this month to come bowling with me, to go out for drinks, to see a movie, a bunch of DVDs. I could sacrifice a little of that down time for the sake of your love life before you start sleeping in the office to get a head start on the working day and unknowingly muttering carbon emission averages beneath your breath.'

Wynnie shook her head. 'It feels like things have fallen into place for me for the first time in a really long time. I *believe* in the organisation with every fibre of my being. Their philosophy is my very lifeblood. To be their advocate is an honour and an obligation. Every hour I spend working for them I feel like I am contributing, and helping and redeeming…'

She shook her head hard and let her voice drift away.

Of all the people she could have talked to about her acute need to make amends, Hannah was it. She'd been with Wynnie the day Felix had disappeared—even finding her a great lawyer through her professors at school. But even after all this time, saying the words out loud felt too raw.

'I'm not asking Dylan Kelly out. Okay?'

She sipped at her drink. All of the excuses were fine but they didn't come close to her main reticence. She'd been known to do stunningly self-sacrificing things for men she regarded highly, and the only way to never let that happen again was not to put herself in the position where it might.

There were only so many times a girl could change her hair, and her name, and leave town. In comparison, putting up with a little sexual tension was small fry.

Hannah leant her elbow on the bar and her head on her hand. 'You done?'

She nodded.

'So you wouldn't mind, then, if Dylan Kelly and I became hot and heavy.'

Wynnie gripped the straw between her teeth. 'Not in the least,' she fibbed.

'What about me and the bartender?'

Wynnie all but bounced on her bar stool. 'Oh, do! He seems nice and sweet, the ideal complement to your rabid cynicism. And he could make you cocktails every night. He's perfect for you!'

Wynnie's bottom bouncing came to a halt when she realised Hannah had been pulling her leg about the bartender to get a true answer about Lady Killer Kelly. And she'd given it in surround sound, with Technicolor and subtitles.

'I have to go,' Wynnie said, finding her shoes with her feet. 'The local farmer's market closes at eight and I'm all out of kumquats.'

She grabbed her battered travel purse from the bar, slid her feet back into her shoes, hopped off the bar stool and pressed her way through the crowd.

'Kumquats? That's one I've never heard before.' Hannah, three inches taller than Wynnie even in her flats, caught up all too easily. 'And just because you thought the sun shone from Felix's you-know-what and he turned out to be a total screw-up that doesn't mean every man you ever meet will do the same. Trust me.'

Wynnie saw a gap open up within a huge group of uni students and took it. Alone.

A screw-up? Felix hadn't just been a screw-up. Her kid brother, her only remaining family, the beautiful boy who'd never even had the heart to step on a spider he was so attuned with the world around him, had done something so heinous, so out of character, hurting people all in the name of saving the planet. And to add insult to injury he'd left *her* to clean up the mess she hadn't even seen coming. And she'd never laid eyes on him since.

Trust was now a four-letter word.

When she reached the sidewalk she bounced on her toes as her eyes scanned the streets for an empty taxi.

'Heard from him yet?' Hannah asked from beside her.

There was no point pretending she didn't know Hannah was talking about her brother. She shook her head so hard her butterfly came loose. She reached out and caught it before it hit the ground. Her heart thundered in her ears at the thought she might have broken it—the only thing she still had that had once belonged to her beautiful, brilliant, progressive parents. She could only be thankful they had both gone by the time Felix changed.

'You will, sweetie,' Hannah said. 'Don't worry. He always

checks in eventually. Though why he doesn't just leave you the hell alone once and for all I have no idea.'

She glared at Hannah, who held up her hands in surrender.

'Fine. I won't say another word on the subject. But if I ever bump into him in a dark alley all he's getting from me is a swift kick up the backside.'

A taxi stopped. Wynnie put her butterfly into her purse and opened the back door. She took a breath and turned to her friend. 'Is that your version of not another word?'

'From this moment on, I cross my heart.' Then she looked back inside the bar. 'A cute bartender who can give me free drinks, or the infamous Dylan Kelly who can buy me the bar. Mmm, how is a girl to choose?'

Wynnie poked out her tongue and jumped in the cab, giving the driver the address of the Spring Hill cottage the CFC had put her up in as part of her irresistible relocation package.

After watching through the back window to see Hannah grab the next taxi that came along, Wynnie leant into the hot fabric seat, let out a long, slow breath and closed her eyes.

Only to be confronted with Dylan Kelly in full colour and three dimensions. This time instead of trying to squeeze him from her brain she let him simmer there a while.

Her breast ached where his fingers had brushed her. Her backside ached where they hadn't. She wished her wrists still hurt and then she might not have noticed the rest, but magical white cream was keeping the most sensible of her itches at bay.

Who was she kidding? They were on two different planes of existence. The audacious, hippy environmentalist and the formidable, filthy-rich corporate giant.

And really, when it came down to it, thank goodness for that.

Dylan sat back from the dinner table, replete. Another rambunctious Kelly family dinner done with.

The minute he'd hit the long table in his parents' over-decorated dining hall, he'd eaten like a man possessed.

Caramelised pork with green papaya salad, duck breast with blood orange & quince marmalade, goat's cheese baklava. He'd not missed an offering, filling his stomach in an effort to quell that other hunger that had cloaked him all afternoon.

Wynnie Devereaux might have been a pain in his behind, but she'd also left him with an ache everywhere else. He'd felt her liquid brown eyes grazing his cheek all afternoon until he'd taken to his office washroom and shaved. His palm had tingled with the feel of her hip sliding against it until he'd purposely scalded himself on a too-hot cup of coffee. No matter the hundred other jobs he'd had to do, he hadn't been able to erase her from his mind.

It certainly hadn't helped that his phone had run hot all afternoon from media outlets looking for quotable quotes about his relationship with the CFC and his opinion on the woman of the hour.

Having to find new and interesting ways of *not* saying he mostly wanted to throw her over his shoulder and give her a good spank had taken its toll.

Food and lots of it had worked for a couple of hours which had made for a nice relief. As had making mention of the incident, every chance he'd had. He patted his tight belly. So long as he didn't make fuelling his sexual appetite with food a habit.

'Are you sure you're done there, bro?' his younger sister, Meg, asked. 'For five bucks I'll let you lick my plate.'

He offered her a shark's grin. 'The day you put in an honest day's work at an honest job, then you'll understand why some of us need big dinners. We often miss lunch rather than make it the focus of our day.'

She poked out her tongue and took off into the next room with her mobile phone already glued to her ear.

'She's almost thirty, right?' he asked his father.

But Quinn Kelly was already pushing back his chair and sneaking outside. Dylan nodded to his parents' butler, James, to make sure the old man wasn't sneaking outside for a cigar.

Dylan sat forward and ran a hand over his mouth. He'd always thought them a tight-knit family. Until a few months back, on the night of his father's seventieth birthday, when they'd discovered a secret that threatened to knock their foundations out from under them.

His father, the true king behind the Kelly Investment Group, the powerhouse who had made their family the most influential in Brisbane, a man they had all thought might defy the odds and live forever, had serious heart problems that had led to him being brought back to life twice.

That night they had closed ranks, and told no one—for the sake of the financial stability of the business, and for the sake of their father's health.

Dylan's position as guardian of the parts of his family's lives deemed not fit for public consumption had only become all the more critical overnight.

It was a job he was more than happy to do. A job he'd needed to do since that long-ago day when the whole city had woken up to find their newspapers filled with pages dedicated to the gory specifics of the horrifically messy breakdown of his engagement.

If he'd been any other jilted man, with any other surname, nobody would have given a hoot. He'd realised that day the precarious position his whole family was in, and he'd taken it upon himself to be all of their safeguards against menace, exposure and innuendo.

Once James came back and intimated that Quinn was not disobeying doctor's orders, Dylan was able to relax. He shook off the dark memories of that long-ago, cloistered version of himself and glanced down the table to find his youngest brother, Cameron, and his new bride, Rosie, finishing off a bottle of wine, not even realising everyone else had gone.

A couple of minutes went by before Dylan realised he was still watching them.

His back teeth clenched and he downed the last swig of

Scotch in the glass held tight in his fist. Of all of his family he got on best with Cam—he was a sharp guy, and he wished him all the luck in the world. But in the back of his mind he worried for him. Odds were Rosie would turn out *not* to be the woman Cam thought she was.

'Aren't they just the sweetest things you've ever seen?'

Dylan blinked, and turned to find his mother standing behind him, a beatific smile on her face.

He stood and turned his back on the couple, hoping not having them in his sights might make the discomfort behind his ribs go away.

'So sweet my teeth hurt. Now when are you going to realise having us over is not akin to a state dinner? You can keep the Wedgwood in the cupboard. Bring out the Ikea flatware for us next time.' He kissed his mum on the cheek, and walked away, hoping to make a stealthy exit.

He headed through the drawing room only to find Brendan sitting at a table with a desk lamp, reading over some contract or other. He'd always been a workaholic, but even more so now that he was secretly running KInG while Quinn was forcibly sitting in his office playing solitaire all day instead of running the multibillion-dollar company that had likely taken ten years off his life in the first place.

Dylan stuck his hands in his trouser pockets and watched his brother a moment longer.

Brendan had been in a long-term relationship himself once, and had been left deeply hurt and alone. True, Chrissy had died unexpectedly, leaving him with two gorgeous young daughters to help fill the gap, both of whom were upstairs now, sleeping like angels, but Dylan still felt an empathy with the guy. If Brendan took a moment to bend, or appear even slightly less than indestructible, maybe they could be stalwarts together, resiliently emancipated from the burden of needing love.

'So that disturbance today,' Brendan said, causing Dylan to leap out of his skin. 'I assume you cleaned it up.'

'Assume away.'

Brendan managed to hold his breath for about three and a half seconds before closing the contract and looking up. 'I saw the news. Handcuffs? Seriously?'

Dylan grinned. He couldn't help himself. Hearing the word *'handcuffs'* come out of his stiff older brother's mouth was almost worth the afternoon chasing the owner of the handcuffs around the deep dark recesses of his mind.

He leant against a twelve-foot bookcase and crossed one ankle across the other. 'Her name's Wynnie. She wants us to help her save the world. I offered to take her to the moon and back instead.'

Brendan frowned even more than usual. 'You didn't—'

'Hey, a good time with me and she'll have trouble remembering her own name.'

Brendan rubbed his fingers over his eyes. 'Why, oh, why did she have to be a woman?'

Dylan grinned. 'It was a fifty-fifty chance and the gods love me.'

When Brendan looked as if he was about to burst a blood vessel Dylan sat in a chair across from him and filled him in on the specifics—Wynnie's new position, the details of her pitch, and the fact that she would not be getting back into the building any time soon.

'The deal wasn't worth considering?' Brendan asked.

'The deal was probably fine. But I have no intention of dealing with someone who all but blackmailed me into giving her the meeting in the first place. It's not a precedent I believe we want to set.'

Brendan's hard face softened into what looked to be the beginnings of a smile. 'You want her to know you're the biggest baddest image manipulator in town, not her.'

Dylan just stared back.

And Brendan shook his head as he opened the contract up again and began to read as he spoke. 'A Trojan horse, that's what she was. Letting her in the building was as good as admitting defeat. But if you think it's best to keep her at bay, then fine. That's the end of that.'

Dylan stared at the ends of his fingernails so long he lost focus. That was the end of that. No more Wynnie Devereaux. No more meetings, no more sightings, no more thinking about her.

Or her tousled hair. Or sweet-smelling skin. Or the blaze of attraction that had grabbed him and not let him go. Or the fact that while she claimed her name wasn't French her accent did have the sexiest tinge of European schooling about it. Or that he'd never met anyone, not even within his own boisterous gutsy family, who had the gumption to put their own pride, their own self-interest, a mile down the line behind standing up for what they believed in.

And she had promised she wasn't yet done with him. He wondered what other surprises she might have in store for him beneath her tough outer layer. Beneath that so-close-to-see-through-it-hurt top, beneath those tight white pants that left little to the imagination, beneath that delicate G-string—

'Another drink, sirs?' James asked from the doorway.

Brendan shook his head without looking up.

While Dylan dragged himself from the chair with a loud oomph. 'Not for this little duck. I'm home to bed.'

He slapped James on the shoulder as he passed. 'You'll keep an eye on them for me, won't you, James? Make sure they don't burn the manor down, or get caught in public naked, or do anything else I would have to clean up in the press the next day?'

'Always, Master Dylan.'

'Good man.'

CHAPTER FOUR

WYNNIE'S knee jiggled and her eyes hurt from staring agitatedly at the sun-drenched glass front of the Morningside café.

Her wrist ached from whipping her chai latte for the past ten minutes. To be more specific, the *muscles* ached. Her handcuff injuries were still swathed in bandages and magic cream; hence the need for a long-sleeved leather jacket over her black and white striped T-shirt.

Her eyes swept past warm orange walls, mismatched wooden chairs and deep purple couches as she glanced at the flat-screen TV on the wall behind the counter. A frothy current-affairs morning show was on, and in the bottom right-hand corner of the screen it told her she'd spent twelve minutes staring. Waiting. Knee-jiggling.

That was twelve extra minutes she could have slept. Twelve extra minutes in which she might have found time to cover the panda patches under her eyes and done something with her hair rather than just run hopeful fingers through it in the cab.

Brisbane's balmy weather, that was what had kept her awake the past few nights. Years spent in more reasonable, temperate climes meant her system was reeling from a little heat shock. Watching the fan spin above her bed, casting long shadows across the moonlit ceiling, while her hot, spreadea-

gled body took every whisper of shifting air it could, she had
finally fallen asleep some time just before sunrise.

Her night sweats had had nothing to do with the fact that
she knew that at seven-thirty this morning she'd be sitting in
this very café awaiting the arrival of Dylan Kelly.

She looked to the TV again, and suddenly there she was in
all her handcuffed glory. A static image over the newsreader's
left shoulder spun to fill the screen showing her strapped to
the inane sculpture while Dylan Kelly paced about her like a
lion baiting his prey.

It was said that a camera added ten pounds. On Dylan
Kelly wherever the camera had added bulk, it had worked. She
shuffled on her seat, heat rising up her back, slithering behind
her knees, pooling between her breasts.

She, on the other hand, with the wind flapping at her hair,
and in her fanciful floral top, her knees knocking, her eyes
locked in on Dylan's every move, did appear the 'eco-warrior'
each outlet had labelled her. She wondered which one had
written the wire and which others had barely bothered changing a word.

Either way, the term didn't sit well with her at all. It
conjured up images of red paint-bombs, and angry protestors
and tear gas.

And Felix. The last time she'd seen him at seventeen years
old, he'd had the gleam of battle in his eye as he'd excitedly
told her he was in Brisbane to protest with a group of mates.
She'd been so proud of his passion. Little had she imagined
the extent of the collateral damage involved in the war he had
been about to wage, all in the name of the environment.

Her hand went straight for her mum's butterfly clip, today
attached to the band of her watch.

Her family hadn't been brought up that way. Their focus
had been living off the land, and leaving as small a mark upon
it behind them as possible. It helped forge a more intimate
community better connected to the world around them.

Finding a way to give the rest of the world just a taste of that idyllic existence was what she was working so hard to achieve now.

The café door swung inwards, a blinding flash of sunlight reflected off the angled glass and into her eyes.

A male form burst into the space, but she knew in an instant it wasn't the male form she sought. It was a more slightly built, younger man in a suit, talking non-stop into a mobile phone.

Her spine relaxed and she reached for her glass— Her fingers curled into her palm before she reached it.

The young man wasn't alone. He held open the door deferentially, and in his wake came another. Pale grey suit, white and grey striped shirt, no tie, platinum-framed sunglasses, broad shoulders, short dark blond hair, a chiselled jaw and lips built for sin. Head down, reading a newspaper held in one hand, this male seemed to suck every ounce of sunshine from the bright room.

As he moved away from the door the light redispersed itself into a more normal pattern and Dylan Kelly came into focus.

No more trying to tell herself that heatstroke had caused the sexual overdrive that had overcome her the last time they'd met. It was all him. She picked up her drink, downing the cooled muck in one hit.

All that was just too damned bad. This meeting was all about the work. It was her second take at chip, chip, chipping away at his rock-hard veneer.

He lifted his head as though he'd only just realised where he was. The man at his side, whom she now recognised as his assistant Eric, mimed that he would get the coffees. Dylan nodded once, then his eyes swept the room.

An equal mix of anticipation and trepidation slid through her body as she waited for him to catch her eye. Dylan wasn't exactly expecting her. She'd started off with the heroine-on-the-train-tracks approach, this time she was going with the sudden-leap-from-behind-a-tree attack.

Then suddenly she wondered if he'd even recognise *her* if he did spot her. What if she'd built up their first meeting into some kind of rare, mythical, sexual awakening when for him she'd been one of a dozen crazies he'd dealt with that day?

The urge to dive beneath the low coffee table nudging at her calves was a strong one…until his head stopped its slow perusal of the room so quickly his cheek clenched, and the newspaper in his hand crumpled beneath a tensed fist.

She took a deep breath and said, 'Here we go again,' beneath her breath, before giving him a jaunty wave.

Eric appeared at his side, noticed Dylan had turned to stone, then followed the direction of his gaze. When Eric saw her with her hand raised, the colour drained from the poor guy's face.

It wasn't as though she'd expected a big hello and a kiss on the cheek from Dylan, but brutal exasperation radiated from his entire body. Pesky as her job meant she could be, she'd never brought about that kind of intense reaction in another person before.

He reached up and slid off his sunglasses. The hit of those glinting blue eyes felt like a sucker punch to the stomach, even this time, when she ought to have been expecting it. Or perhaps that was her very problem. The expectation of seeing him again, of wondering if her reaction to him would be as outrageously vivid as the last time, had grown exponentially with every passing hour since she'd last walked away.

She stood, and waved an arm towards the matching couches surrounding the low-slung coffee table she'd secured for their 'meeting'. This time she'd had two days in which to get completely ready. She had all the information she needed right in front of her—statistics, research, cost-projections. And since the emails she'd sent had bounced, she had pamphlets, proposals and contracts at her fingertips.

Dylan's cheek twitched.

Wynnie's stomach rolled over on itself. Time slowed to a

most painful rate. Her jacket began to feel like a hotbox. *Come on*, she begged inside her head.

And then he smiled. Wide lips. Straight white teeth. His cheeks lifting to create half a dozen deep creases around each blue eye.

When his smile turned to laughter, she called out across the cafe, 'What?'

He began snaking around the haphazard tables in between them until they were separated by the coffee table alone.

'What?' she said again.

'You.'

'Me what?'

'You are one tenacious woman, Miss Devereaux.' His smile eased until it was all in his eyes.

As she drowned in a sea of sky blue, her neck relaxed and her muscles grew loose. Loose enough she smiled right on back. 'The sooner you realise I'm not going away, the sooner you'll stop ignoring me.'

He tossed his sunglasses onto the couch and shucked off his jacket, his shoulder muscles bunching and shifting beneath his light cotton shirt. 'I'm afraid I couldn't ignore you even if I wanted to. We'll be sitting here today, Eric,' he said, and Wynnie glanced over his shoulder to see his assistant hovering.

'Sure thing, boss,' he said, then scurried off to grab their order.

Not quite believing her luck, Wynnie waited until Dylan sat before sitting again herself. Her knees knocked as she leant over to neaten up her presentation and the fabric of her skinny jeans rubbing together sent hot sparks up her legs.

What with her leather jacket, her hot jeans, the chai latte in her belly and Dylan Kelly smouldering at her three feet away, she was very much in danger of heatstroke.

She ran a hand across her forehead to find it was moist. Deciding it was better to appear foolish than to faint, she took off her jacket and all but whimpered with pleasure when her arms were bare to the blissful air-conditioning.

Unfortunately it took Dylan half a second to reach out and grab her hands. 'Now what the hell have you gone and done to yourself?'

Despite the lightning speed of his grab, he held her wrists gently, turning them over in his large hands, running his long fingers over the edge of the bandages. His face was so grave her heart skipped a beat.

When storm clouds began to gather in his eyes, she buckled. 'It was the handcuffs. They were cheap. They flared up a latent nickel allergy. I have to put on stupid cortisone cream three times a day. Happy now?'

So happy he burst into laughter. Peals of loud, free, pulsing laughter. Half the café stopped talking and stared. Everyone recognised him. If not as Dylan Kelly then likely as the guy who got coffee there every morning at seven-thirty. Those who did recognise him as Dylan Kelly quickly slid their eyes to her, the woman who had made him laugh.

She felt darts of envy impale her from about seven different points in the café. If they had any clue he had only laughed at her because she had made a fool of herself, rather than from any kind of friendliness, they might not feel so darkly towards her.

She sat on her hands. 'Are you done?' she asked between her teeth.

'For now,' he said, shifting on his seat and crossing his right foot atop his left knee. 'Now to what do I owe this unexpected pleasure? Or am I to suppose that it is pure coincidence that you are in this exact place at this precise time of day?'

'Mr Kelly—'

'Dylan. If this is to be our second shared coffee, I'd suggest the time has come for us to be more…familiar with one another.'

If she hadn't been on the receiving end of irritation in those daring blue eyes as many times as she already had, she might have thought he was suggesting something altogether more… familiar than he really was.

He was a man with a limited attention span.

She grabbed a hunk of papers from in front of her and said, 'I'm here to give you specifics on how our plan would work.'

'Well, isn't that a great pity?' he said.

And for a moment, taking in the rich timbre in his voice, and a flare of rare warmth in his eyes, she believed him. She blinked, yet felt it still. She breathed deep enough to catch his scent above the sugar and coffee flavours filling the air—

'Sorry it took so long,' a strange voice said instead, cutting so cruelly into her thoughts. 'They forgot your cinnamon again.'

The bustle at the edge of her vision pulled her gaze from Dylan's deep blue eyes to find Eric had joined them, was making a little table picnic for Dylan with coffee, sugar, napkin, spoons and a decadent-looking cream bun.

Once settled in the tub chair at the end of the coffee table, Eric pulled out a tiny laptop, sat it on his knees and looked to Wynnie in expectation.

When she looked back at Dylan, he had his newspaper in one hand, a coffee in the other, and to all intents and purposes he seemed to have forgotten she was even there.

She threw her papers onto the coffee table and thought about leaving. Giving up. Moving on to a new target, or maybe a new city. This was just too hard. Trying to work with this man was proving to be beyond her capabilities.

She closed her eyes tight.

And that was exactly why she had to see it through to the very end. Nothing was worth having if it wasn't a struggle to achieve. The reward at the end would only be greater for the blood, sweat and tears she gave to the endeavour. Maybe this was exactly what she needed to overcome to clear her conscience once and for all.

So she clasped her hands atop her knees and turned to Eric.

'Hi,' she said, offering him a friendly smile.

'Hello.'

Well, so far, in comparison with his astonishingly charismatic boss, he was…not exactly riveting. She managed to not look at Dylan, though she just knew he was smiling.

She had to get to the crunch, and forge a relationship with her new target, and fast.

'Eric, right? I'm Wynnie.'

'I know.'

Dylan's cheek twitched as he flapped the paper loudly and settled back into his seat to read the back sports page.

She leant towards Eric, but not close enough to scare the guy; he seemed a tad skittish. 'I love your suit. What's it made of?'

When he gawped at her, she slowly reached out and ran two fingers down the lapel. 'Worsted wool, right? Perfect choice for Brisbane weather.'

'Unlike leather,' Dylan murmured without looking up.

Wynnie nudged her jacket aside with her knee, and turned the full force of her charm back to Eric, who had at least managed to stop looking so bug-eyed.

'Do you live near here, too?' she asked.

He flicked a glance at his boss, who rolled his eyes in response before waving a defeated hand.

'Chapel Hill,' Eric said.

Having only lived in her uni town for a few months several years ago, her geography was a tad shaky, but Chapel Hill was on the bus route from the big draughty old house she'd shared with Hannah and a half-dozen others while at university.

'But that's a half-hour drive from here!' She poked a thumb in Dylan's direction. 'Does he make you drive all this way every morning to order his coffee?'

Eric's chest puffed out. 'I'm happy to do it.'

'By that he means no, I don't make him drive all this way,' Dylan drawled as he glanced her way. 'The kid's enthusiastic. Something you two have in common.'

Wynnie scowled. Eric blushed. And Dylan's long stare had her blood thrumming.

He wasn't generally nice. He didn't have any kind of natural inclination to do the right thing by the world at large. He was stubborn, antagonistic, cynical and infuriating. Yet she desperately, deplorably, immediately wanted to sleep with him. A futon, a king-sized water bed, the coffee table digging into her calves. She didn't care where. She didn't care when. All she cared was that it would happen. It had to happen. Or she might never be able to think straight again.

Maybe it was his very decadence that grabbed her so hard. His very wrongness and badness. Like her latent nickel allergy, his type was an itch she'd had her whole life that only now had been brought to the surface by circumstance.

Wynnie Gracious Devereaux Lambert, she yelled inside her head. *Present your pitch, get the hell out of here, then get thee to a yoga mat, or better yet an ice bath*!

'So, Eric,' she said, her voice sounding as unnaturally tight as her body felt, 'has Dylan filled you in on our plans?'

'My plan,' Dylan interjected, 'was to read the paper in peace. Your plans are yours alone.'

If only he knew exactly what she'd spent the past minute planning in precise detail!

She crossed her legs the other way so that her body faced Eric, then picked up a simple bulleted list typed on recycled paper. 'We can start out by focusing on simple insulation tricks, lessening plastic waste, paper waste, electrical waste and putting into place greener working methods for the future.'

Like a good little assistant Eric took the page and read it over. 'Seems easy enough,' he said with a nod.

She shot a testing look at Dylan. 'Doesn't it just?'

Dylan lifted his large *paper* cup to his lips and took a long swig. Wynnie found herself concentrating on his long fingers instead. Fingers that had stroked her breast, touched her lower back, caressed her sore wrists, and a hell of a lot more than that in her dreams.

She lifted her eyes to his to find his drinking had stilled and he was watching her. If her pupils weren't the size of dolla coins she had been let off lightly.

'Eric,' he barked and her list fluttered from the kid's hand to the table as though it had burnt his fingers.

'Yes, Mr Kelly.'

'I have the horrible feeling I left the iron on.' Dylan dangled his house keys at the young man.

Eric was on his feet in a second, and gone in another, leaving Wynnie and Dylan alone in the cosy corner of the café.

The clatter of laptop keys, the rich smell of really good coffee, the hiss of steaming milk all became heightened a Wynnie's senses went on full alert.

As did the realisation that below the table Dylan's foot was about an inch from her own, and that through the entire encounter with Eric and the keys Dylan's eyes had neve once left hers.

She reached for her cup to find it had been taken by a wait ress when she hadn't been paying attention. So she looked away instead, anywhere but at his deep, confusing, confront ing, tempting blue eyes.

There were people everywhere—mums with prams, schoo kids with backpacks, other men and women in suits getting an early start to their days.

Nothing nefarious could happen here.

She relaxed enough to say, 'You think you left the *iron* on?

Dylan's intimate, rumbling laughter filled the air and everyone else in the room faded away. 'He's dedicated, and consistent, and likeable, but so damn eager he never question me. The day he does is the day he'll move up in the company.

'So why did you send him away?'

Dylan folded over his broadsheet and placed it on the table He leant forward and she breathed in a nose full of his clean tangy scent. 'You're not going to get to me through Eric.'

She wrapped her hands about her knees, lest she give into temptation and reach out and stroke the hard edge where hi cheek met his chin. But her voice was still giveaway husky as she asked, 'Then how *am* I going to get to you?'

His eyes darkened, his neck tensed and his nostrils flared as he took in a long slow breath. 'That's not your problem, Miss Devereaux. You get to me. Far more than I wish you did.'

She felt it then, as if she was being dipped slowly into a deep hot bath—the sling and slide of mutual sexual awareness.

When she'd thought it had just been her, that had been discomforting enough, but to know, without a doubt, that she brought out a rumble in his voice, a heaviness in his eyes, and who knew what other physical responses, made the ground beneath her feet no longer feel quite so stable.

She breathed in slowly so that he would not pick up on the trembles running through her, and she pretended to misunderstand.

'Then let me in,' she said. 'Let my people in. We can do it in secret. At night. With your people on top of us every step of the way. Let us see how you operate, allow us to come up with a plan to do it greener, and you will be shocked at how cost effective, and beneficial those changes will be in the short and long term. From the extra pride your staff will take in your workplace all the way to how your clients and your city perceive you. If you just opened yourself up to the possibility one tiny little bit, you'd see how perfect we are for one another.'

When his eyes turned dark as night she qualified, 'How perfect the CFC and KInG are for one another.'

His eyes remained locked on hers—hot, dark, as focused as she'd ever seen them. 'Wynnie, you are wasting your time tilting at the wrong windmill.'

She leant right forward, not caring how deeply into his personal space she'd gone. 'What can I say or do to make you change your mind?'

The words 'I'll do anything' seemed to cling to the air between them. Though she hadn't said them, hadn't really thought them, she wondered if the time might be nigh that it all mattered so much that she'd mean them.

His jaw clenched, and his eyes flickered at the ceiling. Then eventually he said, 'All the statistics in the world won't convince me. I'm no pen-pusher, or cheque-signer like those you've come up against before. Think of me as a pit-bull guarding the gates of my family lore. Push me too hard, take one step too close, and I will bite.'

'I'm pushing too hard,' she said, her voice catching on the final word as she found herself caught in the rare moment of candour in his unpredictable eyes.

He nodded, and seemed to lean nearer to her still. His shirt bunched into waves against his stomach muscles. The tendons in his hands stood out in tanned ridges as though he, too, was holding himself at bay.

'I'm getting too close?' She was asking herself as much as she was asking him.

One of his hands braced the coffee table, resting mere millimetres from hers on her knees. If she took too deep a breath their fingers would touch.

'Wynnie, you've been too close since the moment you set foot on my forecourt.'

Wynnie felt the air between them contract and pulse. She took a deep breath through her nose and it bled from her mouth in a most unsteady exhale.

Before she had the chance to come up with anything sophisticated or coherent in response, Dylan's hand slipped away, reached into his trouser pocket and pulled out his phone, which he pressed to his ear. She hadn't even heard it ring.

'Kelly,' he said, his eyes not leaving hers. But as the seconds passed the clarity therein slowly, eventually, completely dispersed. They lit with a glinting smile that, no matter how appealing, felt to her as though the shutters had come down with a clang.

'I can't remember,' he said into the phone, then flipped it

shut. 'That was Eric, wondering in which room I might have been using my iron.'

She slid her hands tight between her knees to stop them from tingling as though he were still close, still within reach. 'If you own an iron I'll walk out of here today and never bother you again.'

His eyes crinkled. 'To think, a hundred bucks' worth of electrical appliance is all it would have taken.'

He could have lied, and she could have gone through with her joke as though it had been a promise. But neither of them did either thing. They sat across from one another, turning a blind eye to their impasse.

She swept a glance to his phone, held between his hands so tight he could crush the poor thing. 'You should ring him back and tell him you were mistaken.'

Dylan slipped his phone back into his trouser pocket. 'Nah. He likes to feel useful.'

'I knew from the moment I met you that you were in league with the devil.'

His smile grew into a grin, but rather than making her head spin, it only made her feel oddly wistful. Now that she'd had a taste of the candour available to her behind the charming mask, the mask would never feel like enough.

Dylan stood and folded his paper beneath his arm. He glanced over her knocked knees, her messy hair and her bandaged wrists before he covered his eyes with his dark sunglasses.

She stood along with him. This was a business meeting after all. 'So I'm assuming today's not the day you're going to sign on with the CFC.'

'Afraid not.'

'Then let me give you one last thought to take away with you. When we run out of water, when your backyard backs onto landfill, when you have to wear a mask so as to breathe the air without choking, you'll be wishing you'd given the bothersome brunette her dues.'

He leant back on his heels, not flinching, not even moving. Until his mouth curved up into a smile. The kind of smile that made her breathe a little harder than normal. Made her heart feel a little more present in her chest.

And then he did the most unexpected thing. He picked up her proposal, and glanced at it for a moment. Just a moment, but it was the most amount of consideration he'd given her yet. Maybe she ought to have imperilled his backyard sooner.

She opened her mouth to tell him to take it with him, but with a shake of his head he let it flutter back to the table.

And this time she had to watch him walk away.

'Damn it,' she swore beneath her breath, kicking the edge of the heavy coffee table for good measure. It hurt her big toe, but it was worth it for the excess energy it sent somewhere other than her stormy stomach.

He claimed she'd pushed too hard, but the way she saw it if she wasn't getting through she wasn't pushing hard enough.

As to getting too close… The memory of the warmth in his eyes as he'd uttered those words washed over her in a flood of sexual awareness.

When he reached the café door he turned and looked her way one last time. At least her skin thrummed as though he had. With his eyes hidden behind those dark sunglasses she couldn't really be sure.

And her deepest instincts when it came to understanding the thoughts and hearts of men had been proven to be disastrously wrong before.

CHAPTER FIVE

THAT night, after everyone else in the office had gone home, Wynnie and Hannah sat on the edge of her glass desk at CFC headquarters.

Feeling like a wind-up toy that had never run out of puff, Wynnie clicked a fingernail manically against her top teeth, and Hannah swung her legs rhythmically beneath the desk as they both stared silently at Dylan's picture pinned to the back of her office door.

In the past few days, in moments when she had been particularly frustrated with him, or with herself, she'd drawn on a Groucho Marx moustache, a plethora of hooped earrings in one ear, a pirate's bandana, and a number of missing teeth.

But beneath the pen marks those blue eyes of his constantly shone through—gorgeous, audacious, mocking her, flirting with her, making her whole body feel as if it were wrapped in rubber bands.

'So he actually read the proposal?' Hannah asked.

'He glanced at it.'

'That's a good thing. A gal won't take a dress off the rack and check the price tag unless she likes the look of it in the first place.'

'Dylan Kelly's no gal.'

Hannah cocked her head as she looked back at the picture. 'No, he's not. And I'm not sure he'd buy off the rack, either.

But he looked. He touched. It's a sign you're getting through to him and that's a good thing.'

Wynnie sat on her hands. *The way he looked at her... The way he touched her*. That might have felt like a good thing, but it certainly was not.

She shook her head. 'More like a sign to say don't call me, I'll call you. Which translates even more specifically into leave me the hell alone before I get my big fancy lawyers to take out a restraining order.'

Hannah's legs stopped swinging beneath the desk, and she slowly turned to face her. 'So you think he's going to call you, huh?'

'I don't know why I bothered coming to you,' she said on a sigh as she slid off her desk, grabbed her purse and Hannah's arm and dragged her from the office and into the long, carpeted hallway lit only by the fluorescent green emergency signs.

Hannah linked her hand through Wynnie's elbow. 'Because I'm such a fun source of moral corruption. Now tell Auntie Hannah what's really bothering you.'

'Okay. I can't believe I'm about to say this. He acts like, well, not as though he likes me, but as though he's finding it really hard not to ravage me on the spot.' She held on to Hannah's arm and squeezed her eyes shut tight, feeling ridiculous now she'd said the words out loud. 'And I know that he's well-practised at the art, and he's likely had every other woman in town and that's the only reason I'm still on his radar, but, still, I can't help but feel it.'

'And this is a bad thing?'

'It makes it extremely difficult to focus.'

Hannah's laughter bounced off the windows and walls until it echoed inside Wynnie's head. She opened one eye.

'That's why they call him the smiling assassin,' Hannah said. 'He blinds with that beautiful face and body and voice and... Well, that's enough really. Then while you're drowning in his eyes he kills your proposal before you've even finished shaking his hand. It's kind of his MO.'

Wynnie let that sink in, all the way to her suddenly heavy toes. 'This is common knowledge? What the hell else are the CFC's researchers leaving out?'

Hannah smiled and nodded.

'And this is the man you all convinced me was the one *I* had to lobby? The same man you have continuously tried to convince me to ask out on a date?'

The nodding and smiling stopped as Hannah obviously saw her point. 'I'm a lawyer. It's my job to be able to argue both sides of the same point with equally compelling reason. Besides which, sweetie, you know better than most that a person's reputation is only a portion of their true self.'

Wynnie shook her head. This wasn't about her, it was about ruddy Dylan Kelly. 'You told me he was a rogue easily enough, why has it taken you until now to tell me *this* is his *business* reputation?'

Hannah sniffed. 'I'm no gossip.'

'Yes, you are!'

'You're right, I am. I truly thought we were mucking about. It never occurred to me that you might really be taken with him.'

'How can I not be? He's all I ever talk about at work, all I ever talk about with my media contacts. He and his business and his family are all I ever think about. I'm saturated by the guy.'

Hannah grinned. 'How much do I love that imagery? Now come on, my young friend, he is wealthy, influential, sexy, and available. If you cut out that entire group as possible dating material what are you leaving for yourself?'

'Helpful, thanks.'

'Hey, I'm a realist. Which is why I'm trying to save the planet, and also why I'm *not* going to rule out any cute guy just because I work with him, or just because he doesn't have the exact same beliefs as me, or just because he has eight toes on each foot.' Hannah jabbed a finger at the security doors. 'It happens.'

Just before the doors opened Wynnie caught her reflection in the glass—her eyes were wide and dark just from thinking about the guy. She was taken with him. But now she was coming to realise how much that sprang from his contradictions. He played the playboy with such panache, but it still couldn't hide the depth of his convictions, and his single-mindedness when it came to protecting his family.

The similarity to her own double life was stunning. How was a girl like her to resist?

They hit the Toowong street to find it bustling with late-night shoppers, locals strolling after eating out, and uni students herding towards the plethora of local pubs.

'So here's my two cents,' Hannah said, 'for which I'd actually charge four hundred dollars an hour if it was anyone else but you, so pay attention. You're a sweetheart and if you like him, then he has to be worth liking. If you're not yet sure if you can trust him, trust yourself.'

Trust. That was what this whole thing was about. Her rabid inability to trust anyone but herself. Hell, her trust in herself had been worn pretty thin, too. She didn't need a psychology degree to know it came from being let down in the worst possible way by the closest person to her in all the world.

The easy ability to love she'd had as a kid had been stripped away the second she'd opened the door of her Sociology 101 class to find herself face to face with the dean and a handful of policemen.

Too bad if she was coming to believe that deep down Dylan Kelly might actually be *decent*.

'What are you doing?' Hannah asked when she realised Wynnie had stopped walking.

'Waiting for the bus.'

'You do this every night?'

'Most.'

Hannah grabbed her by the sleeve and tugged her up the brightly lit street. 'You try too hard.'

'It has nothing to do with trying. I have no intention of hopping in a car every day if I don't even need to.'

Hannah shook her head. 'My car's gonna be guzzling gas anyway. I'll drive you home.'

'Fine. Just let's talk about something else for a while.'

Hannah linked her arm through Wynnie's once more. 'Ah, what fine weather we're having.'

Wynnie laughed. Brisbane almost always had fine weather. But playing along would serve her cause. 'We sure are.'

On Friday evening Dylan sauntered into his office, his eyes skimming over the below-the-fold article on the front page of *The Australian*, a paper cup of fresh coffee warming his other hand, when the hairs on the back of his neck told him he wasn't alone.

Jack Colby, an old school mate, and the best private investigator in the country, was sitting in his office chair, feet on his desk, ignoring the stunning, glittering night view of the Riverside Expressway and South Bank bordering the city straight of the Brisbane River.

'Evening, Jack,' he said.

Jack's silhouette nodded. 'Dylan. How's things?'

'The amount I pay you I'd hope you know the answer to that better than I.'

It took him a second to remember when and why he'd hired Jack this time around.

When? Days earlier. Why? Wynnie Devereaux.

From the moment he'd looked into those soft brown eyes down the lens of Eric's mate's camera he'd found himself in uncharted waters—torn between wanting to slap a restraining order against her stopping her from coming anywhere near his family, and wanting to immerse himself in the heat that flickered deep in her eyes every time they made contact with his, and wanting to do whatever he had to do to ease the aching vulnerability that engulfed her in moments when she let down her guard.

None of those courses of action was ideal so he'd needed to find another way to cut her off.

Since there was no way she was merely the frustratingly sexy tree-hugger she appeared to be, she had to have a hidden agenda, a self-serving reason why he was in her line of sight. They always did.

Indubitably once he knew exactly what her ulterior motives were, she would be rendered far less intriguing. Enter Jack.

Dylan closed his paper and threw it on the coffee table by the lounge suite in the corner. He undid the buttons at his wrists, rolled up his sleeves and dragged a tub chair over to the guest side of his desk.

'What've you got?'

Jack sat forward and opened up a slim, innocuous-looking Manila folder.

'Rightio. Wynnie Devereaux. Twenty-seven years old. Brunette. Brown eyes. Slim build. Average height. Single. Pretty girl.'

Jack didn't know the half of it. Her soft floral scent invaded Dylan's dreams. He could feel the warmth of her skin caressing his palms in the middle of business meetings. Every time he saw a woman with dark brown hair, anywhere, he found himself looking twice.

Dylan raised an eyebrow. 'I don't pay you to editorialise.'

Jack grinned. 'It's rare this job has such perks.' He slid a handful of photographs of her across the desk.

The first was Wynnie walking down a city street the day they'd first met. He'd recognise those thighs in those white pants anywhere. A curly-haired blonde was at her side, hands gesticulating.

As he moved through the photos Wynnie's face was serious, shocked, then laughing. Her wrists were bound in bandages. He ran a finger across his lips to stop from smiling.

In the final picture she seemed to be looking directly into the camera, her brow furrowed, her eyes determined, her dark hair whipping about her lovely face. Eyes like honey. Skin like cream. Her life force bursting from her every pore.

Dylan's whole hand rested across his mouth. If that was all Jack could get…

He threw the photos onto the desk. 'Nothing I didn't already know from just meeting her.'

'I was simply waiting until I had your attention.'

Dylan's eyes narrowed. 'You have it.'

'She studied a range of humanities on a scholarship at the University of Queensland when she was eighteen after being home-schooled her whole life, but didn't finish even a year. She moved to Paris before she turned twenty and once there talked her way into a job with a local parks beautification group.'

So that made sense of the faint accent at least.

'She's worked for numerous organisations since, raising funds, lobbying for government help, last of which was an Arena di Verona Restoration Committee. The money she raised and the profile she built for the Opera house would turn even you on a little bit.'

Dylan shifted in his chair. As if he needed another reason. 'That's it? She's a gifted twenty-seven-year-old lobbyist. You're slipping, my friend.'

Jack just leant back in his chair and grinned.

The hairs on the back of Dylan's neck stood to attention. There was more. And not just more. There was dirt. A valid reason for him to be on his guard and exceedingly wary of the vigorous way he reacted to her.

'One salient thing I might point out before you file that folder away,' Jack drawled.

'Spit it out.'

'Though Wynnie Devereaux is the name on her driver's licence, her passport, her Medicare card, her employment contracts, it's not her real name.'

Dylan placed a finger on the top photo, the one where he could look into her eyes. 'Then who the hell is she?'

Jack stood and cocked his hand into the shape of a pistol. 'I don't want to spoil all the surprises. The rest I'll let you read for yourself.'

He swept from his office, leaving Dylan with a bill, and the thin Manila folder that suddenly seemed a mile deep.

Dylan stared at it, unusually unwilling to dive right in. Because the truth of it was, even though he'd been the one to have her background plundered for dirt, for some ridiculous reason he'd half believed that maybe, just maybe, he'd met the last honest woman on the planet.

It seemed he'd been right all along. There was no such creature to be found.

He opened the folder, flicked through until he found the photocopy of an old news report, and began to read.

CHAPTER SIX

ON SATURDAY night Wynnie and Hannah's cab, a hybrid to keep them both happy, pulled up in front of the Queensland Museum at South Bank. The great hulking concrete and glass building was floodlit by blocks of pink and orange light, the pathway ahead swathed in pink and orange chiffon.

Through the car windows Wynnie watched women in glamorous, barely there, summertime evening dress and men in exquisite tuxedos slip from shiny black town cars that lined the street in front and behind them.

'Charity balls sure ain't what they used to be,' she said under her breath. 'It looks like an orgy waiting to happen.'

Hannah appeared at the window and Wynnie jumped. Then realised she was still inside the cab, whose driver was waiting for her to vamoose. She shot him a quick smile and hopped out, taking care to keep her knees locked as flash bulbs of paparazzi cameras did their all to catch her in a compromising position in case she was a somebody.

She held her sparkly silver purse in front of her face, ostensibly to shield her eyes from the lights, but more truthfully it was a move born of instinct.

Putting herself in the public eye she could handle. But the thousand flashes of a flock of rabid photographers crowding towards her, screaming her name, always took her right back to the time when she had been a 'person of interest' in the bombing of a uni science lab, walking from the police station a free woman but with the life she'd known in tatters at her feet.

Hannah grabbed her hand away from her face. 'I know I look super-hot tonight, but they don't know me from a bar of soap. You, Wynnie my sweet, they lurve. So for the sake of my standing with the bosses, for the sake of the money I spent on this dress, and by George, for the sake of the planet, smile for the cameras.'

Wynnie mentally slapped herself across the back of the head. She was no longer an ice-blonde with pixie-short hair. She no longer wore enough eyeliner to sink a ship. Ponchos and multi-coloured hemp flares were no longer her uniform of choice. And she'd lost the classic freshman fifteen pounds a long time ago.

So she smiled, she twirled, she tossed her hair. She waved to photographers and cameramen she'd met during her interviews so far. She gave pithy sound bites about the Clean Footprint Coalition to anyone with a recording device. And she thanked her lucky stars for cortisone now that her wrists were clear bar a slight pink ring that nobody would see unless they got really really close.

And she acted for all the world as though beneath her short, slinky tomato-red silk dress she had nothing to hide. Her arms were covered to her wrists, but her legs were bare to mid-thigh, and the thing slithered so close against every inch of her skin the world now knew she had an 'innie' for a belly button.

When they walked through the front doors her eyes almost popped out of her head. The long, thin, three-storey foyer was usually empty, bar stunning, life-sized models of a family of humpback whales suspended in the open space above. This night, bringing the same warm, decadent feeling from the outside inside, backlit swathes of pink and orange crêpe draped from the ceiling creating intimate, warm, rosy, golden light over the ornate, candlelit tables scattered throughout.

'Is there going to be any money left over to give to the charity?' Wynnie said out of the corner of her mouth.

'Not our charity tonight,' Hannah said, 'so not *our* concern. Just be grateful the head honchos love you so much they gave us these tickets, and remember we're here to get you some much-needed fun. To get some booze into you. Then a bit of dance-floor action when the party gets going. Maybe you'll even meet yourself a nice, cute, harmless yet wild-in-the-sack philanthropist. Because you can't stay wound up this tight or you're gonna pop. And there's nowhere in that dress for you to go.'

Hannah grinned, picked up the heavy tribal beat of the music booming through the lofty space and boogied away into the pulsating crowd.

But Wynnie's feet had stuck to the floor of the wickedly decorated foyer. She wished then that she'd worn a sack, or a large shawl or at the very least an entirely different dress.

For not ten feet in front of her, looking resplendent in an exquisite tuxedo, stood Dylan Kelly.

Not now, she thought, *not tonight*. Not when she still hadn't come to any logical, sensible, rational conclusions about what she could do with the feelings she had for the guy.

Still she couldn't take her eyes off him. Standing in a group of men about his age, all dressed much the same, all exuding that suave, easy, master-of-the-universe air that came of growing up blanketed by privilege, Dylan Kelly stood out as though he walked through life with a spotlight shining down upon him.

His dark blond hair looked darker, slicked back off his face. He had one hand in the pocket of his black trousers, pulling the seat firmly across a pinchable derrière. He pointed at something in the distance, stretching his snowy white shirt tight across his torso that made the very most of the kind of build that spoke of sit-ups and a lot of them.

Her mouth literally began to water.

As though someone had tapped him on the shoulder and

said 'she's here' Dylan glanced away from the group and his eyes found hers. Hot, dark, stunning blue.

In a nervous gesture she couldn't control, her hand fluttered to her hair, brushing against her butterfly clip tucked within the waves. But rather than feeling grounded, she felt fragile, breakable, small.

Without saying a word, Dylan left the group and made a beeline towards her. The crowd parted. His gaze slunk down one side of her underdressed body then up the other, leaving a trail of enfeebling goose bumps in its wake.

As he came close enough she could pick out the scent of his now all too familiar aftershave his eyes found hers. He conjured the most charming half-smile as he drawled, 'Of all the museums in all the world…'

Wynnie gripped her purse so tight sequins left tattoos on her hot palms. 'Why, Dylan Kelly, what on earth is a man like you doing in a place like this?'

He moved to stand beside her, clasping his hands behind his back as he looked out over the crowd. 'Perhaps I knew you'd be here tonight. Perhaps I've come to see the creature in her own environment, mingling with her own species. Such a scoop would certainly help me to learn a thing or two about how to defend myself against you.'

Wynnie smiled and waved to a woman involved with solar energy research whom she'd met through the CFC when she'd first come to town. The woman waved back, though only after fixing her hair in case Dylan's eyes turned her way, as well.

'You think you need help?' she muttered. 'Between you and me you're doing a bang-up job so far.'

'One must always do what one can to do better.'

She glanced sideways to find he was no longer interested in the crowd. His attention was one hundred per cent on her.

She said, 'It's fifteen hundred dollars per plate. That's an expensive experiment.'

He leant in so close his breath tickled her hair against her ear. 'Somehow I get the feeling uncovering your layers will be worth every cent I've paid.'

Her knees buckled, and her airway all but closed up. Only years of lobbying men as intimidating and less likely to soften any disapproval with a gorgeous smile helped her get by without her voice giving her away. 'I'm sure you're quite aware that you could make an appointment to see me, in more layers than I am wearing tonight, at my office any time. Here, I would have thought the weight of do-gooderness in the air might cramp your style.'

'Nah,' he said, his voice dropping a note, maybe even two, 'my style will be just fine.'

He took a step closer as he looked back out into the seething, sparkling crowd. 'So, which of these poor schmucks do you plan on getting your claws into tonight?'

'It's my night off,' she shot back. 'I'm here to relax and have a nice time. You and your sort are safe from my sticky clutches.'

She felt his eyes on her again, but she knew better than to lock gazes at this proximity. She turned and backed away. 'Do me a favour?'

'Name it.' Dylan slid a hand back into the pocket of his trousers. Wynnie did her best to keep her gaze on his receding face.

'These good people are here tonight because they care about clean energy and that's why *they've* paid good money to be here. Try not to rub off on them.'

And then he laughed. Head back, rumbling laughter that from deep within his belly. Heads turned, all female.

But Dylan's eyes remained fixed entirely on her. 'Wynnie,' he called out, not caring a lick who heard, 'I could ask the same of you. But then we'd both be disappointed.'

The further she backed away, the more the burgeoning crowd surged between them. His laughter, and his smile and the intense electricity that surged through her with simply being near the guy, gradually dimmed to a sweet buzz.

'You'll get a neck crick,' Hannah said.

Wynnie came back to the present to find the Minister for the Environment, Heritage and the Arts had finished his speech and a jazz band had struck up a soft shuffle on stage. She was sucking air through a straw as her mocktail was empty bar crushed ice and lime pulp, and she was staring at the back of Dylan's head as three tables over he had a dozen people in stitches.

Placing the offending glass on the pink tablecloth, Wynnie spun on her seat and glanced at Hannah who was grinning at her over a mouthful of caramel tart.

Wynnie said, 'I know I am officially off the clock, but this is my first opportunity to watch the guy interact with his peers. If I'm going to win him over, I need all the help I can get.'

Hannah laid a hand on Wynnie's wrist. 'If that's the line you're sticking with, then more power to you.'

Wynnie shook out her shoulders and spooned a mouthful of mocktail-flavoured crushed ice from the bottom of her glass before a liveried waiter swept it away.

'Wynnie,' a deep familiar voice said from behind her, 'may I have a word?'

And she almost choked on the ice.

Hannah's chair squeaked loudly against the stone floor. Wynnie, coughing, glanced across to find Hannah had leapt to her feet with her hand outstretched while somehow, simultaneously, leaving barely any daylight between her body and Dylan's.

'Hannah Laskowski,' she breathed huskily. 'It's a pleasure to make your acquaintance.'

Dylan, ever the coolest man on the planet, managed to smile as if he meant it. He took Hannah's hand. 'Dylan Kelly, the pleasure is mine.'

'I'm Wynnie's boss. Sort of. So anything you have to say to her, you can say to me. Here, or elsewhere.'

Wynnie suddenly felt her chair sliding backwards and she had to stand or fall flat on her butt. She spun, and released a loud 'oomph' as she smacked into Dylan who, it turned out, had been the one pulling her chair out from under her.

She grabbed tight to his velvet soft lapels to stop from falling in a heap. He slid an arm around her waist for the same reason. *Funny*, she thought, blinking into his blue eyes, *it doesn't feel like he's trying to keep me from falling at all.*

He said, 'Thanks for the offer, Hannah, but I prefer to keep my business contacts close. The wider the spread, the more chance things can get lost in translation.'

'Fine with me!' Hannah said. Wynnie shot a look over her shoulder to find her friend grinning like a proud fairy godmother.

Wynnie was frowning by the time she glanced back at Dylan. 'Hannah knows the word *"no"* in as many languages as I do. What on earth could get lost in translation?'

His arm slid tighter still, pressing her hips against his with such force her head rocked back. 'Come with me and you'll find out.'

His spare hand found one of hers and soon she was being pulled in his wake. She turned back to Hannah for help, but her friend was sitting at the table, resting her cheek on her palm and licking the last drop of liquid off the end of a flamingo-shaped swizzle stick.

'Mr Kelly,' she said, smiling at those she wriggled to avoid as they surged through the crowd. 'Dylan!'

He stopped so suddenly she slammed into him again. This time she reached out and pushed against his chest before she ended up in his arms.

'Yes, Wynnie.'

'You said you had something you wanted to talk about.'

'I did, didn't I?'

'So talk.' She crossed her arms, and stuck a high-heel-clad

foot out in front of her, pointy toe up, keeping a healthy gap
between them.

Still he managed to grab her hand, spin her out and draw
her back in close, right as the band started playing 'The Way
You Look Tonight'.

'What are you—?'

'Shut up and dance or everyone will stare.'

'Considering we are the only ones on the dance floor,' she
hissed, 'everyone is already staring.'

'Then we may as well make the most of it.'

Dylan tucked her close, moving her around the dance floor
as though he were on wheels. She gave in and followed as best
she could, and soon the crowd faded away as his clean scent,
his hard body, his gentle embrace served to fill up every ounce
of room her mind had on offer.

She was adrift on a cloud of pure pleasure when the fingers
of his left hand wound around her wrist before sliding back
up to wrap about her right hand.

'All better?' he asked.

'So long as I keep away from cheap handcuffs I should be
fine.'

'I can give you the line on where to find a more respectable
brand. If the need ever arises.'

She shot him a sarcastic smile. 'I have no doubt.'

He ducked her under his arm, slid her around his back,
and she was in his arms again before she even knew what
was happening.

'Smooth,' she said, a tad breathless and not from the exercise.
The guy could really dance. And he was smooth. Of course he
was, he was perfect—perfectly bred, perfectly arrogant, perfectly
oblivious to what someone with his infamy could do to look out
for not only those closest to him, but his whole community.

He even smelled perfect.

'Did you say something?' he asked.

She tensed, slowing him down to a soft shuffle so she

could extricate herself before she did something really stupid like leaning her head on his shoulder and sighing.

'Won't your date wonder why you're not out here with her?' she asked.

'No date tonight.'

Her flicker of a glance took in at least half a dozen women watching him from the sidelines looking ready to pounce. 'I imagined you the type to have a little black book the thickness of *War and Peace*.'

His smile was breathtaking. 'I gave the inhabitants a night off.'

'How magnanimous.'

He offered a shallow bow, and the look in his eyes when they found hers again was anything but magnanimous.

The exact reflection of her own absorbing attraction in his eyes might have been real or imagined. It didn't matter. What mattered was how much she needed fresh air and for that she needed to be anywhere but in Dylan Kelly's addictive arms.

'Mr Kelly—'

'It was Dylan a moment ago.'

'Fine. Dylan, if your conscience has finally come to the party and you are ready to sit down with me, properly, and make a deal about how I can change the way you do business for the better—'

'That's a lot of weight for you to carry on such small shoulders,' he said, his hands running over them, his eyes following.

'That's why I need you to share it with me.'

His eyes shot to hers. Deep, reclusive, unreachable.

'One person can make a difference,' she said. 'A hundred people can change the world.'

'Mmm,' he rumbled in her ear as he pulled her close. 'So you keep telling me.'

Her rebellious body melted against him, softening to fit as closely as it possibly could without needing an X-rating.

He said, 'You know what?'

'What?'

'I'm not sure if it was the candlelight or the pink napkins that did it, but the minute I sat down to dinner my heart gave a little twinge I'd never felt before. An inner desire to legalise marijuana, and talk to dolphins, and throw cans of red paint at women in fur coats.'

Wynnie's melting body snapped upright. 'You're an ass.'

She pushed away. She tried to anyway. Dylan's will to hold her seemed to be stronger than hers to be free.

'Stay,' he said, his laughing voice low enough only she could hear. She imagined a lick of rawness. Of the sincerity she had only glimpsed on rare moments few and far between.

She glared at him, but her pushing didn't get any stronger. 'Give me one good reason why I shouldn't kick you in the shin and get back to my caramel tart.'

He took her back into a dance hold and began to sway, his hips sliding against hers, nothing between them but some ridiculously thin silk and tuxedo trousers. It took all of her energy to keep from whimpering.

'You think people are staring now?' he said. 'Walk off this floor before the song ends and our lovers' tiff'll be page three while the coverage of this here party, and any good will towards the charity, will be shunted twenty pages back. You don't want to be blamed for that, do you?'

'You *are* the devil,' she said. 'You know that, don't you?'

His smile was pure sin. 'I admit to nothing. Now stop fighting me. Dance.'

Wynnie took a deep fortifying breath which only pressed her chest flush against his. Not a good idea. Her breasts let her down; swelling, hardening, begging her to stay close to the wall of masculine heat.

She let her breath slowly go, and did her best to relax. There could only be seconds remaining of the song. Seconds for her to wonder what he was playing at. Because she knew as well as she knew her own name, well, both of them, that he wasn't dancing with her because he had finally realised he couldn't keep his hands off her. He had some new angle she couldn't hope to fathom.

The only angle she had the chance to discover was the new angle of his hips as he slid his knee gently between hers. And finally she was undone. Fighting him was all too hard when compared with just giving in.

Her eyes fluttered shut and her breath expelled from her lungs in a soft sigh.

His hand slid lower down her back, the silk of her dress slithering across her skin, and tiny prickles of sweat sprang up in its wake. She didn't have time to worry, for that was when he somehow tipped her off balance. Her left leg gripped his and suddenly she was arched back into a low dip.

There they stayed. One bar. Two.

Her breaths came heavily. The faint edge of a not so recent shave leant shadows to his carved cheeks. A muscle twitched therein. His eyes narrowed. Darkened. His grip on her hand tightened.

Trust. Bad judgment. Decency. Decadence. The survival of the planet. None of it mattered in that moment as much as the fire in his eyes.

The song came to an end. Then she was upright again. Their heavy breaths intermingled as their chests heaved against one another. Every place their bodies had touched felt aflame. Every place they hadn't longed to do so. Suddenly the idea of being on page three of the paper didn't matter a lick. If he leant in, if he closed the gap, if he pressed his lips to hers—

'Kelly,' a loud unfamiliar voice said. 'Thought that was you.'

Wynnie blinked and realised they were no longer alone. In fact, the dance floor was full of couples clapping the band. A gentleman reached past her to shake Dylan's hand, slap him on the back, sequester his attention.

She slipped out of his embrace, ran shaking hands down her dress and put enough space between them that she could breathe.

His eyes were still dark, and still fully trained on her as the gent shouted about market forces and the Dow Jones and some celebrity golf tournament he'd paid a fortune for at some auction.

A Violent Femmes classic started up and the crowd went wild, jumping up and down, rocking the room. Wynnie offered Dylan a slight shrug, then, taking her chance, she slipped away, trying to concentrate on protecting her peep toes from bouncing stiletto heels, when she could still feel Dylan's eyes on her back as she pressed through the boisterous crowd.

With each step away she tried to shake off the feeling that rather than dancing just now she'd actually been tiptoeing around the edge of a volcano.

Only once she was free of the crowd and was heading through the now mostly empty tables back towards her seat did she realise whatever it was Dylan had intended to say to her had never been said.

Then again, maybe the dance had said it all.

Wynnie stood in the corner of the museum foyer, on her tippy toes, trying to spy Hannah's blonde curls from amidst the slick-dos, wishing the girl hadn't had one too many cocktails or her goodbyes would take forever.

'Well, if it isn't Guinevere Lambert.'

She landed back on her heels with a thud, kept her eyes dead ahead and swallowed as discreetly as she could while she pretended that she hadn't just heard someone use her real name.

A body slid in beside her. It felt big and tall and male. It smelt like cigarette smoke and too many hours spent wearing the same clothes.

'It is Guinevere, isn't it? I saw you earlier with Kelly on the dance floor and something pinged in the back of my head. I couldn't place you and then suddenly…there it was. Ten odd years ago. Sweet, little, hippy waif Guinevere Lambert, chin up, lips sealed, surrounded by the boys in blue as they led you from your uni class and all the way to police central.' He held out a hand smack bang in the middle of her personal space. 'Garry Sloane. Allied Press Corps.'

She glanced down at the hand to find it held a digital voice recorder the size of a tube of lipstick. She bit her lip, and pressed her feet hard into the harder floor to stop herself from trembling. She wouldn't lie to the guy, in the end that would serve no purpose but to make sure she never worked in public relations ever again. But neither did she have a clue what to say.

Where the hell was Hannah? She'd said she'd be two minutes!

'Sloane, leave the lady alone.'

Wynnie looked up to find the big man at her side was being overshadowed by an even bigger man. One with pure venom lighting the depths of his dark blue eyes.

'Kelly,' Sloane said. 'This has nothing to do with you or your darling family. So why don't you sashay on away and leave me and this nice lady to our conversation?'

When the reporter turned to face Wynnie she was caught looking him in the eye. His weathered face broke into the kind of expression that ought never to be allowed to be called a smile. 'Am I right?' he asked.

She stared at him, and narrowed her eyes. He was right about one thing—what he wanted to talk to her about had nothing to do with Dylan and neither did she want it to.

She turned to Dylan, and had to swallow before she could manage a word. 'I'm fine.'

He glanced at her throat, which was still working hard to get any kind of moisture to her poor mouth, then back into her eyes. Whatever he saw there had him ignoring every word she said.

'Nevertheless,' Dylan growled, 'I think you wouldn't find it hard to track down cockroaches more worthy of talking to.'

Sloane puffed out his chest and Wynnie had the distinct feeling that this no longer had anything to do with her.

'Surely,' Sloane hissed, 'you of all people know better than to rub me the wrong way.'

'Go,' Dylan said, his voice as cold as ice. 'Now. Out of my sight. Before I do something you'll regret.'

Wynnie backed up a step. Good thing, too, as from no-where the Sloane guy swung, and connected, and big, bad Dylan Kelly spun on his heel to land square on both feet facing his opponent. His eyes were so dark they were no longer so impossibly blue, a smear of blood appeared on his lower lip, and his right fist was clenched into a white ball.

Instinct be damned, Wynnie threw herself between them. Dylan's eyes connected with hers, and cleared enough that he held himself in check.

She shook her head, still slightly stunned. She knew without a doubt he'd have hit back if he'd had the chance. But there were cameras everywhere. He'd come to her defence, it was her turn to come to his.

She blinked, then ran her thumb across his lip. It came away glistening with his blood, and tingling with the sensation of having done such an intimate thing.

She held it up to him. He frowned, then his tongue darted out and licked at the split in his lip. Then he glanced down at her thumb and before she knew what he was about to do he had the end of her thumb in his mouth as his tongue curled around the tip. Once it was clean, he let her go.

She wrapped her other hand around her thumb the second she had it back, but no manner of squeezing could rid her of the heat radiating from the spot.

Wynnie glanced over her shoulder to find a crowd had gathered, but Sloane was nowhere to be seen. Meaning the coward knew he was in deep trouble. And if they hadn't already, she and Dylan had become the talk of the party.

Things couldn't get any worse for her reputation. She grabbed Dylan by the hand and snuck him through the crowd as fast as she could until she found a neat spot behind a mani-cured conifer in the courtyard outside where the decadent light didn't touch.

'Are you okay?' Dylan asked, a hand reaching out to cradle her elbow.

'I'm fine. But I'm not the one who just got myself into a round of fisticuffs.'

Dylan's tongue darted out to the now blood-free spot and Wynnie struggled to stop staring. Such beautifully carved lips, so adept at smiling, so built for kissing. Now marred by a swelling bruise created in an effort to protect her, his lips were even more intoxicating.

'What were you thinking back there?' she asked, looking back into his eyes, only to find that out there in the darkness they were an even scarier proposition than those lips.

'Garry Sloane's a cretin.'

'That's not an answer.' He was far too self-aware to fly off the handle for no good reason.

Though what did she know about him really? He was one of the coolest customers she'd ever known. She wasn't sure his own mother would even be able to decipher one of his smiles, a cheek twitch or a rare flinch.

Oh, what she would have given for a key to those expressions. To know if the man she thought he was might be even close to the truth. To know if the way she felt about him was founded on anything but imprudent desire.

'Dylan,' she begged, instantly regretting the longing twinge in her voice nobody would mistake.

The hand at her elbow moved up her arm, sliding the red silk against her overheated skin. 'Believe me, whatever Sloane wanted from you, don't let him have it. I wouldn't wish the guy on my worst enemy.'

Wynnie planted her backside against the mossy concrete planter box, and Dylan's hand fell away. The seat was cold through her dress. She snuck her hands down to grip it all the same. 'Is that how you think of me? As your enemy?'

He kicked the toe of his dress shoe against the concrete,

and his lips curved into a sexy half-smile. 'What makes you think I think of you at all?'

Her heart skittered manically in her chest at the same time that the rest of her grew warm and loose.

She stretched her shoulders back until the muscles in her arms gave her a pleasant kind of hurt. 'If you didn't think of me a little bit it would mean that I'm in the wrong job. And my salary, the corporate headhunters who have me on speed dial and my gut tell me I'm exactly where I should be.'

Shreds of moonlight poked through the tree behind her, picking out his sharp white incisors as his smile grew.

He snuck a hand into his trouser pocket and leant down to her. 'Fine. I think about you plenty. More than I think you'd really like to know. Happy?'

Happy? Not so much happy as tipped upside down and turned inside out.

He grinned, then swore mightily and spun away to press the back of his hand against the split in his lip that he'd just reopened. The split lip he'd endured because of her.

She stood, her silk dress made a horrible sound as it separated from the concrete. It'd be pilled to bits. Thankfully, like every piece of clothing she owned, it was a designer second and had already lived a worthwhile life.

In her high heels her eyes were level with his mouth. His tongue darted out to his lip, and he winced. Again a mix of guilt and desire had her reaching to touch the wound, but this time common sense came to the rescue and her finger stopped short of its mark.

He took her fingers and gently urged her to do as she pleased. Wrapped in his warm grasp, her finger traced the contour of his lip, slowly, carefully, sliding over the bruised bump.

When his hand dropped away, hers continued its path— mapping the indent of his cheek, running over the edge of his sharp jaw, tracing the line where subtle stubble met the smooth skin of his throat, and finishing by sliding into the soft darker hair at the base of his neck.

There she finally came to her senses, her fingers curling into her palm as she pulled it away, but the warmth of his skin and the texture of his wholly masculine roughness were stained onto her tingling fingers for good.

She looked down at her purse as she said, 'Your lip will feel much better much quicker if you get ice onto it as soon as possible.'

'I suppose so. Where would you suggest I find some ice at this time of night?'

She sucked in a deep breath through her nose, ignored the red flag waving madly in the back of her mind and looked him in the eye as she said, 'How does my place sound?'

CHAPTER SEVEN

WYNNIE opened the small cabinet behind the mirror in her bathroom in the hopes she would find something there which might warrant the fact that, rather than asking Dylan's driver to take him to the hospital, she'd brought him home.

After madly text-messaging Hannah, explaining she'd found her own way home, she'd left Dylan sitting in her small lounge room, draped over her rented chocolate leather couch with its so-new-it-still-had-a-tag-attached red angora throw rug, his shirt undone at the collar, his bow tie dangling from his neck, holding his Scotch on ice to his lip.

She drew in a shaky breath. Could a guy seriously be any sexier if he tried? Maybe that was why he was so sexy. He didn't *have* to try. It just oozed from his very pores. And he was sitting in her lounge room…

Eventually she came out of the closet with make-up-remover wipes, antiseptic cream that had travelled with her over three continents and was probably out of date and Band-Aids with butterfly pictures on them, which she'd been a sucker and spent a third more on than the plain ones when she'd done her first Brisbane grocery shop.

She closed the cupboard door and caught her reflection in the mirror. Hair that earlier had been sleek waves was mussed, as if she'd just rolled out of bed. Her hours-old make-up was less than perfect, smudged about her muddy brown eyes making them look huge. And she looked tired. Tired and wired.

Wired because on the interminable town-car ride to her house she'd realised that even though Dylan had arrived at the exact right moment to get her away from Sloane, it wouldn't be long before he came after her again.

Leaving town was one hell of a strong option. Not facing Sloane meant keeping her anonymity, and protecting Felix—wherever he was. But she'd be letting so many people down. She'd not get the chance to continue rekindling the only real adult friendship she'd ever had or to experience a Brisbane summer after so many winters in Europe. It all felt like a cruel joke.

Not to mention the fact that she'd be walking away from the man currently pacing around her small lounge room. The man who'd leapt to her defence without thought of what it might cost him.

She heard a noise from outside the bathroom, and flinched. Had the noise been a door shutting? Had he gone? No. There was music. He'd found her miserably small CD collection in a drawer of her coffee table. Sting crooned from her rented speakers.

Out there making himself at home was a man brimming with power, self-esteem, brutal sexual energy. She wanted so badly to know what he tasted like, her own lips tasted sweet and salty.

She wasn't going anywhere. Not tonight anyway.

'What the hell am I thinking?' she begged of her reflection.

It practically smirked back at her. She'd brought this on herself. She'd flirted, and pushed, and prodded and made herself a part of his world, so that he had no chance but to notice her above and beyond the hundred odd fresh-faced souls who begged him for face time each and every day. And now he'd noticed her, all right. Now she had every chance of getting up close and personal.

But she wouldn't count her chickens. This might turn out to all be blissfully innocent. She might patch him up, then he might happily go on his way. And a pig might fly into her lounge room and offer to make them both cups of chamomile tea.

'No time like the present to find out,' she said. Then ducked her head, grabbed her medicinal paraphernalia, took a deep breath and opened the bathroom door.

Dylan sat on Wynnie's couch, downing the last of his Scotch as he waited for her to return from wherever it was she'd been hiding.

His eyes glanced over blonde-wood floors, windows looking out over a lush backyard, lashings of moonlight spilling inside creating silver swatches on the floor, and fat gold beeswax candles burning discreetly on a bunch of surfaces.

As far as he could tell there was not another light on in the house. If he didn't know her as well as he already did he might have thought this a scene fit for seduction rather than frugal energy use. As it was, it only made him smile.

The woman might have enough darkness in her past to need to go by an alias, but at least she was no hypocrite.

He stared into the melting ice in his glass and frowned. Why did *that* suddenly feel like an important discovery considering the mound of concrete, black-and-white evidence he'd collected on her already?

Just as Dylan was about to call in a search party, Wynnie reappeared.

She'd changed from her slinky red dress, half the reason he hadn't been able to keep his damn eyes and hands and thoughts off her all night, into loose grey track pants and an even more shapeless red sweatshirt. She'd discarded the sexy high heels in lieu of bare feet.

He bit back a grin. She was so obviously trying her dandiest to appear asexual, but it just wasn't working. Little did she know the pants clung to the curve of her buttocks as she walked, and that the red sweater had slipped off her right shoulder just enough that he could see the edge of a white lace bra strap. The hint of what lay beneath was even sexier than the blatant, smack down, luscious, clingy number that had had him in such a state all night long.

'Nice place you've got here,' he said.

'It belongs to the CFC—they're letting me stay here for the meantime. It was built green. Solar panels, shaded windows, double-glazed glass and the like.'

'Candles included?'

In the silver light of the moon he could still tell her cheeks had pinked. 'They're all mine.'

'Oh, and your phone beeped while you were in there,' Dylan said as she knelt on the other side of the coffee table.

Her golden eyes shot to his. 'Did you check it?'

He laughed, then sat forward, cradling his still-throbbing mouth. 'What kind of man do you think I am?'

'I'm sure I have no idea.'

She laid out a strange collection of wares on the coffee table. His bruise gave a sharp little pulse as he realised she wasn't as pedantically organised domestically as she was professionally—another insignificant snippet that felt as if it held more weight than it ought to have when compared with Jack's discoveries.

He poked his finger at a Band-Aid with a pink butterfly upon it. 'Suddenly I feel a desperate need to know what kind of men you usually bring back to your place to… soothe.'

She afforded him a blank stare. 'Alas your need will remain unassuaged.'

He could have taken that line so many ways. The minx. He laughed again, his lip hurt more, and this time it was followed by a pretty rambunctious oath. 'Jeez, woman. Stop making me laugh and heal me.'

He left his now-watery Scotch behind and lay back on the couch, one leg resting on the seat, the other foot still connected to the floor, his far arm tucked behind his head.

She cleared her throat, a small pucker formed between her brows, telling him at least she planned on trying to do a good job of nursemaid.

Her teeth began tugging at her bottom lip leaving in their wake a sheen that turned his whole body to stone.

'Relax,' she insisted, her voice anything but. 'I'll be with you in just a sec.'

He closed his eyes and tried to do as he was told.

Not as though that was in any way why he was there. Or why she had invited him there. Meaning they were both unhinged.

Now he knew without a doubt that she had agendas above and beyond those she espoused, he ought to have washed his hands of her for good—Wynnie Devereaux, or Guinevere Lambert or whoever she was.

And then bloody Garry Sloane had oozed up from the gutter and pounced.

The second he'd overheard that bastard of all the possible bastards call her by her real name, his instinct had sent him flying in there like a frenzied whirlwind.

True, he'd hired Jack to uncover the skeletons in her closet in case *he* might one day need to use them to protect his own interests. No altruism at all, pure self-protection. That was why he *should* have swept her away from Sloane.

But watching her standing there, panic and pain lighting her eyes as her past was about to be spilled on the floor at her feet, he'd imagined how it would feel if someone like Sloane stumbled upon the truth of his father's failing health, how exposing that news would hurt his family, how it would cut him to the bone…

Blinded by completely soft-headed empathy, he had only been able to think of saving Wynnie from that kind of hurt.

He blamed those eyes, those damned, compassionate, big liquid-brown eyes. It seemed in searching for her Achilles' heel, he'd only ended up exposing his own.

A wave of warmth washed over him, followed by the gentle draw of her floral scent. He opened one eye to find her leaning over him.

She squeezed a big gloop of cream onto an oversized cotton swab-like thing, and Dylan wondered if he ought to ask for a spoon to bite down on before she got any closer.

'So how did you end up working for the CFC?' he asked.

The swab hovered. She'd refused to answer a similar question before. But something made her change her mind. 'My friend Hannah, you met her tonight, she works for their legal department. They needed a campaign. A new image. She begged me to head it up. I loved the concept to bits. I couldn't say no.'

'Why would you have wanted to?'

She sat back on her haunches and her eyes shot to his. Now he knew where her vulnerability and motivation both sprang from, the caution that masked every word out of her mouth was as clear as day.

'I enjoy living abroad.' She reached out to him, dabbing at his lip, and the cold of the cream actually felt nice.

'Verona, right?' he said between dabs.

She tensed, and pressed slightly too hard against his lip. He flinched and so did she. 'You've asked around about me?'

He bit his tongue. 'Someone mentioned it in passing. Something to do with encouraging the good folk thereabouts to give generously to help renovate the Arena. Wasn't it once a colosseum? All lions and gladiators battling to the death? Not the kind of place I would imagine a big softie like you getting all het up about.'

'Every inch of this planet has at one time or another been a place of bloodshed and bad decisions. The nice part about being enlightened is that we can hopefully learn from our mistakes and aim to do better.'

His chest rumbled with laughter. 'Now if that isn't a stump speech you've said a hundred times before, I don't know what is. I can't believe you're trying to sell your proposal to me now, while I'm lying here bleeding.'

'You're not bleeding,' she scoffed, not denying his accusation. 'I'm actually beginning to wonder if he hit you at all or if you just got a fright and bit your lip.'

He laughed all the harder and his lip stung so much he licked it to taste blood. He glared at her, to find her biting her own lip to stop from laughing.

'Anyway, you brought it up,' she said, 'and it's not like your every waking·minute isn't taken up with finding ways to make people believe that putting their faith in KInG is all they'll ever need.'

He licked his lip again and realised her gauze was just waving in the breeze as her eyes were locked on his lip, his tongue. He gave his lip one last swipe, her eyes following it precisely, before putting it away. He wondered if she had any clue how many waking minutes over the past days had been dedicated entirely to her.

He pushed himself up on his elbow. 'So if you don't own this place, where do you have your money invested?'

'Oh, no,' she said waggling a finger at him. 'You are not going to sell me on investing with KInG.'

'There are no rules with what you and I are doing, Wynnie. That's the fun part—we get to make it up as we go along.'

She blinked, weighing his words. 'Fine. My money's in the bank.'

'Putting all your eggs in one basket is never a smart thing to do. To protect yourself, you need to hedge your investments. Diversify.'

She glanced at him from beneath her lashes and grew very still. He searched her eyes, looking for clues as to what she was thinking now that he had more pieces of the puzzle.

But all he got was the distinct feeling that she had already figured him out long before he came close to figuring her out. That she might actually be wondering how soon he might need to 'diversify' if anything actually happened between the two of them.

'Stop talking and lie down or we'll never get you out of here,' she said, pressing his chest until he did as he was told.

But as he gazed into her hot honey eyes he knew, once and for all, that there was no 'if' about it. The only question was when.

She tucked a swathe of her mussed dark hair behind her ear, and her brow tightened in concentration as she sat up on her knees and gingerly angled some kind of cold, wet bandage over his lip, her stomach pressing into his free arm as she twisted, the lower part of her breasts sliding over his ribcage as she twisted again.

Seriously, how was a man to bear it?

Wynnie patted Dylan's lip as gingerly as she could. It wasn't as though she had a single clue if what she was doing was really helping, but he wasn't complaining, or telling her she was doing it wrong, so she must have been doing something right.

The wound wasn't as bad as it had first seemed. Some swelling, which the iced drink had taken down. And she was fairly sure a bruise would arrive through the night. But it, thankfully, didn't require a butterfly Band-Aid.

Tending it, on the other hand, was sweet agony.

His clean scent, his hard body reposed beneath her, and those lips tugging beneath her gentle fingers. If she ever truly required punishment for mistakes of her past, then this was it—the impossibility of wanting Dylan Kelly and the enduring ache it left in the region of her heart.

She shot to her feet, the fresh air swarming between them allowing her to catch her breath.

Then his hand wrapped about her ankle. She got such a fright she dropped everything in her hands. Make-up wipes floated to her floor like snow.

'Dylan,' she warned, her voice husky.

'Wynnie,' he returned, in a voice she'd never heard before. It was so deep, so dark, so blatantly hungry she actually shivered.

'What are you doing?' she asked.

His cheek lifted. His hand slid further up her calf, sliding the wide hem of her track pants with it. 'What do you think I'm doing?'

Something you shouldn't, she thought before her eyes drifted closed and she breathed out hard through her nose.

Accidental touches, touches under the guise of being polite or professional—to this moment that had been it. And each and every one of those innocuous touches had set her nerves alight. His purposeful touch was irresistible.

'What are you doing all the way over there?' he asked, giving her a tug and putting her off balance.

'I'm done,' she said. 'You're on your way to being healed.'

'Honey, we're not even close to done.' He sat up, slowly, his eyes not leaving hers, his hand sliding up her leg till it rested on her outer thigh, holding her in place. 'Tell me why you brought me here?'

'To fix your war wounds. You stood up for me and I felt beholden. I always pay my debts.'

Dylan just laughed, the sound trembling down her thighs into the backs of her knees. He tugged, she twisted and she was beside him on the couch.

'You don't owe me a thing.' He reached up to sink a hand into the hair at the back of her neck. 'And you brought me here because this has been inevitable.'

'What?' she asked, the word barely making it past her lips.

'This.'

He pulled her to him, his lips sliding over hers, a perfect fit, as though they'd been there a thousand times before.

Every other sensation bombarding her, on the other hand, felt entirely new. The way her whole body melted against him like a fire had been lit beneath her. The need to wrap her arms tight about him so that she could be as close as she could possibly be. The build-up of relieved tears behind her eyes.

Then she remembered his split lip. She pulled away as

quickly as she could, which was embarrassingly sluggish. Her finger hovered above his lip. 'Doesn't it hurt?'

'Not a damn bit.'

He sank his face into her neck—it lost all bone structure and fell back to give him all the access he would possibly need.

'You taste like heaven,' he murmured near enough to her ear lobe that she shuddered deliciously.

'Say that again,' she begged.

She could feel his smile against her neck. And this time as he said the words his breath deliberately teased her ear and she let out a groan she could no longer suppress.

He slid her sweatshirt over her head. She tore so furiously at the front of his shirt several buttons popped right off. The sound of them hitting the polished wood floor felt like pebbles pelted hard against the inside of her head.

She let go of his shirt, and sat back with her hand over her mouth. 'Oh, God, I'm so sorry! I broke your shirt.'

He didn't even look to check; his eyes remained locked on hers. 'Not to worry. I have more.'

Of course he did, but that wasn't what had psyched her out. Her own wild abandon, the effortless loss of control—how deep could those untapped dimensions of herself possibly go?

In the resultant silence, she realised she wasn't the only one who was caught in the deep end. Dylan's breaths came thick and fast. The tendons in his neck stood out as if the blood flowed through his body at twice its normal rate. His eyes were so dark she wouldn't have known their true colour if it weren't permanently etched on her mind.

Her hand dropped from her mouth to grab the edge of the couch cushion for balance. Strands of her hair were stuck to her neck with sweat. Her heart rate was frantic. Her legs were wrapped about his hips and from the waist up she wore nothing but a delicate lace bra.

But she might as well have been naked for the way the look in his eyes made her feel. There was nowhere left to hide. Not behind her job, her name, her past. And for the first time in her life she felt herself living, right smack bang in the middle of the moment.

And then he slowly undid the rest of his buttons, and slid his jacket and shirt from his back.

Her eyes roved hungrily over his chest. His tanned skin was sculpted, smooth and perfect. The arrow of dark blond hair beginning at his navel and disappearing into his black trousers made her mouth turn completely dry.

No one human being had the right to look the way he looked. And she knew he was no angel. The fact that her skin felt hot, and slippery, as if it were tugging from her body, certainly assured her of that.

But now she had the taste of him in her mouth, the scent of him in her nose, on her clothes, constantly wafting across the back of her mind, reason took a backseat.

He reached out, his hands sliding around her waist, and he pulled her more fully into his lap. What little breath remained in her lungs left in a heady whoosh.

'No regrets,' he said, his voice rough.

She shook her head. She wouldn't be sorry for this. It was inevitable. It was chemical. It was nature's intent. And who was she, a hippy child from Nimbin, to argue with nature?

Wynnie slid her hands over his shoulders, the heat and curve of hard muscle giving her strength. She let temptation continue to guide her as her fingers delved into the short thick hair at the back of his neck. It fluttered through her fingers like velvet.

Then she leant in and kissed him. Open mouth. Tongue. Eyes closed. Luscious. Wet. Decadent.

He groaned into her mouth as he wrapped his arms so tightly around her she could barely breathe. But she didn't care. All she needed was his hot skin, his undisciplined grip.

Only this time she really let go, and just let whatever would happen happen.

Every sensation heightened. Every touch, every shift of skin on skin, every catch of breath, every aching groan, every tantalising breath that whispered across her neck, her ear, the swell of her breasts, her hot lips. She imagined this must be what it felt like to be high.

Dylan Kelly was her drug of choice. And, despite the pleasure bombarding her from every angle, she knew he was the most dangerous kind of addiction she would ever know.

His hands moved to the clasp of her bra, unlocking it with practised finesse. He'd done it before. Many times if rumours were to be believed.

She closed her eyes tight to shut out the thread of doubt that brought on. The extent of his experience was the only hope she had that they'd be able to find a way to be professional after they were through.

Slowly, deliberately, his thumbs traced the outline of each and every rib as though it was something he'd fantasised about doing. His fingers slid around her sides to press firmly into the always tight muscles below her shoulder blades causing her to arch towards him.

Then his mouth moved to her breast, his breath washing across the taut peak sweeping every thought from her mind but pleasure. She cried out her thanks and arched closer.

The feather-light touch of his tongue circling her nipple was too much. But then it was nothing compared with the heat that rocketed through her body as he took her breast in his mouth.

She bit her lip to stop from crying out that he take her then and there. Because no matter how great the ache, it was an ache she found herself imagining she could live with for the rest of her life.

His teeth scraped painfully around her breast before pulling away. The cooling night air tickled at the moist spot and she broke out in an array of goose bumps.

His brow furrowed, and then he set to righting the wrong, his hands again running over every exposed inch of her.

'Your skin,' he rumbled. 'It's like fresh butter. I've never in my life felt anything so soft.'

He slid from the couch and sank to his knees before her. Then he leant in and ran his tongue along the curve of her lowest rib. She breathed in deep as it curled into her navel and along the top of her track pants. He nudged them downwards so that he could scrape his teeth gently along her hip bone. She wasn't sure whose moan was louder.

'God,' he groaned, running his thumb along the smooth skin an inch below her hip bone, 'could you possibly taste any better?'

'Caramel tart,' she said on a sigh. 'Tonight at the ball, there was a spare seat next to mine. I had seconds. By now it's probably leeching through my skin.'

His laughter reverberated through her bottom half. The delectable shudder that followed was worth it.

His breath whispered against the rise of her belly as he said, 'Mmm. I'm not sure that's it. I have the distinct feeling the taste I can't get enough of is all you.'

Using the finger stroking her hip, he tugged at her track pants and her bottom shifted lower on the couch. Another tug and they were gone, leaving her naked in the moonlight, bar a nude, seamless, barely there G-string tiny enough not to have shown under her silk dress.

Before she had the chance to even wonder about her bikini line, the G-string was gone—sliding down her legs, scraping delectably along her calves, and over her feet, and gone. Flicked away. Hanging from a palm frond in the corner of the room.

If she hadn't known she was in the middle of the most decadent night of her young life, that clinched it.

Her eyes were drawn back to his. And it was only then that she realised he was still covered from the waist down, and thus, to all intents and purposes, dressed.

Her knees pressed together and she pulled herself into a more dignified upright position. 'Somehow the balance of power has gone all your way,' she said.

'Wynnie, my sweet, you have got that all wrong.' His eyes roved over her body, adoring it, worshipping it as he said, 'You have me in your complete thrall.'

She crossed her legs, and crossed her arms. 'So if I brought out a certain contract and waved it before your nose…'

His eyes turned so dark she thought she might have pushed her luck a centimetre too far. Until he grinned like a shark and lay his hands upon her knees, drawing them back apart. 'How could I hope to hold a pen when my hands are so pleasantly occupied otherwise?'

How indeed.

Ignoring her round-about request that he disrobe, he instead returned to focus on her. He caressed her right leg, from her knee to her toes, massaging, melting. Then when he had her completely boneless he lifted her leg and lay it atop his shoulder.

The pure audacity sapped her breath from her lungs and her wide eyes shot straight to his. He smiled, and waited. Making sure she was okay.

She wasn't exactly sure how to tell him she was more than okay, bar smiling back. Her cheeks felt shaky, her lips swollen and halfway numb. But it was obviously enough.

His mouth hovered at the juncture between her legs. It took every ounce of strength she had not to delve her fingers into his hair to guide him.

He looked up, and his eyes pierced hers. 'Now tell me why you really brought me here.'

She slapped a hand over her eyes and bit back a scream. 'Are you truly going to make me say it?'

'I'm the devil, remember. It's par for the course.'

She licked her lips as his breath washed across her thighs. 'Fine,' she croaked. 'I brought you here because I wanted this. All of this. From the second you came strolling through that crowd outside your great big phallus of a building and saw me handcuffed to your statue like dinner waiting for you on a plate, I wanted you.'

And any other words she might have had in store were lost in a groan as he lowered his head.

Her arms shot out and her hands gripped the back of the couch. Her eyes slammed closed and her head snapped back.

His absolute tenderness astounded her. His deftness did not. It met her expectations and then steadily blew them out of the water.

Sweet agony lapped at her core. Wave after hot, liquid wave swelled and surged until she no longer had any control of her mind, or her body.

'I can't do this.'

'You can,' he murmured, kissing one thigh, then the other, letting her come down off the crest of the wave just long enough to catch her breath before taking her higher still.

Her skin prickled with sweat, her fingers grew numb from hanging on so tight, and every nerve felt aflame as the pressure inside her built to a beautiful crescendo.

And on and on it went. Higher, harder, deeper, bliss. Building still until she was sure she would faint from the violence of the pleasure rising inside her.

And just when she thought she couldn't take it any more numbness overcame her, the eye of the storm giving her respite, making her feel as if she were floating above the couch.

Then pleasure as she had never known crashed over her, and she shattered into a thousand hot, dark, beautiful pieces.

Cruel as he was, Dylan didn't even give her a chance to live out the waves cascading over her. He kissed her thigh, stroked her hip, ran his tongue up her waist and the edge of her left breast. It was torture, pure and simple.

He ran his hands along her arms, uncurling her fingers from their death grip of the rug-covered leather, and slowly lay her back on the couch.

Replete, boneless, weak, she stretched her arms over her head and twisted her body back into a more normal shape.

Dylan, now standing over her, watched her with his hand

on his fly. 'Why do I get the feeling you have no idea how beautiful you are?'

Wynnie curled onto her side, still warm and buzzing. 'Flattery will get you everywhere.'

'Maybe so, but I've never found cause to use it.' He pulled down his zip, then after that his trousers, until he stood before her—naked, ready and godlike.

Silver moonlight caressed his muscled form as though it had merely been waiting for the chance to do so. Every dip and depression seemed caved from marble. Every curve and rise all man.

He was right. He'd never need to use flattery to get what he wanted. He just had to ask.

She pushed herself up on one arm and held out her other hand. He knelt over her. She wrapped her arms about his torso, arching into him as he pressed her back on the couch. And their kiss was like nothing she had ever known.

Heat exploded through her body, spot fires sprang up all over her skin. She wanted him so badly, but even though she could feel the tension in his arms, in his legs, in his kiss, he still spent every second making sure her pleasure was paramount.

Sweeping her damp hair from her face. Tugging at her bottom lip, which made her moan every time. Sliding his free hand down her side, teasing, lightly caressing the outside of her breast when she wanted his whole hand thereon. Brushing her hip bone with his knuckles with a whisper-light touch that had her arching higher towards him, wanting more. Then from nowhere sinking his fingers deep between her legs, drawing her back to the brink of destruction again and again.

Need and desire were the only two things keeping them on that couch. The fact that he had a condom on hand now felt like a miracle, as well.

He sheathed himself. She wrapped her legs around him. And finally he sank into her with a shuddering sigh.

He filled her and then some, stretching every part of her

until she felt more, on every level there was, than she'd ever felt before.

Her breath came in gasps. Her fingers dug into his back. Beauty and exhilaration overcame her. Time expanded and compressed as her world shrank to the size of her couch as she rocked with him, pressed into him, enveloped him, took of him everything he had.

With the brakes off it felt as if they were careening down a steep hill. She could barely breathe; she could barely think. It was terrifying and exhilarating and she didn't want it to end.

And then the rhythm changed, hastened. Power surged through her, giving her the knowledge that it was her turn to bring him release.

She looked deep into his eyes, the deepest ocean blue, and he looked right on back as together they reached the highest heights before sliding into oblivion.

And as she fought her way back into consciousness Wynnie felt the heart whose life force had long since been compartmentalised to care for greater causes, the heart she had been sure would never truly be touched again, make a hot, heavy return to life.

CHAPTER EIGHT

As Dylan sat upon the overly soft green couch on the set of the Sunday-morning chat show, eyes closed tight as his face was powdered, he tried his very best to concentrate on what he had to say over the next ten minutes, and not on Wynnie as he'd left her less than eight hours earlier.

Standing in the doorway of her home, a short satin robe barely wrapped about her deliciously naked body, her bare legs twisted together, her dark hair cascading over her slender shoulders, her hand wrapped loosely around the doorframe as she leant up to kiss him goodnight.

It had all been so civilised. As civilised as he'd ever known it to be. So why then did he feel more like a tightly coiled spring than he had before releasing every ounce of energy he had inside him with the best sex of his life?

'Dylan!'

He blinked and the bright lights of the TV studio came back into focus to find Rylie Madigan, the anchor of *Daybreak*, and one of his sister's best friends, slapping him across the upper arm.

'Where the hell are you?' she whispered between her perfectly capped teeth.

He thought cooling thoughts, flapped his suit jacket and repositioned himself on the over-soft couch. Through gritted teeth he said, 'Same place I am every Sunday morning, my backside parked on this exact spot as I prepare to pass out the good investment word to your loyal viewers across this fair land.'

Rylie tilted her chin so her long blonde hair could be fluffed and coiffed. 'Sweet cheeks, don't go acting like you are here out of the goodness of your heart. I should be getting a finder's fee for the mum-and-dad clients who flock to your business because I let you and your pretty face charm the sense out of them on my show.'

Dylan grunted. She was right. He never did anything unless it served the family's interests.

So why then had he gone and slept with the woman who was doing her everything to make them all seem like avaricious jerks? Why? Because he was a man not nearly as in control of his hormones as he'd always thought he was, that was for bloody sure.

He reached out and pinched Rylie's cheek. 'The fact that you don't even think about trying to take advantage of us like that is the reason we let Meg keep you around.'

'Nice. Oh, and did my producers tell you they found a super-fun way to mix things up a bit today?' Rylie's green gaze slid past his shoulder. Something in her smile put his muddied instincts back on high alert. He tensed and turned.

And as if he'd dreamt her up out of the most wretched, disobedient, self-flagellating depths inside him, Wynnie Devereaux stood in the wings shaking hands with the producers, hand to her heart, smiling, flirting, winning them over as easily as she won over every poor soul who stood in her path.

A young guy in jeans, T-shirt and headphones tapped her on the shoulder and pointed to the soft, fat couches on which he and Rylie sat.

She squinted in their direction, saw him there and nodded. He offered a subtle bow in response. If he wanted to know how civilised things could truly be, this set-up would show him.

She touched each cohort on the arm as she took her leave,

then lifted her high-heel-shod feet as she skipped over the thick electrical cords gaffer-taped to the floor.

Dressed in a blousy cream top, a cream skirt hugging her curves to just below her knees, a loose bronze belt skimming her hips, with her hair loose and soft, she looked like an angel, meaning in comparison in his dark grey suit, sharp white shirt and red tie he'd look like the poster boy for corporate greed.

And the closer Wynnie got, the clearer it all became. The outfit, the lack of surprise in her eyes—she had to have known she was coming here today. And all the night before, as they'd danced, as he'd come to her rescue, as she'd played nurse-maid, as they'd come together naked, she *had* to have known he was going to be here, too.

And she'd never once mentioned a thing.

He uncrossed his legs and dug his fingers into his thighs. The marks they would leave would be nothing on the red weals across his back from where her fingernails had dug into him as she had climaxed in his arms.

He allowed himself, and her, a break. Maybe this had been a last-minute arrangement. Maybe she'd only found out about it that morning. Maybe in the heat of the moment it had simply been forgotten.

Or maybe she'd unscrupulously taken him for the great cuckold he seemed determined to prove he could be.

'You all right, hon?' Rylie asked from somewhere to his left. 'You look like you've seen a ghost.'

Wynnie hit the patch of hot light beaming down upon the small stage, caught his eye and smiled. Cool, calm, confident, with not a lick of vulnerability to be seen.

'No ghost,' Dylan said. But certainly a tunnel of light.

Wynnie sashayed past Dylan and made herself known to the host of the show.

At least she hoped she'd sashayed.

From the moment she'd clapped eyes on him, lounging in

the couch, cool as you please, right at home under the glaring down lights, nothing about him registering the wildly intimate night they'd shared the night before, her feet had felt like lead, her knees as if mini earthquakes were erupting beneath her kneecaps with every step, and her clothes felt as if she'd put them on backwards.

She'd known he'd be here. It was in the brief the producers had faxed to her that morning, which she'd read in the cab on the way to the row of TV stations atop Mt Coot-tha.

If she'd known he'd be there before she was halfway up the mountain? If she'd known the nerveless reaction she was going to get? For the first time in her career she probably would have feigned the mumps.

'So glad you could come,' Rylie Madigan said with a grin, and Wynnie was glad for the change of focus. 'Nothing like fresh blood to shake up a comfortable old city like ours.'

'Happy to oblige.'

'I read a bit about you in the papers over the past few days. I'd love to take you to lunch sometime to pick your brain about a few things.'

Rylie glanced at Dylan. Wynnie felt as if she was missing something.

Dylan grabbed his glass of water, took his time sipping, then placed it on the coffee table and stood, stretching his arms over his head, and said, 'Say yes, Ms Devereaux, she's not hitting on you.'

Wynnie's cheeks pinked in an instant, less from the sexy rumble of his voice, and much more from the unduly cool Ms Devereaux remark. 'I didn't… Of course I…'

Rylie laughed. 'Ignore him. He's a fiend. He takes his greatest pleasure from winding women up and watching them spin away as fast as possible. The lovely Lilliana's fault right there. That's what a succubus for an ex-fiancée will do to a guy.'

A succubus? *And* an ex-fiancée? Wynnie silently fumed as these new snippets sank in. Hannah needed a good talking to about timely revelation of important information. And her researchers were going to have a little meeting with her all on their own.

She couldn't help herself; she looked to Dylan again. He seemed not to have heard a thing, but she saw his fingers curl into his palm. She knew that feeling—clenching was the only way you could keep the bad things locked up tight inside.

Her first instinct was to soothe his pain. Again. But there was nothing in his bearing to give her any indication that she now had that right. She wasn't his girlfriend. She wasn't even really a friend. She was barely a prospective business associate.

'So, lunch?' Rylie asked. 'We'll get Meg to come, too. She's out there in the audience somewhere, playing her portable PlayStation thingie while she waits for me to finish. It'll be a riot.'

'Sure. That'd be lovely. Call my office and we'll make a time.'

Rylie's brow then furrowed, her lips turned down and Wynnie got the feeling she was doing her best impression of solemn. 'Now, back to our regular programming. I know that your agenda is a serious one. Saving the planet and all that. Go you! But remember we're a super-relaxed show. Our viewers aren't tuning in for anything hard-hitting or ultra-political. So best thing is to keep it light.'

'Can do,' Wynnie said as brightly as she could while her stomach felt as if it were trying to digest a pound of lead.

Rylie grinned, and somehow didn't wrinkle, then moved Wynnie to a soft couch on the other side of the stage from Dylan's.

She sat, crossed her legs, and suddenly the floor manager was flapping a two-minute signal, and the eyes of the cameras grew large as they zoomed in close. Wynnie's heart rate made itself known as adrenalin surged through her body.

Though the last thing she needed two minutes before a live TV interview was adrenaline on top of her adrenaline, she shifted her gaze a fraction until she found a pair of daring blue eyes.

The night before those eyes had roved over every inch of her naked skin, drinking her in as though he were quenching a lifetime of thirst. But now the level of indifference he was maintaining even as their eyes held for second after second made her body clench from top to toe.

She wasn't his girlfriend. She wasn't a friend. And the harsh truth that was finally dawning on her was that she wasn't even really his lover.

She'd been warned, more than once, and she'd known it deep down inside all along. But she'd blithely ignored it until the truth slapped her hard across the face.

She'd said it herself. Dylan was a flirt. The art was his greatest weapon.

In their game the sell was not nearly as much about showcasing the high points of a product itself as much as it was about creating a blissful buying experience. It was their job to be memorable, delicious and addictive. To make sure that even while they were shaking their head 'no' a prospective client was thinking ahead to when they might come back for more.

Looking into his cool dark eyes, she wondered *how* she'd let herself go so long without remembering that.

'Today we have something special for you,' Rylie's sing-song voice rang out and Wynnie realised they were on.

She blinked, found a smile, found a camera and found her centre. She'd sort the other stuff out later, when there weren't hundreds of thousands of people looking in.

Rylie continued, 'Not only do we have our regular financial advisor, Dylan Kelly, head of Media Relations for the Kelly Investment Group, we also have Wynnie Devereaux, a representative for the Clean Footprint Coalition who has come along with some advice of her own. Welcome to the both of you.'

Dylan smiled for the people, and even Wynnie, who knew better, had flutters in her stomach at the flirtatious light in his eyes. When he turned that light her way, her heart tumbled, twisted, second-guessed itself and then went back to pumping blood and left confusion to take over her head instead.

She blinked, then somehow beamed at Rylie. 'Thanks for having me, Rylie.'

Rylie leant forward, draping her manicured hands over her knees. 'Now, is it true that you first met our Dylan when you handcuffed yourself to a statue outside his building?'

Wynnie laughed to cover the fact that she was barely registering Rylie's words. 'I'm afraid it takes more than a polite phone call to get the attention of a representative of a big firm like KInG. And considering the changes I believe they could make in order to help reduce energy consumption in this city are beyond compare, this girl had to do what a girl had to do.'

The small studio audience cheered. She just knew any woman at home watching would be cheering, too. Putting themselves in her shoes, imagining the day they might find reason for a showdown with a man like Dylan.

She glanced at the man in question to find he certainly did not look in the mood to cheer. If the women at home knew the havoc a showdown with such a man wrought, they might change their minds.

Rylie's sharp gaze swung to him and Wynnie drew in a deep breath. 'Did you really refuse to return Wynnie's phone calls? How could you? She's adorable!'

Dylan's returning smile was beautiful enough for the people at home, but Wynnie knew he was struggling not to throttle Rylie, their good host.

'Yeah,' Wynnie threw in, to all of their amazement. 'How adorable does a businesswoman with a great idea have to be to get the great and wonderful Dylan Kelly to call her back?'

His gaze slid to hers—hot, dark, menacing. Warning her to back down. But she had to take out her frustration on somebody, and he was so perfectly positioned to bear the brunt.

He shuffled forward on his seat, seemingly not the least

bit intimidated by the dual front. And then his eyes locked back onto hers.

'Ms Devereaux,' he said, his voice as smooth and hot as melting wax, 'being that you are so new in town, perhaps you didn't realise that we are a financial institution whose job it is to look out for the interests of our clients. If you had an investment query, I'd be happy to take a meeting with you. Any time.'

Wynnie licked her dry lips. She wondered if anyone else thought that by *'meeting'* he meant hot, sweaty, naked, sex. Any time. By the twitters and sighs pouring from the studio audience she figured they probably did. She only wished she knew if his offer was good, or just for the cameras.

'Mr Kelly,' she said, her voice huskier than she would have liked, but now she'd gone down this road she couldn't turn back. 'Book me a room, and I'll be there.'

It took a few moments of dead air, but then Dylan smiled. 'I might just do that.'

It was the first real smile she'd had from him since she'd walked into the studio. It was beautiful, breathtaking, real, and all for her.

She smiled right on back. In fact, she had to bite her tongue to stop from laughing out loud. Somehow it eased her tension and ramped it up all at the same time. She only hoped the sudden heat in her cheeks was lost in the wash of hard white light.

'My one good deed for the day,' Rylie said, and then Wynnie remembered where she was.

'No good deed goes unpunished,' Dylan warned, plainly having never forgotten for a second that he was on show.

Rylie looked down the barrel of the camera as she said, 'Now, my lovelies, let's go through Wynnie's list of ways we can each and every one of us reduce our energy consumption and save money at the same time, then Dylan can give us some advice on how to start saving now for Christmas.'

She glanced at Wynnie, then at Dylan, waggling her

long fingers at the two of them. 'Now who could have possibly guessed that your interests would converge so beautifully as all that?'

'Not this little duck,' Dylan said.

Wynnie somehow bit out a smile.

And Rylie's eyes gleamed as bullet points of Wynnie's list came up on the screen.

Fifteen minutes later, Wynnie sat in the green room, waiting for the producer to come by so she could press some flesh, and thank him for the spot.

The door bumped on its hinges, and her heart rate kicked up a notch, hoping instead it might be Dylan. The last thing she wanted was a 'we have to talk' talk, but some kind of clarity was only fair.

The door swung open and closed and a petite brunette, wearing the kind of cute chocolate-brown cocktail dress not usually seen on a person so early on a Sunday morning, slumped onto the couch next to her.

'Hi,' she said, 'I'm Meg.'

Meg Kelly. She hadn't even needed to drop her surname. Her blue eyes were the same as her brother's—bright, mischievous, and, if you looked harder, guarded. But unlike him she was also obviously as sweet as pie.

'I'm waiting to take Rylie out to brunch,' Meg said, 'but I had to pop back here to tell you how much fun that interview was. I've never seen anyone get to my brother like that.'

'Is he around somewhere do you know?' Wynnie slipped in.

'God, no. He snuck out a back exit before the floor manager had barely yelled "clear".'

Wynnie slumped back into her chair.

Meg continued unabated, 'I thought he was about to pop a vein when you said only eight KInG employees out of eight hundred actually car pool to work. You are my new favourite person in the whole world.'

'I don't think I've ever been commended for causing vein popping in anyone before. Maybe a new line for my résumé?'

Meg laughed and held up a fist. 'Rock the establishment!'

Of course Wynnie liked her, and so instantly she almost allowed herself to ask about the succubus ex-fiancée. To find out if he still had feelings for the woman and that was why he was so reticent. To ask if she perhaps knew of a magic pill she could take that would make her forget all about the Kellys forever.

Meg lay a hand on her knee. 'Now, the other reason I'm here is that my parents are having a little get-together at the house this afternoon, just family and a couple of friends, and I'd really love it if you could come.'

It took Wynnie a moment to compute what Meg had just said. 'Oh, no, no, no. If you were really paying attention to that interview you'd know that there is no love lost between your brother and me.'

Her choice of words rang a bell deep inside her, which she thought it best to ignore.

She continued, 'If I set foot on your family's property he would have me shot for trespassing.'

'Rubbish. He's a Labrador. All bark. So you'll come as my guest. Would it help if you knew my reasons were purely selfish? Having the family not entirely focused on why I am not the vice president of some fabulous company like the rest of them are would be nice.'

Meg certainly had the same charisma as her brother; Wynnie could feel it tugging her to do things she oughtn't to want to do. But she shook her head. 'It's very sweet of you to ask, but I just can't.'

Meg sat back, adorably vanquished. She lifted her feet off the floor and seemed to find her bright purple toenails fascinating for several long moments before she said, 'He was talking about you, you know?'

Wynnie slid her butterfly clip from her top, needing something to occupy her while she reeled from having the second female close to Dylan pick up on vibes between them.

'I'm sure my name has been used in vain in the hallowed halls of KInG many a time over the past week.'

Meg dropped her feet, then looked Wynnie square in the eye. 'Maybe so, but I don't hang out at the family biz so I wouldn't know about any of that. This was at a family dinner. He kept bringing the conversation right back to you.'

Wynnie blew warm air on her butterfly and polished it on her skirt.

She said, 'That's what a woman in handcuffs will do to a conversation, I'm afraid.'

But her heart raced. Her mind whirled. And her imagination ran away with itself. Maybe she'd been thinking about this all wrong. Maybe what had happened between them had already been going on longer than one hot spring night.

'I know this might not seem like it's my business,' Meg said, 'but Dylan is my business, and he's been different this week. He's been spry, and twitchy and far less of a pain in the butt than he has been in years. I have the feeling I have you to thank for it.'

Wynnie's hands shook as she put the butterfly in her purse. 'Perhaps he's so chipper as he's planning on new and wonderful ways of telling me "no". In a professional capacity,' she added as a dismal addendum.

Meg held up a hand, and, being that she was of the same Kelly stock, Wynnie found her words drying up in her mouth.

'Then look at it this way; he's not the be-all and end-all when it comes to making decisions about KInG. My father is the CEO, and our older brother Brendan is all set to take over…' Meg's hand dropped into her lap. 'One day a long, long time from now. So if you're game, I'd love you to come with me as my guest. Give yourself one last chance to make your case.'

Meg Kelly was a clever girl. She'd made the temptation far too great.

Wynnie had one last chance to find out if Dylan was all she so deeply thought he was, or whether her usual bad judgment made her just another notch on the smiling assassin's bedpost.

And one last chance to convince KInG to join with the CFC.

Her cheeks flushed as she realised her first thought had been Dylan, and not how precipitous an opportunity she had just been thrown to get her job done.

Either way, Wynnie couldn't turn Meg down.

'I'd be delighted.' Wynnie smiled at Meg over the top of her drink. 'So why aren't you the vice president of some fabulous company?'

Meg's mouth twisted into a smile. 'If I'd been this age in the eighties—the days of three-hour lunches, junkets overseas and perks up the wazoo—then who knows?'

The door swung open and Rylie flounced in, obviously having heard the tail-end of a story she'd heard before. 'You'd never have carried off the shoulder pads.'

'Oh, well. Too bad. A life of leisure and avoiding making excuses to the fam is to be my lot. Here's my mobile number.' Meg handed over a shiny white business card with a large bold embossed letter '*M*' above a mobile number and an e-mail address in bold hot pink letters. 'Message me your address and I'll swing by and pick you up at yours at say three o'clock and we'll head to the manor from there.'

'Sounds good.'

Meg stood and Wynnie did the same.

'You coming?' Rylie asked Meg, and the two of them bounced out the door, waving their goodbyes.

Wynnie slumped back onto the couch and stared at Meg's card, wondering how on earth she would explain her presence at his family's home to Dylan, and wondering what else she could possibly think to say to him after that.

CHAPTER NINE

DYLAN hid on his hands and knees behind a manicured hedge in the centre of the park at the rear of his parents' Edwardian-style home, ostensibly counting backwards from thirty-eight. That was as high as Olive, Brendan's youngest, knew how to count.

'Ready or not, here I come!' he bellowed after enough time seemed to have passed, and the direction of the squeals that followed told him the girls were both in the exact same places they had been the week before. Didn't mean he couldn't take his time finding them.

It took a loud oomphing sound to make getting up easier.

'Don't do that,' Cameron said as he wandered over, carrying a bone-china plate covered in crumbs that told of intensely delicious hors d'oeuvres, which Dylan was missing out on.

Food had worked a treat the last time he was here and trying to stop thinking about what lay beneath Wynnie's outer layers. Now that he knew the answer in brilliant, intimate detail he feared he might need a table full all for himself.

'You're older than me,' Cameron said. 'You're giving me a bad image of what I might be like in two years.'

Dylan brushed grass off the knees of his casual, hide-and-seek-ready trousers. 'You're married now, remember. I'll give it a year before everyone starts thinking you're older anyway.'

'Nah. My love's glow will keep me ageless and this good-

looking forever. You, on the other hand, as a ridiculously determined single man, will wear mismatched socks and lose
your car keys and your sentences will be replaced by mumbles. But you'll still be welcome at Rosalind's and mine.' Cam
added a slap to the back as he said, 'Old man.'

'Leave me be, I have pre-teens to entertain. Only the cool
uncle gets that job. But first tell me where I can get my mouth
around some of that food. My stomach needs filling and fast.'

'Not just yet. Meg's here, and she's brought a little friend,'
Cameron said with just enough of a smile in his voice Dylan
knew the joke was about to be on him.

Dylan glanced up at the house to see his sister and…

His empty stomach went into free fall and landed somewhere
in the region of his knees. 'You have got to be kidding me.'

Cameron laughed. 'Don't tell me she's brought an old
flame here to haunt you again.'

When Dylan said nothing but continued to stare, Cameron
added softly, 'Or perhaps it is a new flame.'

If the fire in his belly had anything to say about it, Cameron
was spot on. So much for splitting from the TV studio quick
smart to give himself the chance to clear his head of her—to
remove himself from her soft warm body, her delectably sharp
tongue, her expressive eyes that told him right there on live
television that, despite the games, despite the professional gulf
between them, she hadn't had enough of him any more than
he'd had enough of her. Now the mere sight of her in the distance deluged him with all those intense feelings again like a
sudden summer storm.

Nevertheless he rallied to shake his head. 'Less of a flame,
more of a thorn in my side.'

Since that morning she'd pinned her fringe from her
forehead, leaving her face open and guileless, her waves
curling softly against her cheeks. A pale blue and cream lace
top gently draped over her shoulders, whispering across her
breasts, veering in to show off her small waist and stopping

ust below the beltline of tight jeans. Her flat silver shoes gave
a bounce to her steps.

He'd never seen her look so pretty, so utterly feminine. The
latent he-man instincts she always seemed to conjure up flew
into overdrive and his skin began to tighten and prickle and hurt.

He curled his fingers into his palms. So far the only way
he'd found to make those persistent and highly inconvenient
feelings go away was having her naked skin flush against his
own. Meaning either he had to make love to her every night
for the rest of his life, or this unhealthy relationship had to
come to a swift end.

'Dylan,' Cameron mumbled, apparently still beside him.

'What?' he barked.

'Would I be completely wrong in thinking that *you* might
be glowing?'

The bark turned to a growl. 'So wrong it makes me wonder
if your new wife is not beating you about the head as you sleep.
It'd be a fast way for her to come into a quick fortune, you know.'

Cameron's glare was baleful, and Dylan knew he'd over-
stepped the mark. He patted his brother on the back and added,
'Though if you snore the way you used to at camp I wouldn't
blame her if she did.'

Cameron forgave him with a smile, before moving off in
the direction of his new bride. The two of them couldn't seem
to be apart for longer than five minutes.

As though Dylan were in need of any other means to add
to his now almost constant discomfort, he took a step Wynnie's
way but stopped when his mother cut them off. Wynnie's
smile seemed genuine as his mother kissed her on the cheek.
She said something then that made his mother laugh.

Her hair was fluttering across her face, the breeze sucking
her filmy top to her skin shaping every delicious curve until
he had no choice but to remember the sheen and tone of every
inch of skin.

And those big brown cow eyes just made him melt in

places he didn't know it was possible for a grown man to melt
Thank God the rest of her made the rest of him rock-hard.

He took another step towards the house and stopped again
when his father appeared from nowhere to join the welcome
party. She shook his hand, looked him in the eye and cocked
her head to one side as he told her some story or other. likely
about golf, or sailing.

She listened. As though she just knew there was no greater
way to Quinn's good graces than to make him think he was
fascinating.

As the rest of the gang, bar him, joined in the welcome
Wynnie's melodic laughter rang across the lawn. Her bright
eyes shone, even from this distance. She showed no fear of
the usually amply intimidating group. And as one they bowed
towards her like sunflowers to the sun.

Each and every one of them on the board of the Kelly
Investment Group.

'Oh, crap,' he said aloud as his blood began to chill in his
veins.

No wonder her eyes were yet to seek him out. He was the
very last person she had come here to see.

Damn Meg and her meddling. He had to clean up her
messes more than everyone else's combined, and right now
he wanted to ring her little neck. But she'd have to get in line
Wynnie Devereaux was right up front.

Since the hideous, unscrupulous, malicious break-up with
Lilliana, his eyes had been wide-open to the fact that every
woman he'd ever known had wanted something from him.
Wynnie was no different—she'd just been so upfront about
wanting to get into bed with KInG his usually rock-solid
guard had slipped. And he'd spent the past week following his
groin rather than his gut. Shame on him, twice over.

Brendan, who was leaning against a pillar on the outer rim
of the circle, caught his eye over a cup of coffee. He raised
an eyebrow before tilting his head in Wynnie's direction.

The Trojan horse might not have made it back inside the building, but she had made it smack bang into the middle of the inner sanctum, and it was entirely his doing.

It all came back to the small pile of photocopied news stories Jack had left him with; Wynnie questioned day after day for twelve days, not because there was any evidence she'd had anything to do with the attack on the laboratory, but because she'd refused to say a word about where her brother might be. Twelve days she'd kept her mouth shut. Not giving up her family to save herself.

He'd held on to that, tightly, as he'd called in a favour to get a ticket to the museum ball. It had thrown him in the way of a swinging fist, and sent him to her bed.

But the truth was he actually had not one clue if she had been involved with radical, violent, environmentalist saboteurs. Video footage and witness evidence said her brother most certainly was. Seven people had been injured that day, including one who was put into a wheelchair for life. And here she was in his home, mixing with his family. He didn't know which direction to step first.

The family split in all directions, and Meg's arm linked through Wynnie's as she took her down onto the grass. Wynnie's eyes skimmed the park until they found his and there they stayed.

Her soft pink lips curved into a private smile, and even from twenty feet away he could see the pink rising in her cheeks.

He gritted his teeth and fought back the urge to throw her over his shoulder and drag her the hell out of there as fast as his legs would carry them.

When he realised he wasn't sure if his desire to do so was about keeping her from getting any closer to his family, or because he wanted to get her alone, he managed to squash his inner Neanderthal, and find enough calming breath to appear cool.

'Dylan,' Meg said, smirking as if she were eight-years-old

and had caught him kissing Katie Finch in the cloisters at the front of the house. 'I believe you know my new friend Wynnie. I picked her up in the green room after Rylie's show. Already I love her to bits.'

'How could you not? She's a jewel.'

He glanced at Wynnie. Her big brown eyes were lit up from the inside. Questions and newfound nerves and attraction skittered behind her gaze but far too quickly to decipher exactly what she was thinking. He blinked at her, his expression a blank mask, hopefully letting her think he didn't care.

'Now we had a great talk in the car on the way here,' Meg babbled, 'all about her work, and I just love what this girl has to say. She's smart, and I know you appreciate smart. So why aren't you being a good boy and doing exactly what you're being told and agree to turn off some lights and fork out on ceramic mugs rather than plastic cups in the office, for Pete's sake?'

Why? Why indeed? Put like that it seemed like the simplest thing in the world for him to do. Hell, he could write a memo in ten seconds flat, and Eric would make it happen before lunch.

But with Wynnie Devereaux standing there before him looking like a wood nymph who'd skipped out of the Kelly Manor's small forest, looking like the woman who'd fallen apart, twice, in his arms less than twenty-four hours earlier, looking like the woman who had skirted the rules again and again to get around him to get to his family, there was no way on God's green earth he was going to say yes.

Wynnie sat on a white cane lounge on the Kellys' immaculate back lawn, shaded by a large cloth sun sail, sipping at a glass of iced tea.

She only listened with half an ear as Quinn Kelly told a story about the time he went on an African safari. Squeals of delight kept her mind focused on the action occurring somewhere over her right shoulder.

The one or two glances she had managed afforded her glimpses of Dylan playing with his two young nieces.

She bit at her left thumbnail, her brow tight from over-furrowing. If she'd had any concerns about the extent and breadth of her feelings for Dylan after the way he'd made love to her the night before, the image of him running in random circles chasing down two adorable girls in pigtails, not caring if he got grass stains on his trousers or their gorgeous pastel dresses, magnified every trepidation tenfold.

The back of her hair suddenly began to itch, and she was sure she was being watched. Not only watched, *stared* at.

The burning feeling moved down her neck, between her shoulder blades, over her hips, caressing her thighs. She sucked in a deep shaky breath and willed herself not to turn around, not to check to see if it was all in her head.

Her will was obviously not nearly as strong as her curiosity. She flicked her hair off her face and shot a quick glance over her shoulder to find Dylan throwing a soft ball from one hand to another, watching her as the girls ran off in opposite directions.

She searched his eyes for the heat she'd felt, but they were closed to her. She gave him a discreet nod. It took longer than was in any way comfortable for him to do the same back.

Maybe if she'd been able to corner him for a minute before his family had cornered her she could have told him this was all Meg's idea. That she'd never had any intention of storming the family compound on her quest to rid the world of incandescent light globes. Perhaps he might not look at her quite so darkly.

Her heart reached out to him. Imploring her to let it do its thing. To care, to want more for herself, to love… To give him the chance to do the same, no matter how great the probability her job, his stubbornness, her fear of getting close, whatever lingering issues he still had with his ex-fiancée all meant that she would get hurt as usual.

She'd never felt the way she felt with Dylan when she'd been with any other man. Or with any other person, for that matter. With him she felt as though parts of herself that had never seen the light of day were now in full bloom.

His dark eyes slid past hers as though she were of no more interest to him than the chair she sat upon.

Her heart sank. Then again, maybe a minute's conversation wouldn't make a lick of difference.

'Don't you think?'

Quinn's deep drawl echoed on the periphery of Wynnie's mind. She turned back to find him watching her with a question in his pale blue eyes.

The only answer she could think in that moment was, 'Right. Of course.'

Brendan leant forwards to grab a napkin, his eyes barely touching hers before he said, 'Dad I'm not sure if you realise this was the one who handcuffed herself to our sculpture a few days back.'

Wynnie felt her neck warm. Dealing with Dylan might have been like bouncing between a rock and a hard place, but she certainly had no ally in Brendan.

Meg grinned at Wynnie, her eyes twinkling as she silently encouraged her to leap in, but as far as she could tell Meg held little sway. She was treated like the princess; not allowed to lift a finger even when she wanted to.

The silver fox, Quinn Kelly, might be her only hope.

'Ah-h-h,' Quinn said, looking at her as though for the first time. 'The Trojan horse.'

She glanced back at Meg hoping to make sense of the comment, but Meg just shrugged.

'Okay, Ms Devereaux, you've made it further than anyone else in your position has ever made it before. I'll give you props for ingenuity. So tell me, why should we spend our time and money reorganising the meticulously efficient way we believe we do business when the largest, richest industrial states in the world aren't bothering?'

Her last chance. With Dylan, and with the Kellys. Dylan

was sending burning arrows into the back of her head; Quinn Kelly was giving her five minutes. The way she saw it she didn't have a choice.

Wynnie sat up straighter in her high chair, clasped her hands atop her knees and looked every one of them in the eye as she said, 'I love ice cream.'

'Ice cream,' Brendan repeated, deadpan, but at least she knew he was listening.

'I lo-o-ove ice cream,' Meg said. 'I'd eat it for breakfast, lunch and dinner if I had my way.'

'Vanilla ice cream is my all-time favourite,' Cameron said, before sending goo-goo eyes at his wife.

She opened her mouth to move on when the scent of clean linen and fresh-cut grass washed over her in a wave of heat.

A large hand curled over the back of her chair, fingers stopping against her shoulder blade, the effect of the touch sluicing much further.

'What did I miss?' Dylan asked from behind her.

'We were having a lovely discussion about ice cream,' his mother said, all politeness.

Wynnie leant forwards ever so slightly but enough that she could focus on her pitch. Four minutes. She could see in Quinn Kelly's eyes that was all she had. And even with Dylan glowering and breathing down her neck, she was in so deep already she was going to use every one of them.

'I love ice cream,' Wynnie repeated. 'In fact, my love affair with the stuff could be considered counter-productive.'

Dylan snorted. Her cheeks warmed, she gritted her teeth, and crossed her legs away from his general direction.

She smiled at Mary, who was smiling at her. 'So I always buy low fat. My friend Hannah rolls her eyes and tells me if I truly wanted to make a difference to my waistline I wouldn't eat the stuff at all. But I know myself too well for all that. I will eat ice cream. So I figure if I can do a little bit of good by choosing low fat, then that's a step in the right direction.'

'Here! Here!' Meg shouted, winking at her.

Wynnie gave her a quick smile before directing her next words to Brendan, to Cameron, to Quinn. 'The same logic applies to all sorts of occurrences in our daily lives. We all use clothes dryers when it's wet outside, we heat our towels on the column heater before getting out of the shower on a cold winter's morning, we buy plastic packaging, we get our bills in the mail. But if we all also remembered to unplug any appliances that aren't being used, if we recycled our newspapers and milk bottles, received bills and memos via e-mail not envelope, that's a step in the right direction. Just by doing a little bit of good.'

The table was quiet. Too quiet. Her heart began to thud as she tried to decipher from the brilliant poker faces around her if she'd made it through.

With thirty seconds up her sleeve she uncrossed her legs, sat forward knocking her knees and letting her hands talk for her. 'I grew up in a place where the people were drawn to the principles of permaculture, of living off whatever the community could produce. My family saw this as a way of taking responsibility for their existence, so this stuff is not new to me. But I'm just like you. I eat meat. I wear leather. I like fishing. I'm not suggesting we all live in eco-bubbles and eat nothing but spinach. I just think we can *all* try a little harder to think not only of ourselves but the wider community, as well.'

Quinn's eyebrows slowly rose. 'To not only think of ourselves, did she say?' He shot a look at his wife. 'Do you think that was a direct jibe at our lot?'

Mary's smile was wide and genuine. 'If so, it was a fair one.'

Wynnie released a long slow breath and planted her shaking feet firmly on the ground. She'd been accused once upon a time of pushing too hard, of getting too close, she could only hope she hadn't done it again. Or if she had, this time it had worked.

When Quinn clicked his fingers and a man appeared as if from a hole in the ground, he asked for more iced tea, and Wynnie knew she wasn't about to be kicked out on her rear.

Quinn turned back to her, his eyes smiling. 'So, Wynnie, tell me, where did you grow up?'

The question was so unexpected she sat there in stunned silence. She had brought it up, in a round-about kind of way, but the details were something she'd much prefer not going into lest her past and her present begin to intersect—

'Nimbin.' Dylan's deep voice rang loud and clear in her right ear as he leant over and grabbed a condensation-covered glass of his own. He took a long slow sip before adding, 'She grew up in Nimbin.'

'Get out of here!' Meg hollered, cutting into her thoughts. 'The land of milk and hemp. I always thought that place was some kind of myth.'

'So Nimbin's where they grow consciences nowadays,' Quinn said with the kind of smile that would have made Wynnie blush if her cheeks weren't already so filled with a rush of blood they felt as if they were burning.

'Her parents were newlyweds,' Dylan continued, leaning lazily against the arm of her chair—filling her personal space with his warmth, his size, his shadow. 'They attended the Aquarius Festival on their honeymoon and stayed, living off what they grew themselves and home-schooling their kids.'

'Oh,' Mary said, 'so you have brothers and sisters?'

Wynnie's feet suddenly felt as though they were no longer touching the ground. She had to grip the arms of her chair lest she slide right out of it onto the grass.

But Dylan didn't, he couldn't *possibly* know—

'One brother,' he answered for her, and her throat burned as though it suddenly filled with bile.

She glanced up at him to find his face was haloed by the bright light of the setting sun. But he was no angel. He was the devil incarnate. Somehow he knew her darkest secrets. How long he'd known them she had no idea.

But she did know that in that moment he was showing his

cards. If he saw the need to do so, he would use her secrets in any way he saw fit.

As if realising she was close enough to physically hurt him if she saw fit, Dylan drifted away.

'I'm glad to hear it,' Mary Kelly's voice murmured in a fuzzy corner of Wynnie's shut-down brain. 'Family is everything. If more people realised that, then feeling a part of a wider community would naturally ensue.'

Quinn stood, his wife was at his side in a lightning flash, cradling his elbow. Wynnie lifted slightly off her chair wondering if he needed help.

But Mary's beatific smile made her realise it was love that had her at her husband's side, not anything more sinister.

'I like you,' Quinn said, patting her on the shoulder. 'I hope Dylan sees the light and lets you in. KInG has become far too stuffy these past months.' And then he and his wife were heading slowly back to the house.

Dylan? she repeated in her head. *He hoped Dylan would see the light? But—*

Brendan cleared his throat and shot her a quick smile as he stood, as well. 'Nice pitch, Ms Devereaux. Inventive as all get out. If you're ever looking to get a real job, give me a call.'

Meg glanced over her shoulder before flouncing away from the table. 'Don't go anywhere,' she said. 'I'll be back. I just have to make a phone call. Great job, though. A whole afternoon and I haven't been the centre of attention once!'

Cameron and his wife, Rosie, had quietly disappeared some time around the first mention of ice cream, meaning Wynnie had been left alone to try to pick up the pieces of what had just happened.

She pulled herself from her chair and spun to find Dylan a metre away. His eyes were blank, his stance far too cool for a man who had just quietly proven he could ruin her life with a word if it suited him.

Her fingers curled into her palms so that she didn't do as

she so wanted to do and slap some life back into his beautiful aloof face.

'They never had any intention of giving me a chance, did they?' she asked, her voice husky, skirting the subject that truly ate her up.

'Of course not. They'd never side with someone outside the family over me.'

A glint lit his eyes. She reacted to it physically as she always had. She slapped down the rising heat and thought cold thoughts, such as how it might feel if she encased his large bare feet in concrete and dropped him to the floor of the Arctic Ocean.

She waved a hand towards the big house which was mostly hidden by the sun sail above her head. 'Yet you just stood there and let me make my pitch to them, knowing it wouldn't make a lick of difference.'

'Would you have kept mum if I'd asked you to?'

She knew the answer was no, so she bit her tongue and just glared at him instead.

'And how the hell did you know all that other stuff about… me?' She paced back and forth and waved her arms about her head so fast she felt like a helicopter preparing to take off.

He sipped at his drink. 'I had you investigated.'

Her blood turned to acid in her veins. 'You what?'

Then she realised if it wasn't because she'd slipped and told him more than she should have in her weaker moments around him, then he probably knew everything.

He slid his spare hand into his pocket and downed the last of his drink, his tanned throat working with every swallow. The fact that she could still find him sexy, even now, scared the hell out of her.

'There's no point in being all sanctimonious about this, Wynnie. I'd bet my house on the fact that you had me researched to the nth degree before deciding I was the one you had to have.'

Her pacing range shortened but didn't lessen in fury one bit. 'So when you leapt in all heroic and saved me from the big bad reporter who knew my real name—'

'You mean, last night.'

She flapped a hand at him, as if it didn't matter that it had been less than twenty-four hours since he'd spent hours kissing every inch of her that he possibly could. As if that weren't the crux from which all this new tension between them had sprung.

'You knew everything,' she continued. 'You weren't protecting me from him. You were saving the information for when you might need it yourself.'

This time he didn't argue, didn't interject. Because she'd hit the mark dead centre.

The moist grass squished beneath her shoes and she replayed every conversation they'd ever had, every time she'd thought she'd had the upper hand, every moment he'd treated her body as if it were the most beautiful thing he had ever seen.

Her pacing stopped; she faced him, crossed her arms and asked, 'Tell me the truth. Right here and now. Have you been playing me all along?'

He blinked. The shutters cleared. The man behind the dangerously charming mask appeared.

Her heart reached out to him, begging him to stay, to break through. But all too soon the glint in his eyes returned and he was lost behind the practised blue haze.

She said, 'From the moment you walked out into that forecourt and gave me that seductive little smile, from when you sent Eric to check your iron to get me alone, and our dance, when you let what's-his-name punch you first, and let me play nursemaid, and let me…' She had to stop to take a breath. Letting him see how important last night had been was not in her best interests in that moment. 'Has every second been a game to you?'

His cheek curved, her stomach dropped and he said, 'Have I ever done anything to make you think it hasn't?' He took a second to let his eyes rest on her left shoulder, the curve of her waist, her right thigh. His hot dark eyes were locked right on hers as he finished the thought.

She blinked up at him, the memories flooding over her, replacing bad thoughts with good. No man who made love like that could possibly be all bad.

'Dylan,' she said, her voice imploring.

But the shutters came back down over his cold blue eyes—bang, bang.

She threw her hands in the air, spun on her heel and stalked away towards the side of the big house.

Coming here had been a mistake. To badger him into listening to what she had to say about her life's work was one thing, to allow him to see her in a moment when her heart felt as if it were beating outside her chest was just plain reckless.

She heard his footfalls right behind her. 'Stop following me.'

'I'm not, we're just going in the same direction and you're so small my strides eat yours for breakfast.'

'Ha! Like you'd have a clue what I eat for breakfast. You were out of there so fast last night you left skid marks in your wake. Oh, sorry. I'd forgotten, your investigator probably gave you a rundown on how I like that, as well!'

His fingers wrapped around her elbow, slowing her down. She twisted her arm away. He slid an arm about her waist instead, turning her to face him, and the guy had such a hold her only way out would be to slip to her knees and crawl.

She pushed her hands against his chest, dug her toes into her shoes and glared at him. Let him speak next. Let him find another new way to prove to her that she was damned to choose very, very badly when she chose to love.

She squeezed her eyes shut tight lest he see the startling realisation that had been slowly dawning on her all the long day.

He said, 'We both knew what we were getting into last night.'

Her laughter was slightly hysterical.

'Look at me,' he demanded.

Her eyes flew open; she glared at him for all she was worth.

'We are combatants on a field of play,' he said. 'And last night we simply took a moment's armistice. If that's all it was, then there is nothing wrong with that.'

He reached out and tucked his hand into her hair, and again she felt his eyes looking for answers in hers while only he knew the question.

His suddenly hot gaze trailed down her face to rest on her lips. 'Nothing at all.'

Before she even had the chance to draw breath, he drew her in, and he kissed her. Hard, soundly, in a way meant to wipe anything from her mind but him.

She fought against the instant rising waves of heat lapping against her stomach, her breasts, her throat. But when her hands began to soften against his solid chest she was gone.

Her fingers curled into his T-shirt and pulled him closer as she pressed herself along his pitilessly rock-hard length.

They kissed as though every word, every smile, every clash between them thus far had been foreplay. Wild, unchecked, hopeless passion sent Wynnie's senses spiralling away from her and over the edge of reason.

When there was nothing reminding her who and where she was but a speck of sunlight far, far away in the corner of her mind, she somehow managed to drag herself back to the surface. Not nearly soon enough.

She glared at his rising and falling chest as sense returned like a slap to the back of the head. 'I knew you were hard,' she said, her voice red raw, 'but I never thought you could be cruel. No matter how much you might want me gone, you should never have used sex as a weapon.'

His smouldering eyes cooled until they were lit as though by chips of ice. 'Honey—'

'Don't call me "Honey",' she shot back, 'like I'm some kind of interchangeable body to warm your bed. Like I'm not important enough for you to bother knowing my name.'

'Fine,' he said, 'Guinevere.'

She reared back as though slapped, and he let her go. She stumbled now he no longer held her up.

A butterfly fluttered past her nose. Beautiful, fragile, its days numbered. With it she found her centre.

'If I'm right,' she said, 'and you have all sorts of juicy information in that dossier of yours, you'll know that I am an abnormally forgiving person, even of those who have used me and hurt me more than one person deserves to be hurt. But right this second, I am looking forward to the day you rot in hell.'

Energy surged through her, giving her the impetus to finally walk away.

Wynnie all but ran as she rounded the side of the house. She'd send Mary a note thanking her for lunch, but right now she couldn't face a one of them.

As always happened when she walked away from him she felt Dylan's eyes burning a trail down the length of her body.

Only this time it didn't fill her with the kind of sexual energy that would keep her going all day. This time it felt like goodbye.

CHAPTER TEN

ON THURSDAY evening Wynnie trudged up her lushly over-grown footpath, her eyes feeling full of grit after not having slept properly in days, her feet sore from wearing high heels for twelve hours at a time as she worked herself senseless, her throat dry from the hundred odd cold calls she'd made in the past four days trying to line up preliminary interviews with the heads of every big company in town.

That was all she deserved for screwing up so badly with the only company she'd even thought about reeling in. Falling into bed with the target; what had she been thinking?

She slammed open the mouth of her neat white mailbox and grabbed the mail as vehemently as such a thing could be done.

Once inside the cottage, she kicked off her slinky red high heels, checked her phone messages to find the one from Meg from a few days back had *still* not been deleted from the ruddy machine.

'I saw you kissing after lunch,' Meg's lilting voice called through the small speaker. *'Don't worry. It was only me peeking out the window. The rest of them are far too self-involved to have noticed a thing. I just wanted to say "yay"! And even though D's a right pain, he needs someone like you to keep him in line. See ya soon!'*

She jabbed a finger at the machine, several times, until it read zero messages. But, knowing she'd only have to hear the damn message again the next day, she pulled the cord out of the wall.

Punishment. That was what her life had become. An endless round of paying for her mistakes.

It had been four days since she'd laid eyes on Dylan Kelly. Four days since she'd heard his voice, been witness to his sexy smile, and her heart still felt as bruised as if she'd walked away from him five minutes ago.

Absently rubbing her right foot up her aching left calf, she threw her mail on the dining table and flicked through it. Junk mail, pay-TV-overdue-account reminder addressed to the previous tenants, and the thick familiar feel of a postcard.

Her foot slid to the floor. She needed them both flat on the ground for this. Her blood thundered in her ears and her breath released on the one word: 'Felix.'

She ran her thumb over the shiny picture on the front. Palm trees. Blue water. White sand. Tahiti.

She didn't need to turn the postcard over to know it was from him, but she did anyway. As always hoping for a message, some kind of word on where he was, what he was doing, that he was safe.

And as always the back side was blank, bar a stamp, her address written in someone else's hand, and a postmark from of all places, Lima. It would only lead to a dead end.

She slumped till her backside rested against the dining table.

More punishment to add to the rest. A teasing reminder that she had someone out there who was meant to be on her side no matter what, but she couldn't have any contact with him. And a thump to the heart reminding her that she had let herself be denigrated, torn apart, broken down all to save his guilty hide.

And all she ever got for her troubles was a batch of blank postcards.

She flicked her hair off her face and her eyes fell on the chocolate-brown couch with the red angora rug draped lazily over it.

Postcards and a string of bad decisions when it came to knowing who to trust. And for the first time in her life the ache to see her brother again had less to do with love for him than it had to do with wanting to shake the breath out of the little punk and make sure he had a clue how he'd messed up her life.

She threw the postcard onto the pile of junk mail, and headed into the kitchen. There she found a bottle of red wine and a large glass and took them both into her bedroom.

Wynnie cradled a glass of red wine, her third, in her palm as she sat cross-legged in the middle of her bed, still dressed in the off-the-shoulder, belted, short black dress she'd worn to work.

Her phone lay at the tip of her bare right foot, Felix's postcard at the top of the left, and a phone number scribbled on the back of an old receipt clutched in her spare hand.

She'd been staring at the phone number for a good hour already. She'd even managed to get halfway through it before hanging up twice.

She put her wine on the bedside table; it only sloshed a very little before steadying. She shook out her hands, cricked her neck, picked up her phone and dialled.

It rang once. She took such a deep breath she started to see stars on the edge of her vision.

It rang twice. She closed her eyes and bounced up and down on the spot to try to release the influx of energy surging through her body.

An all too familiar male voice answered. 'Hello?'

She stopped bouncing, her eyes flew open. Her voice cracked, just a little, as she said, 'Dylan?'

A long pause. Then, 'Wynnie.'

The sound of his voice was like an elixir, warming all the cold places inside her. She drew her knees to her chest and wrapped her arms about her shins, trying to keep the remarkable feeling locked inside as long as she could.

She closed her eyes and a stray tear slid down her cheek. She hastily swiped it away, knowing it would probably taste of Cab Sav. 'Look, I'm truly sorry to ring you like this. Mortified, in fact. But I called Meg and asked for your number and she gave it to me.'

She thought she'd sounded perfectly fine but he must have picked up an off note as his voice came back to her strong, determined, and most of all, protective. 'Wynnie, what's wrong? Are you all right? What's happened?'

'Nothing's wrong.' Nothing new anyway. 'I just had a question that couldn't keep. It's not a work question so I didn't want to bother you during work hours.'

'Since when did propriety become your catchphrase?' he asked, his voice now liquid sex, as if he hadn't been a cold-hearted bastard and she hadn't told him to rot in hell when they'd last seen one another.

It hurt, it ached, it made her hold herself tighter, but at least he hadn't hung up.

Not sure she would be able to cope with any more complications to her life in that minute she decided to get to the point. 'It's about you having had me investigated.'

'We've been over this,' he said.

She waved her hand in front of her face as though he could see her. He stopped talking as though he could, too.

'I know,' she said. 'I just... There's something...'

'Just ask.'

She closed her eyes and this time tears poured down her face. 'My brother. Do you know where he is?'

'Wynnie—'

'I don't care how you know,' she said on a rush of garbled air. 'I don't care if you have my bank account passwords, statements from my kindergarten teachers, or my bra size on file. I really don't give a flying hoot at this point in time. I just need to know about Felix. I have to see him. I need to talk to him, to know if he's all right.' *To let him know I'm not*. 'So if you know anything, anything at all, I need you to tell me.'

Her breaths came laboured and deep and she gripped so tight to the phone her fingers ached, and years worth of sorry tears continued pouring down her cheeks.

His voice was gruff when he asked, 'Where are you?'

'Home.' She sniffed.

'Don't go anywhere.'

'Dylan—'

'I'm coming over.'

He hung up.

She stared at the phone through her steamy eyes. She gave a great big sniff, wiped frantically at her face and tried calling back, but there was no answer.

She threw the phone on the bed and rubbed her face hard.

Why had she ever thought she might get what she wanted from him, ever? He was so damned contrary!

The moment she'd reconciled herself to not having him she got him. And when she knew how much she wanted him, she couldn't have him.

She lay back on the bed with a thump and stared at the wide, still ceiling fan.

But when she *needed* him…he came.

Fifteen minutes later Wynnie was pacing the living-room floor, her bare feet making sharp slapping sounds on the wood, when a loud rap sounded at her door.

Her disobedient heart rapped even louder against her ribs. Four days. Four days without seeing him, and despite everything her heart raced like an excited puppy.

She took a deep breath. She'd open the door, she'd show him she was fine, tell him she'd had a glass too many and should never have called, and then he'd think badly of her—nothing new there—and leave.

She opened the door, expecting to find herself faced with

he pitiless suit. But there he stood in a crushed white long-sleeved T-shirt poking out of the bottom of an old-fashioned black blazer and old jeans that fell soft at the knees, frayed and splayed at the hem, and clung lovingly everywhere else.

In a suit he was devastating. Dressed down, as though he was trying to blend in with regular folk, only showcased how truly beautiful he was.

'Dylan,' she croaked, 'go home.'

His blue eyes were dark. His cheeks tight. His mouth a thin horizontal line. 'Not until I know that you're okay.'

She shrugged. 'That's not your concern.'

His cheek twitched. But he didn't contradict her. Her heart gave a sorry little tug.

'Either way, I'm here now, so why don't you just let me in?'

And then from behind his back he pulled a bucket of ice cream. Dairy Bell's Nuts About Chocolate, the most decadent ice cream in the history of ice cream. 'You never mentioned your favourite flavour but this was always Meg's favourite when she was having a "crapola day". Her words.'

She took the ice cream and cradled it under her arm, the cold good for her. It helped keep the heat he aroused in her veins from going to her head.

'I shouldn't have called.'

'Yet you did.'

Her next breath in was unsteady. The fact that this man knew *everything* about her was a relationship she'd never experienced before. Hannah knew pieces. But Hannah didn't know her grief and her guilt. This man did.

Yet he wasn't her friend. He wasn't even her lover. He was a compulsion, an illusion, a threat.

But she was so tired. Tired of keeping secrets, and watching her words, and holding on so tight to her life lest all the disparate pieces got carried away by the lightest gust of wind.

He knew everything. Telling him more couldn't hurt. Maybe, with his connections, it might even help.

'I could do with a coffee,' he said, his eyes boring into hers. 'And your ice cream's melting.'

She stood back and let him in.

They sat at the dining table. Dylan at the head, silently watching Wynnie on her chair pulled at an angle from the side of the table. Her knees were hugged to her chest, the spoon with which she'd eaten half the tub of ice cream resting against her mouth, her eyes roaming over a spread-out stack of mail on the table.

Her black dress draped from one shoulder leaving it exposed. Her hair was pinned off her face, her long fringe sweeping across her brow. Her eyes were dark and smudged. Her skin as pale as milk. Her lips bare.

She'd never looked more beautiful, or more fragile. And that was the combination that got him into trouble with her again and again.

Dylan held tight to his cold coffee mug to make sure his hands didn't rove anywhere else, and questioned himself for about the tenth time what he was doing there. Even though looking back he was conscious he had overreacted and over-complicated what had only been a night of great sex, the result, their parting, had been for the best.

'When Felix was little,' she said as though they were mid-conversation about the guy, not that it was the first time his name had been mentioned since Dylan had arrived, 'he couldn't pronounce Guinevere. He called me Wynnie. So when the police finally told me they were done with me, when I knew I had to have a fresh start, somewhere to wash off that whole experience, I began by shedding the name that had been splashed all over the papers, took my grandmother's surname and chose a new path.'

She stuck a finger in her mouth and nibbled on the end. Her lips shone with moisture. Her eyes blinked languidly as her memories took her far away. Dylan pressed his feet hard into the floor, and kept his focus from the couch lurking just over her bare right shoulder. From their one night of phenomenal sex.

'I like the name Guinevere,' she said, her eyes suddenly focusing and swinging to his, full of accusation.

He held up both hands in surrender. 'It's a beautiful name. French?'

She blinked again, and then her cheek lifted into a slow half-smile. 'I think the name is old French but I have no idea beyond that. What's with you and the French thing?'

'It's the accent. It speaks to my G-spot.'

'Mmm. Well, all I know is that Guinevere means fair and smooth. Does that work for you?'

'Don't ask. And Felix?' Time to bring the conversation where it needed to be. Flirting, though so very difficult not to engage in around this woman, was not helpful.

'Happy,' she said on a ragged sigh.

He furrowed his brow.

'His name means happy. And he was as a kid. Joyful, and interested and just the sweetest thing on the planet. But after my parents passed away I moved to the city to go to uni and he stayed behind to finish school with his friends around him and… I don't know. He must have fallen in with some radical types who saw Nimbin as a breeding ground for their bio-nomical army.'

She frowned at the pile of mail again.

'Then what happened?' he asked.

He knew the nuts and bolts. He'd read the papers Jack had given him, more than once in an effort to figure her out. But she *needed* to tell him. *That* was why she'd called. And despite his warnings to her on the contrary, it seemed they both somehow recognised she'd be safer telling him than anyone else.

Her finger slid from her mouth to slowly swipe her fringe back from her eyes, but one stray lock fell straight back down. 'He broke into a science lab attached to the uni, in an effort to let the lab rabbits free. Rabbits, of all things. Environmental pests in Queensland. Anyway, the lab was ransacked, chemicals mixed, an explosion occurred, injuring seven. One man…' She paused, swallowed. 'One man lost the use of his legs. Eco-terrorism, they called it, and they had it all on security tape. They showed me his sweet face. And when they couldn't find him, they came after me.'

'Where did he go?'

She shook her head, shrugged, her eyes turning the exact liquid brown that made his heart feel as if it were sinking and flying all at the same time.

'Our parents had money before they moved to Nimbin and left us the lot when they died. Enough Felix could travel, and hide, his whole life if he so desired.'

'Have you heard from him since?'

Her eye twitched. He felt her drawing inside herself, away from him. He knew that feeling. Closing ranks against all but family. It was an instinct that was hard to break.

She said, 'If I hear from him I am supposed to call the police immediately.'

It was an answer that Dylan philosophically understood. But it didn't stop his stomach from contracting in disappointment as she gently pushed him away.

He ran a hard hand across his mouth. It wasn't as though he deserved her trust. He'd threatened to abuse it so many times.

Then she held up a postcard. A tacky beach setting that ought to have had nude sunbathers on it. 'Every few months I get one,' she said. 'Meaning he knows exactly where I am and what I'm doing. But they never give me one damn clue as to where he is.'

'This is from him?' He took the card, turned it over, frowned at the lack of message. This was the thanks she got from the brother whose life she probably saved by giving him the chance to get the hell out of Dodge?

She nodded. 'It came today.'

So much for pushing him away. Her life had hit a hurdle too high to climb alone and she'd called on him.

This woman had the kind of guts he couldn't even imagine. What she'd done for her brother and how she'd created a life from the ashes of her family splitting apart showed courage. But now, the blind faith she showed in him that she trusted he was man enough not to screw her over, knocked the wind from his sails big-time.

He silently gave the card back. She flicked at a corner, again and again, then held it in her lap.

She watched him down the last of his second cup of coffee. She sniffed in deep and let her feet fall to the floor. She sat on her hands and leant forward, her dress draping and shifting across her pale skin.

Finally she looked down at her bare toes, hot-red toenails blinking back up at her. 'I've never told anybody what I told you just now.'

'I can understand why.'

'And you do realise you could run me out of town with what you know.'

He nodded, his mouth turned down. 'I could. But then I would never again wake up in the morning, wondering if you might be about to leap out of my laundry basket. My life would become ever so dull.'

She lifted her head, squinted at him through one eye, and even managed half a smile.

He didn't take his eyes away. He couldn't.

He'd tried to put her from his mind after Sunday's fiasco. He'd tried immersing himself deep into the job that had kept him more than satisfied his whole adult life. He'd tried to appear attentive when Eric gave him the briefs on each new Wynnie wannabe who called, or wrote requesting a formal meeting with him.

But everything seemed to remind him of her strapped to his sculpture with her crazy cheap handcuffs. Of her turning up at his at his coffee shop with bandages wrapped about her tiny wrists. Of how deeply she believed in what she did. Or how thoroughly she had given herself up to him the moment she'd decided that was what she wanted.

She'd called and he'd come. There hadn't been any hesitation. And now that he was here he suddenly wanted to be the man she obviously thought he was. He needed to be.

He leant forwards and held out a hand. She placed her small hand in his. He looked her square in the eye as he said, 'I'm really sorry but I don't know where he is.'

Her throat worked, her eyes shone, her hand in his turned cold. So cold, he wrapped both of his around hers. He saw the torment in her eyes, and wanted to make it his own. But he just couldn't. His plate was overfull looking after those in his life who were his to take care of whether he wanted to or not.

No wonder he'd railed against her when she'd so neatly backed him into a corner the day they first met. It wasn't altogether fun being shown with such clarity how he'd spent his entire life doing the very same thing to himself.

'Okay,' she said on the end of a deep breath in. 'Then that's that.'

She pulled her hand away and leant back in the chair.

He curled his empty fingers into his palm. He hadn't done enough. And he never could.

He was smart enough to have figured out over the past couple of hours what *enough* might entail. That which he now sensed she wanted from him was simply not his to give. He could be tough if she needed tough, he could be self-deprecating if she needed a smile, he could be kind if she needed a break.

But not even for those demanding liquid brown eyes could he again be naïve enough to promise himself to one woman and mean it.

Yet if he walked out of there and didn't at least give her back half the trust she'd given him, he'd never be able to look himself in the mirror again.

He leant his elbows on the table and looked into his coffee mug as though hoping to find the words therein.

'I'm not claiming to have a clue what you went through back then. But I have had had my dirty laundry aired in public once before.'

She leant her elbows on the table, as well, her chin rested on her upturned palms, and she waited for him to go on.

He said, 'I was engaged once, before.'

He flicked her a glance. She gave him a short smile.

'Lilliana Girard was her name.'

'French?' she asked.

He coughed out an unexpected laugh. 'She would have given her right thumb to stake that claim, but no.'

'Sorry. I couldn't help myself. Go on.'

'We were together for three years. Engaged for one of those. And six weeks before the wedding it hit the papers that she'd quizzed a nightclub full of patrons about which European beach resort she ought to move to when she scored millions in the divorce.'

Wynnie cringed and sucked in a slow stream of air between her lips. Soft pouting lips the colour of dusky pink summer roses. Lips that Lilliana would have killed for. Or had they married she would have used his good money to pay for.

'That's harsh,' Wynnie said. 'Are you sure it wasn't a stupid joke? We girls can do silly things after too many drinks. Add a working phone and I'm living proof.'

He shook his head. 'If only it was the alcohol speaking. Once the story broke, people came out of everywhere quoting conversations had, conversations heard, money owed all over town on the proviso she would take care of it all once she was a Kelly.'

Her eyes grew large with shock. 'She *was* a succubus.'

He laughed again. 'That she was. Now I just feel sorry for her. Three years of her life she spent with a man she didn't really love all for the sake of the *stuff* that came with the name of Kelly.'

She dropped one hand to the table. 'And you didn't have the luxury of changing your name and moving away.'

He looked into her eyes. Deep as an ocean. Warm as a blanket. Clear as a summer sky. 'No, I did not.'

Her other hand slid into her chocolate-brown hair, and his fingers began to tingle. 'It can't be easy assuming every new person in your life just wants something from you.'

She'd hit the nail so directly on the head his whole body clanged like metal on metal. Habit had him leaning lazily back in his chair so she wouldn't notice. 'You know what, it's easier than you think.'

Her arms stretched out straight in front of her. This time it was his turn to lay a hand in hers.

'Thank you,' she said, her brow furrowed, her expression earnest.

'What for?'

'For coming over. For not trying to prolong my hope about Felix, thinking that might help. For telling me about Lilliana.'

'You're welcome.'

'You're a good guy.'

'Now don't go thinking nice things about me. You'll only be disappointed.'

She shook her head. 'You have a good heart. You should use it more often.'

'For the betterment of mankind?'

'Why not?'

Her fingers curled around his, weaving in and out, warming them, leaving them bare, creating enough friction in his hands alone to set the rest of him ablaze.

Her constant ability to believe he had a noble side to him was one of the rare pleasant surprises of believing the worst. And one of the reasons he had to slide his hands away and stand.

'Now it's getting late.'

'So it is.' She tilted her head and smiled up at him and it took every ounce of self-control he had not to kneel down before her and kiss his way up those cruelly tempting bare legs, starting with the hot-red toenails.

'And it is a school night,' he added.

'Right you are.' She pushed herself upright with all the energy of someone who'd just run a marathon.

She padded to the front door. He followed. Her petite form filled out her tiny dress to perfection. Her hips swayed adorably with each footfall. Against the black of her dress her pale skin glowed. The nakedness from her neck to that one bare shoulder cried out to be stroked.

She turned at the door, her hands behind her back clasping the handle. But the door remained closed.

He clenched his back teeth and shoved his hands into the pockets of his jeans. 'Are you going to be okay?'

She nodded, shrugged, then shook her head. 'Eventually.'

She blinked fast as her eyes focused in the middle of his chest. When she looked back at him he knew what she was going to say before she even said it.

'Wynnie—' he warned, trying to cut her off.

But she pushed away from the door and padded to him, stopping only when she was close enough he could make out every eyelash, every fleck of colour in her beautiful eyes, every nuance of desire she felt for him.

Her voice cracked when she said, 'I don't want to be alone tonight.'

All the blood in his body shot to the region of his fly. Well, almost all—enough oxygen flittered around his brain for him to give himself one last shot at actually being noble. 'I left out the fact that I now know there was good reason for Lilliana to have never loved me, you know.'

She blinked up at him, unmoved.

'I'm a cold-hearted bastard. I'm insular, I'm jaded, a workaholic, I'm ruthless and I'm self-serving. I don't do forever, I rarely even do "I'll call you tomorrow". And just because I'm here now it does not mean if you ask me to stay I will.'

She reached up and placed a soft hand on his chest. He breathed in deep, which only filled his nostrils with her sweet scent. This woman, this persistent, tangled, beautiful woman who saw him not just as a Kelly, but as the man who could help her save the world.

She repeated, 'I don't want to be alone tonight.'

The breath bled from his lungs, and his self-control along with it. 'Then you don't have to be.'

CHAPTER ELEVEN

WITHOUT another word, Wynnie took Dylan by the hand and led him into her bedroom.

White furniture, white linen, white lilies in a vase on the dresser. The only splash of colour came from a fat potted palm in the corner.

She reached up and stroked a finger down his cheek and his eyes slid back to her. 'But I need you to know I didn't go to your parents' place on Sunday to pitch the proposal to them.'

He brushed her hair behind her ear. 'I know.'

Her right cheek lifted into the sexiest smile he'd ever seen. He ran his thumb over the dimple it left behind. 'And I didn't have you investigated so that I could use your background against you.'

'You didn't?'

His smile was rueful. At least she was smart enough to doubt him—that made him feel slightly less of a cad. He slid the butterfly clip from the chignon at the back of her head and let her hair fall through his fingers. 'You intrigued me to the point of distraction. I needed something to make you go away.'

She swallowed. 'I'm guessing you found one or two.'

His hand cupped her chin as his eyes slid to hers. 'You're guessing wrong.'

'For a pair of professional communicators, we both have a lot to learn.'

'Mmm. Let this be lesson number one.' He leant down to her, slowly, carefully. His tongue darted out to wet his lips, and just as her eyes fluttered closed he kissed her. Feather-light.

The subtlety of the touch was the most exquisite kind of hell, and no less than he deserved for giving into his irrepressible desire for her right when she was at her most vulnerable.

He kissed her again, barely touching, playing, teasing and taking her breath and her warmth in the tiniest increments he could handle.

When suddenly she pressed up onto her tiptoes, grabbed handfuls of his T-shirt and kissed him back.

Lights exploded behind his eyes as her soft warm body melted against him. Her mouth opened wide beneath his, welcoming him in. He'd made himself forget just how good this felt, as though remembering the taste and feel of her would mean he might not be able to give her up.

But, God, this was even better than everything he'd tried to forget. It was as though he could hear her very thoughts. He felt every emotion she had whirling inside her in that kiss— her anger at Felix, her frustration with herself, her confusion about how she felt about him, and how he felt about her.

She snuck a hand behind his head, changed angles and kissed him deeper, harder, more lushly. He almost lost complete control of himself then and there.

He wrapped his arms about her small form and lifted her off the ground. They tumbled onto her bed, legs intertwined, lips joined, hands grasping and clawing and trying to find skin where there was none to be found.

'Wait,' she called out and he all but leapt from on top of her.

The reprieve was like a life ring to a drowning man. He ran a fast hand through his thick hair, leaving it spiking in goodness knew how many directions.

Then he was forced to watch as she lifted her hips off the bed, slid the thick belt from her dress and threw it across the room before whipping her dress over her head, leaving herself naked, bar a pair of innocuous black underpants.

He barely had the chance to take his fill of her soft curves before she dragged him back into her arms.

But suddenly he was wearing far too many clothes.

He dragged his blazer from his back and whipped his T-shirt over his head between kisses. Her groans as he left her lips unattended were the most unendurable siren calls. But he knew this building tension, he knew her body so intimately, he knew it would all be worth it in the end.

He flipped onto his back, his fingers on the top button of his fly, when her hand stilled his progress.

The primal roar of defeat that built up inside him would have burst every window in the house.

Until her fingers peeled his back and took over. She was on her knees beside him, her breathing rate calm considering the circumstances, her dark eyes on the job at hand.

One button. His head fell back onto the bed.

A second button. He curled his fingernails into the bedspread.

The third button snapped and he jerked as the backs of her knuckles scraped against his erection.

She swung a leg over his thighs until her centre nestled against the bottom of his fly. She shifted closer, her legs spreading wider and her eyes turned to coal.

This is insane, he thought. *Pure sublime insanity.*

She leant forward, her small full breasts tipping forward, their pink peaks making his mouth water. Then her hand slid between his open fly and his cotton boxers and she cupped him as her teeth bit down on the softest part of his ear lobe.

He lasted about ten seconds before the fire inside him became too much. Even though he fought against the wrongness of what he was doing, he wasn't near ready for it to end. If they were going to do something foolish, they might as well do it right.

In one smooth move he tilted his ear out of reach of her

transcendent teeth, grabbed her blessed hand, lifted a knee between her thighs and rolled her onto her back.

Her adorable frown as she realised she'd been usurped was almost his undoing.

'Trust me,' he growled.

Time ticked by. Time in which he could have decided to be a better man and left her to get over him in peace.

But when her brow cleared, her eyes turned to molten gold, and she lifted her arms above her head in complete surrender, his position on the dark side was forever cemented.

He rid them both of the last of their clothes.

He slid her left knee to a right angle and pinned it to the bed with his leg, then set to teasing his tongue over every inch of her that had drawn his eye at any time since he'd first met her—the inside of her delicate wrists, the sexy dip above her clavicle, the tiny crease at the corner of her luscious lips.

He slowly drew her breast into his mouth. Then as she began to writhe beneath him his tongue circled her nipple. He didn't stop until she cried out from the pain of it.

Then when he knew she could stand it no longer, and with his leg still pressing hers apart, he cupped her.

He knew her so well. Every whimper, every flicker of pleasure lighting her golden eyes, every jerk beneath his hand. He knew her as if she'd been made to be pleasured by him and him alone.

The beauty and instinct of her response to him took him on the ride right along with her. Every whisper of heat that curled through her undulating body curled through him. Every catch of breath seared his own lungs. Every time their eyes connected he felt as if he knew her as well as he knew only himself.

His need soon became too great to ignore. He stroked his thumb against the perfect juncture between her legs and she bucked against him, grabbing his arms for support as she spilled apart beneath his touch.

But he didn't stop there. He couldn't. The moment her

breaths grew comfortable he brought her to the brink again. The look in her dark eyes as she clung to him was almost furious but at the same time she silently begged him to never stop.

When her own body gave way beneath the billows of pleasure, Dylan kissed her hard, drinking in her every breath, every moan until he was beyond ready for his own release.

How he'd managed to keep so long from doing so he had no idea. His patience, his absolute need to draw things out as long as he possibly could, even while he ached for her, while his erection remained strong and ready, was coming from somewhere other-worldly.

He glanced at his jeans. Too bloody far away. There was a condom in his wallet. He needed it now. But before he had the chance to tell her, she wrapped her legs about his hips and drew him in.

He slid inside her, a perfect fit. The sensation of skin on skin a phenomenon. The combination of friction and heat, and passion, and abandon and the wild, natural beauty of the woman in his arms took him somewhere he'd never been near before; she took him to the edge of heaven.

Clear, perfect, flawless, blameless, aspiring heaven.

And they made love as though they both knew it would be the last time. As if a lifetime's worth of pleasure had to be reaped from that one experience.

Dylan closed his eyes and tried not to imagine that he would never have an experience like it again. He let everything go bar the feel of her, the scent of her, the taste of her and finally, eventually, relief came.

Dylan woke up, stretched his arms over his head and opened his eyes. A wide-brimmed ceiling fan sent long shadows across a white ceiling. He was not in his own bed.

He glanced sideways to face a curtain of silky dark hair splayed across a white pillow and a pale naked back glowing in the moonlight.

Wynnie....

He reached out to run his hand down her beautiful back, then stopped himself just in time. Making love to her had been selfish enough, prolonging any kind of connection would be plain cruel.

He pushed the sheet aside, slid from the bed, stepped into his jeans and collected the rest of his clothes before padding silently from the room.

He stopped at the doorway, allowing himself one last glance. She looked so young, so fresh, so unsullied. He'd always thought himself a cut above his whole life. A Kelly with the privilege, smarts, sense and pride that came with it. But looking at that peaceful face he knew Wynnie deserved far better than him.

He moved into the kitchen and finished dressing. And that was when he saw the postcard that had set this unexpected night in motion propped on the bench by a bowl of loose change.

So innocuous looking. So tactless.

If Jack ever did track her brother down he'd ring the kid's skinny neck for what he'd done to his sister. Not just the once but over and over again for every time he reached out, yet gave her nothing real to hold on to.

Dylan grabbed the postcard, found a pen, turned over the card to its blank white back and did what the kid ought to have done himself.

He wrote: 'Sun's shining. Having a blast. Wish you were here.'

Once it was too late to take them back, he ran his thumb over the words, hoping she would never guess that, for the five seconds he had taken to write them, the words could well have come from him.

He propped the postcard writing side out where she'd left it and he walked out of her cottage and out of her life just as he'd warned her he would.

Dylan shoved his hands in the pockets of his jeans, and

urned the collar of his jacket up to stave off the cool night air
s he jogged out to his car.

That was it. Enough was enough. The time had come for
im to snap back into focus and get on with the life he'd
nown before she came along.

Because the corner he'd backed himself into—the titanic
esponsibility of protecting his prodigious family from every
ind of harm, no matter what he might have to sacrifice in
rder to do so—was so large a part of who he now was, going
ack there was all he knew how to do.

Wynnie trudged into the office late Friday morning, feeling
ke a wrung-out rag.

The postcard, half a bottle of wine, half a tub of ice cream,
Dylan, the postcard… How she managed to get out of bed at
all was a testament to her dedication to her work.

She pushed her sunglasses higher onto her nose to cut out
he glare of the overhead lights and wondered how on earth she
ould stand going another round of phone calls to CEOs and
managing directors who didn't want to give her the time of day.

Dedication, schmedication. After she checked her mes-
ages she was going to take a sickie and that was that.

Because last night… She'd shown Dylan exactly how she
elt about him. She knew he'd seen she was in deep, and that
was why he'd stayed. He'd all but told her he wasn't in the
ame place, and that was why he'd left.

Still, when she'd seen the fresh handwriting on the postcard
er heart had leapt. Till she had realised his sweet words had
een his way of telling her he knew why she'd been so stead-
ast with Felix even though the kid didn't know it himself.

Family first, that was what he'd been telling her. For her.
And for him. It had been his way of setting her free.

And now her heart felt as if it had been bruised, stung,
oisoned and flicked with sharp fingernails. It seemed she'd
ever learn.

She turned the corner into her office and was met with standing ovation from all the staff. She stumbled backwards knocking over a potted mulberry plant and losing her sun glasses down her top.

Once she'd righted herself she looked over her shoulder t see what she was missing.

Hannah stepped forwards from the crowd. 'Where the he have you been?' she whispered through a massive toothy smile

'Errands,' Wynnie said, rather than, *I slept through my alarm because I was up much of the night having hot break-up se with a possible client of ours who I was never really going ou with even though I'm fairly sure that I am actually crazy in lov with.* 'Do you want to tell me what on earth's going on?'

'It's been one hell of a morning. Faxes, e-mails, the phone have been ringing off the hook.'

'And…?'

Hannah stepped back, spread her arms at Wynnie as if sh were the prize on a game show and shouted, 'And Eric Carlisl from the Kelly Investment Group just rang to say that a terms proposed by you have been agreed to and that he wi be the new point man on the CFC/KInG joint venture.'

The office went crazy once more, this time throwin confetti at her made of crushed two-minute noodles they' probably found in the staff kitchen. When champagne cork started popping Wynnie ducked her head and made a beelin for the washroom.

She wrapped her hands around the edge of the cold sin and waited until her heavy breathing settled into a non fainting type rhythm. Then she let go, and pulled her hair o her face and looked at herself in the mirror.

Somehow she looked just fine. Her hair was neat an bouncing. Her make-up was flawless. Her deep purple velve top with its plunging neckline, and her skin-tight, pre-love designer jeans were just saucy enough for her workmates t shake their heads and think, *Wow, weren't we clever to hir this spitfire.* She didn't look as though she'd been to hell, and heaven and back again in the past twenty-four hours.

She was so damned good at her job of making people think what she wanted them to think nobody even knew when she was a raging mess.

Nobody except Dylan. Barely three words into the phone call and he'd known.

The washroom door swung inwards, and Hannah's head popped through. 'Sweetie. Whatcha doing in here?'

She squinted at her picture-perfect reflection in the mirror. 'It's a really long story.'

Hannah shut the door behind her and locked it. 'The champagne's a-flowing. They won't even notice we're gone. I've got time.'

Wynnie turned and leant her backside against the sink. And she filled Hannah in on the briefest update possible. Leaving out certain things. Leaving out Felix and his postcard, and Dylan and his succubus. She found she couldn't find the words to talk to Hannah about her family, even though she'd lived through the worst of it with her. Yet last night, with Dylan, the words had spilled out so easily she'd wondered how she'd ever found it hard before.

'Sheesh,' Hannah said.

'I know, right? And right now, I've just been given what I wanted all along—the biggest client the CFC could have landed. And it was all my doing. I should have been doing cart-wheels and demanding high fives of everyone in the office.'

'But not so much?'

'Not so much.'

Wynnie looked down at the pointy toes of her shoes. Actually she felt a lot like crying. Again. 'I didn't earn it. He's given it to me as a consolation prize.'

It was Dylan's way of saying thanks but no thanks, only this time not to her proposal but to her.

'I'm such an idiot.'

'You're a trouper.'

'And you know what? I'm angry! For him to do it this way, and through Eric… If there weren't so many other people involved with the deal, and if the outcome wasn't so bloody fantastic, I'd rip the contract up and eat it piece by piece while standing in front of his bloody building.'

'Don't be ridiculous. You'd recycle the paper it was printed on.' Hannah moved over and leant on the sink next to hers. 'I did try to warn you, hon. He's a hard man from a hard family. And you are so very, very soft.'

That was just it. His family was lovely. And he was kind, and gentle and caring. Or maybe it was exactly as Hannah said and she was just too soft to assume the worst. Always had been. Always would.

Wynnie leant her heavy head on her friend's shoulder. 'I think I deserve a long weekend.'

'I think so, too.' Hannah gave her a nudge with her hip. 'Go. Right out the front door now. And don't come back till like Wednesday. I'll cover for you.'

Wynnie gave her a quick kiss on the cheek, grabbed her purse and fled before she changed her mind.

As she hit the pavement outside the building, warm spring sunshine beating down on her face, she wondered if Dylan had any idea the good he'd done by approving the deal. Not for her, but for the city. She doubted it. So much she wanted to ring him and blast him and tell him off and applaud him and kiss him all at the same time.

Argh, he was so frustrating! Even now, even after it was all said and done. He was one great hulking clueless walking contradiction. And *that* was why she loved him.

He was beautiful; he was challenging. But most of all she loved him for his principles. She loved him because of the strength of his loyalty to those he loved. He was everything she hoped she could be.

He just refused to see it.

But she couldn't tell him. The deal was now in the hands of the CFC ground crews, and Eric. And she knew that this time he wouldn't take her call.

Wynnie was so mentally, emotionally and physically exhausted she slept all Friday afternoon, and most of the day Saturday, feeling as if jet lag had finally hit.

Then bright and early Sunday morning, she got a phone call that woke her up better than a bucket of iced water over the head.

On Sunday morning Dylan sat slumped in his office chair staring out of his large window, looking past the view of South Bank and out into nothingness.

He still wore the same clothes from the day before. His head felt as if a jackhammer had taken up residence inside it, and with Eric not about he had to make his own coffee, the one life skill he readily admitted he sucked at.

His office phone rang.

As he had every time the phone had rung the past couple of days, for a moment he imagined it would be *her*—wanting him, needing him, gently urging him to be a better man.

The very thought of her made him feel tight and loose and wasted. But that was too bad. She was a smart woman, he had no doubt that she knew that postcard was his last hurrah. She wouldn't be calling him again.

By putting Eric in charge of the CFC deal, he'd made damn sure he'd left no avenue for her to even try.

The phone rang again. Loudly. He spun on his chair, flipped it from the cradle and yelled, 'What?'

'Kelly, it's Garry Sloane. Of the Allied Press Corps.'

Dylan gripped the phone tighter. As if he didn't know the exact tones of the scum-sucking cretin who'd been the first to spill his worst day all over the Sunday papers years before.

It was the one downside of his job, that he had to play nice with the sod. Strangling a journalist with his own computer keyboard cord would make it a tad difficult to remain the head of Media Relations.

'Sloane,' he growled, relishing the fact there was someone in the world he disliked more than he currently disliked himself. 'I must have missed the roses and chocolates you sent in apology for assaulting me last weekend.'

'Yeah,' he shot back. 'They're in the mail.'

'What do you want?'

'I'm running a story tomorrow I thought you might like to comment on.'

'Go on.'

'It's not a new story as such, more like a "where are they now" piece. It's about a woman called Guinevere Lambert who got herself into a bit of trouble with the law several years back, and has now suddenly become one of our fair city's favourite daughters. You might know her better as Wynnie Devereaux.'

Dylan shot his chair upright and slammed his fist on his desk so hard his coffee mug jumped and slid off the edge, landing on the carpeted floor with a pathetic thud.

'Shall I continue?' Sloane asked.

'Not over the phone,' Dylan said, his mind whirring a million miles a minute. He shot a look at his watch. 'Meet me at my place in say…three hours. Until then don't call another living soul about this piece.'

'You'd better have something good.'

'You'd better hope I don't slap you with a lawsuit the size of my bank account for the pain and suffering of my split lip.'

'Three hours,' Sloane said.

Then Dylan slammed the phone down so hard it snapped in two.

CHAPTER TWELVE

ON MONDAY morning, when she ought to have been getting ready for work, Wynnie instead sat on her back deck, sipping from a cooling cup of green tea and staring out through the palm fronds filling her small leafy backyard.

The sun was shining, the sky was cerulean blue, a light breeze picked up the scents of the myriad spring flowers dotting the undulating hills around her Spring Hill abode.

This was Brisbane at its best. Something she'd only experienced for about nine months in her late teens before Felix had fallen and her whole life had been whipped out from under her.

The 'beautiful one day, perfect the next' nature of the place hadn't been enough to salve her heart then, and so far it wasn't doing all that much to salve it now.

Knowing she couldn't put off the inevitable for much longer, she moved her glass of orange juice off the top of the folded newspaper, not caring that condensation had left a wet dark ring over the sports section.

She slowly opened it up, her fingers shaking as she turned to the front page, ready to slowly flick through until she found her photograph, her true story, her ticket to unemployment and ridicule and humiliation.

Her hands shook and she kept the paper closed a minute longer. She squeezed her eyes shut, took several deep breaths and tried to meditate her way to a happy place.

When the happiest place she could think of was being wrapped naked in Dylan's strong arms, it didn't help her heart rate settle in the least. Her muscles tensed, her nerves twitched, her skin began to overheat.

Her eyes flew open and she pinched herself on the back of the hand. *Enough*. If she was that worked up before she read the article she might as well knock herself out now.

She gripped the newspaper in both hands.

When Sloane had called, looking for information about her past, she'd told him to go bite himself. Then after pacing the house for twenty minutes she'd called her bosses at the CFC and told them everything, offering her resignation. She'd then called a female reporter who she'd built a relationship with since the handcuff stunt and given her the exclusive.

For the time had come to stop running—from her past, and from her desires. She wasn't Felix. She would never hurt others in the pursuit of getting what she wanted. She was a helper. She was a guardian angel for the planet. But she was also a woman with needs that deserved to be fulfilled without constant concern that an incident in her distant past could ruin it all.

She took a deep breath, opened the paper…

And didn't get past the front page.

She leapt off her chair and stood staring at the headline. Above a photograph of Quinn Kelly it read: The King is Dying, Long Live the KInG.

She sped-read the article so fast she got whiplash.

Quinn, Dylan's gorgeous father, had major heart problems, had suffered two heart attacks in recent months, he no longer ran the family business as everyone thought he did, all of which the family had kept under close wraps. Until now…

The timing rang a bell inside her head. But she had to keep reading. She had to know everything.

A full-page story on the front led to several more inside, all about Quinn's failing health. She held a hand to her heart as she read that he was doing as well as could be expected, but had already taken a large step back in the business and would be retiring as of that day. Brendan had been secretly running the empire for months. There was a special interest piece from Mary Kelly's point of view with a photo of her whole beautiful family that must have been taken recently as Cameron's new wife was in the shot.

But what caught at her most was quote after quote from Dylan. His name was mentioned so many times she wondered if he'd written the article himself. She checked the byline.

Her backside slumped onto the chair so hard she bruised.

'Garry Sloane?' she read aloud in case she was imagining it.

And then everything came together as if a hurricane had passed and she were left surveying the damage in its wake.

She hadn't been the only one with a secret. Hers had been about to be revealed. Sloane was such a sleaze he must have called Dylan after she'd told him where to go. And Dylan had somehow, for some reason, chosen to sacrifice his own intensely held privacy in order to keep hers safe.

To keep *her* safe.

She leapt off the chair and ran inside, grabbed her house keys, realised she was wearing sheer pyjamas and a see-through robe and ran back into her bedroom.

She stripped off her pants, threw a navy velvet jacket over her lacy pyjama top, tugged on jeans hanging over the back of a cane chair, and slid her feet into her handiest shoes which happened to be red high heels.

Whipping her hair from its scrunchy and slapping some sunscreen onto her cheeks, she scooted out to the deck, grabbed the paper, checked she hadn't been imagining the whole thing and then took off out of the front door.

It wasn't yet seven in the morning.

Monday? Yep, Monday.

She knew exactly where the great hulking fool would be.

Dylan stood in line to buy his own double-strength white chocolate mocha with extra cinnamon. It was almost enough for him to rescind Eric's promotion and get the kid back to do his grunt work.

The café door swung open, and something made Dylan turn. Whether it was the shift of chocolate-brown hair on the edge of his vision, the stirring of sexual tension in the air, or just plain instinct, he found himself looking into Wynnie's big beautiful brown eyes.

She stood in the entrance, brandishing what looked like a third of a scrunched newspaper as though she might slap him over the back of the head with it the first chance she had.

And he knew why.

With his father's news out there, he was sure he'd hear from her in the next few days. Or that evening. Or before lunch. Actually if she hadn't called within the next two hours he was going to turn up on her doorstep with a chai latté and a pair of cream buns.

'Wynnie,' he said, his voice as cool as he could hope for it to be considering two steps would put her within touching distance. And that was a mile closer than he'd thought he'd ever get to her again. To that luscious skin, those edible lips, this woman.

'Don't you Wynnie me,' she said, her voice coming to him as though she'd swallowed sandpaper.

He stepped out of line and weaved through the small, and extremely attentive, crowd to manoeuvre her out of the way. 'Well, now I'm confused,' he said with as disarming a smile as he could muster. 'Which name would you prefer I use?'

Her face was livid. Her chest rising and falling. Her hair a shaggy mess. Her eyes wild. He'd never been as turned on in his entire life.

'Stop changing the subject,' she hissed. 'What have you gone and done?'

Their fan club was growing by the second. One young guy even lifted his mobile phone, which gave off the distant click of a photo being taken. Dylan glanced around for an alternative exit, when the girl behind the counter caught his eye, madly waving at him as she was.

She cocked her head to his left, and mouthed, 'Back door.'

He gave her a nod. She smiled and shrugged. And he reminded himself to tip her everything in his wallet the next time he came in.

When Wynnie opened her mouth to rant anew, he grabbed her by the upper arm and half pushed, half dragged her through the crowd, down a small hall, past the kitchen and out of the back door.

A small, hopelessly untended garden stopped sharply at a cliff's edge. Dylan took them down a series of old stone steps until he and Wynnie stood on a secluded jetty jutting out into the Morningside stretch of the Brisbane River. Tall reeds and weeping willows created privacy, a thick fall of jacaranda flowers carpeted the wooden jetty at their feet, and sunshine blasting through thick tufts of flowering yellow wattle leant a strange golden glow over everything.

'Now,' he said, 'what was it you were trying to say?'

She threw the newspaper at him and it scattered to the soft purple ground in slowly wafting pieces. 'Your father is really sick.'

'I know.'

Her face softened. 'I'm so sorry. Please tell your mum if there's anything I can do, I'll do it.'

'Thank you.'

She looked from one eye to the other, the strength of her feelings for him seeping from her very skin. And instead of feeling trapped, or suspicious, or terrified, or unworthy, finally it just felt right.

Then she reached out and slapped him hard on the arm.
'Ow!'

'Oh, shut up. Don't you think I know what you did? Don't you think Garry Bloody Sloane called me first?'

She pushed away from him, paced a step till she hit the water's edge, then spun back. A shaft of sunlight split the glade, lighting on her alone. She appeared to be naked beneath her jacket bar some tiny pieces of lace that flashed at her stomach when she moved. All it seemed he'd have to do was flick open that one button at her waist and all would be revealed. The bruise forming on his arm told him the time was not yet right for such a move. The thickening of his blood told him the time was coming.

'You've kept your father's health concerns private for a very good reason,' she continued, 'so that he has the space to stay healthy. I've kept mum about my past because I feel humiliated that I didn't spend enough time with my own flesh and blood to see the bad coming and people were hurt.'

'People would have been hurt if we didn't tell the truth soon, too.'

'People,' she repeated, again looking deep into his eyes. 'What people?'

'Friends, colleagues, investors, the business itself. It was the right thing to do.'

'And yesterday. You tell me, and I want to hear it from your lips, why suddenly yesterday?'

'You were right,' he said, sliding his hands into the pockets of his black suit trousers so that he could get through this part without touching her, holding her, kissing her. There were things that had to be said first. 'Sloane called me yesterday morning. He told me what he was planning to write about you and he wanted my input.'

She looked so worried, as if maybe she was putting herself on the line for him again, and he was going to let her down again. As if she believed in him so much it physically hurt her to think she could be wrong about him still. He'd never wanted to hold her so much.

'All I knew was that I had to do everything in my considerable power to make sure he didn't do it.'

'Why?'

Hell, had his stubbornness wounded her that badly?

He took a step towards her. 'Wynnie, honey, you know why. You've known why far longer than I have. I did it because you are braver and stronger and far more honest than I will ever be.'

She swallowed hard.

He reached out and took her arm. She didn't flinch. She didn't pull away. He took her other arm, and though it was physically nearly impossible, he left enough space between them for her to breathe.

'I called a family meeting yesterday afternoon,' he said. 'I told them I had accepted your proposal on behalf of KInG as it was smart and necessary and up until that moment I had been acting like a horse's ass. I also told them that the time had come for all of us to stop hiding behind the walls of Kelly Manor and to come clean. If we were going to move forward, as a business, and as a family, we needed to unburden ourselves of everything holding us back.'

'You said all that?'

He took a small step closer. She had to tilt her head to look him in the eye. Her exposed neck was almost too much temptation. Almost. He knew there was better yet to come.

'I told them all that, and I could feel the relief sweep through the room. As it turns out I can be rather persistent when I want to be and since damage control is my area they've agreed to keep mum for my sake all this time.'

'So it's all okay? With your family, I mean? They're not angry with you?'

'It's better than okay. Because I also told them that I hadn't come to that conclusion lightly. I told them that Garry Sloane, of all people, had forced me to prioritise my life in a split second. And it had been so easy it was ridiculous.'

He made sure he had a good grip. He'd had time to process all of this. Still his voice was very slightly shaky as he said, 'I told my family that I realised in that split second that I had met the woman I wanted to spend the rest of my life with. That I would do whatever it took to make her see that, despite the many things I had done in a foolish effort to prove otherwise, I am the man she thought I was. I told them that woman was you.'

He was glad he'd held her tight as her knees gave way. He hauled her into his arms. Her hands rested on his shoulders so that the length of her was pressed against the length of him. Now he was ready to get to the good part.

'Wynnie Devereaux,' he said, 'I am in love with you. I think I have been in love with you since the moment I saw you hooked up to that ridiculous sculpture, smiling, laughing, trying your dandiest to look comfortable while nickel burnt your wrists.'

Tears filled her eyes as if she'd turned on an inner faucet. As he always had the moment those eyes of hers gleamed, he went into protector mode. His hands cupped her face, as gently as possible.

'You love me?' she said on a gulp.

'I do love you. So deeply it hurts. But the hurt is so far overshadowed by the good I barely notice it.'

She put a hand over his and leant into his palm. 'I love you, too.'

He nodded. 'I know you do, beautiful girl. I know you do.'

She smiled, radiantly, and the brightest of lights burst inside him, filling him with so much pleasure, so much happiness he wasn't sure he'd ever know what to do with it.

'Now back to that statue,' he said. 'I've been thinking all morning about tearing the thing down so I can mount it in our front yard. It would be the kind of talking piece the neighbours would hate.'

'*Our* front yard?' she repeated.

For the first time since she'd come looking for him, Dylan faltered. Not having ever been in this exact place before, where he knew his heart was on the line and he was deliberately putting it there anyway, he wasn't sure if he was moving too fast. Or if it was even possible to move too fast.

He slid his hand into the back of her hair, and let her see the full truth of his feelings. 'I'm not sure the CFC would approve of you sticking it up in front of their cottage. And my place has so much room.'

'How many rooms?' she asked, her cheek lifting into a soft, sexy smile that slid through him like molten lava.

He wrapped an arm tighter about her waist and pulled her closer. Her head lolled back and her breath released on a sigh. His body temperature went up two degrees.

'Too many,' he rasped. 'But there's only one you need to familiarise yourself with for starters.'

She slunk closer still, her knee sliding between his, her breasts pressing in against his chest until he was certain she wasn't wearing a bra. 'If you say the kitchen we have issues, my friend.'

He raised an eyebrow. 'There is a perfectly good bench in the kitchen, which might serve our purpose one day. But for starters I thought we might try out the bed in my room. I had the mattress shipped over from the Four Seasons in Paris. You have never felt anything like it.'

'Your room?'

He wet his suddenly dry lips. 'If you're game, how about we go ahead and make it our room?'

'Our room. I don't think you have any idea how much I love the sound of that.'

'Yeah,' he said, nudging her nose with his. 'I think I do.'

She tilted her head, he tilted his and they kissed. Slow, sensuous, disarming.

Being that they were them it soon dissolved into something hotter, harder, deeper. Dylan slid his hand between them, unbuttoned her jacket and groaned as his hand closed over her breast. If any boats had chosen to sail on past at that moment they would have been in for quite a show.

Wynnie pulled gently away and said, 'Now this all works out just beautifully for me, you know, considering I'm probably about to lose my job, and therefore my house.'

He slid his hand down her back to cup her buttocks, pressing her against his rising hardness. She didn't seem to notice. His beautiful tease.

But then she pushed away far enough that she could look him directly in the eyes, and so that she could make sure he was doing the same. 'In the spirit of full disclosure—'

'You were once a man and your real name is Kevin. I knew there was a reason why you didn't throw yourself at me the moment I unshackled you and your hands were free.'

She held her hand over his mouth, and he was hard pressed not to nibble at her fingers. To slide them into his mouth and scrape his teeth along each and every one.

'While you were giving your story to Sloane, I gave my story to another reporter. It had obviously been usurped by more pressing news. But it will come out.'

By the look in her eyes it was as though she thought that would make a lick of difference to him. Newfound strength made him stand up straighter as he planned on spending his life making sure she felt secure every day of hers.

'Sweetheart, it's time you realise that all you did was stand up for the brother you loved. The CFC are far too smart a bunch of people to let you go for something that was never your fault. And as for me, if that's as dark as your secrets get then I'm hoping we can hurry up and start to forge some much darker ones of our own.'

He buried his nose in her hair. Her fingers gripped his shoulders hard. And he knew without a doubt that the best sex of his life, and hers, was yet to come.

'I read the paper and I came straight here,' she said, trying with all her might to find her way back to the subject. 'I haven't even showered.'

'You smell great.' Boy, did she smell great. Like cotton sheets, and spring flowers. So great he kissed her neck, and gave it a soft lick. God help him, she tasted even better au natural.

'Your family—'

'Aren't anywhere near here, thank God,' he said, moving to stoke gentle kisses along her décolletage.

'But they are so important to you and—'

'And what?'

'And me.'

He pulled back so that he could look right into her beautiful brown eyes.

When he'd told them about how he felt for Wynnie they'd reacted with tears, hugs, phone calls to distant relatives, wiped brows, bets paid out, and wedding plans begun. Dylan thought it best to ease Wynnie into the hard, fast, no-holds-barred Kelly way of doing things. Now he'd enchanted her he wasn't going to do anything to make her wish otherwise.

'Brendan wants to hire you,' he said. 'Dad wants to adopt you. Mum wants to introduce you to everybody. Meg wants to know where you get your clothes. Cameron is pretty much still in a newlywed haze so might not even remember he's met you before, but the odds are in your favour.'

'I wish Felix was around so you could meet him. You'd drive one another crazy and it would be so much fun to watch.'

Dylan lifted his head and looked into her eyes, knowing that he couldn't miss the chance at seeing again the love she had therein, even if this one time it wasn't directed at him.

'I had planned to save this bit for later…'

'What bit?'

'I might have a small addendum to add to your reporter friend's story.'

Wynnie's brow furrowed and he could feel the deepening

of her breaths through his chest. Her hand gripped his shirt tight, and she nodded, just the once. 'Tell me.'

'I've had conversations with a colleague of mine in the federal prosecutor's office about Felix's case. Over time, after tracking down several others involved in the caper, they downgraded his charge to an accessory. They have known for some time that he was a wide-eyed kid roped in at the last minute and that he had no say in the planning, and little in the execution, bar being a lookout.'

Her spare hand slapped over her mouth and tears welled in her eyes.

Dylan held her tight for the next part. 'My friend agreed that if he comes back to town and turns himself in, he will be charged as a minor, given probation and his records will be sealed.'

'He'll be free?'

'Wynnie, I'm hoping you'll both be free.'

'But we don't even know where—'

'Jack, my investigator mate, found him. He's spoken to him. Felix knows the deal. He's on a plane as we speak. He'll be here tomorrow.'

The tears that had threatened to spill were suddenly gone. In their place, radiance. Pure unadulterated sunshine, and this time it was all for him.

She slid a hand through the hair above his ear, and he breathed in deep.

'I told you that you were a good man,' she said.

'Yeah, you did. And for some silly reason I've begun to believe it.'

'How can I ever repay you?'

'My gorgeous girl, you'll never, ever have the need.'

He leant in to kiss her and she pressed a hand to his chest. He rolled his eyes and growled at the sky. 'What does a guy have to do to get some appreciation around here?'

Her voice shook with laughter as she said, 'I was just about to thank you for signing KInG on with the CFC.'

'Actions not words are the way to thank a man for such a thing.' He nipped at her ear lobe and she shivered.

'And why is Eric the contact at KInG?'

'Did I know you could talk this much?'

'You did, you just love me so much you forgot.'

'Hopefully we can continue in that vein.'

'So why Eric…?'

Dylan let Wynnie go. Holding her so close but not getting any closer was pure agony. He took a step back and held an arm between them when she stepped his way. 'Now you've closed the deal will you be the contact at the CFC?'

'If they let me keep my job, then still no. My job's to ring 'em in. It's someone else's job to follow through.'

'Well, that was the first reason. The second reason is that Eric called me a cretin.'

She took another step towards him, her shoes crunching in the purple flowers. His hand landed upon her waist. She slid until his hands slunk beneath her jacket, opening it to reveal the sheer lace top, and the naked gorgeousness beneath.

'He said that to your face?' she asked.

'To my face,' he growled.

'Why? I mean, not why did he say it to your face, but which of the thousand asinine things you do each day finally made him crack?'

He dragged his eyes from her beautiful torso to look her in the eye. 'I let you go.'

The sass dissolved into sweetness as she said, 'Oh.'

And if possible he loved her all the more.

'Mmm. So I fired him as my assistant and moved him into development. More money. More autonomy. He sent me flowers. Crazy kid.'

'Not so crazy,' she said, her voice a husky whisper as his thumb grazed the edge of her breast.

As her body grew pliant and soft he slid his hand around her back, drew her close and let himself just revel in the fact that this woman had come bursting into his inert world, clearing the mist from his eyes, showing him how to breathe deep of life, and now he would get to touch her like this, feel her, be near her, joke with her, kiss her, make her melt as long as he remained smart enough to realise what he had.

His last secret was that he hoped that would be for the rest of his days.

Wynnie blinked up at him, then into the bright sunlight. Her brow furrowed and she glanced down at the purple flowers sticking to their shoes, and through the bright yellow wattle and across the river, and only just seemed to realise where they were. 'Now how on earth did we end up—?'

Dylan silenced her with another kiss. The kind of hard, fast, thorough kiss that ought to give her something else to think about for a few minutes.

When he pulled away it took her a few moments to open her eyes. They fluttered up at him, all liquid and dreamy.

He loved this woman. He loved her vivacity, her bravery, her impudence. It was so obvious, now the light had been switched on he knew it would never turn off again.

'This spot is so romantic,' she said, her voice husky as all get out. 'Who knew you had it in you?'

'Complete accident, so don't get any ideas that I'm the romantic type.'

She held a hand to her heart. 'I'm shocked to hear it.'

His cheeks warmed. He could actually feel them turning pink. What other changes could this woman possibly bring to his life? If he started singing Pavarotti songs in the shower that was the end of him.

He cupped her cheek, and looked into those eyes that always told him so much. 'But in a funny kind of way telling my family's story was my version of a love letter to you.'

'On the front page of the paper?'

He grinned. 'I'm a Kelly. I don't know any other way.'

Wynnie slid a hand through his hair, making a mess of the slick 'do. 'I do love you, Dylan Kelly. And not because you stood up for me, but because I always knew you would.'

'Even though I'm insular, jaded, a workaholic, am ruthless and self-serving?'

'Save that for the paying public,' she scoffed. 'You are a marshmallow. My marshmallow. My beautiful, generous, big-hearted, loyal marshmallow.'

Every word out of her mouth sank in and stuck until he began to really believe she was right.

He held her chin between his finger and thumb and waited until she was looking him in the eye. 'You once said to me that if one person can make a difference, a hundred people can change the world.'

'That sounds like something I'd say.'

'Well, I'm thinking perhaps you underestimated people.'

'I did?'

'Mmm. There's only one of you and yet you managed to change my world all on your own.'

He pulled her to him, or maybe she leant towards him. Either way, they kissed. It was beautiful. It was melting hot.

And Wynnie was not the only one to take a sickie that day.

* * * * *

ONE NIGHT WITH THE REBEL BILLIONAIRE

BY
TRISH WYLIE

Trish Wylie tried various careers before getting the one she'd wanted since her late teens. She flicked her blonde hair over her shoulder while playing the promotions game, patted her manicured hands on the backs of musicians while working in the music business, smiled sweetly at awkward customers during the retail nightmare known as the run-up to Christmas, and has got completely lost in her car in every single town in Ireland while working as a sales rep. And it took all that character-building and a healthy sense of humour to get her dream job, which lets her spend her days in reindeer slippers, with her hair in whatever band she can find to keep it out of the way and makeup as vague and distant a memory as manicured nails. She's happy she gets to create the kind of dream man she'd still like to believe is out there somewhere. If it turns out he is, she promises she'll let you know... after she's been out for a new wardrobe, a manicure and a makeover...

For Sharon W—friend, reader
and fellow admirer of hot and gorgeous horses.
Luv ya, babes!

CHAPTER ONE

'EXCUSE ME. I'M SORRY. This is a private beach.'

Roane Elliott stepped tentatively closer. A full moon lit everything around her in shades of silver and grey, with black shadows that seemed to breathe with the ebb and flow of the tide. But her surroundings didn't worry her as much as the presence of the stranger; she might have known every rock, every path, every place the sand sank deeper beneath her feet—but she also knew she was too far away from a 911 call for it to help if she got into trouble...

Her footsteps faltered. But it wasn't the sudden 911 thought that had done it; it was because she was now standing close enough to see he was—

Her eyes widened. Oh, dear Lord. *He was naked!*

More than that, he was an Adonis. In the silvery light every tight muscle was defined in shadowy dips and shimmering planes from wide shoulders to tapering waist to taut... Her mouth went dry.

He turned around, so Roane swiftly averted her gaze, and mumbled under her breath, *'Look at his face.'*

When she glanced at him from the corner of her eye her errant gaze didn't do what it was told. Well, who could blame her? He was sensational. She damped her lips as if she could taste him on the air before forcing her gaze sharply upwards, her palms itching with an almost primal urge to reach out and *touch*.

'This is a private beach,' she repeated with a little more force, lifting her chin to make her point. 'You shouldn't be here.'

'The ocean belongs to everyone.' Even the tone of his voice was magical.

Well, he could take that deep, rumbling, deliciously masculine voice of his that was doing something completely undiscovered to her pulse rate and—

Her thought process stalled. Wow, he had the most amazing muscle definition on his chest and upper arms. Not pumped up, steroid induced definition, oh, no. He looked like the kind of man who worked at something very physical for a living. Or was a natural sportsman of some kind, a swimmer maybe—no, not lean enough for a swimmer. Not that he was fat anywhere she could see, which was pretty much everywhere if she chose to take a good long look. And she could have, because he wasn't the least bit embarrassed about being naked—in fact, he placed his hands on his hips, almost daring her to go right ahead and look.

Thankfully the silent arrogance brought her gaze north to his shadowed face rather than travelling south, which, deep down, it *really* wanted to do…

She cleared her throat. 'You're not in the ocean; you're standing on the beach. And it's *private*. You have to go. There are security patrols.'

It was a lie. But he didn't know that.

In the shadows the suggestion of a crooked smile appeared, 'Your beach, is it?'

'It belongs to the family I work for. I—' She'd been about

to tell him she had a place a few hundred yards away. No doubt she'd be casually discussing the weather with him next. 'I have permission to be here.'

When he took a step forwards she instinctively stepped back. 'I know self-defence, so don't try anything. I'm a black belt in ju-kwando.'

A brief chuckle of deep laughter preceded the dropping of his hands and another forward step. 'My clothes are behind you. And for future reference it's ju-jitsu or tae kwon do. Nice try. But I won't bite you.'

Roane moved to the side as he stepped closer, colour rising on her cheeks when he inclined his head and added a low, 'Not unless you ask me to.'

She opened her mouth to say something cutting in return and couldn't seem to get her brain to work well enough to form a sentence. But she liked to think any red-blooded female would have been the same when confronted with such temptation. He was one of those men that would take what he wanted when he wanted, wasn't he? She could *feel it.* There was just something very erotic about that—in the darkness—when he was naked... For a girl as inexperienced as Roane it was quite the realization. But what kind of woman was turned on by a naked stranger in the middle of the night? She tried to think of a reason why she was still standing there.

Making sure he leaves, she told herself.

Liar, an inner voice replied.

The rasp of a zipper invited her to glance back at him. His elbows bent as his hands worked on the belt of his jeans, he asked, 'You live here?'

'Answering that would hardly be a good move on my part, now would it?'

'I'd say you left the region of good moves when you approached a stranger to begin with, wouldn't you?'

When he turned his face towards the ocean the moon lit his face. For a brief moment Roane was struck by how *beautiful* he was. Not a word normally used to describe men, she knew, but he was. There was no way to tell what colour his hair or eyes were in the restricted light, but she had a sneaking suspicion they'd merely be icing on the cake.

His face had a symmetry to it that she'd never seen before—almost as if he'd been artificially created. Twinned dark pools that suggested large deep-set eyes, a perfectly straight nose, a mouth—dear heaven, that mouth; full lips practically calling out to be kissed. He even had a square jaw.

Roane was just the teensiest bit smitten.

He looked at her and smiled the most sinfully sexy smile. Because he knew, didn't he? Looking the way he did, how could he fail to know women were smitten by him? Judging by the beast of a motorcycle she'd discovered parked at the top of the wooden walkway down to the beach she'd bet he drove all over the country leaving trails of smitten women behind him. There was an addictive sense of—freedom—to him too; as if he belonged where he stood and nowhere else. Nothing would stop him from going where he wanted when he wanted, from swimming naked on a private beach or seducing a woman in the moonlight…

He could reach out and haul her to him, press those practised lips to hers, lower her to the soft sand beneath their feet, surround her body with his and—

Erotic images flashed across her brain, her body aching low inside at the very thought of that kind of an encounter. Just once in her life. She could almost hear the ragged breathing; feel the sweat-slickened skin…

Roane choked out the words, 'Please leave.'

His answer was slow, voice so husky she felt her breasts grow heavy in response. 'Scared, little girl?'

Roane frowned at the words. Why did they sound familiar? She didn't know who he was, but a part of her suddenly felt she should recognize him. 'Do I know you?'

'No one here knows me.'

When he turned and bent over to retrieve the rest of his belongings a shadow tracked the line of his spine, disappearing into the slight gape at the back of his jeans. The muscles in his shoulders worked as he moved, large hands reaching out and casually lifting what looked like a shirt and a jacket and boots. No underwear, she noted. And then he was turning to face her again, tucking the items casually against his hips.

'Taking a chance approaching a naked stranger on a beach in the dark, you know that, don't you, little girl?'

Why did he keep calling her that? Okay, so compared to him she *was* little. He had to be six feet two easy; Roane was five feet five. And beside all that defined muscle and inherent strength she was positively sylph-like in comparison. But being called a little girl at the age of twenty-seven should surely have felt patronizing to her. Instead it felt distinctly…sexual…and Roane was certain he knew that.

'I told you, there'll be a security—'

'No, there won't.'

She felt a flicker of panic. 'You don't know that.'

'Yes—' he continued looking at her '—I do.'

Who *was* this guy? The end of Martha's Vineyard they were on wasn't known for a large influx of motorcycle-riding bad boys. Frankly, anyone unfamiliar with the island would never have found the beach to begin with. But the main house on the bluff was certainly rich pickings for thieves. Maybe he'd been checking out the Bryant place? Was that it? Had he been filling in time on the beach while he waited for everyone to go to bed?

Roane had always had a very active imagination.

The stranger moved his clothes to the same hand as his boots, before reaching out to her. When she flinched back from it his low voice sounded irritated. 'I won't hurt you.'

'I don't know that.'

'You're still stood there so you must feel it or self-preservation would have kicked in.' He beckoned with long fingers. 'Come here.'

'Why?'

'I want to see you.'

'Why?'

Sighing impatiently, he stepped forwards and lifted her chin with the crook of his forefinger, turning her face to the light while she looked sideways at him with wide eyes. She didn't move—she couldn't seem to find the strength to move. It was surreal.

Trapping her chin between his thumb and forefinger he angled his head and examined her face at a maddeningly leisurely pace; thumb smoothing back and forth almost absentmindedly. Then he let go—leaving the heated brand of his touch against her skin.

'Grew up some, didn't you, little girl?'

Roane blinked at him as he turned away, her feet carrying her forwards as he stepped silently onto the end of the wooden walkway. 'Who are you?'

He didn't look back, his deep voice carrying on the night air. 'Night, Roane.'

* * *

'Hey, Jake?'

Roane jogged across to her friend's side when she spotted him on the laneway between the main house and the guest quarters the next morning. 'Wait up.'

He turned, a broad smile in place when he spotted her. 'Morning, sunshine.'

'Morning.' She couldn't resist stopping for a similar smile in return before falling into step beside him. They'd been friends since they'd been in nappies. And whereas most women were immediately struck by his tall, dark and handsome good looks Roane had long since outgrown the stage of being anywhere in the region of starry eyed. He was like a brother to her.

'Do you have a visitor on the estate? There was someone on the beach on my way home last night.'

Jake lifted dark brows. 'Was there?'

'Yeah—it was the weirdest thing.' She pushed her hands into the pockets of her jeans and skipped over the bigger details, like naked male glory and a soul-deep feminine reaction to that nakedness. There were some things a gal just didn't discuss with a brother. 'He seemed to know me.'

Jake's chin jerked up a little, his gaze on the guest house. 'Did he? Well, then—let's just see if it's who I think it was, shall we?'

Roane frowned in confusion as Jake slung a long arm over her shoulders and tugged her close to whisper conspiratorially in her ear, 'We *do* have a visitor…'

Roane kept her hands in her pockets and allowed Jake to steer her up the grassy path and through the open doors of the house that her own home could have fitted inside at least a dozen times. Guests at the Bryant estate were treated to the kind of luxury most folks would be hard-pressed to find in a five star hotel.

Exquisite views over the ocean from the custom-built, architect-designed house were the first treat. The fact it was nestled in fifteen-odd acres of mature trees and established gardens overlooking a private cove was the next. Then add ten thousand square feet of house with five bedrooms, gourmet kitchen and countless luxury amenities, including master suite with Jacuzzi and great room with cathedral ceilings and two-storey stone fireplace and, *well...*

Modern-day European royalty probably lived in less.

'Hello?' Jake released her as they stepped through into the beechwood kitchen, bright light streaming in through the many windows to bathe the room in golden warmth. 'Anyone home?'

He stopped so suddenly Roane almost walked into the wall of his back. Frowning, she stepped around him, ready to make a comment about a little warning being a good thing when her jaw dropped.

Her mystery man gave her a cursory glance before turning his attention to Jake. 'Coffee?'

'Yeah, please.'

He turned and poured two cups while Roane continued to gape. She'd been right about the hair and eye colour being icing. In fact if anything he was even more stunning in sunlight than he was in moonlight. She now knew his cropped hair was dark blond, the bright light in the room picking up lighter strands in the spikes that looked as if they'd been formed by long fingers raked casually from front to back. As for his eyes...well, she might have to be a little closer to be sure, but they looked pretty good to her...

Jake was talking again. "Found the key, then?"

'Looks like it.' He turned and placed a mug into each of

their hands without asking Roane if she wanted anything. 'Add what you need—it's all on the counter.'

Then he caught her gaze for a moment, a knowing light sparkling in the stunning green-flecked brown of his eyes. 'Morning, Roane.'

Suddenly she knew who he was. *'Adam?'*

While Jake moved over to the kitchen table Adam smiled lazily, lowering his head to whisper, *'Now* she remembers me.'

Before Roane could say anything in reply, he turned away and slid onto the curved bench facing his brother. 'The detective agency was a bit much, don't you think?'

Jake shrugged. 'It wasn't like you sent Christmas cards every year so we'd know how to reach you.'

'And there was possibly a reason for that…'

Jake pursed his lips as Roane slid onto the bench beside him, immediately feeling the need to ease the tension by teasing him. 'You hired a detective agency to find him? You didn't mention that. Was he a raincoat-wearing private-eye type?'

Jake smiled. 'No; I was disappointed actually.'

'If you'd told me we could have searched for one. It would have been much more fun.' She smiled back at him. But a part of her was hurt he hadn't told her he was searching for Adam. It was a huge deal. She could remember a time in their lives when they'd talked about everything and anything.

When she glanced across the table she found the prodigal Bryant lounging casually, one long arm slung along the back of the wooden bench while sunshine glowed off the deep tan on his skin. But the nonchalance was a façade, wasn't it? Roane could *feel* the intensity in him while his impossibly thick lashes flickered as he studied the interaction across the table.

His gaze crashed into hers for the space of two heartbeats and Roane felt her breath hitch. How did he *do* that with just a look?

He turned his attention to Jake. 'How bad is he?'

'He has good days and bad.' Jake leaned forwards, cupping his mug between his hands and idly turning it while he spoke. 'We try to keep him to a routine; that helps.'

Roane's voice softened. 'He'll be glad to see you.'

Adam glanced briefly at her again, then back to Jake. 'Lucid?'

'Short-term memory loss initially—confused some days; angry, prone to mood swings—'

Adam's mouth twisted wryly as he turned his profile to them and looked outside. 'Not much change, then…'

Jake didn't smile. 'Still Dad, yes. But it's only a matter of time before we're looking at language breakdown, long term memory loss and a general withdrawal as his senses decline. Once diagnosed they give them an average life expectancy of seven years. And they diagnosed him two years ago. So if you want to make your peace you'd best make it now.'

Roane frowned when Adam didn't respond. Surely he wouldn't have come home if he hadn't intended to make his peace with his father before it was too late? She knew very little about why he'd left, but then Adam had been an enigma long before that. When he'd left she had barely been fifteen, Jake a year older—and they'd been thick as thieves. But the rebellious Adam had been twenty-one. Six years wasn't that big a gap for adults, but back then it had seemed like a lot more. Adam had been a young man, and a deeply unhappy one at that. He hadn't wanted to spend time hanging round with two carefree teenagers during their endless halcyon summers.

Jake pushed again. 'If you want to look the business over before you make any decisions, then—'

'There's a hurry, is there?'

God, he was so *cold!* Roane felt a chill run down her spine, fighting the need to shiver at his reaction while he calmly lifted his mug to his mouth. If he didn't give a damn why had he come home at all? Why not stay as lost to his family as he'd been for the last twelve years?

'Yes,' Jake informed him.

Roane blinked at her friend. What was going on?

Adam apparently knew. 'Gonna buy me out, are you?'

'If I have to.' Jake nodded once.

Roane leaned her elbow on the arm of the wooden bench and rested her forefinger along the side of her face, hiding her mouth behind the rest of her fingers. Adam Bryant might be pretty amazing to look at, but he wasn't much of a personality, was he? Didn't he feel the least bit guilty that he'd left everything on his younger brother's shoulders? She might not know much, but she knew Jake had been tense of late, preoccupied, *older* somehow… Running the Bryant empire alone had been taking its toll.

As if he could sense her disapproval, Adam's gaze flickered briefly towards her again, then back to Jake just as fast. Frankly it was starting to bug Roane. It felt as if he was dismissing her presence—as if he didn't feel she should even be there. But if Jake thought that he wouldn't have brought her in with him, would he? With the benefit of hindsight, she knew he'd probably felt the need for moral support.

'I'll take a look at the figures,' Adam told Jake.

'There's a board meeting at three in Manhattan. Roane can fly you in, can't you, Ro?'

Did she have to? She smiled. ''Course I can.'

Adam didn't look at her. 'I'll drive.'

'It's at least five and a half hours by road—you'd need to leave in an hour,' Roane pointed out. 'It's less than two hours by air; you wouldn't have to leave til noon. I'm sure you'll want to spend time with your dad before you go…'

When he looked at her again she quirked her brows. Not that it had any effect on him. Instead he held her gaze steadily, as if to prove he could having spent so little time looking her directly in the eye.

'You fly?'

'Yes.' Silently she willed him to make a comment about it being a step up from the chauffeur-cum-handyman position her father had held for most of his life.

He didn't. Instead he took a deep breath that expanded the material of his dark green T-shirt while his gaze shifted back to Jake. 'When's the next board meeting?'

'Two weeks.'

'Right.' Adam looked out the windows, his jaw tensing while he thought, eyes narrowed against the bright light. Then he nodded briefly. 'Fine. I'll fly.'

Roane lowered her hand and looked at Jake. 'I'll book the slot. You coming?'

'No, I'll go ahead. I already have a slot.'

Which meant she got to fly down with Adam on her own. Fantastic. That should make for a chatty flight. Roane couldn't remember ever spending time in close proximity to someone she found so intensely physically attractive yet didn't like at the same time.

Jake nudged her to indicate he wanted to slide out. 'I'll take Adam over to the house.'

'I remember the way.'

Roane pursed her lips at Adam's reply as she slid off the

bench and walked to the sink to toss her untouched coffee away, Jake's voice calm behind her.

'I'm going over anyway.'

When he joined her at the sink she looked up at him, mouthing a concerned You okay?

He winked and mouthed back, Fine.

Automatically she took his mug and rinsed it out after she'd done her own, adding a plate and a couple of pieces of cultery that were lying on the side too and not noticing Jake had moved away until she turned—and walked straight into the solid wall of Adam's chest. One large hand shot up to grasp her elbow as she staggered back, her spine bumping the edge of the counter as she looked down at his hand with wide eyes.

Because it was like being touched by a live wire.

A spark of electricity shot up her arm, under her skin and into her veins where it picked up speed with the rapid beat of her heart. The tingling then radiated outwards, licking over her bare shoulder and down over her chest where her nipples beaded into tight buds against the lace of her bra.

Adam let go so suddenly her gaze shot upwards.

When his eyes narrowed an almost imperceptible amount Roane blinked at him. He'd felt that? What in the name of heaven *was that* anyway? It couldn't even be put down to static electricity—not when it was bare skin touching bare skin. Could it? Science had never been her thing, after all.

'Ro? You coming?' Jake's familiar voice sounded from the open doorway.

'Mmm-hmm, yeah.' She frowned as she stepped around Adam, absent-mindedly rubbing where he had touched her as if to remove an invisible mark.

Adam took a half step in her direction so that her shoulder

brushed his upper arm, the rumble of his voice low and steeped with innuendo.

'Be seeing you. *Little girl.*'

She stopped and smiled sugary sweet. 'How long did you say you were staying?'

'I didn't.'

A quick glance at the doorway showed that Jake had already stepped outside. Suddenly Roane felt edgy without him there. Her hesitation didn't help either, because when she looked up at Adam it was in time to see he'd noticed the same thing.

'Finally caught him, did you?'

What? She gaped when she realized what he meant, 'I wasn't ever—' She frowned at the sudden need to defend herself. 'My relationship with Jake is none of your business.'

When she stepped away he reached out and grabbed her wrist, lifting her hand to study it. 'No ring.'

Roane tugged her arm. 'Let go.'

He held on. 'How come?'

Not that she had all that much experience with men, but Roane had never met such a Neanderthal. For goodness' sake, the man practically *grunted* a conversation!

She tugged again, harder this time, determined not to pay attention to the low thrumming of awareness in her abdomen. 'That's still none of your business.'

Adam repositioned his fingers, his gaze studying her wrist for a moment before he looked sideways at her and a smile began to play with the corners of his mouth. The way the green in his eyes had darkened, the way that half a smile was forming—it threw rational thought clean out of her head. Until she realized what he was smiling about…

He'd just felt her pulse jumping about in her wrist. He

knew what he was doing to her disobedient body. More than that—he was *pleased* about it! The arrogant great—

Adam let go.

So Roane did the mature thing and practically ran from the room. Let him go right ahead and think she was with Jake if he wanted to. It made her reaction to Adam even worse than it already was, but at least she wouldn't have to deal with it, because surely he wouldn't make a pass at his brother's girlfriend?

Cowardly, the voice said inside her head, using Jake as some kind of protective shield. But she ignored it. Caveman had never done it for her before, and it sure as heck wasn't starting to now.

Even if Adam Bryant looked like the kind of bad news every girl secretly dreamed of finding.

CHAPTER TWO

'MVY TOWER...MERIDIAN five eight nin-er two November ready to taxi with mike...right turnout southeast bound.'

Only when they were cruising at five and a half thousand feet did Roane truly experience all that she loved best about flying: serenity, control and exhilaration. All around them were blue skies, below them the mirrored aquamarine of the ocean. Things were so calm she could have switched to autopilot. But that would have left time for conversation with her passenger, and it was bad enough he'd got in the cockpit instead of sitting in back where she could have pretended he wasn't there. So she didn't.

Unable to resist, she glanced to her side and noticed long fingers tapping restlessly against the taut trouser-clad thigh that was moving to the rhythm of a bouncing heel. An errant smile immediately blossomed in her chest as the realization hit her.

'Not that good a flier, huh?'

When she bit down on her lower lip to control the smile Adam frowned. 'I'm good. *Thanks.*'

'Mmm-hmm.' She nodded, letting his sarcastic 'thanks' roll over her head. 'The tapping foot is a sure sign of relaxation.'

The tapping of his foot abruptly stopped, long fingers

curling into a fist. His knuckles were just white enough for Roane to suspect he was forcibly keeping his leg still. It was the first time since she'd met him on the beach that she'd felt she had the upper hand—it was empowering, especially considering every time she laid eyes on him her hormones seemed to go into overdrive. When he'd turned up at the airport she'd surreptitiously rolled her eyes at how good he looked in a dark suit. One glance at him and every part of her that had ever been attracted to intelligence and wit and congeniality went straight to hell. Apparently to be replaced with a cell-deep genetic need to mate with the strongest of the species for the sake of the human race…

But his reaction to being in the air meant her pilot's conscience insisted she make small talk to help take his mind off it. Sometimes Roane truly wished she had a meaner streak.

'Clear skies from here to New York; we won't even hit turbulence. Honest.'

'Right.'

Roane studied his tense profile, then took a breath and decided to throw caution to the wind and just say what she thought. 'You're not much of a talker, are you?'

Adam's reply was so low she mightn't have heard it if they weren't wearing mikes to go with the matching head sets. 'The secret of being boring is to say everything.'

Roane stared at him in amazement. He couldn't be serious. 'And where did we pick up *that* excuse?'

'Voltaire.'

Her brows lifted. 'Quote of the day?'

The vaguest hint of a smile appeared. 'No.'

Well, that went well. If Roane didn't know better she'd have said he was enigmatic on purpose. But before she could steer the conversation in a direction where she might glean some insight, Adam exhaled loudly and leaned back into his seat, his chin dropping as he studied the array of dials and readouts.

'Tell me how it works.'

He wanted a flying lesson? In Roane's experience it wasn't how people who were afraid of flying tended to react. Maybe he meant the theory of it? Okay—she could do the *basic* theory of it.

'One sec.' She engaged the autopilot and leaned back, turning and folding her arms across her breasts. 'It's flying itself now. But if the ground suddenly starts looking bigger, yell.'

'Funny,' Adam said dryly.

'Let's see.' Roane considered the ceiling for a moment, starting with something she'd read somewhere. 'Basically it all centres around Newton's idea that for every action, there is an equal and opposite reaction.'

Then she ad-libbed, warming to her subject, 'So you know when you let go of an inflated balloon and it flies all over the room? That's kinda like thrust in an airplane engine; it propels the plane into the air…' Unfolding an arm, she made a sweep with one hand to highlight the 'plane into the air' part; quite pleased with the analogy until she found him studying her with hooded eyes.

His deep voice held an edge of barely concealed disgust. 'When did you decide I was an idiot?'

Finding her mouth dry, Roane swallowed before coming back with a pathetically weak-voiced, 'Short Neanderthal grunted answers might possibly have done it.'

'I understand Newton's theories.'

A nervous bubble of laughter formed in her chest, but with effort she managed to keep her reaction to a teasing smile. 'Maybe you could explain them to me some time. I just keep the thing in the air. I've never felt the need to know the science that goes with it.'

She batted her lashes innocently.

'I'm sure to get your pilot's licence you had to be a step or two up from dumb blonde. How long have you been flying?'

'A long time—and I haven't killed anyone…' she paused for effect, shrugging one shoulder '…yet.'

The fleeting smile twitched the corner of his mouth; brown softening the green of his eyes. For a brief second, to Roane's astonishment, there was even a hint of deep laughter lines fanning out from the corners of his eyes, suggesting he laughed more often than she'd had evidence of so far. Leaving her wondering what it would take to make him laugh out loud—without holding back the way he was.

She *really* wanted to hear that sound.

But the fleeting smile was gone as fast as it arrived. When she studied him he studied her right back and then jerked his head in the direction of the controls. 'Run me through the basics.'

'Of actual flying rather than the theory of flight?'

'Yes.'

Roane sucked her bottom lip in and let it go with a slight 'pop', the words coming out before she could stop them. 'It's a control thing for you, isn't it?'

Adam blinked lazily, 'Could be.'

She couldn't really work him out, and it was disconcerting. But then it wasn't as if she were all that worldly-wise. She had met a fairly diverse selection of people in her time, but Adam? Adam was something new. Adam was *fascinating* to her if she were honest about it, which she wasn't about to be. At least not out loud.

She adjusted her mike, and when she spoke she heard the

distorted version of her own voice echoed louder in her ears. 'On the floor are pedals that operate the brakes and rudder. Push the right pedal, the rudder turns to the right. Push the left pedal, the rudder turns left. With me so far?'

Adam had dipped his chin and moved his knees apart so he could see the floor. But when she asked the question he glanced sideways, his tone still dry. 'I'll try and keep up.'

Roane smiled, turning away to check the readouts while she continued, 'The pilot controls the airplane by using a control wheel—the stick. This lets you move the elevators on the tail and the ailerons on the wings, which in turn move the airplane. Still with me?'

A deep sigh was magnified by the mike.

Still smiling, Roane shifted positions so she was leaning her upper body closer. 'Hands on the stick.'

Adam swiped his large palms across his thighs before lifting them and placing them tight on either side of the stick, his knuckles white. So with a roll of her eyes Roane couldn't seem to stop herself from asking, 'Jeez, Adam, would you grab hold of a woman like that?'

He shot her a sideways glare.

'Let me know when you want to find out.' He flexed his fingers and looked down at the controls. 'Keep going.'

The throwaway invitation sent a thrumming pulse of anticipation to the centre of her body, even though Roane knew instinctively it had been a knee-jerk reaction to her runaway tongue. 'Towards you the nose comes up—away the nose goes down. But I warn you, you touch the throttle at any point I may have to kill you myself before we hit the ground…'

He swallowed. 'And that's where exactly?'

Roane somehow managed not to laugh. She knew he wouldn't appreciate it, even if she did tell him her urge to giggle was partly because she was finding the chink in his armour so humanizing. Adam wasn't the kind of man who would like being told vulnerability was appealing, was he? So instead she reached for his large hands, her smaller ones nowhere near able to cover them as she curled her fingers around his.

'Between us.' She kept her gaze focused on their hands when he turned to look for the throttle, the heat of his skin beneath her cool fingers mesmerizing beyond belief to her. What would hands that size feel like on her body? Images immediately flickered through her brain in answer to the silent question, so that when she spoke her voice sounded embarrassingly breathless to her.

'There. That's it. A little forwards the nose drops…a little back…and…erm…'

She'd made the mistake of glancing up at him. When she found his face disconcertingly close to hers she faltered; his intense gaze focused on her mouth as she damped her lips. The man really did have the most ridiculously thick eyelashes.

'The—uh…the nose comes up…' She swallowed and forced air into her aching chest. Then his scent hit her. She'd been aware of it since they'd closed the cabin doors, but up close…up close and with the heat of his skin to magnify it. *Dear heaven…*

Roane was no expert, but she was a long-time fan of scented candles. There were notes of citrus in there, maybe blackcurrant…and then there was a hint of sandalwood, a suggestion of mulberry and just possibly a whisper of amber. It was the most *enticing* combination…

She breathed deep and practically sighed with contentment as she exhaled.

He was staring at her.

And he continued studying her with silent intensity, leaving Roane floundering. 'Okay, well, erm…left is left and right is right. Basically…'

The smile started in his eyes. 'Said that too…'

Well, how was she supposed to concentrate with him sitting as close as he was, looking the way he did and smelling as good as he was? Letting go of his hands, she sat back in her seat.

'Don't move the stick a minute.'

The change was so smooth it would have taken an expert to notice it. Then Roane was in control again. If Adam *was* seeking control by asking for the impromptu flying lesson, then she could understand that, she supposed. Having control of her plane again immediately made her feel better. He might be able to take possession of her body's reactions simply by breathing in and out. But by distracting herself with the everyday business of flying Roane could focus her mind elsewhere. She *could*.

'Just relax and feel my movements through the stick. That's it. Smoothly…'

Suddenly the control she had took on sexual undertones for her. She'd never been in a relationship with a man where she'd had the courage to be one of those women who took control. She'd never asked to be touched a particular way or in a certain place; nothing that might have made the experience better for her. Nope, Roane's method had always been more along the lines of making approving mumbles and hoping he got the message. But in her plane, where she was totally in control of her environment, even giving instructions to a man like Adam Bryant seemed like the most natural thing in the world to her.

Unfortunately the fact it was a man like Adam made her think about what it would be like to give him a different set of instructions. Like a breathless, Kiss me, Adam. Or, Touch me, Adam…

Since when had she been so obsessed with sex?

Feeling the vibration of the engine through the stick Roane stifled a moan, squirming on her seat in an attempt to ease the unfamiliar tension she felt between her legs. Thankfully when she glanced at Adam he seemed engrossed enough with flying not to have noticed so she damped her lips and told him, 'Okay. Now you try.'

His fingers flexed around the stick while Adam took a breath and tried to ignore the move she'd just made—he'd seen that shimmy of her hips on the seat. She was more distracting than the flying lesson.

Of all the things he'd mentally prepared for there had never once been the scenario of being instantly viscerally attracted to his little brother's woman. And woman she was, no matter how much the 'little girl' tag he'd given her as a kid still seemed appropriate. Everything about her was little: little fine-boned hands, little wrists he could circle comfortably with his thumb and forefinger, little waist he could probably have spanned with both hands, little breasts that would easily fill his palms…

Yet everything she did and said belied any air of fragility her body intimated. Not that she came across as tough— quite the opposite. She had an air of vulnerability to her that Adam found compellingly fascinating. Not a bad thing considering where he was.

Adam hated small planes.

Her softly feminine voice filled his ears. 'There you go. You're flying.'

While Adam focused on the combination of what he was doing and his physical awareness of the woman sitting beside him Roane took the silence to mean she could try making conversation again.

'Is it weird being back?'

'At the Vineyard?'

'Yes.'

'No.'

'How can it not be? You've been gone a long time.'

Adam didn't take kindly to being called a liar, even subtextually, frowning as he spoke. '"My witness is the empty sky."'

There was a brief silence.

'Voltaire?'

'Kerouac.'

When he looked sideways at her she was staring at him and Adam liked that she couldn't figure him out. It could stay that way as far as he was concerned.

'You have dozens of these, don't you?'

Adam felt his mouth twitch. 'A few.'

'As a way to avoid making conversation?'

Nope, he could make conversation when he *wanted* to.

'You're not good with silence, then, I take it.'

'I'm fine with silence.' Said the woman who had babbled nervously at him all the way through the airport concourse. 'It's rudeness that bothers me—I'm just trying to figure out if that's what you're doing.'

'So short sentences make me an idiot—the lack of idle conversation makes me rude.' Adam took a breath. 'Anything else?'

There was another moment of silence and then a mumbled, 'You really couldn't be any different from Jake if you tried…'

She might not have meant it with quite the same level of contempt his father had any time he'd used similar words, but they had the same effect. Adam felt the echo of adolescent anger roll in on him like a tsunami—destroying any sense of reason or tolerance in its wake the same way it always had. He'd heard the words a million times; said with impatience or frustration or resentment or in disappointment. But the result was always the same. Jake had been the son their father wanted. Adam had fallen short of the mark.

Well, not any more. Maybe Roane Elliott should be the first of them to understand that.

Adam turned his head, dropping his gaze to look her over at his leisure. He heard her sharp intake of breath when he watched the rise and fall of her breasts long enough to see two distinct beads appear against the soft material of her blouse. Then he smiled a slow smile as he looked up at her parted lips, at the flush on her cheeks and finally into the darkened blue of her eyes. Only then did he quirk his brows, his voice a low rumble in the headsets.

'Ready to find out just how different, little girl?' He angled his head a little and studied the way her honey-blonde hair curled against her cheek. 'I saw how you looked at me on the beach last night. Manners and IQ weren't high on the list of things you were interested in then, were they?'

When she stared at him with widened eyes he leaned a little closer, deliberately looking down the 'V' of her blouse at the rapid rise and fall of creamy half-circle breasts above the lace of her bra. He watched the beating pulse on one side of her elegant neck, the way she damped her parted lips before sucking in a shaky breath. Then his gaze locked firmly with hers again. 'You're right. It *is* about control with me. But you want to lose it, don't you? In a way you obviously don't with my brother or you wouldn't react to me the way you do. You know I'd take you the way you want to be taken. Hard. And slow. For hours on end…'

There was a brief narrowing of her eyes before he continued, 'Maybe you should make sure you chose the right Bryant, little girl…'

Roane's breath caught, she swallowed hard and then her eyes sparkled with a mixture of outrage and desire. 'I'm not some *little girl* you can intimidate.' Her chin lifted defiantly, the husky edge of her voice giving away her physical reaction to his words as much as her body already had. 'Let go of the stick. *Please.*'

Adam frowned. 'Wh—?'

Without warning her knee jerked, and the plane veered violently to the left, throwing Adam away from her. He released the stick as if he'd been burned, his stomach lurching and a violent expletive leaving his mouth. When the plane eased smoothly onto an even keel again he glared angrily at her.

'What did you do?'

Roane was facing forwards, both hands on the stick and her fine-boned jaw-line set with determination. 'I'm sorry. My foot must have slipped.'

Meaning she'd kicked the rudder, right? Adam would have laughed at her audacity if she hadn't just taken a year off his life. His brother had gone and got himself quite the little firecracker.

'Clever.'

The compliment didn't earn him any brownie points. 'Feel free to take your lack of conversational skills to the extreme from here to New York. Or I can give you a demonstration of just what this plane is capable of if you'd prefer…'

Adam knew she wasn't just referring to the plane. She'd clearly told him not to mess with her. It was a nice try, he'd give her that. It would have worked better if she'd denied anything he'd said about wanting to be taken hard and slow and for hours on end…

The knowledge did several things to Adam.

But what it did most was bring out the primal strand to his DNA code. One that now felt a deep seated need to tame her…

Adam had never backed down from a battle of wills. It had been half his problem for most of his life. So she might have got the upper hand on him this time, but she wouldn't do it again. She should understand who she was dealing with. All of them should.

She'd just get a more pleasurable version of the lesson…

CHAPTER THREE

'Do I have to?'

Jake's brows rose, 'You don't like him much, do you? I thought you liked everyone.'

Under normal circumstances she did. Roane was a glass-half-full kinda gal. Not till Adam had she met anyone who made her believe irredeemable people existed. Feeling that way and being so physically attracted to him at the same time only made her dislike him more than she already did…

But he'd basically called her a gold-digger!

More than that—she was an unfaithful gold-digger who would stoop to having hot, sweaty, emotionless sex with her supposed boyfriend's brother! He was slime. No. He was lower than that. She scowled harder. 'He's not nice.'

Jake stifled a smile, but not convincingly. 'Okay. You got me. What happened on the way down here?'

Ooh…now where to start with that one…?

Idly swinging the office chair back and forth, she searched the air for something safe to say. 'He thought I thought he was an idiot…'

Yes, she was pretty sure it started there. No—hang on—maybe sooner. He hadn't been happy with her knowing he was afraid of flying. 'By the way—did you know he's not good with planes?'

Jake shrugged, flicking through a file on his desk. 'It's not surprising. Hitting the ground harder than normal when you're in one would do it.'

Roane's jaw dropped. 'What?'

'Charter flight, if I remember it right; Adam and his mother were flying in from a week in the Hamptons when Adam was three or four—Dad had visitation rights. It was a rough landing.' He shrugged. 'No one got hurt but it was edge-of-the-seat stuff.'

To a child it must have been a nightmare. No wonder he wasn't a good flier. Would it have killed Adam to possibly mention that? 'Jake, it didn't occur to you he mightn't be that good a flier when you suggested he *fly* down here?'

'He should've said if it was such a big problem.'

'Does he strike you as the kind of man who would confess to a weakness like that in front of a brother he hasn't seen in twelve years? Between the two of you there was enough testosterone in that kitchen this morning to sink a schooner.' There was no way she was getting caught in the middle of that battle of wills so if Jake thought—

He looked up at her. 'Now you're defending him? Thought you didn't like him.'

'I don't.' She fought the need to pout.

'Well, calling him an idiot wasn't one of your better moves. What did he say to that?'

'I didn't call him an idiot. He *assumed* I thought he was. And he was—*surly*...'

Jake chuckled. 'Yeah, I'll bet he was.' He checked his heavy wristwatch and closed the file before pushing his chair back. 'You know he's got a genius level IQ? One fifty or sixty;

something close to the highest level they measure it at. Bugged the hell out of me when I was a kid; made me feel real dumb in comparison.'

'You're kidding me, right?'

'Nope.' He lifted his jacket off the back of his chair and pushed his arms into the dark sleeves. 'Dad reckoned it was part of his restlessness. No matter how many grades he skipped he was still bored. He didn't want to be groomed as a child prodigy, so he rebelled. I think Dad blamed himself for never being able to keep his mind actively interested in anything long enough to stay out of trouble.'

When Jake chuckled at her expression a realization hit her. So Roane dropped her face into her hands, her voice muffled. 'Oh, God.'

'What did you do?'

She peeked over the tips of her fingers, opening them a little so Jake could hear her. 'He quoted Voltaire and Kerouac at me.'

'And you said?'

Dropping her hands, she sighed heavily. 'I asked if they were quote of the day.'

Jake snorted with laughter, then saw her woeful expression and controlled it, his dark eyes still sparkling with amusement as he reached for a hand to draw her out of her chair. 'I can't believe he's here less than twenty-four hours and you've already had a fight with him. You're s'posed to be the friendlier one of the two of us. I have more to argue about with him than you do and *I've* managed to stay calm.'

Yeah, but he didn't have the same issues with Adam she did. Not that she could tell him that.

'Just promise you'll be nice until he signs the papers. Then you can say whatever you want to him. I know I intend to.'

She let Jake guide her to the door. 'Do I have to?'

'You do. For me. If I didn't have you to be nice to guests and clients while I'm up to my eyes in work I'd have to go out and find myself a wife, wouldn't I?'

Roane rolled her eyes. 'Poor you.'

'Exactly.' He held open the door and stepped back to let her through. 'You're as near to an actual Bryant as be damned, Ro, and you know it. That makes it your *duty*.'

When he nodded wisely Roane chuckled, lightly punching his upper arm as he fell into step beside her in the corridor. 'I hate you.'

Jake swatted the back of her head with his file. 'No, you don't. You love me. You know you do. I'm adorable.'

Her smile faded when they rounded a corner and found Adam standing by the doors to the boardroom, his hands pushed deep into the pockets of his dark trousers.

His dark gaze crashed into hers. Immediately she felt a flush rising in her cheeks. Damn him. She really didn't like him one little bit. Regardless of the new information she now had to explain a very small portion of his behaviour.

Feeding the façade, she turned on her heel and stood on tiptoes to press a kiss to Jake's cheek, smiling at the surprise in his eyes. 'I do love you. But you owe me for this one. Big time.'

Jake blinked at her. 'O-kay.'

With a deep breath she turned and walked towards Adam, her chin held high despite the sparkling of silent amusement in his stunning eyes. 'I'll be back after the meeting. Jake tells me you're staying at the penthouse.'

'Will you be acting as tour guide?' He smiled lazily, his deep voice lowering. 'Or making sure I don't skip town again?'

Roane blinked innocently, unable to resist baiting him with a small pout. 'Babysitter possibly?'

Adam's gaze rose to watch the people filtering into the boardroom. Then he took a step closer, invading her personal space to within inches and surrounding her with his enticing scent while he lowered his head.

'Nice to see there's as much fire in your relationship with Jake as there is in ours.' He turned his head closer to her ear so she felt the movement of his lips against her hair. 'Let me know when you're ready to upgrade…'

Roane took a deep breath, ignoring her dancing pulse while she turned her face towards his. 'I'm not so sure it would be an *upgrade.*'

When a smile threatened the corners of his tempting mouth she took another breath, reminding herself that she'd told Jake she would be nice to his brute of a brother. 'Have fun at your board meeting.'

When she impulsively patted his arm, Adam's chin dropped, disbelief lifting his brows and furrowing his forehead when he looked back up at her. It was a very, very small victory, but somehow it was enough for Roane.

His eyes narrowed when she smiled a little brighter, but then Jake interrupted, 'You ready, Adam?'

'Yeah.' He glanced down at Roane. 'Later.'

Roane scrunched up her nose with feigned glee. 'Can't wait.'

Adam had to grit his teeth through the majority of the board meeting. They'd dumbed it down for him. Assuming he wouldn't have a clue about anything they were talking about was a serious mistake on their part. But he remained silent throughout.

Let them think what they wanted.

'So you see the problem.' Jake waited for the room to clear before he turned towards him.

'I do.'

Adam looked at his sibling with new-found respect. The kid knew his stuff. He'd led the meeting with a firm hand and was savvy about every aspect of the company's businesses. Where someone had to open a file to quote figures, Jake was able to correct their mistakes off the top of his head. He gave credit where credit was due for good work, was able to hand out recrimination with a glare. There was no doubt who was the captain of the good ship Bryant. Good for him. Just a shame so many members of his crew were useless.

'And you hire this lot or are they inherited?'

'Some are inherited.'

Adam bet he could name them without Jake's help. 'So cut the dead weight.'

'It's not that simple.'

'Never is.'

'Some of them are shareholders.'

Well that explained that, then. Losing the majority hold on shares was Jake's biggest threat. It was the reason Adam was there. He doubted Jake would have bothered looking for him otherwise. Especially if he knew the truth.

Jake stared calmly at him while Adam moved his head from shoulder to shoulder to ease imaginary tension in his neck. 'What do you want to do, Adam?'

'Are you going to give me options?' Adam stopped what he was doing and looked his brother in the eye. 'See me here with a nice little corner office, do you?'

'No.'

'Good. I've never spent a day of my life in an office, and I'm not starting now.' It would be suffocating.

'You'll sell to me, then.'

'Maybe.' He laid his palms against the gleaming table and

pushed his chair back, stretching his long legs out in front of him. 'Where are you getting the money?'

When Jake studied him with suspicion Adam thought he'd overplayed the nonchalance card. So he leaned forwards, bending his knees so he had a place to rest his forearms. 'It'd take time to liquidate enough assets and you'd need permission from the board for that—which you're not going to get if anyone stands to make any money with a takeover bid. So where would it come from?'

Jake pursed his lips.

So Adam pushed off his knees into an upright position, 'You either want me to have the full picture or you don't.'

'What difference does it make?' Jake's voice remained calm. 'You don't need to know where I get it any more than I need to know what you do with it.'

Fair point. Except he did want to know. If his little brother wasn't going to tell him, then he'd find out on his own.

Adam glanced around the large room, taking in the changes since the days he'd been dragged along for the obligatory heir-to-the-kingdom tours. Instead of heavy oak and opressive panelling there were shining modern surfaces and spotlights immitating stars in a jet-black ceiling. He'd bet his father hadn't initiated the changes, which made him wonder just how long Jake had held the reins. And how much of the conglomerate's current problems were actually his doing...

'Four years.'

Adam looked at Jake.

Who leaned back in his chair and formed a tent with his fingers. 'I've been running it four years. That's what you were wondering.'

Adam hid his surprise at the unexpected spark of insight. 'You were young.'

'I didn't have much of a choice, did I?'

'Everyone has a choice.'

'Not if they give a damn, they don't. Then they make decisions based on what matters. Or what *should* matter.'

Adam shook his head, exhaling a soft snort of derisive laughter as he pushed to his feet. 'Don't pretend to know what mattered or didn't matter to me, Jake. You don't know anything about me.'

'And whose fault is that?' Before Adam could reply Jake pushed to his feet, gathering files together as he continued, 'You might not care about this company, Adam, but I do. So if you're selling, let me know. If you want to learn more before you decide, then say so. The door has always been open.'

He looked Adam in the eye on his way past. 'Whether you thought it was or not.'

Adam stood in the empty room for a while after Jake left. He'd been there one day—hell, not even that long—and already he felt as if the walls were closing in. Dropping his head back, he scowled at the ceiling; it was as if he'd stepped back in time and hadn't learned a single thing in his twelve years away.

Turning on his heel, he dropped his chin—and met Roane's gaze through the vertical blinds. She was standing still in the middle of the bustling hallway, watching him. Lit by the bright light streaming through the office windows, her skin glowed, her hair shone like ripe corn fields in summer sunshine—and wearing a red jacket she stood out in the sea of greys, blacks and charcoals like a beacon.

For a split second he almost smiled at her. But instead he frowned at the fact she might have seen even a hint of how he was feeling. He didn't want anyone to see. It was a weakness. So with a silent mental shake he gathered himself together, stepping out through the doorway and striding confidently towards her, determined to pick up where they'd left off. But before he got to her a middle-aged man from the meeting stepped over.

'Good to see you, Adam.' His voice was laced with thinly veiled disrespect. 'We thought you were dead.'

Adam was a step away from him when he stopped. He clenched his jaw. Talking a measured step backwards, he turned his face towards the man, his voice cold. 'Sorry to disappoint.' He looked him over. 'Jeffries, right?'

The man swallowed hard. 'That's right.'

Adam nodded, slowly turning ninety degrees to tower over him. 'Well…*Jeffries*…a word to the wise…'

He paled. 'Y-yes?'

'Ever treat me like a fool the way you did in that meeting again and you'll wish I *was* dead.' When he lifted his arm the man flinched, and Adam smiled inwardly as he swiped an imaginary piece of lint off his shoulder before lowering his head to add, 'Have a nice day.'

Roane blinked wide eyes at him as he walked by her, her voice choked. 'Bye, Malcolm.'

'Roane…' Malcolm Jeffries was too busy scurrying away to pay much attention to her.

A quick glance over Adam's shoulder told him she was following him to the elevators, so he punched the button and waited. When she got to his side Adam glanced sideways at her, 'You got something to say, then spit it out.'

'Nope. Nothing to say.'

'Good.'

'Except he probably deserved it,' she said after a moment of silence. 'Malcolm can be a bit of a jerk. Office lech too, from what the girls say. Wandering hands…'

Adam's face jerked her way so fast he almost put his neck out. 'He *touched* you?'

One arched brow rose as she rolled back onto her heels. 'That would be your problem because?'

Damned if Adam knew. But it took a gargantuan effort not to turn round and go right back down the hall for another tête-à-tête. The elevator better get a move on. He glanced up at the numbers: forty-two, forty-three... It was the slowest elevator in New York.

'Jake didn't have a quiet word?' Bitterness rolled off the tip of his tongue. But if he hadn't, then he'd just dropped in Adam's estimation.

'Why would he—? Oh...' When she faltered Adam turned to study her expression, the fact she wasn't able to look him in the eye making him suspicious even before a hint of colour started to appear on her cheeks. 'I didn't say he touched me—I said the office girls mentioned it. It wouldn't have been Jake's problem even if he had. I can look after myself.'

Adam turned towards her, calmly folding his arms, 'Anything else you want to set straight?'

She looked up at him, her luminous blue eyes filled with curiosity. 'How come you didn't tell me the reason you don't like flying?'

She'd been asking questions about him, had she? That was interesting, but, 'That wasn't what I meant.'

She blinked blankly at him.

One of the things Roane Elliott needed to learn about him quick smart was that he wasn't that easily diverted. 'Are you or are you not involved with Jake?'

'I am.' She nodded firmly.

Adam knew he'd worded it wrong. *'Sexually.'*

Her eyes widened, gaze darting nervously around them and her voice lowering. 'Do you *mind*?'

As it happened, yes, he did. He minded a whole heap.

They stepped into the elevator together, Adam waiting until the doors closed before he moved and effectively boxed her into a corner with his body.

'Yes or no.'

The small space between them seemed to crackle. From the change in her breathing and the sharp intake of breath she took Adam knew she could feel it as keenly as he could. He couldn't remember the last time he'd felt so much heat radiating from a woman. He'd felt it on the beach, he'd felt it in the kitchen, he'd provoked it on the plane...

If she wasn't involved with Jake, then she was in way over her pretty little head. She was exactly the kind of distraction Adam needed from the things he currently felt he had a fleeting control over.

The doors behind him slid open and he saw Roane angling her head to look around him, the small grimace on her face telling him they had company. So he casually leaned a shoulder against the wall and lowered his tone.

'Yes or no.'

Roane glared at him, answering in a similarly low tone, 'None of your business.'

'I'm making it my business.'

'Why?' She seemed astounded by the notion.

Surely she couldn't be that naive? But if she wanted to have the discussion in front of an audience, then so be it. 'Why do you think?'

Taking a moment to smile weakly at the other occupant of the elevator, she flicked her long lashes upwards again. 'I'm not interested.'

Adam's smile was slow. 'Liar.'

The elevator doors opened again and for a brief second Adam thought he heard her moan. Probably mentally willing their visitor to stay. But by the time the doors closed the spark of fire had returned to her eyes.

'I *meant* I didn't want to know why.' She cocked her head to one side, the curls at the end of her shoulder-length hair brushing the collar of her jacket. Then she grumbled, 'If your ego gets any bigger you'll have to give it its own name.'

'So why did you tell me you're in a relationship with my brother if you're not?'

Roane growled at him. '*You* are the most—'

Adam calmly folded his arms again. 'Want to know what I think?'

She lifted her arms and flopped them down into a similar folded position, pouting in a way that drew his attention to her mouth. 'No.'

Adam continued to stare at her mouth. 'I think you were hiding behind him.'

When she worried on her lower lip it drew his hand out of the crook of his arm, his thumb pressing against it to still the movement. 'Don't do that.'

When his gaze rose he found her staring at him, the blue now clouded with—he frowned—was it fear? It made him study her closer, the realization slow to filter through to the front of his brain. 'This is new to you.'

How could someone with so much fire not have experience of sexual attraction on its most basic level? There was no way she'd got to her age and not— He almost laughed in disbelief at the idea. There was no way she was a virgin.

When the doors slid open he dropped his hand and glanced over his shoulder, frowning when they were joined by several men and women in suits. He knew there was another reason he hated office environments. Too many damn people.

He looked down at Roane again, the flush on her cheeks and the laboured rise and fall of her breasts telling him just how affected she was by their topic of conversation and the proximity he'd forced on her. There was one thing he was sure of—she *was* turned on. He'd bet she was ready for him already.

He breathed deep as if he might catch the scent of her arousal in the air, then stated the obvious with deep satisfaction. 'It's a no to you and Jake.'

'Well, that genius IQ obviously isn't wasted on you, is it?' She glared up at him, then looked away.

'Was it ever a yes?'

'No. Happy now?' Another glare.

Ecstatic. For the first time since he'd laid eyes on her Adam let go. He experienced anticipation thrumming through his veins, the rush of adrenalin pumping his blood harder. It had been a long, long time since he'd been so turned on by the thrill of the chase.

He wanted her. He wanted her bad. Adam always got what he wanted. Had done for a long, long time. He'd built his new life on his ability to make things happen…and on never taking no for an answer…

Roane's gaze flickered upwards, her eyes widened and then she whispered huskily, 'Please stop that.'

'Stop what?' he whispered back, leaning in a little closer and allowing his gaze to drop to her mouth.

The mouth she dutifully prepared for him with the tip of her tongue. 'You know what.'

Yes, he did. He knew exactly what he was doing.

The doors slid open at street level, so Adam pushed his

shoulder off the wall and waited for the other occupants to leave before swinging an arm in invitation. 'Miss Elliott.'

She glared sideways at him on her way past.

He fell into step beside her, matching his long-legged stride to her fast paced clicking of heels on the sheen of the foyer floor. Then he let her go through the swinging doors first, his gaze dropping to the rounded curve of her rear.

On the bustling sidewalk of Park Avenue he casually reached for her elbow, swinging her sharply around. Her hair arced out from her head, she scowled in annoyance. Then Adam hauled her in, pressing his mouth to hers.

When she tried to pull back he lifted his other hand, wrapping his fingers around the back of her head and adding enough pressure to still her. She moaned in complaint. He smiled against her lips. She was the sweetest thing he'd ever tasted. All the sweeter because she didn't fight.

Her lips were warm and soft beneath his, full and irresistibly inviting. When she didn't open to let him in he sucked her lower lip between his, teasing it with the tip of his tongue. Her sharp gasp garnered such a deep sense of victory in him he did it again, purposefully keeping the kiss soft and persuasive—lips coaxing as his tongue caressed. She shivered, he nipped her lower lip. Silently demanding she succumb to him.

Roane made a strangled noise in the base of her throat. When she opened her lips to let the noise out, Adam dipped the tip of his tongue into her mouth, curling it to tease the tip of hers. Suddenly she was leaning into him as if her legs couldn't quite hold her up… It was all he needed to make his point. For now.

He dragged his mouth from hers and set her back a step, smiling as she swayed and her heavy-lidded eyes gradually blinked him into focus.

'I can find the penthouse on my own unless they've moved it since my day.'

Her brows wavered, her breathing laboured as questions formed in her expressive eyes. 'Why did— How— You can't—'

Adam pressed his forefinger to her mouth, lowering his head to look deep into her eyes. 'Just something for you to think about, little girl.'

Roane began to frown, but Adam smiled lazily. The battle lines were drawn now.

He moved the tip of a blunt fingernail over her swollen lower lip, his gaze watching the movement as he told her in a low, rumbling voice, 'When you've thought about it you'll find me. Or I'll find you. It's that simple.'

Roane blinked at him with wide eyes.

Good girl. That's more like it. He rewarded her with a small smile, his voice low and steeped with promises of what was to come. 'It's gonna be hot, little girl—trust me. This kinda chemistry? It's rare.'

Then he dropped his hand and turned on his heel, letting a full-blown smile loose as he walked away…

CHAPTER FOUR

HE WAS SITTING in a café when Roane caught sight of him hours later, his elbows on the table and his chin resting in the palm of one large hand while he looked ahead.

He looked as if he had a lot on his mind. If he'd been anyone else she knew Roane would immediately have walked over and pulled out a chair to talk to him. But he was Adam. She didn't want to help him feel better when he'd walked away before she could form a sentence!

Why-oh-why did it have to be *Adam* who kissed her better than she'd ever been kissed before? Who left her standing on the same spot long after he'd walked away—blinking while she tried to figure out why it suddenly felt as if the world had tilted on its axis beneath her feet. And that it was a man like Adam who had done it was just…it was…well…it just didn't make any sense to Roane. She didn't even *like him*.

He was arrogant, blunt to the point of rudeness, overbearing… She had a long list of what he was.

Pursing her lips and scrunching up her nose, Roane turned on her heel to walk away. She didn't care what was on his mind.

A whimper of frustration sounded low in her throat as she wavered on the balls of her feet—trying to force herself to walk away. If she went over there he would just be Adam. It had taken her the rest of the afternoon and most of the evening wandering around Manhattan to feel like herself again.

She grimaced, attempted to go left and bumped shoulders with someone. 'I'm so sorry.'

She tried going right and managed two steps before she stopped again, stamping her foot in frustration. She really had had enough. Adam Bryant needed to understand he couldn't just stride in on those long legs of his and ride roughshod over her. She wasn't going to be bullied, or intimidated or harassed or—*tempted,* darn it. He needed to get that.

She needed to have the guts to tell him.

Yanking determinedly on the bottom of her fitted jacket, she turned on her heel and marched across the street to his table.

'We need to get a few things straight.'

His hand dropped from his chin, ridiculously thick lashes shifting upwards as he looked at her with a confident calmness that made her want to slap him. 'Pull up a chair…'

When he jerked his chin at the chair in front of her Roane frowned down at it, then looked back up, a thought side-tracking her. 'You got changed.'

When she'd left him he'd been wearing the dark suit he'd looked so good in, now he was in jeans and a dark navy T-shirt that he looked just as good in. But she didn't remember him having a bag with him.

How could one man look that good in every item of clothing he ever wore?

'I picked something up.' He reached over and pulled the chair out. 'Sit.'

Roane had to move back a step to make room for it. 'See, that's one of the things we need to talk about—you can't keep giving me orders. I don't work for you.'

'You're on the Bryant payroll, aren't you?'

'Yes, but—'

'Well, contrary to popular belief I'm still a Bryant, so therefore by default…' he pulled the chair further out '…you *do* work for me. Sit.'

She didn't want to sit. 'If I worked for you I'd probably be looking into a harassment suit about now. I really don't appreciate being talked to the way you talk to me. It's—'

'Rude; yes, you said. Don't sit then. What do you want to drink?'

'I don't want a drink.' She frowned at him when he looked around for a waitress.

'Nothing quite like sitting outside with a cold one in New York City on a warm night, is there? Sit here long enough and you'll see the world go by.'

Roane had always thought that too, but even so… 'I don't know where it is you've been the last twelve years, but back here in civilization—'

'I moved around a lot. In the last few years I've split my time between the places I liked best: San Francisco, New Orleans, here…'

Here? He'd been in New York? But that didn't make sense. 'Why didn't you visit your family if you were close by?'

Adam shrugged. 'Never got round to it.'

A cop-out if ever she heard one. 'Didn't it occur to you they might want to know you were still alive?'

'If anything happened to me they'd have been told. I have strict instructions laid down. I had a lot of things written down after Katrina…'

Roane's eyes widened when she put two and two together from what he'd said. '*Hurricane* Katrina?'

'Yep.' He grinned, dazzling her with perfectly straight

white teeth before he winked. 'Now there was a gal to make
you think long and hard about life.'

Roane blinked at him while he smiled at the waitress, who
smiled in return. 'Same again.'

'You got it.'

Adam raised his brows at Roane, who gave him a wide-
eyed glare of recrimination before glancing down at the beer
bottle in front of him. She sighed heavily before drawing the
chair back the last few inches. 'I'll have what he's having.'

When she was seated Adam leaned back, his forearms
resting on the table while he idly turned the bottle in circles
between his long fingers. 'Never tempted to leave the island?'

'I like it there.'

'There's a big wide world out here, little girl—didn't you
want to see any of it?'

'I still have a few years left. And I've never been all that
keen on the idea of hurricanes myself…'

Adam's mouth quirked, his gaze rising from the bottle to
study her face. 'Planning on leaving it till retirement, are
you? I hope we got you a good pension plan in that employment contract.'

'You did. The family more than looks after me; they have
done for a long time.' She folded her arms and flumped petu-
lantly back into her chair. Why was she sitting having a drink
with him? How had that happened?

'Does your dad still work the estate?'

Roane felt the familiar sense of loss at the mention of the
man she still missed so badly. 'He died three years ago. He
had a heart attack.'

'I'm sorry.'

The softer tone to his deep voice brought another ache to
Roane's chest, but she shrugged. 'It happens.'

'He was a good man. We used to talk some.'

Her gaze was accusatory. 'I don't remember that.'

'You wouldn't. You were either at school or tagging around after Jake like a puppy.'

'I did *not* tag around after Jake like a puppy.' They'd been joined at the hip for a long time, yes, but he made it sound as if she'd had some kind of schoolgirl crush on him. 'We were *friends*. We still are.'

'That's not how I remember it.'

'I remember you as a latter-day James Dean who didn't give a damn about anything or anyone—how accurate an assessment was *that*?' She jerked her brows.

Lifting his bottle, he tilted it in salute.

When he set the lip to his mouth Roane took the opportunity to notice a few things. Like the two thin strips of leather knotted around his wrist, a matching one tied round his neck and disappearing into the neck of his T-shirt, the wide silver band on the ring finger of his right hand...how his throat convulsed as he swallowed...the flicker of his tongue over his wide mouth to remove any lingering moisture...

Then her gaze rose and met his again, the green in his eyes merging into the brown with silent knowing. He'd seen her checking him out, hadn't he? Well, he could think what he wanted—she hadn't been thinking about the kiss. *Much.*

The waitress reappeared with their drinks, setting napkins down before she removed the bottles from her circular tray and bestowed a wide smile on Adam for his word of thanks.

Roane lifted hers, wiped the top with the napkin and took a sip, frowning at how easily he seemed to have charmed the brunette. He liked to keep his options open, didn't he? That really shouldn't have bugged her as much as it did, but—

She looked around, the sound of distant sirens and a loudly honking horn telling her a fire truck was going to work a few blocks away—then she glanced at Adam and found him studying her with hooded eyes.

'What?'

'You're mad at yourself for sitting down, aren't you?'

She sighed in exasperation. 'Who wouldn't want to spend time in your charming company?'

A lazy smile curled his mouth, deepening the grooves in his cheeks. 'You really don't like me much, do you?'

'You've not given me much of a reason to.'

'You just don't know me well enough yet.'

'And you're planning on sticking around long enough for that to happen, are you?'

Shifting his gaze to the people on the sidewalk behind her, he shrugged again. 'I haven't decided what I'm doing yet.'

Something in his tone made Roane delve into an area that really wasn't any of her business. 'How did it go with your father this morning?'

'He didn't know me.'

Roane grimaced inwardly because it had to have hurt, even after so many years. How could it not? Her voice softened as a result. 'Mornings aren't good for him. Until he gets into the routine of the day he can be disorientated—and in fairness it'll have been a surprise to him. He doesn't do well with surprises. If we'd known you were coming home we could have prepared him for a few days to—'

Adam looked sideways at her. 'Spend a lot of time with the old man, do you?'

'Yes.' She wasn't put off by the flat tone of his voice. 'We all share the time between us. We have to. It's a full-time job.'

He looked back at the crowd.

But Roane still felt the need to help. 'He'll know you. Give
it time. He talks about you every day.'

The burst of low laughter was bitter. 'Yeah, I'll bet he
does.'

She shook her head, confused. 'Why come back if you
hate him so much?'

He frowned as if he wasn't happy saying the words out
loud. 'I'm here for me, not him.'

Edward Bryant wasn't an easy man, Roane knew that. But
neither had she any experience of him being as awful as
Adam seemed to think he was. She'd always thought he was
more of a pussy cat inside than he let the world see. Roane
being Roane, she immediately felt the need to try and mediate
in some way. A father and his son should never be as es-
tranged as they were.

She couldn't stop the words from slipping free. 'It must
have been quite the bust up you had with him…'

Adam smiled wryly as he lifted his bottle to his mouth. 'It
wasn't exactly an episode of *The Waltons,* let's put it that way.'

'You used to argue a lot. I remember that.' There had been
times when their raised voices could be heard echoing
through the large house, times when Jake had frowned and
dragged her outside into the open air where they couldn't hear
it. Adam might not have known it, but those arguments had
upset his kid brother just as much as they probably had him—
maybe more—because Adam's leaving had placed a rift
between the father and his second son too…

Again it probably wasn't her place, but he needed to hear
it. 'Jake blamed him for you leaving.'

Adam's head turned sharply. 'I was always going to leave.
It was just a question of when.'

'Why?'

His brows lifted in disbelief. 'Why?'

'Yes. Why?'

Adam was staring at her as if she'd just dropped in from another planet. 'You think it's that simple? I'm supposed to spill my guts and you'll dish out some words of wisdom to make everything all right? I'm going to lay my head on your shoulder afterwards and we can shed a few tears—share a chick-flick moment. Is that how you see this working out?'

She smiled at him. 'Yet after one itty bitty kiss I'm s'posed to fall at your feet and jump straight into bed with you. That any simpler, is it?'

To her amazement he smiled back, nodding his head and pursing his lips as he lifted his bottle again. 'I get it. You're here to psychoanalyze me in search of redeeming qualities. Then you'll feel better about being attracted to me.'

'I think you want me to hate you.' She lifted her own bottle. 'It's the easy way out. Sex for sex's sake and you don't ever have to get involved with anyone, right?'

'Well, you know what they say, sweetheart: it's better to be hated for what you are than loved for something you're not…' He had the gall to continue smiling at her over the lip of the bottle. 'You're still not denying you're attracted to me though, are you? Hate me all you want. It's just going to make it all the hotter when it happens.'

Roane set her bottle back down with a dull thud.

Before she could say anything Adam leaned closer, his voice low. 'Ever have angry sex, little girl? I'm betting you haven't. I'm betting there's plenty you haven't tried. That's what's got you here when you don't want to be, isn't it?'

His gaze shifted, his head angling so he could study her closer. 'There's a part of you—deep down inside—that wants to experience what you've never experienced before. I'm the key to a door you've never dared open. But you're burning with curiosity to know what's on the other side, aren't you?'

Roane's mouth was as dry as a desert, her throat raw when she attempted to swallow. She could feel the heat building inside her body, could feel her skin tingling as if it were being touched by the whisper of his seductive words. Heaven help her. Everything he said was true. She burned. And he hadn't laid a finger on her.

His gaze slid leisurely down the V of her jacket to the breasts that immediately seemed to swell against the confines of lace cups. 'You want to know what it's like to have my hands on you—to have my mouth on your skin—what it'll feel like when I'm inside y—'

'*Stop.*' She exhaled the word on a note of pure agony, her heart slamming against her breastbone. No one had ever spoken to her the way he was. The fact it was seriously doing things for her was shocking. She'd never thought of herself as the kind of girl who was turned on by a man who could talk dirty.

Adam's gaze rose sharply to search her wide eyes. 'Why so scared? That's what I don't get. You're too old to be a virgin. You're curious or you wouldn't be here. You can't tell me you're not turned on. Like I said before, I'm not an idiot.'

Roane forced her vocal cords to work. 'You *are* the most arrogant man I've ever met.'

'Not arrogance, sweetheart—*confidence.* Life experience brings you that, along with a healthy dose of "life's too short." You want this as much as I do. You know you do. Why fight it?'

'Why?' The whispered question rose up from deeper inside her than she'd ever looked before. '*Why me?*'

Surprise flickered across his hypnotic eyes. '*Why?*'

Roane could only manage a nod.

To her utter astonishment, one large hand lifted to push her hair back and cradle the side of her head, his thumb smoothing over the skin on her cheek with impossible gentleness. Then his deep voice rumbled low. 'I'll tell you why, little girl, it's because I want to be the one to teach you the things you've obviously been missing out on.'

Roane blinked at him in wonder.

The smile he gave her was devilishly slow and sexy, creating a coiling knot low in her abdomen. 'Life should be filled with unforgettable experiences. I promise I'd make this one of them for you.'

Roane was drowning in a sea of seduction so deep she could barely breathe, her very soul yearning for an *unforgettable* sexual experience. She wanted to be shown what all the fuss was about, why some people spent days in bed, what it was that had driven the human race to such extremes in the name of passion. The kind of passion she'd never come close to experiencing; not that she hadn't tried, but she'd been left feeling empty and, well—*unfulfilled*, quite frankly.

Just *once* in her lifetime. Was that so very much to ask? She didn't think it was.

Adam was the perfect candidate if she decided to do something as completely crazy as accept the offer. Not only was he hotter than Hades, he wasn't the kind of man to put her through all the angst and self-doubt of dating. He wouldn't ask for any kind of a commitment. Not liking his personality meant there wasn't any chance of her falling for him and having her heart broken…

All right, so call her shallow; part of her attraction to him was the way he looked—she wouldn't even try to pretend it

asn't. Having such an astonishingly good-looking man
ursue her was an undeniable thrill. She was only human.

After an endless moment, she found herself silently
odding, a curl of apprehension tying into a knot in her
tomach when his eyelids grew heavy and his smile turned
angerous.

He's going to kiss me again, she realized instinctually. A
econd later his gaze dropped to her mouth and she knew she
vas right, her pulse dancing in anticipation and her tongue
lickering out to dampen her lips in preparation.

Hurry up and do it, then! She needed to know the first one
adn't been a fluke, made memorable by the element of
urprise. It wasn't too late to back out. Women changed their
ninds all the time.

Adam moved his hand, nudging her chin up with his fist.
hen he kissed her. He took advantage of her submission to
art her lips with his tongue and sweep inside, taking her
harp gasp of cooler night air and replacing it with raw heat.
n a mist of sensuality Roane was only vaguely aware of him
vrapping his arm around her waist and tugging her closer to
ne edge of her chair. Her arms lifted, hands sliding around
ne column of his neck to hold him tight as their knees
umped together. Every doubt, every fear, every voice of
eason in her head short-circuited except one.

Why haven't I been kissed like this before?

It was *so* unfair. Twenty-four hours ago she'd thought she was
appy, contented even. That her life was exactly what she
vanted it to be. Now she knew what she'd been missing. She
elt cheated. If this was just the kissing part, then *heaven help
er…*

So much for changing her mind. It was already too late.
Ier body knew what it craved.

Tentatively she kissed him back, her moves becoming bolder when a growling noise of approval vibrated deep in his chest. She parted her knees and tugged herself closer, feeling the erotic sensation of the rough seams of his jeans sliding up the insides of her soft cotton trousers. But it wasn't enough. Somewhere in her darkest thoughts came the idea—no, the *need*—to climb onto his lap and press her breasts tight against the wall of his chest.

One kiss and she was ready for the kind of public display she would never even have contemplated before.

With considerable effort she leaned back, running her tongue over her swollen lips the second they parted from his. As if subliminally she felt the need to lap up every last taste of him before she opened her eyes.

When she did Adam was staring at her. 'Quick study, aren't you?'

Roane smiled a little shyly. 'You think?'

'I *know*.' He released her and lifted his hands to hers, freeing her fingers from behind his neck. Then he placed his hands on either side of her waist and lifted her up and back—dropping her unceremoniously into place before he pointed a long index finger.

'Stay there. Before you get us both arrested for public indecency.'

When he reached for his beer bottle and downed half its contents Roane's smile grew. 'You started it.'

Adam looked at her from the corner of narrowed eyes. 'Careful, little girl. Or this is gonna happen faster than you're ready for.'

Squirming a little on her seat, she felt her cheeks warming at just *how* ready she was…

Adam's voice was gravelly. '*Quit that.*'

Roane's cheeks burned, so she aimed a scowl at him, 'I'm confused. One minute you're all "I'm gonna teach you" and now you're telling me to behave?'

The beer bottle froze halfway to his mouth, was lowered carefully to the table—then Adam turned at the waist and looked her in the eye. 'As of now lesson number one is about anticipation. I'm going to make sure you're so ready for this you'll go insane if it doesn't happen.'

Roane couldn't help it; she gulped.

Adam slowly nodded his head, 'Mmm-hmm. Lesson two has a lot to do with lesson one; sex isn't just about the body— it's about the mind. It's the largest erogenous zone the body has.'

Said the guy with the genius-level IQ? Roane's brows wavered. Oh she was in *so* much trouble. How was she supposed to compete with that? How did a girl like her engage the mind of someone like him?

The smile started in his eyes. 'What?'

Roane had never been all that good at hiding things. Jake had teased her countless times about wearing her heart on her sleeve and saying a million words with just one look. But Adam didn't know her that well.

'Nothing.'

'Liar.'

She felt a hint of a headache forming behind her eyes. He was hard work. 'You're obviously more experienced with this than I am…'

When she waved a limp-wristed hand in the space between them Adam smiled indulgently. '*Obviously*. Though frankly? Your lack of experience baffles me.'

Roane frowned a little. 'It does?'

'Yes.' For a moment he looked as if he was holding back

a larger smile, then he controlled it and studied her face wit
open curiosity. 'The island's population jumps from what
Fifteen thousand off season to a hundred thousand in th
summer—give or take? You can't tell me there haven't bee
opportunities.'

Well, yes, there had, but, 'It makes for short-term relation
ships, though, don't you think?'

'Meaning there *were* opportunities…'

'Not everyone looks at people from the point of view o
whether or not there'd be great sex,' said the girl wh
probably wouldn't know great sex if it drove over her in a bu
with the words 'great sex' written on the sidings.

Adam blinked a couple of times. 'So you've been waitin
around for Mr. Right. You should know from the get-go–
I'm not him.'

'*Obviously.*' The corners of her mouth twitched.

'I mean it. Don't fall for me.'

Roane rolled her eyes. 'Do you ever actually listen to wha
comes out of your mouth? I mean, *seriously*?'

'Just laying out the ground rules…'

'Uh-huh.' She blinked at him. 'Do I get a say in any o
these ground rules?'

'That depends.'

'On what?'

'On whether or not I like what I hear…' he smiled in chal
lenge as he lifted his bottle to his lips again, eyes sparkling a
her '…though never let it be said I'm not open to sugges
tions…'

When he waggled his brows a burst of incredulou
laughter left Roane's mouth. 'You're unbelievable.'

'I told you you'd learn to like me when you knew me better

That was just it, though. She couldn't. Not if she stood an

chance of coming out of the other end of whatever they were doing with her heart still intact. It was a survival thing.

Adam Bryant was *way* out of her league…

CHAPTER FIVE

ADAM TOOK AS deep a breath as his lungs would allow, his chin low and his gaze focused straight ahead. He could beat this. He'd been in New Orleans when the full force of a furious Mother Nature had sent the world crashing down around his ears so he could most certainly beat the violent need to throw up when faced with a pretty little blue and white light aircraft.

Ignoring the trickle of cold sweat working its way down his spine, he set his shoulders. *Mind over matter.*

'I checked the weather; we might hit a little light turbulence before the approach to the Vineyard, but that's it…' Roane's voice was softly feminine and confident at the same time.

But still smacked of sympathy to Adam.

'We could have another flying lesson, if you like.'

He looked at her from the corner of his eye. 'Yes because the last one ended so well for me.'

Roane looked back up at him with sparkling blue eyes, her teeth catching one side of her lower lip before a smile broke free. 'Well, you see, last time you didn't understand the most important ground rule. Or sky rule.' She shifted her gaze upwards and considered that for a moment. 'I'm not quite sure which one it is when we're up there…'

They stopped at the tip of one wing, Adam turning to look down at her. 'Okay, I'll bite. What's the rule?'

Her chin jerked up and a more mischievous smile appeared. 'Up there, *I'm* in control—you're on my turf—any control I give you is on my terms. Therefore rubbing me up the wrong way isn't the brightest move you could make.'

When she added a determined nod to the end of the sentence Adam lifted a brow. She was sassy when she set her mind to it. Adam had always been a sucker for sassy. And feisty. And frisky. Frisky most of all…nothing quite like a frisky woman, he felt…

He allowed himself another leisurely examination of what she was wearing—his sixth or seventh since she'd met him that morning. Again he wondered how she'd managed to stay so inexperienced. The woman dressed in a way that suggested she was way more sexually confident than she actually was.

Not that she was blatantly sexual in the way she dressed. Knowing what he did of her, he knew the very fact it was sexual was probably unintentional. Being five feet five at best, she chose heels to boost her height, heels that made her walk the way women did in heels: with the gentle sway of hips that drew a man's attention. Then there was the way they made her legs appear longer, the zips and tassels on her low-hipped burgundy combat trousers inviting a man's imagination to explore, unzip, untie…*remove*…

But it was her jacket that had him most fascinated. She had a thing about fitted jackets. Bit buttoned down for Adam's preference under normal circumstances, but on Roane they were different—they cinched in at her impossibly small waist, lovingly hugged her pert breasts… created the kind of silhouette that said she might be small, but *man* was she beautifully formed.

The one she was wearing was a dark purple, long-sleeved, high-collared, with seams that ran vertically to highlight that tempting silhouette. Fairly conservative, until she was facing forwards—then it changed completely. Large circular rings lined the front edges, but Roane had left the hooks that held those edges together undone at the top and the bottom. There wasn't just the tempting V down to the valley of her breasts but an even more tempting inverted V at the bottom that showed mesmerizing glimpses of the feminine curve of her stomach. It made Adam's palms itch to reach out and touch, to push the edges back so he could splay his fingers and feel how soft her skin was.

But if he touched he knew he wouldn't stop. Not when merely looking at her was enough to have his body thrumming with awareness and his jeans too tight for comfort.

Roane hooked her thumbs into the belt loops of her trousers, cocking her hip just enough for him to drag his gaze back up to her face. She lifted an accusatory brow at him.

'Is there any chance you could stop looking at me like I'm chocolate-coated?'

'Actually, that I could work with…' His gaze tangled with hers. 'I did say I was open to suggestions.'

When her mouth dropped open he blinked lazily, allowing his gaze to rove down over her body and back up, 'You should be used to it when you dress like that…'

Her chin dropped. 'What's wrong with it?'

'Oh, sweetheart, there's nothin' *wrong* with it.' He felt his body grow painfully hard as another thought occurred to him. 'You're wearing something under that jacket, right?'

There was a moment of hesitation and then she looked up at him from beneath long lashes. 'It doesn't really need anything under it.'

He was half a step closer when she grabbed hold of his wrist and turned him towards the plane, her voice firmer. 'If it helps to distract you from flying, then you can wonder if I have on any underwear at all. Knowing you, that should keep your mind occupied…'

'Remember we talked about you pushing me?'

'Oh, I remember.' She opened the door to the cockpit and stepped back to make room for him. 'But you also said the mind was the largest erogenous zone. Maybe I'm just testing that theory.'

'You know what they say about payback, don't you?'

'I'd heard a rumour. Get in the plane, please.'

When she let go of his wrist he folded his arms and studied her face with hooded eyes. 'And once I'm in there you're in control.'

'Uh-huh.'

He stepped closer. 'I have to do whatever you say.'

'You do.'

Adam thought it over for a second, his fear of flying taking a back seat to a sudden plethora of possibilities. 'Okay, then.'

Unfolding his arms, he set his hands on her hips; his thumbs on the curve of her stomach as he yanked her closer. When he dipped his thumbs beneath the waistband of her trousers her eyes darkened, the muscles in her abdomen trembling. 'If you're looking to distract me I have a challenge for you…'

Her eyes widened with a sexual awareness she didn't try to hide from him. Learning already, wasn't she?

Adam smiled a slow smile. 'What I want to know is just how far you're prepared to stretch this window of opportunity.

'Cause call me weak, sweetheart—but I'm not prepared to chance another *accidental slip* of your foot on the rudder…'

Roane looked repentant. 'You deserved it.'

'Maybe.'

'No maybe about it—you were an ass.'

'You rattled my cage—' his fingers tightened on her hips '—so if I'm stepping onto your turf and relinquishing control I'd like to know just how far you're prepared to go to distract me this time…'

Curiosity shimmered across her expressive eyes. 'What exactly are you suggesting?'

'It's a one-time offer. I'm putting myself in your hands. Consider it lesson number three…'

She watched as his arms returned to his sides, unable to believe what he was saying judging by her expression. 'Wouldn't you prefer it if I devoted my attention to flying the plane?'

'You said clear skies for most of the way.'

'I did.' Her voice was filled with caution.

'Well, then, you can use that autopilot thing of yours again, can't you?' He rocked forwards and quirked his brows in challenge. 'And a little imagination…'

Her eyes widened. 'You're asking me to—'

'Take charge. Yes, I am.' He rocked back and nodded firmly. 'I'm guessing that's something you've never done with a man before.'

The familiar flush on her cheeks was answer enough.

'Yeah, I thought so. You've never told a man what you wanted or what felt good. Consider this a test run. In the air I'm your temporary slave—emphasis on the word temporary. *Remember that.*'

The uncertainty radiating from her was palpable, so Adam

reached out and tilted her chin up, his voice as low as he could allow it to go to still be heard over the ambient airport sounds surrounding them. 'Do anything you want. Or don't…and I'll just go right ahead and focus on how much I hate planes…'

One small hand shoved him hard in the centre of his chest. *'That's* emotional blackmail.'

'If you say so.'

'I should white-knuckle you from here to the Vineyard for that—it would serve you right.'

'But you won't.' He stepped back and rubbed his palms together vigorously. 'Can't say I've ever looked forward to a flight as much as I am right this second…'

Roane stood on the tarmac for a while after he folded his large frame into the cockpit. She frowned as she closed the door behind him. Then she took her time walking around the tail, glad she'd completed her pre-flight check before he got there. There was no way she'd be able to concentrate properly after his challenge. And challenge it was.

More than he could know.

He was leaving it all down to her: the method of distraction, the execution of it—he wasn't going to do *anything?* So if she wanted to touch him he would just sit there and let her? If she wanted to kiss him he wouldn't kiss her back? Or he would but he wouldn't initiate it?

It was like being given a tiger to play with.

But, boy, was it tempting!

It would just be so much easier to give into temptation if there weren't a very real chance of her making a complete fool of herself. What did she know about seducing a man?

Imagination, he'd said. Okay. She just needed to think about it for a bit. She would focus on the everyday business of getting them safely into the air and out of New York airspace and by the time they got to clearer skies she might have had a stroke of genius.

Mentally she crossed her fingers as she stepped into the cockpit. 'Buckle up, Bryant.'

'Yes, ma'am.'

Roane shook her head as he saluted her.

It was the low tuneless whistling that eventually galvanized her to action. Apparently even thinking about what she might come up with had been enough to settle Adam's nerves. He'd only gripped his knees a little during take-off, swiped his palms a couple of times as they'd ascended to their designated altitude, been pursing his lips just enough for her to know he wasn't one hundred per cent comfortable. Roane found each and every one of the telltale signs endearing. *Worryingly*…

But the whistling made her crazy. 'That sound is magnified in the headsets, you know.'

'What sound?'

'You're whistling.'

'Am I?' He stretched as much as the cockpit would allow. 'Must be passing the time till my distraction gets here…'

'You can be as irritating as a rag-nail when you put your mind to it,' Roane complained beneath her breath, checking all the readouts before she reached for the autopilot. Then she turned to consider him, her mind reaching for a possible solution in the absence of any imagination. What to do… hmm…and how to do it without giving away just how nervous she was?

Adam turned her way, resting his back against the door while he smiled a smile that softened the green in his sensational eyes. 'Don't know what to do, do you?'

'I'm weighing up the options.'

'Chicken.'

She cocked a brow and angled her head. 'I can make you reach for a sick bag in about thirty seconds, you know. The Meridian is a versatile little plane.'

When his eyes sparkled with light she found it hard to stop the smile from making its way onto her face. Darn it. Even when she was supposedly in charge he still had the upper hand on her. Then somewhere out of left field came a glimmer of an idea. Work with what you've got, they said. She'd always found flying sexy so maybe she just needed to transfer some of that to Adam?

Okay. She could do this. She just needed to give it a try. Nothing ventured, nothing gained.

'Put your hands on the stick.'

'You've had all this time to think of something and the best you could come up with was another flying lesson.' He shook his head. 'Man. We've got a long way to go with you, don't we?'

'This is my turf—remember?' She scowled at him. He wasn't making it any easier. 'You have to do as you're told.'

'Bossy can be sexy. That's a start.' He moved back into place and reached his hands out, curling his fingers around the stick with more care than he'd used the first time.

'You have to be quiet so I can concentrate.' She placed her hands over his and adjusted the angle, her body leaning close to his and her breast pressed against his upper arm.

She could feel the heat radiating off him through her clothes, the responding jump of awareness in her pulse. It was just like last time. Except this time it wasn't Adam backing her into a corner and forcing her to feel things she didn't want to feel. This time it was Adam *inviting her* to feel those things, to explore, to take what she wanted…

It was the most erotic thing she'd ever experienced.

Adam's voice was deeper above her head. 'I don't remember being told not to speak…'

'Adam?' She said his name somewhat huskily, then leaned back a little and looked into his eyes, her voice deliberately low as she smiled at him with meaning.

He smiled back at her—that lazily, deliciously sexual, slightly lopsided smile of his. 'Yes?'

'Shut up.' She batted her lashes, beginning to enjoy her position of control over him.

The smile remained, so with a shake of her head Roane went back to checking everything before she removed one hand long enough to reach over to the autopilot. 'You have the stick now. Just keep it even. Now don't move from there. You see this dial?'

She pointed to one and looked at him long enough to smile at his frowning nod. 'That's your horizon. Keep the line straight and we're good. Got it?'

He nodded again.

Okay, so far so good. Leaning back and letting go of his hands, she checked to make sure he was focusing on what he was doing before starting. She damped her lips. She could do this. No matter what the violent thudding of her heart, her dry mouth and her suddenly clammy palms said to the contrary.

Adam had his profile to her, his ridiculously thick lashes flickering as his gaze shifted from the stick to the horizon to the sky and back to the beginning again. So Roane took a deep breath, her voice husky even to her own ears.

'Now I'm going to tell you a few things about the airplane. So listen up.'

He glanced at her with raised eyebrows that furrowed his forehead.

And Roane nodded. 'Yes—the plane.'

When he rolled his eyes the way she normally did Roane chuckled, leaning in so her face was closer to his. 'Focus on what you're doing; feel the vibration of the engine through your hands and underneath your seat…and listen to my voice…'

Adam glanced briefly at her from the corner of his eye and Roane could see the combination of suspicion and curiosity there. She'd sparked his interest, hadn't she? It was quite the confidence booster.

So she kept her voice low and the words slow, not caring if her own rising arousal was showing. 'You are sitting in two million dollars' worth of precision engineering. She's a thing of great beauty and strength and has more than enough under the hood to make an aficionado shudder with pleasure…'

When he glanced at her again she saw the darkening of his eyes. It told her he knew what she was doing—that he could read the subtext where Roane told him about the kind of woman she would dearly love to be. It gave her a sudden rush of adrenalin, so she swiped her tongue over her lips and let her lower lip slide between her teeth. 'A plane like this comes with a beautifully glossy brochure. I read it from cover from cover. Shall I tell you my favorite part?'

He nodded.

'*Anything is possible…*' She breathed the words, her eyelids growing heavy as she inhaled his sensuous scent and continued, 'People are said to reach a meridian in their lives—a time at which their powers and prowess are at their apex. A time at which anything is possible, and all the objects of desire are suddenly within reach.'

When she glanced down she saw his throat convulse, so she kept going. 'It is a height hard-won, and deeply satisfying. A height from which one can see into the light of things…'

Further down she could see that his breathing had changed, his wide chest rising and falling in shallower breaths, so she let herself get lost in her passion for the subject. 'It's how this plane makes me feel when I'm flying. Up here I'm free, I'm exhilarated, I'm *turned on* by it…Every. Single. Time.'

As free and exhilarated and turned on as she was by what she was doing with Adam…

His breathing stilled while Roane resisted the temptation to allow her gaze to slide down to his lap, instead following it back up to the column of his neck where she could see his pulse throbbing temptingly just beneath the collar of his shirt.

'Then we have the stats—' she took a measured breath '—like horsepower…lift…flight speed…*thrust*…'

The last word was whispered and while she stared the throbbing pulse sped up. So before she could talk herself out of it, she pushed her mike back to make room and bent forwards, pressing her lips to the spot.

Adam's low hiss of pleasure thrilled her, a smile forming against his skin as she lifted her hand and set it on his knee. He tensed. She leaned back just enough to be heard in the mike.

'Cruise speed is two hundred and sixty knots…' Another kiss a little further up. 'She can rise to a maximum altitude of thirty thousand feet…'

Impulsively she flicked her tongue out, running the very tip of it over his skin and closing her eyes to savour the combination of warm skin and hint of saltiness on her lips. He was delicious.

Adam let out a low growl.

'You're wondering about the range…' She slid her hand a little higher up his leg, feeling the muscles in his thigh

unch beneath her palm. 'It's got a thirteen hundred kilo-
meter range…over a thousand nautical miles…'

Simultaneously she ran her tongue over the sensitive skin
below his ear and slid her hand a little higher up his thigh, his
body heat seeping through the material of his jeans and into her
palm. 'We could cross the Atlantic with this plane, Adam…'

Then an undiscovered vixen within her asked, 'How long
do you think you would need?'

'*Roane?*' Her name was said on a harsh note.

She moved back enough to be heard and to study a muscle
clenching in his jaw. 'Yes?'

'If you keep doing that in about thirty seconds I'm gonna
crash this plane.'

'No, you won't.' She smiled drunkenly, intoxicated by
his reaction.

'Oh, yes, I will.' A short burst of deep masculine laughter
sparkled into the air. 'And when we die I'm gonna haunt you
for all eternity.'

'No, you won't.' Roane's smile grew, her gaze tangling with
his. 'I'd have had to disengage the autopilot for that to happen…'

Adam frowned. 'You reached over.'

'Mmm-hmm—doesn't mean I did it, though.'

There was a comical moment of uncertainty when Adam
frowned harder at the stick in his hands and then back to her,
realization narrowing his eyes. 'So if I let go of this thing we
won't plummet into the ocean.'

'No plummeting.'

His voice deepened as he loosened his fingers. 'Sweetheart, you're in so much trouble about now it's not even
funny…'

'Ah-ah-ah.' She leaned back and waggled a finger at him
when he turned her way, joy bubbling effervescently inside

her at her achievement. 'No, you don't. You're all mine, remember? Temporary slave. At my command.'

'I'm calling a do-over due to foul play.'

Roane grinned. 'What are you, *seven?* You can't call a do-over. The rules were set before we left the ground.'

'You're a con artist, Elliott.'

'No-oo…it turns out I have hitherto unknown talents… who knew?' She shrugged a shoulder and continued grinning ridiculously as she checked the readouts and how far they were from home. 'I think I might just get to go to the top of the class for this one. Go me.'

When Adam didn't say anything she looked over at him and found him studying her with hooded eyes, the smile he aimed her way enough to melt her into a puddle on the floor. Then his voice rumbled huskily over her headset.

'Two words, little girl…'

Roane lifted a brow.

'Pay…back…'

'That's one word,' she calmly informed him while her body flamed in anticipation.

Adam shook his head as he turned forwards in his seat. 'The amount of it coming your way merits more than the one word.'

It sent a shiver of excitement up Roane's spine. But she'd known what he'd do if she was successful, hadn't she? Maybe it was why she'd put so much effort into it. It had taken very little, surprisingly. Whether that was because his mind had already been engaged on the subject before she'd ever got started or because she'd let him read innuendo where he chose to on an otherwise innocent subject she didn't know.

But the sense of empowerment it engendered in Roane was unparalleled except for the day she'd gained her pilot's licence—and her freedom along with it.

Adam's idea of payback suddenly felt more like a *reward*…

The plane shook a little and Roane disengaged the auto-pilot to begin their decent through the mild turbulence. She glanced at Adam and saw his large hands gathering into fists on his knees again.

'Adam?'

'Mmm-hmm?' He made the sound almost absent-mindedly. As if his mind was already engaged on methods of payback…

'Just out of curiosity…'

The edge to her voice got his full attention. 'Yes?'

Roane noticed he didn't seem bothered by the second bump they hit. 'If I had kept doing what I was doing—just how long *would* you have needed?'

There was a moment of silence—then laughter. The deep, rumbling, very male sound was mesmerizing to Roane. It changed him. Light danced in his eyes, laughter lines made crow's feet at the outside edges of his dense lashes, the deep grooves in his cheeks framed his smile while ridiculously white teeth flashed at her. He was the most gorgeous man she'd ever laid eyes on. And pretty soon he was going to make love to her. She didn't know when or where, her imagination was now having one heck of a time with the how—but it was a certainty, a fait accompli…

Roane had always had very fixed opinions on the idea of falling into bed with a man she didn't know. But it didn't feel wrong to her; she felt as if she'd known Adam a lot longer than she had, that he wouldn't judge her for caving in so easily. With him she felt free in a way she never had before. It was addictive. As if doing away with all the associated un-certainties of dating and building a relationship removed all the pressure at the same time. She could just be herself and consequences be damned. It was a rare form of emancipation.

'You're a very different woman on your own turf. You know that, right?'

Roane thought about that, her voice low. 'I guess. I've never really thought about it before. On the ground I'm… *grounded*…no pun intended.'

When she accompanied the last word with a wry smile Adam smiled devilishly at her. 'Well, then, we'll have to see what we can do about making you soar when you're on terra firma, won't we? 'Cause this version of you? It's *somethin'*…'

It was the nicest compliment anyone had ever paid her, a part of Roane blossoming and growing under the warmth of his praise. And *that* feeling?

That was *somethin'*…

CHAPTER SIX

ADAM WATCHED AS his father considered his chess move. Roane had been right; further into the routine of the day he was vastly more lucid than he'd been the first morning Adam saw him. By late afternoon he was giving Adam a run for his money.

Playing chess was the one thing they'd done that Adam remembered with any degree of fondness. It had been an especially important break during the times when they'd disagreed on pretty much anything and everything else. The arrogance of youth had begun butting heads with the self-perceived wisdom of experience by Adam's early teens...

He sighed lightly—as much at the new perspective on the past as the amount of time the old man was putting into considering his move. Stubborn old bastard. Despite the fact he was much frailer than Adam remembered, the description still held true. Adam had heard the way he talked to the nurse, who obviously had the patience of a saint.

His father reached out a pale-skinned hand and moved his rook. Adam calmly reached out and moved his knight.

The old man frowned. 'Been practising.'

'Every now and again.'

'You always were too smart for me, boy…'

Adam frowned. Where had that come from?

'Your mother was smart. Get it from her. Look like her too.' He smiled down at the board. 'Beautiful woman…'

Adam watched as his father's chin lifted, a look of confusion on his face. 'She here?'

'No, she's not here.' It wasn't the fact the old man was confused enough to ask about the ex-wife who'd died when Adam had been ten that surprised him. It was the fact he looked so stricken when he was told she wasn't. 'It's your move.'

His father looked into the middle distance. 'She never liked the island. Couldn't settle…'

'I know.' Adam's mother had viewed the island as a desert rather than the oasis, especially during the off season.

'Tried. Both tried. Didn't work.'

'I know.'

He looked Adam in the eye. 'She took you away.'

Adam clenched his jaw. 'I visited. You taught me to play chess.'

He smiled wistfully. 'You learned fast. Beat me when you were seven.'

Adam nodded. 'It had patterns I liked. They made sense.'

'Always good with math. Made money that way, didn't you?'

The statement made Adam's eyes narrow. 'How do you know that?'

But his father's attention was waning again, his gaze searching the room. 'Dinner at five.'

When Adam checked his wristwatch and found it was ten to, the nurse magically appeared to announce, 'Mr. Bryant needs to get ready for dinner now.'

'Dinner at five,' his father repeated.

'That's right, Mr. Bryant. Now, let's get you to the table, shall we?' She smiled warmly at Adam. 'Will you be joining your father?'

'No, I have a few calls to make. But I'll come back.' He helped the nurse to get his father to his feet, surprised at how much shorter he was compared to Adam's memories. He'd always remembered Edward Bryant as an imposing bear of a man. 'We have a game to finish.'

His father smiled, lifting a hand to pat Adam's forearm. 'We'll play chess, boy. I'll teach you.'

Adam went for a walk to fill in time. He was restless, and not just because his father was so changed. Feeling restless wasn't anything out of the ordinary for Adam. He got itchy feet several times a year. The difference was he was usually in a position to do something about it. Like visiting one of his projects or driving across country to a different city to see friends or check out something he'd found interesting enough to invest in.

But within a few hours of stepping back onto the island that day he was restless in a way he hadn't been in a long time. The thing was, it had very little to do with the location—if anything he quite enjoyed revisiting some of his favorite places on the estate.

No, this had more to do with the woman who was thousands of feet up in the air taking businessmen to Boston. Something she'd neglected to tell him she was doing until they'd been safely on the tarmac and his thoughts had been focused entirely on a very sensual payback.

So he'd left her with a kiss that had barely scratched the surface of how turned on they both were by the game she'd played in the air. And walking away from her had cost him his first cold shower in…for ever…

When his phone rang he frowned—the sound seemed so out of place where he was. Time for a reality check from his new life, it seemed.

'A.J.—it's Sol.'

Adam's gaze strayed towards the main house as he made his way up the grassy, tree-lined laneway. 'You get the information I wanted?'

'I did. He's been trying to buy up shares for the last eighteen months. But you still hold the majority.'

'Does he know that?'

'Not that I can tell. You're pretty well hidden. You wanted it that way.'

'I still do.' Adam breathed deep. Then he asked the question that had been bugging him for the past half-hour. 'Does anyone else know?'

For a brief second it had felt as if the old man knew what Adam had been doing since he left. It suggested he'd kept tabs on him. But if he had then why had Jake needed to hire people to find him?

'Not unless they've been doing a lot of digging.'

'How would we find that out?' The thought of someone poking their nose in his business irritated the hell out of Adam. He didn't like his privacy invaded. Being judged because of his name had never appealed to him, nor had the associated publicity. His mother had been hounded by scandalmongers until the day she died.

Sol hesitated. 'I honestly don't know.'

Meaning Adam would have to try and find out from the old man—without giving anything away. He didn't want to play his hand yet.

After running through a few things with Sol he made his way back into the house, and found his father asleep. The

nurse appeared beside him. 'He gets tired after dinner sometimes. He'll nap. I left the pieces on the board if you decide
to continue the game.'

Adam nodded, frowning at what could have been an
analogy for other things.

'I'm sure he'd like you to stay. He talks about you all the
time.'

It was the second time someone had told him that since he
came back. It was still hard for Adam to believe. But he
nodded and made his way to the end of the room where there
were bookcases jam packed with everything from books on
economics to the classics. Sitting on an ancient leather chair
with a high wing back, he stretched his legs out in front of
him, his gaze randomly discovering a pile of old photo
albums. There to help jog the old man's memory, most likely.

Lifting one, he opened it.

Roane came into the room so silently he didn't know she
was there until his father stirred. 'That you, girl?'

'It's me, Edward.' Her voice was impossibly soft and Adam
looked around the edge of his chair to see her bending over to
place a kiss on the old man's forehead. 'I've come to read to you.'

'You're a good girl.'

Roane smiled at him, reaching for a book on the night-
stand. 'We're still reading Dickens. *Great Expectations,*
remember?'

'You weren't here.'

'I know. I'm sorry.' She pulled an armchair over. 'I had to
fly to New York. But I'm here now.'

Adam watched as she tucked her hair behind her ear and
opened the book, her voice clear and mesmerizingly feminine
as she began to read.

It had been a long time, if ever, since a woman had wound

him as tight physically as Roane had and then left him
hanging. Adam hadn't liked it. But what he liked even less
was the sudden realization that he'd spent the rest of the day
thinking about her. She'd been in the back of his mind the
whole time—like whispered words just out of earshot. It
wasn't supposed to be that way.

His distraction was proving too distracting…

In the soft glow of a reading lamp she was incredibly beautiful. Not in a classical way, not in a supermodel way, but in a
completely fresh and…untouched-by-the-world way. She had
the same timelessly serene beauty as the island, as if she were
a product of her surroundings rather than genetics. In New
York he'd told her she should see the world. But Adam had
the feeling she would never be quite the same anywhere else.
She *belonged* where she was…in the very place Adam never
had…

He leaned back into his chair, careful not to let the leather
creak. Then he continued to look through the album, watching
his early life unfolding until something she was saying caught
his attention. Lifting his hand from the album he randomly
toyed with one of the thin leather bands on his wrist while he
listened to her voice as she read.

That was a memorable day to me, for it made great
changes in me. But, it is the same with any life. Imagine
one selected day struck out of it, and think how different its course would have been.

Her voice wove as much of a spell over Adam as the words
she was quoting.

Pause you who read this…and think for a moment of
the long chain of iron or gold, of thorns or flowers, that

would never have bound you, but for the formation of the first link on one memorable day.

Like when he chose to take a dip in the ocean after a long drive across country to the stretch of beach he had gone skinny dipping on countless times in his late teens? Where Roane had found him; *the first link on one memorable day*...

Adam frowned at the thought. Why did it suddenly feel more important than it was? He'd never been a romanticist. His mind wasn't built that way.

'Where's the boy?'

Roane's voice was infinitely patient in reply. 'Adam's not here. Not right now. But he's home. He came to see you. He'll come see you again.'

Adam leaned forwards and saw her take his father's hand in hers, a gentle smile on her lips a she reassured him, 'Really this time. You didn't imagine it.'

'Gone too long…'

'I know. But he's here now.'

Adam was still coming to terms with the idea of having been talked about with Roane before he'd even 'met' her—he wasn't sure how he felt about that—when something happened that he never thought he'd see: his father began to silently weep.

His voice cracked on the words, 'Where's the boy, Grace?'

Adam's mother's name…

Roane had to clear her throat. 'He's—'

'Here.' Adam set the album to one side and stood up, his gaze finding Roane's and noting the surprise in her eyes before he used the word he hadn't used in a long, long time. 'Dad—I'm right here.'

Still aware of her gaze following his every move he walked

to his father's bedside and placed a hand on his shoulder. A cold hand rose to his, the old man's voice threaded with emotion.

'Sorry, boy. I let you down.'

'It's all right, Dad.' He nodded at Roane's lap. 'Keep reading.'

The even tone was absent from her voice when she started reading again, indicating how unsettled she was by his appearance. So when Adam stepped back and pulled a chair over to sit opposite her he purposefully kept his focus on his father. After a while her tone evened out, taking on the hypnotic edge that eventually lulled his father to sleep.

When it did Adam looked at Roane, her gaze rising from the book to tangle with his. It might only have been seconds they stared at each other, but it felt like longer to Adam. Then they rose at the same time, met at the door, and walked through the house to the outdoors—not talking or touching until they got to where the air felt infinitely lighter than it had before and Adam felt as if he'd shed twenty pounds.

'I didn't know you were there,' she said on the gravelled path to the laneway between the main house and the guest house. 'I'm sorry.'

'How long have you been reading to him?'

'A little over a year; he likes the classics best.'

They stopped in the laneway, the sky a stunning display of ochre and gold over their heads as the day faded. Then Roane turned to face him, her chin rising and the luminous blue of her gaze searching his. 'He really did miss you, Adam. When he's his most confused he gets emotional and says he has to find you to make it right. You're the one thing he left undone. You being here, it means more to him than you realize…'

Adam looked over her head, staring into the distance as

e fought to assimilate the information. The old man was dif-
erent. Maybe at some point Adam had mentally exaggerated
he image with the perceptions of the archetypical angry
oung man he'd been back then. Maybe it was simply
ecause of the illness he seemed so changed. Adam didn't
now. The thing was, they were both stubborn. He was more
ike his father in that respect than he'd probably ever have
dmitted.

Roane stepped closer. 'There's still time.'

Adam frowned. He'd thought he had it all planned out. But
hings were different. He hated the lack of clarity. So much
or the plans he'd made…

One small hand lifted to turn his face, her palm sliding
pwards to allow her fingers to spread against his cheek.
Then she stood on her tiptoes and surprised him by pressing
n all too brief kiss to his lips. 'You did good.'

Was she patronizing him? Adam's brows jerked upwards
n disbelief. He searched her eyes for confirmation as her hand
dropped back to her side. No. She wasn't. She'd been helping
o care for his father for at least a year so she knew what
worked to soothe him and what didn't. She was simply telling
im his words and his tone and his presence had helped…

But somehow knowing that didn't help Adam's mood. In
act if anything it made him angry. He didn't need her to
soothe him.

Moving swiftly, his large hands framed her face, fingers
hrusting into the soft curtain of her hair as his lips crashed
down on hers. She rocked back a step but he didn't make any
attempt to support her. Instead he took. He demanded. He
devoured and in a heartbeat her whimper of protest morphed
nto a moan.

Small hands lifted to grasp onto the anchor of his open

shirt. Then she kissed him back, tangling her tongue with his. It was frantic and primal. It was the tension that had been building between them let loose without any hint of coherent thought.

Adam smiled with satisfaction before lifting his head and reaching for her hand. 'Come on.'

Her voice was husky as she let him guide her across the lane. 'Where are we going?'

Adam stopped and turned, towering over her while she looked up at him with eyes darkened several shades by desire. 'Where do you think we're going?'

It took a moment, but then her lips formed an 'o' and her eyes widened, her gaze darting past him to the guest house and then back to his chest. 'I can't…I mean…well, it's just that…'

Adam attempted to read between the lines. 'You're not sure? You're having second thoughts? All of the above?'

'No, well, yes and no…I just…' Indecision shimmered across her eyes and she shifted her weight from one foot to the other before glancing up at him. 'You're gonna think this is pathetic.'

Adam flexed his fingers around hers. 'Try me.'

'It's just that the guest house…'

When she grimaced and waved a hand in the direction of the house behind him Adam had a sudden flash of insight; it was about *location*? The idea made him smile.

His smile made her frown, her hand slipping free from his. 'I told you you'd think it was pathetic.'

Adam forced the smile off his face and folded his arms across his chest while he attempted to keep the amusement from his voice. 'So what's wrong with the guest house exactly? It has five bedrooms—you can take your pick.'

She shot him a scowl before looking at the house again. 'There's nothing wrong with it. It's just it's…well, it's impersonal. Like a really fancy hotel impersonal. And this is already—'

'Impersonal?' Adam's brows rose in surprise. That was how she saw what they were doing? 'There aren't too many things in this world as personal as sex, sweetheart. When you get naked in a bed with someone it's *personal*.'

'With me it is. But you're the guy who gets naked at the drop of a hat.' When Adam angled his head and eyed her with suspicion she clarified what she'd meant. 'I don't need to remind you how we met, do I?'

Roane took a breath and tried again. 'The guest house. Well, maybe it's the word guest. It's not a home, it's impersonal and that makes this, well, it—'

'Cheapens it.' He didn't make it a question.

Roane exhaled her reply as if she was relieved he understood. '*Yes*. I'm sorry. I just don't want it to feel like that…'

It wouldn't. He'd make sure of it. 'So you'd be more comfortable in your own space.'

'Comfortable is possibly a stretch, but yes.'

Adam could feel her nervousness shimmering in the space between them; mixed in with the heat she naturally radiated it formed a tantalizing glimpse of things to come. He knew instinctively she would tremble when he touched her, that the awakening of her body would both frighten and arouse her at the same time. Every bone in his body ached with the need to watch her as it happened, his arms unfolding and hands reaching out to insinuate their way under her jacket the same way they had earlier. With his gaze fixed on hers he set his palms against the curve of her stomach, a smile toying with his mouth as he felt her tremble. Then he splayed his fingers, adding a little pressure as if to help still her inner shaking as he stepped in and lowered his voice to say one word.

'Where?'

Roane stared up at him as if mesmerized, long lashes flickering as she studied each of his eyes in turn. Adam could feel her wavering indecision; the fine line between sensible thought and physical need wobbling like images caught in the heat waves radiating off a road through the desert. She breathed shallow breaths—her soft skin warmed beneath his palms—she damped her lips in preparation for his mouth…

So Adam leaned in and kissed her. Taking his time to soothe and cajole and tempt while hunger spiralled inside him again. Roane fed that burgeoning hunger with calming touches of her velvety soft lips. She made his animalistic instincts growl with tentative strokes of her sweet-tasting tongue. When Adam fought for breath she breathed air into his lungs with whispered sighs, until the kissing became softer and slower still and he could feel something give inside her.

'Where?' He asked the question against her mouth.

'I live in the beach house.'

Silently stepping back, Adam turned, hooking her forefinger over one of his little fingers. But he didn't make an attempt to reach for anything firmer, as if he was aware of how little it would take to change her mind. The touch was tentative, even when they stepped off the end of the wooden walkway onto the deep sand of the beach—it could have been a metaphor for their relationship.

When her finger almost slipped free he hooked the tip of his ring finger to hold on; Roane smiled nervously in response when he glanced her way and a breeze from the ocean whipped tendrils of her hair against her cheeks. God he wanted her. He craved physical closeness with her the same way the incoming tide craved the touch of the shore.

The small beach house caught his gaze when he looked forwards; its pale blue painted boards and white trim were indicative of houses dotted from one end of the Vineyard to the other. And a thought occurred to him. 'You were going there the night you found me?'

She nodded, studying him as she walked as if she was trying to figure something out.

Adam looked back at the house. They were less than fifteen yards from where she lived now—where she slept— from her *bed*. They were getting closer with every step. The thought made Adam's body stiffen painfully in anticipation. Fourteen yards, thirteen, twelve, eleven…

He looked over at her profile and found her staring out to sea, the deep breath she took lifting her breasts. Then she turned her head and looked up at him and out of nowhere Adam heard his own voice.

'Do you trust me?'

The reward for his question was a dazzling smile, one that had him smiling back in an instant. His smile was then rewarded with a gentle nodding of her head. So he let out the breath he hadn't noticed he was holding to say a husky edged, *'Good.'*

He'd needed to know. There was no going back once they got started; Adam knew that. He just needed to know she knew it too. Her open gratitude that he'd taken the time to ask her an added bonus…

When they reached the foot of the wooden steps to her small porch he stepped close and broke the contact of their hands to set his hands on her hips and draw her close.

She slid her arms under his open shirt and around to his back, pressing her breasts against the wall of his chest and sending a jolt of electricity to his groin. Then she kissed the side of his neck the way she had on the plane, igniting remembered sensations to add to the new ones he could feel growing inside him.

Adam growled appreciatively above her head. 'Fond of that spot, aren't you?'

He could feel the smile on his skin. 'Mmm-hmm…am…'

Decision long since made, he started backing her up the steps, his hands sliding under the bottom edge of her jacket to touch warm skin again. 'You've got buckets full of payback coming your way for earlier…'

'I know.' She rained kisses up the column of his neck and mumbled near his ear, 'I've done nothing else but think about that since I left you…'

Every fibre of Adam's physical being throbbed with the need to feel her moist heat surrounding him, to hear the noises she would make as he moved inside her, freeing the sexual being he knew was hidden within. He hadn't lied. He wanted to be the one to teach her what she could feel, what it could be like when that one intangible was there between two adults. For her to understand how rare it was to have that much chemistry from the get-go…

Tightening his fingers, he lifted her off the ground, setting her down on the top step so she was at eye level with him. She lifted her chin and looked deep into his eyes, and for a brief second Adam had honestly never felt so naked. Not even when he'd been standing in front of her that first night.

He angled his head and leaned forwards, his mouth hovering over hers as he watched the play of emotions crossing her expressive eyes. One at a time they were easy to decipher. But he had a suspicion the knack of reading them when they were so mixed up was beyond his reach. It would probably take a lifetime to understand the nuances.

But with a complete certainty born of instinct alone he knew that none of them was doubt. She was giving herself to him. It garnered a sense of elation in Adam that made him want to throw his head back and howl in victory.

Instead he leaned over and took his time kissing her, paying particular attention to her lower lip before sweeping his tongue in to taste her addictive sweetness. The second she joined the dance things changed; she kissed him as if she were starving and he were a feast, as if she were dying of thirst and he were a cool drink of water. There was no way Adam could fight it, he couldn't help but devour her right back—because she wasn't the only one who'd been thinking about it all day, was she? He could hear the whisper now, the one that had been in the back of his mind just out of reach—it said her name. As if she was calling to a part of him no one else ever had.

When her hands began to move frantically against his back, reaching under the edge of his T-shirt to touch his skin, Adam tried to find something to focus his mind on; to help slow things down. If he didn't then he knew he would take her. Harder and faster than he knew she was ready for. Later, he promised himself. Not this time. The first time she needed him to exercise some of that control he was usually so good with.

'Adam—' She wrenched her mouth from his to plead breathlessly as he plied kisses to the neck she arched for him. 'Adam, *please*—I want—'

'I know.'

'But I need—'

'I know.'

When he punctuated the words with kisses and nips she shuddered against him. 'You're making me crazy!'

Lifting his head, he smiled down at her. 'Am I now?'

He was glad he was. He wanted her crazy for him.

'Yes.' She frowned. 'I just—I need you to—that is, I want…'

'Tell me.' He looked steadily into her eyes, his voice vibrating low in his chest. 'What you need, what feels good, what you want. Every last request…'

Roane's answer was barely above a whisper. 'I want *you*. I *burn*—for you—you *make me* burn…'

'Door. *Now*.' He kissed her hard, the need to consume her so powerful it took everything he had in him not to rip her clothes from her body.

They practically fell through the door, Adam making a cursory examination of the room before asking the obvious. 'Bedroom?'

Roane walked backwards, mumbling between kisses. 'This. Way.'

Adam reached for the hooks on her jacket, his mouth still fused to hers. It felt like he'd imagined undressing her a thousand times and yet now that he was his fingers were shaking. What was with that? It had been a long time since any woman had made his damn hands shake. It added to his frustration, because their movement coupled with his lack of dexterity meant it took twice as long as it should have to undo the hooks.

Roane removed her mouth from his long enough to look where they were going. While she did the last hook came free, the edges of the jacket opening to reveal smooth, creamy skin only partially covered by deliciously feminine lace. Adam's mouth went dry as he imagined trailing kisses over her skin. He could see her puckered nipples through the thin lace and he swallowed to ease the rawness in his throat.

'You're beautiful.' His voice was gravelly as he slid the jacket off, his thumbs trailing over her shoulders. 'Have I told you that?'

'You haven't.' She looked up at him, her eyes dark in the dying light.

'I should have. You are.' The jacket was tossed aside, Adam's formerly dry mouth watering at the thought of capturing her nipples with his lips. So blinded was he by the thought that he hadn't noticed she was pushing at his shirt until she shoved it off his shoulders and down his upper arms.

'So are you.' She murmured the words in a low, sexy voice that shot another surge of heated blood to Adam's groin. But then the fact she'd divested him of his shirt and reached for his T-shirt—her knuckles grazing his abdomen in the process—probably had just as much to do with it. The thought of her hands on him, around him, squeezing his hard length and guiding him to her—it was almost too much…

'Men aren't beautiful.'

'This one is.' She looked up at him as she lifted his T-shirt.

Adam smiled when she scowled and added, 'You might have to help me with this—you're too tall.'

He yanked it unceremoniously over his head and tossed it in the general direction of her jacket. By then Roane had backed through a doorway and her light summer breeze scent surrounded him, stronger than before. *Her bedroom.* But he didn't look around him beyond discovering the bed, he wasn't the least bit interested in his surroundings—the woman in front of him was all he could see.

She took a shaky breath, he saw her hesitate, and then she reached out a hand. When he dropped his chin he saw her fingers tremble and then they touched, tentatively—like someone holding their hand out to an open flame. Her fingertips traced his chest almost reverently and Adam sucked in a sharp breath, forcing himself to stay still and let her explore.

It was torture.

Groaning low down in his throat with a combination of arousal and a sense of defeat, Adam tried unsuccessfully to find a shred of sanity to cling to. But when she stepped forwards and pressed her lips to a point directly above his heart it was gone in a second; incinerated in the white-hot intensity of one butterfly-soft kiss. She stepped in close, tilted her head back in invitation, so Adam claimed her lips and drank deep.

Lace-covered breasts pressed against his bare chest and he was sweeping his hands up to cup them before he realized he was doing it. On his lips she tasted of sweet, soft woman—on his body her hands splayed across his abdomen, making him suck in a sharp breath that tensed the muscles beneath her fingers. In his hands she was the perfect palm-filling curve he'd known she would be. Thanks to the combination of all those things his jeans were so tight they were painful.

She was killing him. He was *trying* to go slow. But the last vestige of control was slipping fast.

Adam wondered if she was even aware of what she was doing to him. Surely no woman on earth could be so naturally seductive in every way and not be aware of her effect on a man? Each gentle touch of her small, fine-boned fingers, each sweep of her tongue against his, each sigh she made or low hum of approval echoed from her lips to his sent molten fire through him.

Maybe she did know what she was doing to him and was doing it on purpose? He hoped for her sake she wasn't.

Without warning she found the fly of his jeans and cupped his heavy erection. Adam immediately forced himself to pull way, breathing hard from the effort as he gently removed her hand and set her back from him.

'You need to slow down, little girl.'

Roane's voice shook. 'Did I do something wrong?'

'Hell, no.' He set his hands on her shoulders and silently persuaded her to step backwards towards the bed. 'It's what you're doing right.'

The smile was immediate and so bright it lit her up. 'I'm glad. I want to do to you what you do to me.'

'Sweetheart, if you do then my reputation for being any good at this is going to go down in flames.'

'I doubt that.'

Adam scooped her up and laid her down as if she were something infinitely fragile and precious. Then he followed her, his knee dipping the mattress as he lay down beside her and brushed her hair back from her cheek. 'Just let me do all the work the first time.'

Roane's voice came out on a squeak. 'The *first* time? How many times were you planning on there being?'

He smiled a slow smile. 'You thought there'd only be the one?'

'I didn't—I mean I hadn't—I—'

'This isn't a one-time thing.'

She gulped, bringing a wider smile to Adam's face—the combination of seductive siren one minute and nervous innocent the next unbelievably intoxicating.

'Don't hold back, little girl, you hear?'

Roane nodded.

So Adam dipped his head.

CHAPTER SEVEN

'DON'T HOLD BACK, little girl…' Adam had asked Roane in a
deep silken tone that wreaked havoc on her nerves.

He had no idea what he was asking of her. But she'd
nodded. She wondered if he had any idea how much power
he wielded over her. How could he not? He was vastly more
experienced and sexually confident than she was…

When he'd kissed her in the laneway with so much pent-
up emotion let loose it had rocked her to the soles of her
feet; literally. She'd panicked when he'd led her toward
the guest house, a part of her still recoiling from the idea
of sex for sex's sake. But when he'd understood her hesitation there'd been a stronger sense of inevitability that had
motivated her to do something she'd never done before.
She'd allowed him to take her by the hand and calmly lead
her to bed…

Adam slowly lifted his mouth from hers and began to
blaze a trail down her neck, the fingers on her stomach
splaying and pressing downwards as if staking a claim. *Mine*
that hand said. *Don't move, I'm in charge—I'm going to take
you the way you've dreamed I would.*

Roane couldn't seem to find her voice and when she did

all she could do was ask shakily, 'You won't hold back either, right?'

He lifted his head and smiled; a slow, sexy, lopsided smile that sent every nerve in her body humming and created a dull ache in her chest. His fingertips trailed over the curve of her stomach to the button on the waistband of her trousers,

'I don't plan on holding anything back,' he said in a voice as heavenly as velvety smooth dark chocolate.

Roane knew instinctively that he hadn't meant the same thing she had. But that wasn't what they were doing, was it? Holding back physically was very different from holding back emotionally. Perversely, since it was the one thing she'd told herself she didn't want from him—she suddenly felt the loss of the emotion; darned fickle heart.

Adam bent and nuzzled her ear, which did nothing for her control over her vocal cords.

'Trust me,' he murmured huskily, the button on her trousers popping free and the zipper lowering.

His tongue traced the shell of her ear. 'Breathe, little girl…'

Roane exhaled, then inhaled sharply, unaware she'd been holding her breath. That explained the ache in her chest, then. Where had her bravado gone—the unwavering certainty that it was right to let him lead her to where they were? The same inner sense of possible recklessness that had loosened her tongue to tell him she'd done nothing but think about what they were now doing all day long.

Gone the second she'd been struck by the reality of what she was doing, that was where. When she'd feasted her eyes on the perfection of his naked chest again and had felt the same cell-deep need to reach out and touch. She'd faltered then, her physical need for him so strong it had floored her.

That was before she'd brazenly cupped him through his jeans and been momentarily terrified by the logistics of what they were about to do. He was so big. She was so much smaller than him.

She stifled a moan when he ran the tip of his tongue down to the beating pulse at the base of her neck, his hand smoothing her trousers downwards.

'Relax,' he breathed. 'Lift up for me.'

Again she did what she was told, trying her best to relax only to have him move further down the bed when she lifted her hips, making her tremble all over again. When he kissed his way down her shoulder and arm she could have gone limp with relief if his other hand hadn't been sliding up her thigh at the same time.

Then her trousers were gone and he was kissing his way across her collarbone. 'And make noise.' He lifted his head and smiled down at her. 'I want to hear it. Every sigh, every gasp, every moan—let it all out.'

When he lowered his mouth to her other ear a whimper escaped before she could stop it. Between the things his mouth was doing to her ear and where she was afraid his hand was headed—oh, come on, *afraid*? Who was she kidding? *Hopeful* his hand was heading—it was hard to form coherent thought. But she gathered all her will power and tried anyway.

'Do you have—you know? With you?' She heard herself ask the question that could have done with being asked sooner. If she hadn't been half pinned beneath the heavy weight of him she would have kicked herself for not thinking about it before. How stupid was she?

Sleeping with a man within three days of meeting him was insane enough for Roane. Having a baby with him? Beyond insane and into the realms of sheer stupidity…

It didn't explain why her body reacted so strongly to the powerful thought of it, though, did it? For a second she convinced herself she could feel her womb clench.

Adam chuckled, gently nipped her shoulder and Roane jumped, clutching his shoulders as a rush of heat spiralled through her body. But she couldn't stop the disappointment that rose inside her when he pulled back and his hand left her leg.

She'd just messed it up, hadn't she?

When Adam's eyes met hers, he didn't look at her as if she'd ruined everything by bringing up the subject of contraception—or lack thereof. Instead he took her hand and brought it to his lips, turning it over and placing a kiss on her palm before setting it to his chest and sliding it down over his skin. Roane allowed a small moan to escape as she felt the hard muscles under the heated covering of silky smooth skin; it was as addictive the second time as it had been the first. He really was beautiful.

'I have one in my wallet.' He guided her hand over his chest, as if her hand had become an extension of his own. Then he pressed her palm over his heart, on the very spot where she'd kissed him.

'I'll be better prepared next time.' He released her hand and cradled her cheek with what almost felt like tenderness. 'All the more reason to take our time…'

Roane's heart kicked hard against her breastbone when Adam lowered his head and coaxed her lips apart. She slid an arm around his neck, whimpering wantonly when his tongue caressed hers and drew her into a leisurely dance. Frankly she hadn't known what she'd expected of him— heat, passion, fire, strength; all those things and more, yes. During the day she'd mentally toyed with all of the associated images of those things. But the last thing she'd expected from him was tenderness.

He tasted her as if he had all the time in the world and intended to make the most of every single second. Roane had no emotional defence from that, a part of her reaching out for it and trying to clasp it tighter to her fickle heart. Rough-tipped fingers traced her cheek, the arch of her brows, the curve of her lashes when she closed her eyes. Then they threaded into her hair, bending at the knuckle to brush it out into a curtain on the pillow beneath her head.

Roane's hand was still where he'd left it, the beat of his heart reverberating through his skin and into her palm. She felt the rhythm, her heart matching beat for beat when she felt it quicken. Then she slid her hand upwards, over his shoulder, around to his back—suddenly feverish with the need to touch him, to learn every last inch of him as if there would only be the one time for them despite his silken promise.

Adam's muscles jumped as she impulsively trailed her fingernails over his skin. Roane felt a thrill shooting through her at the effect her touch had on him. Had she really done that to a man like him? He drew her closer, his breathing speeding up as the kiss spun endlessly on and on.

With a deft flick of his thumb and forefinger she felt the front clasp of her bra come undone and then a large hand un-erringly found her naked breast making her arch and moan out loud. It was the most intense sensation. His touch sent shivers radiating outwards from her breast to the rest of her body. Then he rolled her nipple in his palm and kissed her again in that slow, relentless tantalization he did so very well.

She began to writhe restlessly against the covers, the hand not clinging to Adam bunching the material into a fist. But Adam simply continued endlessly caressing her and kissing

r until she thought she'd explode into a million pieces if
didn't do more.

'*Adam.*' She moaned his name when he pulled back to kiss
s way along the line of her jaw.

'I know,' he whispered roughly in reply.

Then he bent and caught her nipple between his lips,
awing it into his mouth and gently grazing it between his
eth. The soft bite effectively short-circuited Roane's brain,
e one leg not pinned under the weight of his moving fran-
cally as she grasped the covers tighter and twisted them.

'God—Adam.' Her throat was raw from gasping in air, her
eart beating so fast that her chest ached. Down below, dear
eaven, she had no idea what that was. It—well, it almost
urt. She was hot and tight and tingly and—

Adam continued to bestow his expertise on her breasts
ntil Roane honestly thought she would die of longing if he
idn't touch her lower down. It was too much and not enough
t the same time. She had no idea what it was that was hap-
ening inside her abdomen or how she was supposed to
ontrol it. It was as if every muscle in her body was strain-
ig to grasp onto something that was just out of reach.
omething her very life depended on.

The hand on his back slid up into his short hair, fumbling
lindly for a hold.

He rested his chin on her ribcage, his voice sending a
ooling whisper of air over a heated nipple as he made the
oft demand: 'Tell me what you want, little girl.'

Lying in bed with him, Roane discovered the nickname
ook on deeper sexual undertones. She twisted her hips and
ound the words were easier to say when she craved his touch
o very badly. 'Lower. Touch me lower.'

'Here?' His hand slid down over her ribs to her hip.

'Lower.'

The hand moved to her thigh. 'Here?'

Roane frowned at him, her voice strangled. 'You *kno* where. You know what you're doing to me. *Please.*' She f emotion clogging her throat. 'Please don't make me beg yo

Adam moved back up, resting his head on the pillo beside her and turning her face towards him with one lo forefinger. 'Anything you give me you give me freely.'

Roane felt tears welling up in her eyes, her answer exhaled whisper. 'Thank you.'

He smiled at her in the silvery moonlight, moving hand down her throat, over her breast, her stomach, h abdomen and then—finally—beneath the band of lace push it down and away. Roane knew to bend her knees a lift her hips, she knew to wriggle just a little and to hook h toes to slide the lace off her ankles and away. Then Adam fingertips were moving back up her leg, over the sensiti skin behind her knee, the softest part of her inner thigh— where she desperately needed his touch the most.

When his fingers dipped into the pool of wet heat s turned her head and arched back into the pillows, her hi rising off the bed as she bit down on her lip.

'You really have been thinking about this all day, haver you?' he asked with what sounded like a sense of deep s isfaction in his voice.

'Um…' She managed to gasp.

Talented fingers dipped and swirled. 'You've been like th all day. For me.'

Roane gritted her teeth, hissing back, *'Yes.'*

'I wish you could se how beautiful you are right now.' H took a breath. 'Look at me. I want to see you.'

She was focused so intensely on the movement of h

ngers it took him to make the softly spoken demand to her
second time before she turned her head. But having him
ok into her eyes while he did what he was doing made her
el more vulnerable than she ever had before.

He was studying her intensely as he slid an exploratory
nger deep inside her, the question forming in his eyes before
e spoke. 'You're tight.'

'Tell me what to do.' She moaned and bared her soul to
onfess: 'I don't know what to do.'

Adam's thick lashes flickered as he searched her eyes, the
uestion still hovering on his raised brows before he told her
an impossibly tender voice, 'Take a deep breath, relax your
ody—let the air out of your lungs slow. And. Let. Go.'

She kept looking at him as she followed each step, her body
aking from the inside out as she took a deep shuddering
reath, tried with all her might to relax her body and then—

He moved his thumb to her most sensitive spot as she
xhaled. He circled, flicked over the swollen nerve ending—
nd her world fell apart.

Her spine bowed up from the covers, her head pushed
ep into the pillows and with her eyes closed tight she could
e a myriad of colours flash briefly across her eyelids while
e let out a long keening moan. One that seemed to come
om the very place he was touching.

Her hips jerked as the waves pulsed outwards. And then
ter what felt like an eternity she flumped lifelessly against
e covers, an almost manic burst of husky laughter escaping
om low in her throat. "What the hell was that?"

Adam moved his hand and was brushing his knuckles
ack and forth over her highly sensitized abdomen, the
uscles beneath still jerking with miniature aftershocks when
e asked, 'You don't know?'

'I've never. Well, it's just never—' She swallowed to ea[se] her aching throat, then swiped her tongue over dry lips. [I] mean I've tried…I just didn't know…'

Adam's face rose above hers, incredulity in his deep voic[e.] 'What kind of guys have you been with?'

'Ones who didn't know what they were doing.' Sh[e] laughed again—the sound softer this time. '*Obviously.*'

Adam repeated the word: '*Obviously.*'

Before she could get herself out of a potentially emba[r]rassing conversation he added, 'So that's the first tim[e] you've ever—'

'Yes,' she interrupted before he said it, colour rapidl[y] rising on her cheeks. How did she even begin to explain h[er] disastrous love life to a man like Adam? It wasn't as if sh[e] hadn't tried, but she'd never felt what he'd just made her fee[l.] 'I think I'd have noticed if *that* happened before.'

Grimacing at how ridiculously shy she suddenly felt, sh[e] looked up at him from the corner of her eye. 'That's suppose[d] to happen every time?'

'It is if you're doing it right.' He brushed her hair bac[k] from her cheek. 'And that's just the pre-show…'

Roane's breath hitched. 'Pre-show?'

When he kissed her again she was stunned at how fast h[er] body responded even though the heat built slower than befor[e.] Somewhere in the midst of roaming touches and gentle sigh[s] and murmurs of encouragement Adam was as naked as sh[e] was and Roane was looking up at him as he returned to h[er] having sheathed himself. He kissed her throat, her collarbon[e,] found sensitive places she didn't even know she had, wo[r]shipped her breasts until she was writhing against the cover[s] again. She would never have believed a man could master h[er] body the way he was.

Then he smiled at her and kissed her hungrily, his hand
sliding down to her waist and over her hip before rising to
cup her breast. Any semblance of protection Roane had left
shielding her heart melted as he rested his forehead against
hers; eyes closed, his skilled fingers tracing the soft mounds
of her flesh and his deep voice rumbling into the heavy air
with words that surprised her,

'I don't want to seduce you, little girl.'

Roane blinked up at him with wide eyes. He didn't? Had
he done something wrong? She wanted him to feel the same
way she had, or even a quarter of it. It was only fair. But more
than that—she needed him to feel it, to want her beyond
reason the way she did him. What would it take to make a
man like him feel that way? she silently asked—so desperate for an answer her voice shook.

'You don't?'

Adam opened his eyes and the corner of his sinfully
tempting mouth rose in a hint of his devastating lopsided
smile. 'Oh, I want you, sweetheart—don't doubt that.'

As if to make sure she got the point, his thumbnail traced
a slow circle around her nipple, her entire body tightening
in response as he continued speaking in the rough-edged
tone that did the most damage to any shred of microscopic
resistance she might have had left. 'I want to show you everything you've been missing. I want to be deep inside you.
I want to feel you wrapped around me and to hear your
moans in my ears. I want to spend days doing this now I
know what it feels like.'

The fire in her blood boiled like molten lava at the mental
images his words created.

'But?' She choked the word out. 'Cause there was a 'but'
in there somewhere, wasn't there?

Adam's hand left her breast and cupped her cheek, his gaze intense. 'I don't want to *seduce* you.'

Reading the confusion on her face, he traced her cheek with infinite tenderness. 'So tell me you want this. No looking back and regretting it. Last chance…'

Roane stared at him, dumbstruck. He was calling a halt to make sure she wasn't swept away by the heat of the moment? He really wanted her to make a rational decision about something as completely irrational as how much she ached for him? How much she'd ached for him since the second she'd laid eyes on him.

'I can't think straight when you kiss me the way you do. Don't you know that?' she whispered, taking the weighty complication of actually choosing to *make love* with him—a phrase so much more dangerous than 'have sex'—out of her hands.

Adam leaned down and grazed his lips over hers. 'You do that to me too.'

Sliding her hands up his muscled arms and over his broad shoulders, she listened to his rasped intake of breath and smiled in amazement. 'Really?'

'Really.'

It made her look beyond her own physical reactions to his. She could feel exactly what she did to him. It was hard, hot and pressed against her hip. But more than that his breathing was ragged, his body was covered in a fine sheen of perspiration, his muscles trembled where she touched—and Roane was shaken by how badly she wanted to keep doing all those things to him.

But only if he would keep doing it back to her…

'*Show me.*' She made the request more confidently, her palms sliding down over his chest and lower still—the need to take him in her hands so strong she shook from head to toe.

With a sudden move that caught her off guard, he removed er hands and pinned them above her head—the submissive osition ramping up her desire several notches. He could ake her if he wanted to and she knew she wouldn't be able o stop him. Why didn't that scare her the way it should? If nything it made her more excited than she'd been before…

'Say it.'

Removing responsibility from him if she got emotionally nvolved and had her heart broken the way she inevitably vould. Roane bit down on her lower lip and saw his thick ashes lower as he watched the telltale movement.

It was already too late for her. 'Yes.' She had to pause to lear her throat, her heart pounding with a mixture of trepi-ation and agonizing arousal. 'I want you to make love to me.'

When he lowered his head to kiss her again Roane fully xpected ferocity from his kisses as a reaction to her sur-ender; sizzling fire that would wipe every thought from her nind and make her forget the aching in her chest. But his full ips brushed hers in a feathery caress that both amazed and errified her.

It wasn't enough, not after he'd made her take complete esponsibility for what was about to happen. Her fingers hreaded forcefully into his short hair and she bit his lower ip with a growl that stunned even her. Since when had she urned into such a wanton woman in the bedroom? She hadn't nown she had it in her.

Adam groaned, his arm tightening into a steel band around er. When he kissed her again she forgot to breathe. Endlessly he kiss went on, his heart pounding heavily against her reasts as her fingers tightened in the soft spikes of his hair. Nothing had ever felt so right in her entire life. Making love vith him wasn't a mistake; she knew it with all her heart.

His mouth left hers to blaze a hot path down her throat making her arch and moan with complete abandon.

'You're so damn beautiful.' Adam mumbled the words before capturing one peaked nipple in his mouth again.

Roane cried out, arching into his mouth as her hands cradled his head to hold him in place. Each flick of his tongue drew another gasp or moan from her. When she dropped her chin to look down at him she was transfixed by the sight of his head bent over her. He had his eyes closed, was making low growling noises that suggested he took as much pleasure from what he was doing as she was receiving. He made her *feel* beautiful. It was the most amazing feeling.

He transferred his attention to her other breast.

Roane had to touch him. So she slid her hands over the back of his head, down the taut line of his neck, skimming across his back while she marvelled at the play of muscle and heated skin slick with a cooling sheen of moisture. Then over his lean hips, up his sides, across his broad chest, back over his shoulders—in a restless, almost frantic exploration that only made her want more of him.

Because he was still holding back. All of his incredible strength of body and spirit held in careful check. Her heart pounded, ached, twisted, she arched upwards with each pull of his hungry lips. Still not enough. *More.* It echoed so deep inside her she thought she might die without it.

Roane moved her hands back to his hair and pulled his head back from her breast, claiming his mouth while revelling in the glorious slide of his body against hers.

He reached down and pushed a long finger inside her, drawing another moan from her that mingled with his groan of frustration. 'You need to relax for me or I'll hurt you.'

'You won't. I know you won't.' She prayed she was right. He was just so big…

When he eased open her legs to form a cradle for himself he shifted over her, leaning his elbows on either side of her head so she could see how much effort it was taking for him to hold back in the straining of his shoulders.

He kissed her long and slow, then rested his forehead on her shoulder and balanced on one arm while he guided himself to her. As he slid forwards the first inch Roane tensed, gasping at how amazing the intimate invasion felt despite the stretching her body had to make to accommodate him.

When she gasped he tensed, his voice rough. 'Relax.'

She took a deep breath and let it go—he slid an inch deeper and froze, staring down into her eyes as if she was the only thing he could see. 'Again.'

Nothing had ever felt as incredible to her as the excruciatingly slow slide of his body into hers. When he slid deeper she struggled for breath. He rocked forwards and the movement drew another gasp from her lips—Adam's head lifting sharply in reply and his large body frozen over hers.

'Did I hurt you?'

'No.' Her voice was breathless. 'Don't stop.'

'You're so damn tight.' His voice was strangled. 'You should have told me—'

'*Please.* Take me, Adam.' She heard the pleading tone to her voice and moaned at how desperate she sounded. 'You were right about my fantasy. I want you to take me.'

To make her point she pushed her heels into the mattress and lifted her hips, forcing him deeper, a low moan leaving her lips. It was apparently all the proof he needed to slide home in one sharp thrust, both of them moaning in unison when his pelvis hit hers.

Adam kissed her again, his mouth claiming hers and drinking deep as he started to move. It was making love in the truest sense and Roane felt the difference with each and every touch, emotion rising up inside her and spilling out of the corners of her eyes before she knew it was happening.

But by then all she could do was hang on tight to him as he rode her hard and slow, then harder and faster—as if he couldn't stop himself; each deep thrust drawing her closer and closer to the same ecstasy he'd already given her. He didn't release her lips, taking her cries and feeding her his groans. Only when the universe exploded around her again—even stronger than it had before—did Roane tear her lips away to cry out his name with the sheer unmitigated joy of how it felt.

Adam's shuddering groan was muffled in her shoulder, his body statue-still for a long moment as he pulsed inside her. Then he collapsed on her. For a long while he stayed there, dragging deep breaths of air into his lungs while Roane fought to control the hot tears streaming from the corners of her eyes into her hair.

He must have felt the change in her, because his head lifted and his gaze searched her face.

'Are you okay?'

God, why was he so obsessed with the idea of hurting her? She allowed a sob to break free since it was pointless trying to hide it when he already knew she was crying. 'Yes. I just I had no idea.'

She sobbed again and smiled tremulously at him, letting the tears fall unhindered. 'I didn't know it could be like that. Why didn't I know?'

One large hand cradled her cheek, his thumb brushing the tears away as he rumbled his reply. 'Because it's not always like that. I told you this was rare.'

Had he? Roane didn't remember. But being told didn't make her feel any better. If anything it was worse. What if it never happened to her again? What if Adam was the only one who could make her feel that way? How could she ever have a relationship with someone else and not feel as if something was missing?

Dear Lord. What had she done?

Was love enough on its own without this? Because with Adam there was this but there could never be love. He wouldn't stay—he didn't have it in him. He was as free on the ground as she was in the air. But she was only capable of that freedom because she was grounded. She knew where she belonged in the world, where she was happiest. It was on the Vineyard. The one place Adam had left behind him twelve years ago and had never once been tempted to revisit. There was no future in Adam. Not for her. But she'd known that when she made the decision to sleep with him, hadn't she?

So why did it hurt so much?

She turned her face towards his shoulder and let the first racking sob loose. Adam shifted his weight, circling his arms around her and drawing her close.

'Come here.'

Roane curled into him, her arm tight around his lean waist as she tried to get closer still, as if she could draw from the strength of his body and make it hers…

She felt his lips press against her hair. 'I've got you.'

It was the very thing that scared her most.

CHAPTER EIGHT

SHE SOBBED IT out, then quieted and finally fell asleep in his arms. Adam couldn't remember anything ever affecting him the way those tears did.

He seriously contemplated hunting down the guy who'd left her feeling less than she should after she'd trusted her body to him. He doubted there was more than one given her level of inexperience. Not that he'd managed to complete the act—at least not properly—Adam knew that now. A man who left a woman feeling as unfulfilled as she'd been deserved at least one well-aimed swing, Adam felt.

One of the driftwood logs he'd found on the shoreline crackled and spat sparks into the air. When Roane had fallen asleep he'd slept with her, lulled into the kind of peaceful, dreamless slumber he hadn't experienced in well over a decade. But when he woke up a couple of hours before dawn he gently extricated himself from her and went for a walk to clear his head. Not that he was leaving her. He knew he didn't want her to wake up and feel as if it had been a one-night stand to him. She was worth more. And Adam was nowhere near done with her. If anything he'd only got started.

So he walked the beach the way he used to when his insomnia first started at nineteen, randomly collecting pieces of driftwood that eventually became a big enough pile to make a fire near the rocks outside her house. Sitting on the soft sand staring into the flames was as good a place as any to figure out what had happened. And what he was supposed to do about it…if anything…

At thirty-three he'd had his fair share of great sex. Not that he was promiscuous—only a fool would be in the age they lived in and Adam was no fool—but then neither was he anything resembling a saint. But he'd never had an experience that lived up to the description of making love quite the way it had with Roane either. He'd never been a woman's first lover the way he knew he was for her. It brought out a possessive streak in him a mile wide…

The thought of being the one to show her all she could feel only to walk away left him feeling ridiculously angry. But it wasn't as if he could stay. Thing was, if what had happened was difficult for Adam to understand with experience, then how overwhelming must it have been for Roane with virtually none?

She was just so very—delicate. Not in a weak way. He smiled as he thought about how sassy she could be when riled. Nope, definitely not weak—delicate and soft and innately feminine; all things he found incredibly sensual. When she let down her guard and Adam saw glimpses of the passionate woman inside it enthralled him. He wanted to know everything about her. He wanted to step into her head and see the world through her eyes. He wanted to discover all her secrets, was hungry to learn it *all*.

Maybe that was part of what happened? She'd engaged his mind in a way no other woman had. Like a puzzle he had to unravel. By doing so she'd intensified his physical reaction to her. That made sense to him.

Then there was the way she'd looked him in the eye and told him she trusted him. *'You won't. I know you won't,'* she'd said when he'd told her he'd hurt her if she didn't relax. So much faith in a man she didn't know. So much belief in him. Maybe that was part of it?

After a long time spent staring alternately into dancing flames or out over the ocean, Adam finally had to admit that part of his frustration lay in the inevitability of hurting her *emotionally*. He would. He knew that now and was regretting it in advance.

'Nickel for them…'

Adam jerked his head up and found her standing a few feet away. She'd dressed in a long white nightdress with a soft-looking cowl-necked sweater on top, long sleeves hanging below her wrists. She was ghost-like, surreal and so beautiful she made him ache to have her again. And that was rare too. Usually taking what he wanted was enough to dull the need in him. But he wanted her bad; again and again until the need was dulled if that was how it had to be… He didn't care how many times it took.

He held out an arm. She stepped forwards and accepted the silent invitation, sliding her smaller hand into his. Then Adam leaned back against the rocks and settled her across his lap; circling her with his arms. She leaned her cheek against his shoulder as if she'd done it hundreds of times, tilting her chin up so she could examine his face.

'Couldn't sleep?'

Adam looked down at her without lowering his chin, 'You thought I'd left.'

He didn't make it a question and she acknowledged the fact by nodding. 'I did until I saw the fire.'

'What woke you?'

'I got cold—I don't usually sleep naked.'

'You should stay naked all the time.'

'Not really an option.'

'Pity.'

When he moved a hand to her thigh her fingers toyed idly with one of the leather bands on his wrist. 'What woke you?'

He shrugged, his gaze travelling to the ocean. 'I don't sleep so good. I haven't in a long time.' He glanced down at the top of her head. 'Active mind.'

'Ah.' She nodded. 'It wasn't that I didn't do a good enough job of tiring you out, then.'

'No.' But he knew she needed the reassurance so he added, 'I slept six hours. That's a record.'

'I'm glad.' Leaning back against the support of his arm, she looked up at him with sparkling eyes.

Adam studied her face for a moment before looking back out to sea again. He felt her gaze on him and then she snuggled into his shoulder and took a deep breath. 'I love the ocean. It's good for the soul.'

Something they agreed on, Adam silently admitted, especially when it came to the stretch of ocean they were looking at. When he'd been his most troubled he would sit on the sand while he thought things through. When he'd first been sent to live with his father, new stepmom and half-brother it had been his hideaway. It still had the ability to calm him, even now, his mind wandering to details the way it so often did.

'You know the Indians called the island *Noepe*? It means "Amid the waters." Something to do with the conflicting tidal currents they could see offshore. It wasn't till the English got here that it was called Martha's Vineyard…'

Her head nodded against his shoulder and he heard the smile in her voice while her fingers continued to play at his wrist. 'I did know that. I even have a quote about the island for you to add to your collection.'

'Go on.'

'"Everything that ever happened on earth has happened on the Vineyard at least once. And some things twice…"'

'Who said it?'

'Haven't a clue.' The leather she'd been toying with caught her attention. 'Are these friendship bracelets?'

'That's what some people call them, yes.'

'You have friends?'

Adam briefly squeezed his arms in warning. 'Very funny. They're from people I know in New Orleans. We worked together on a rebuilding project.'

The words brought her chin up, her gaze flickering over his face. 'You stayed after Katrina?'

Adam nodded. 'Lots of folks did. I still go back. Coming through something like that ties you together in a way nothing else can.'

'Were you hurt?' The fine arch of her brows wavered on the question so he could see her concern.

It lowered his voice to a deep rumble. 'I was one of the lucky ones.'

Nodding, she dropped her chin, her gaze falling on a spot at the base of his throat and her hand lifting from his wrist to capture what she saw. 'What are these?'

'Which one are you looking at?' There were two on the thin strip of leather fastened around his neck.

Roane turned it towards the firelight. 'It looks like a little tooth on a blue stone in—pewter maybe?'

'Silver. A shark's tooth.' He smiled with meaning when

she glanced up at him from beneath long lashes. 'For strength and stamina…'

She rolled her eyes, her fingers moving to the second one. 'And this? It's beautiful.'

He felt her turning it over to look at each side in turn. And he knew what she was seeing; antique silver—one side set with an eight-pointed star, the other with an intricate pattern of interweaving circles.

'Open it,' he told her.

'It opens?' She was already lifting her other hand and when it opened Adam could hear the surprised delight in her voice. 'It's a compass—a perfect little miniature compass. Where did you get this?'

He'd thought the pilot in her might appreciate it. 'It was my great-grandfather's—on my mother's side. He was a schooner captain, sailed up and down the coast for most of his life when the Vineyard was still a busy harbour. As the second son he could do what he wanted until his brother died and he had to give it up.'

While he explained the history behind it Roane moved her head, leaning back against his arm and looking up at him with a curious expression. 'Are you making this up?'

Adam lifted a brow. 'Do I strike you as a big fan of fairy stories?'

She crinkled her nose. 'Not so much.'

'Well, then.' He looked out to sea, the sky on the horizon hinting at fingers of amber morning light while he contemplated how far to go with the story of the compass. With a deep breath, he looked down at her from the corner of his eye. 'Wanna hear the rest?'

There was a chance she might read more into it than was there, but she'd trusted him so Adam could trust her in return.

The boundaries of their relationship had already been set, she knew where she stood. Somehow he knew she'd appreciate the story, even before she nodded with enthusiasm.

When she batted her lashes at him he shook his head. 'There's no once upon a time so don't get too excited.'

'Spoilsport.' She pouted.

Adam smiled at her antics. 'He gave it to my great-grand-mother as a wedding present. Every time he went to sea she would put it around his neck. So he could find his way back to her, she'd say. Then when he came home he'd put it back round her neck because—'

'Because he'd found his way home…'

When Adam looked down at her she was staring at the compass, a wistful expression on her face. He frowned. Women tended to read between the lines. But before he could backtrack any she closed it over and let it go, leaning back against his shoulder. 'Sounds like they were very much in love.'

They'd certainly been devoted to each other their entire lives; they died within a week of each other he'd been told. But he didn't tell her that. Instead he told her another part of it. 'He found a poem with a compass in it—part of it was engraved on their tombstone here on the island. Smart guy, my great-grandfather—knew how to wrap a woman round his little finger with words.'

Roane snorted gracefully, her fingers playing on his wrist again. 'I bet she let him think he did. What was the poem?'

'Shakespeare.'

She echoed his earlier demand. 'Go on.'

When he hesitated she looked up at him and he saw the flash of realization in her eyes, swiftly followed by what looked like amusement to him. 'I'm not gonna end up wrapped round your little finger with words, Adam.'

'Ah, but I already found a way of wrapping you round my little finger *without words,* didn't I?'

Her chin dropped and she ran her hand down his wrist to his finger. 'Tell me about the ring, then. I'm guessing there's a story to go with it if everything else you wear has one…'

The story behind the ring was out of bounds, especially to her. He didn't need her pity. So Adam pushed his hand underneath her thigh, out of reach; gaining a shudder of awareness from her when he spread his fingers and kneaded her soft skin through the light material of her nightdress.

'It's a famous love poem.'

'The story behind the ring?'

'The Shakespeare.' He looked out at the ocean and smiled, nudging her with the arm supporting her to get her attention. 'Sun's coming up. Look.'

She turned her head, so he shifted her round a little to see better, lowering his mouth to just above her ear to tell her, 'Sunrises fall into the unforgettable experiences category.'

'I know.' Her tone had softened again.

Adam breathed in her light scent—moving his chin against the neck of her sweater to press his mouth against the sensitive skin below her ear. 'Let's see what we can do to make it more unforgettable, shall we?'

'Hmm.' She angled her head to make room for him.

When her hand slid up the inside of his leg Adam felt the rush of adrenalin through his veins. Shifting his hand from her thigh to underneath the edge of her sweater, he sought out her breast, filling his palm. She sank into him in response, her nipple beading as he rolled it; she was so responsive it was becoming a drug to him.

When he lifted his lashes he saw the fiery ball of the sun breaking the horizon.

'I don't remember all of it—' he didn't care if she knew it was a lie '—but it starts with: "Love is not love which alters when it alteration finds" and then moves on to say something about "it is an ever-fixed mark…"'

She turned her face and looked up at him while he looked back at her and continued lightly caressing her breast as he added, 'The bit about the compass is further in…'

Roane searched each of his eyes in turn, her breathing becoming shallow. Then she shrugged back her sleeve and curled a hand around his neck to draw his mouth down to hers. 'No wonder she wanted him to come back to her.'

Adam resisted the last inch that stood between their lips, his gaze locked with hers and his voice a husky rumble. 'Handsome devil too.'

Roane's eyes smiled at him. 'Just would be.'

'Probably a girl in every port…'

He leaned in and brushed her lips with his. Roane in turn lifted her other arm and wrapped it around his neck, light now dancing in her darkening eyes as her voice took on a seductive huskiness.

'Don't ruin it for me.'

Adam studied her eyes and then asked what he'd been burning to know for hours, his voice low and rough. 'Why didn't you tell me?'

'Tell you what?'

'How inexperienced you were.'

When doubt crossed her eyes and she avoided his gaze he leaned back a little, his voice firmer. 'Look at me.'

Her lashes lifted, blinking slowly as she looked into his eyes. Then she took a deep breath. 'Would it have made a difference?'

'No.' Adam tightened his hand against her breast, brushing

his thumb over her nipple and earning a gasp from her parted lips as her eyelids grew heavy. Smiling with satisfaction, he kept his tone deliberately low. 'You thought it would?'

Roane didn't answer him.

Moving his hand, he caught her nipple between his thumb and forefinger, the move arching her spine away from the band of his arm and drawing a soft moan from low in her throat. 'It wouldn't. You've got fire in you. I could see it. Wanted it. Still do.'

'You put the fire in me,' she breathed.

'No. You already had it in you. You just make me want to bring it out. If you tried holding it back I'd work harder for it.' Any man who considered himself a man would do the same in Adam's opinion.

Roane was looking at him as if she'd never seen him before or as if he was something completely new and fascinating to her. It was momentarily unsettling. So Adam moved his hand over her breast again and smiled when her eyes closed and she offered her neck to him.

Tilting his head to one side, he lowered his mouth to her skin and kissed his way up to her ear. 'Ever make love outdoors?'

She groaned. 'We can't.'

He was already moving his hand down her body and dragging her nightdress up her legs. 'Yes, we can.'

'No, we can't.' Her body made a lie of the words by parting her legs as he trailed his forefinger up the inside of her thigh. 'We don't have anything…'

Adam lifted his head to look down at her languid eyes, her full lips parted and waiting. 'Still have a lot to learn, don't you?'

He began lowering her to the blanket he'd brought down

from a swing seat on her porch. When she was lying on her back looking up at him he studied her face, temporarily floored by what he could see in her eyes. She was giving herself to him openly and completely. Even when the flicker of her lashes told him how unsure she was of herself. He brushed her hair back from each of her cheeks in turn, savouring the feel of her soft skin beneath his fingertips. Then he traced her mouth, his gaze lowering to watch as her lips parted and the brush of her exhaled breath whispered warmth over the back of his hand. When he looked back up there was wonder in her eyes too, a sense of awe that he could make her feel what she felt? She really had no idea how much of a siren was buried beneath her cloak of inexperience.

Adam wanted to strip that cloak away and let the siren out to play. He was going to tempt her out…

So he lowered his mouth to hers and sipped from her lips, as if she were the finest of wines and every single drop were nectar. He felt her small, cool hand against his cheek, her fingers splaying out against the skin warmed by the heat of the fire in front of them and between them. When he lifted his mouth he turned his head and kissed her palm, framing the back of her hand with his and threading his fingers through hers as he angled it back and kissed the beating pulse at her wrist before gradually working his way up her arm.

Lifting their joined hands above her head, he got to a point where her sleeve was in the way.

'I told you, you should stay naked,' he complained. 'Up.'

Tugging the sweater unceremoniously over her head, he smiled a small smile at her rumpled hair and shining eyes, balling the soft material in his fist and setting it under her head for a pillow. 'There.'

Gaze locked on hers, he unbuttoned the pearl beads down

the front of her nightdress, his palm pushing the edges apart so he could look at her. Adam had always had a deep and abiding appreciation of the female form, but with Roane it was more than that. He ran his fingertips from the base of her neck, through the valley of her breasts to the indentation on the slight curve of her stomach. She was perfection.

When she shivered he looked into her eyes. Was she cold? No, not cold. He'd made her shiver with desire. *For him.* It made him feel like a god.

Moving his flattened palm, he cradled her hip as he kissed her again; drinking deeper, suckling on her bottom lip until she opened her mouth on a sigh. When he moved his palm upwards, letting it learn the inward curve of her waist, she shifted on the blanket to get closer. But when he let his fingertips whisper over her ribs she squirmed, and he felt the low echo of muffled laughter in her throat. Ticklish. He smiled against her mouth. He liked that.

Kissing her deeper still, he sought out her tongue. Then he filled his hand with her breast again, growling at how perfect a fit she was, the bead of her nipple dead centre in his palm. As if she were made for him, or born from his imagination.

Moving over her and settling into the cradle she'd formed for him he dragged his mouth from hers and kissed down her neck, feeling her arch up into him as he kissed his way to her breast and held it up in his hand to draw her nipple into his mouth. She moaned—and when he caught it between his teeth, she gasped. Adam felt like a musician playing a delicately strung instrument. Each place he kissed brought forth a different sound that then vibrated through him and echoed in empty spaces he hadn't known he had. And when he did know, it felt as if the hollowness had to be filled with her.

Pushing an arm under the upward curve of her spine, he dragged her upright, rocking back on his bent knees and hauling her onto his lap. When he looked up at her he saw wide eyes filled with a combination of arousal and surprise, so he yanked her closer; the material of her nightdress bunched tight between her legs as she came into contact with the ridge of his erection.

Awareness flushed her cheeks. She rocked her hips experimentally against him, her sharp intake of breath and the way she bit down on her lower lip distracting Adam from the rush of blood to his throbbing groin.

'Adam—'

When she breathed his name like that it did him in. Didn't she know that?

Thrusting his fingers into her hair, he angled her head back, using the arm around her waist to control the backward arch of her body as he lowered his head to her breasts. Every pull of his hungry lips earned him another rock of her hips against him, her hands clinging to his shoulders and her fingernails pushing into his skin. He could almost feel the siren struggling free…

He pushed the material off her shoulders, down her arms, letting it pool around her waist as he twisted it around his fist behind her back and pulled it tighter between her legs, adding to the friction of her movement. But when she realized what he'd done she froze, her body trembling from within.

Adam kissed her neck and turned his head to whisper roughly into her ear, 'Don't stop.'

Sliding his hand down, he cupped the back of her neck between long fingers and his thumb and lifted his head—the tip of his nose almost touching hers as he looked into her eyes and tugged the material tight again. 'Take what you need from me.'

Roane swallowed hard, her voice husky. 'I can't.'

'Yes, you can.'

'But you won't—'

'Not this time.' And if she had any idea what it was costing him she wouldn't look at him the way she was. 'I want to watch you.'

'I can't.' The agony in her eyes came through in the wobble of her soft voice. She wanted to please him. What he didn't know was her pleasure alone pleased him. He could wait. For now…

'You can.' He angled his head, his mouth hovering over hers. 'I can make you.'

Still looking into her eyes, he dragged her lower lip between his teeth and let go. 'I can wind you up so tight you won't be able to stop yourself. Your body belongs to me now.'

He kissed the lip he'd tugged when a flash of fear crossed her expressive eyes. 'I can make you do it with words alone if I want to…'

Moving his head again, he set his cheek to hers and spoke into her ear again, his voice low and even, the words purposefully slow. 'I can tell you what it felt like when I was deep inside you. I can tell you what it was like when you came around me…'

Her hips moved restlessly against him, her breathing ragged in his ear.

'I can tell you how amazing it was.' He pressed his lips to her ear lobe. 'I can tell you how much I want to feel it again. And again. And again. I can tell you how many times I want to come inside you the way I did…'

Roane whimpered and moved rhythmically against him.

Adam smiled, holding the material in place and feeling the shudder of her body as she got closer to the edge. 'Take what you need. I want you to.'

'Oh, God—'

She wrapped her arms around his neck and held onto him as if her life depended on it, her breasts rubbing against the wall of his chest and making him wish his T-shirt wasn't in the way. He wanted her skin to skin with him, nothing between them, nothing in the way. He wanted to drive deep into her body and get lost in her. He wanted her screaming his name. He *wanted*.

He was consumed with need. He'd never felt that before. She was like a fever in his blood.

She rocked her hips forwards, grinding herself onto his erection. Then she stilled. A low moan pushed upwards from inside as her body shook uncontrollably.

Adam leaned back, his fingers in her hair so he could pull her head back and see her face. Her eyes were hooded, glittering and so very dark it was almost as if she wasn't there. Her lips were parted, the air she dragged into her lungs making her lower lip tremble. Her cheeks were flushed—a strand of hair was stuck against her damp forehead...

She was *sensational*.

Adam's heart thundered in his chest, his breathing ragged, his gaze so intensely focused on her he was frowning in concentration. He *burned* for her.

Her breasts heaving between them, Roane's eyes slowly returned to a closer shade of the luminous blue he knew so well. She damped her lips, dropped her gaze to his mouth and then leaned forwards—the voice of a seductive siren making a determined demand: *'Now you.'*

Adam groaned as their mouths fused together. *Hell, yes.* She could do what she wanted. He was all hers.

CHAPTER NINE

WHEN HE TOSSED the helmet at her she scrambled to catch it and looked up at him with wide eyes, laughing nervously. 'Oh, I don't think so.'

'Trust me, sweetheart. You'll love it.'

Her gaze shifted to the shining black metal of his beast of a motorcycle, then back to Adam. She didn't know which one gave her more of a kick to look at, frankly. The motorcycle was dangerous and risky and would probably be the experience of a lifetime—and Adam... Actually in fairness there was very little difference between them. She liked to think Adam was less likely to kill her, though...

He was buttoning up his trademark shirt-worn-over-T-shirt, long fingers moving with the same dexterity he'd used on her body for hours on end. Roane felt a newly familiar rush of heat prickle over her skin as she watched him. How could she still want him that much when he'd pretty much pleasured her into a languid puddle? She had muscles that ached in places she hadn't even known she had muscles, but since each and every ache came with a memory...

On second thought maybe he did have the means to kill her. *But what a way to go.*

He patted the seat of the bike. 'C'mon.'

Roane wavered, grimacing. 'Do I have to?'

The hesitation seemed to surprise him. 'You can fly a plane but you're afraid to get on a motorcycle?'

Cocking a brow, she made a circle with a limp-wristed hand. 'Do we want to turn that one round and take another look at it? Planes are statistically safer than motorcycles.'

He took a long stride towards her and grabbed her elbow tugging her forwards. 'Have you ever even been on a motorcycle?'

'No. I don't know anyone who owns one.'

'You do now.' He lifted the helmet out of her hands and set it on the seat beside his before reaching out to button up her jacket. 'Consider it one of many firsts I've brought your way. I'm broadening your horizons.'

Roane found it difficult to focus on excuses when the backs of his fingers were working their way up from her stomach, over her ribs and lingering on her breasts. But when he lifted his chin and smiled lazily at her she sighed heavily, fully aware of the fact he knew what he'd just done to her.

'If you kill me I'm never speaking to you again.'

'I'll keep that in mind.' He placed a swift kiss on her mouth and reached for the helmet.

'Please do.' She laughed. ''Cause I'm not much use to you if—' The rest of the sentence was muffled as he pushed the helmet onto her head, patting the top of it with a grin when she scowled at him.

'There.' He buckled the strap under her chin while she set her hands on her hips. 'You're good to go.'

Roane tugged the front of it down a little to tell him, 'You white-knuckle me and this is gonna be the shortest relationship in the history of mankind.'

With a low chuckle, Adam turned and lifted his helmet before casually swinging a long jean-clad leg over the heavy duty touring bike with ease. He then kicked the stand back and lifted it upright as if it weighed as much as a feather—which Roane seriously doubted. She briefly wondered why it was he looked so damn good on it while she was standing feeling like a complete idiot. There was just something about a sexy male on a large motorcycle, wasn't there?

He held out an arm. 'Climb on.'

'I bet you say that to all the girls,' Roane mumbled as she attempted to do as she was told. She wasn't nearly as graceful as he'd been. In fact it took a couple of attempts and some bouncing around on one foot as she tried to keep her balance. All of which Adam found highly amusing, his sensational eyes sparkling at her when he looked over his shoulder.

'Put your feet up. That's it. Arms round my waist.'

All right, so there were certain fringe benefits. Roane was revelling in the sensations of her hips wrapped around his and her breasts pressed tight to the hard wall of his back when he gunned the engine.

Dear Lord. They could just stay where they were. She closed her eyes and let out a low moan she knew he wouldn't hear over the loud rumbling purr of the engine. The vibration sent a rhythmical pulse through the seat to her rear, making her squirm her crotch tighter to the seams of her jeans. She smoothed her hands over his taut stomach, squooshed her breasts tighter to his back so she could feel the heat of him through their clothes… Oh, yes…now this was suddenly *very* interesting.

Adam's head turned and she smiled as he raised his voice above the noise. *'Behave.'*

Roane smiled impishly. She was enjoying her personal

sexual revolution. Now that she knew what she'd been missing out on she was determined to enjoy every single second of it. She wasn't even going to allow herself to think about how brief a time it might be with Adam. All that mattered was the here and now.

When the bike moved smoothly forwards she clung to him, stomach lurching and heart pounding. They bumped cautiously down the laneway, onto the narrow tree-lined road and when they hit the better surfaces she started to relax. Okay. This wasn't so bad.

She knew he was going slower than he probably did normally but she appreciated the thoughtfulness. He wouldn't let any harm come to her. She knew that. It was the same blind faith she'd had in him when he'd made love to her—she knew he wouldn't hurt her. Oh, he might be rough-edged, but Adam Bryant had an honourable streak underneath it all, didn't he? It added to his overwhelming maleness, Roane felt—was a potent combination when added to everything else.

Women fell for men like him.

The worrying thought made her focus her mind elsewhere, her gaze taking in her surroundings from a totally new perspective. She'd driven along the Vineyard's roads a million times, in a station wagon, as a passenger in Jake's convertible, in her own little compact. But the view from a motorcycle was so very different. She felt closer to nature somehow; a cooling breeze on her face, the scent of freshly mown grass and the salt sea air in her nostrils, the sunlight that danced through gaps in the foliage of the trees creating an arch above their heads. It was glorious.

Then the trees gave way to the ocean, white foam randomly appearing to froth towards the pale sands of the ristine shoreline. Roane held onto Adam's strength to lean back a little so she could smile up at the blue skies.

He threw a smile over his shoulder and she laughed. He'd known she would love this because he knew how it felt. She wondered if he ever got tired of knowing her better than she apparently knew herself. But at the same time she wished she could share her joy of flying with him the same way he was sharing the joy of his freedom on a motorcycle.

It felt as if she was getting more from him than he was from her. Which begged the question of just what it was he got from being with her beyond sex?

By lunchtime they ended up in Vineyard Haven. The boat-filled harbour protected by East and West Chop, promonto-ies that formed a natural enclosure for one of the busiest harbours in the heydays of coastal schooners. It made Roane wonder if Adam's great-grandfather had sailed his schooner from there, with the compass around his neck and his wife waving him goodbye. She smiled at the thought. Then felt an ache at how far back Adam's connections to the Vineyard went. It was sad, especially when he'd left it all behind without a backward glance.

They drove past schooner captains' houses with their bright white porches and heavily laden planters and hanging baskets, then along the tree-lined main street where Adam parked and held out a hand to help her down. Roane was fussing with her hair after removing her helmet when he took her hand.

'Hungry?'

She threaded her fingers with his and smiled at the fact he was holding her hand. Pleasure in the simple things, she supposed. *More to do with the man attached to the hand,* her inner voice admitted.

'Starving.'

'We'll get it to go. Eat at one of the lighthouses.'

When most of the staff in the small general store greeted her by name Adam shook his head. 'I had no idea you were famous.'

'Not famous. *Friendly.*' She adjusted the basket on her arm and scanned the shelves for fresh rolls, smiling as she added, 'You should try it some time. When you first meet someone you can be…surly.'

'Surly.'

'Uh-huh.' She found rolls and moved down the aisle, cocking her head and looking up at him from the corner of her eye. 'And brusque.'

'Surly and brusque.' He looked back at her the same way, then smiled cockily. 'And adorable. You forgot to add adorable.'

Roane snorted. 'It wasn't high on my list.'

Something caught Adam's attention and he set his hands on her hips to turn her. 'That's right. You didn't like me. I'd forgotten.'

'It's been four days. How did you forget that fast?'

'You did. You like me now.'

Good point. Because, darn it, despite the danger she did like him. She more than liked him. It would be so much easier if she didn't…

She searched the shelves to see what he was so interested in. 'What are we—? *Oh.*'

'Ladies' choice.' Leaning down to lower his voice to a deep rumble, he added, 'Just make sure we have plenty. Think strength and stamina…'

He had the gall to slap her rear—firmly—making her jump and scowl at him as he walked away. 'Where are you going?'

Turning on his heel, he walked backwards. 'The produce section. Gotta keep our energy levels up.' He grinned broadly and winked at her. 'Meet you at the checkout.'

Smiling, Roane shook her head, then looked back at the baffling array of contraceptives in front of her. It wasn't something she'd ever spent a whole heap of time looking at in a store. She really wasn't sure she knew where to begin. A ring caught her attention and she lifted it to figure out what it was—swiftly setting it back down when she read the back. It was official—she was a prude. The thought made her frown.

Then she considered the possibilities of some of the items in front of her and felt the heat rise in her body. It was because every image involved Adam. He'd turned her from a prude into a sex maniac in one night.

She glanced up and down the aisle and smiled weakly at someone she knew. Nope. Still a bit of a prude. But she bravely hid a small pack of condoms beneath the bread rolls and silently prayed she could manage to pay for them without blushing. She was a twenty-seven-year-old woman having incredible, mind blowing sex, for crying out loud! She should be holding a parade in the main street.

Several picnic items later she met Adam at the checkout, a large handful of fresh fruit added to their basket as he charmed the middle aged woman behind the counter with a smile.

'Hi, there—' he glanced down and back up '—Mabel.'

Roane rolled her eyes, as much at who was ringing up their purchases as the beaming response he got. Well, if the world didn't know she was sleeping with Adam it was going to inside a matter of minutes. Mabel loved a good gossip. 'Mabel is a sensible married woman with four kids. That won't work on her.'

'Oh, I don't know, Roane.' Mable giggled like a school-girl. 'Nothing wrong with being friendly…'

Adam smirked smugly and Roane couldn't help but laugh. She'd been the one to tell him to try being friendly after all. It was just a rarity for him to do anything she suggested outside the bedroom.

He glanced down, cocked a brow at her and shook his head. 'I'll be right back.'

'Where'd you find *him*?' Mable asked in a whisper. 'He's gorgeous.'

And knew it too. But Roane couldn't help smiling again, the reason why suddenly hitting her. She was happy. With a pang of regret, she wondered how long it would last.

'We're friends.'

It wasn't a complete lie. They were getting on better than she would ever have imagined. Even more ridiculously she knew she would miss him when he was gone. Surely it was too fast to feel that way? Yeah, thought the girl who'd slept with him after three days. The usual rules didn't apply to someone like Adam and it seemed to have had a knock-on effect on Roane. She was behaving so completely out of character she felt a little lost for a moment.

Then Adam dumped a load of things into their basket and looked her straight in the eye.

Almost in slow motion Roane managed to forcibly drag her gaze away from the intense heat radiating off him. She looked down at the basket, stifling a groan and immediately feeling a wave of heat rise on her cheeks as she looked at Mabel's smiling face.

Who lifted the first bumper pack of many and rang it up on her till, without saying a single word. She didn't have to. The condoms said it all.

There was a loud crunch beside her and Roane glared at Adam as he chewed a mouthful of apple and spoke with his mouth full, waving the apple at Mabel as he stared at Roane. 'And this, Mabel.'

Roane continued to glare at him as he reached for his wallet. She was going to kill him.

Outside in the sunshine she lifted her chin high and informed him, '*You* are in *so* much trouble right now.'

He swallowed another mouthful of apple, studying his surroundings as they walked. 'You've never actually bought condoms, have you?'

'I've bought them *discreetly.*' She scowled at him, her cheeks still ridiculously hot. 'I haven't felt the need to announce to the entire island that I'm having—*sex!*'

When she looked around her and lowered her voice to hiss the word 'sex' at him he stopped and turned to consider her with hooded eyes. 'People have sex every day. If they're lucky they get to have it…'

He lifted a hand and made a show of counting his long fingers, the corners of his devilishly sexy mouth twitching as he gave up, dropped his hand and added, '*Lots.*'

When she couldn't stop looking at his mouth he tossed the half-eaten apple in a nearby receptacle and placed his hands on her hips, tugging her closer. 'In our case they only stop out of necessity. And, sweetheart? If I have my way—which you know I will—you'll be buying plenty more of that very necessity pretty damn soon. So you need to get used to it…'

Roane's jaw dropped. 'Are you kidding me? We just bought enough for a month.'

'No, we didn't. Couple of weeks' worth—tops.'

Ridiculously even the fact he was handing her a couple of weeks made her heart soar. 'Is that a fact?'

Adam nodded firmly. 'It is.'

Roane managed a shaky breath as he lowered his head and kissed her. Oh, Lord, she was in trouble. She couldn't possibly feel something so strong for him so fast. It wasn't how things were supposed to be.

His hand lifted, his knuckles brushing a strand of hair from her cheek when the wind caught it. Then he stepped closer, forcing her to tilt her head further back as he deepened the kiss and sought entry with the tip of his tongue. There it was: the instant spark—the spiralling knot of desire. The need to have his body joined to hers. If anything it was even stronger than it had been twenty-four hours ago, because now she knew what came next. She knew what it was like to have that warm mouth and his large hands on her body. How it felt when he pushed inside her. She could practically feel the weight of his body on hers as he drove her to the edge and beyond.

How was she supposed to survive without it now she knew what it felt like with him? How was she supposed to breathe without it hurting when he left? When every breath she currently took was filled with his enticing scent as he stole her heart piece by piece.

She knew nothing about him. *Nothing*.

She was falling for him. *Hard*.

When he lifted his head she forced a smile onto her face and gently extricated herself from his hold to step around him. 'Well, in that case…'

She bit her lip and smiled impishly over her shoulder. 'There was this ring thing in there that I think might have possibilities…according to the back of the pack it's for him *and* her…'

Deep laughter erupted from his chest as he reached for her

hand and yanked her back to him. 'We don't need it. Haven't you learned that yet?'

Laughing in reply, she stumbled as he slammed her body into his, his feet spreading wider to balance them both. 'And here I thought you liked it when I got adventurous. I don't remember you complaining when I—'

'Afternoon, Roane.'

Adam lifted his head as the owner of the voice passed them, Roane looking to see who it was. She scrunched her nose up and closed her eyes. 'Hi, Peter.'

When she opened her eyes Adam's were filled with silent sparkling laughter. 'Who was that?'

'My bank manager.'

'Ah.'

Ah indeed. But she didn't care, her chin jerking upwards as she huskily demanded, 'Kiss me.'

Another chuckle of deep laughter vibrated his chest and Roane smiled at him. She loved it when he laughed. But the firm kiss he gave her was all too brief and then he was slinging a long arm over her shoulders and tucking her into his side, lowering his head to her temple to promise her, '*Later.*' He steered them towards the motorcycle. 'Let's go build up an appetite first…and I don't mean for food…'

Roane leaned her head back against his shoulder, moving her arm around his lean waist and hooking her thumb under the belt loop of his jeans. 'We're having an early night, though, right?'

He chuckled again. 'I've created a monster.'

Roane was laughing with him when another voice sounded, 'A.J.? It is you. Thought so. What the hell you doing here, man?'

Adam changed in a heartbeat, releasing Roane and

frowning at her before he stepped forwards and shook the fair-haired man's hand. 'Just visiting. Didn't know you knew the island.'

'Wife's folks have a holiday place here. You should come out and see us. Lucy would be glad to see you.' He looked pointedly at Roane. 'Bring your girl over. Hi—Steve Rowland. I do business with A.J.'

Roane shook the hand that was offered to her. 'Roane Elliott.'

'Roane—lovely name.'

'Thank you.' She let go of his hand and stepped closer to Adam, looking up at his unreadable expression with a lift of her brow. 'How long have you known A.J.?'

'Too long.' He laughed as he looked at Adam. 'I meant to thank you for that last tip you gave me. You were right on the money—as always.'

'No problem.' Adam placed his palm on the small of Roane's back and exerted pressure to nudge her forwards. 'We've got to go. Tell Luce I said hi.'

'Stop by. We're in Oak Bluffs. You've got my cell.'

'Do. Bye, Steve.'

'Bye, Steve.' Roane leaned her head to one side to smile at him as she was firmly ushered away. 'Nice to meet you.'

'You too, Roane. Make him bring you along.'

'Oh, I will.' She looked up at Adam with open curiosity when they were a few steps away, 'A.J.?'

'It's how most people know me.'

'What's it stand for?'

He didn't look the least little bit pleased to be telling her. 'Adam Jameson.'

'Middle name?' She hadn't known that. The clench of his jaw made her smile. As middle names went she didn't think it was all that bad. But it obviously bothered Adam.

'And mother's maiden name.'

The words had been said on a flat tone that made Roane wonder what the problem was. Then it came to her. 'You don't use the Bryant name, do you?'

'No.'

They stopped beside the shining motorcycle, Roane frowning in confusion. 'Why?'

'Because it's easier.'

And because when he left the island he hadn't just left his home behind? He'd left everything. Had he really hated his father that much?

Roane's voice was low. 'I don't understand.'

'I wouldn't expect you to.' He shrugged, opening one of the storage cases at the back of his bike to stow away their purchases.

Reaching a hand to his outstretched arm, she gently squeezed to get his attention. 'Then make me. Did you really hate them that much?'

His gaze focused on her hand. 'Who?'

'Your dad—Jake—everyone who has the Bryant name. People would say the name opened doors for you…'

The words seemed to make him more tense than he already was, his spine straightening as he dropped his arm to his side and freed her hand. 'I'm not interested in opening those doors. Never was. I don't make my living piggybacking on a name. I do it my way.'

Instead of being intimidated by his change back to the surly man she'd met just days ago Roane stepped closer, her hands lifting to his waist and her voice still soft. 'Okay. So what *do you* do?'

He smiled, but his eyes were serious. When he spoke his voice shimmered with authority, hinting that whatever it was

he did he did from a high position. 'I dabble in whatever inter
ests me. And I do it well.'

Meaning he didn't want her to know.

The sense of rejection must have shown in her eyes
because his hands immediately lifted to frame her face, his
thumbs tilting her chin up as he leaned down to look into her
eyes. 'It's complicated.'

Roane frowned. 'You don't think I'm clever enough to
understand, do you? I might not have a genius IQ like you
do, Adam, but that doesn't mean—'

He kissed her to shut her up. 'I know it doesn't. That's not
what I meant.'

'So what, then—you're a spy?'

The corners of his mouth twitched. 'Not a spy. It's much
less interesting than that.'

'Then wh—?'

Another kiss. Much as Roane enjoyed the liberties he was
taking to distract her from the subject, she was starting to get
annoyed. What was the big deal? Was he really so deter
mined not to let her into a single corner of his life? It wasn't
as if she was going to stalk him all over the country after he
left!

'I'll tell you. Just not now.' He took a deep breath that
brushed his chest against her breasts. 'Do us both a favour
and don't push.'

Who *was* this man? It hit her that she was sleeping with
a stranger. Surely that should have scared her more than it
did?

'It's nothing illegal.'

'Nothing illegal.' He looked amused at the idea.

'Or unethical…'

'Nope; not my style.'

'Or immoral.'

Adam shook his head, a lopsided smile appearing to addle her thoughts. 'Good to know you have such a high opinion of me. No—nothing immoral—and you're pushing, sweetheart.'

When he reached for her helmet and set it against her breasts she cocked her head and smiled at him to cover up how confused she suddenly felt. A day with Adam was quite the magical mystery tour, wasn't it? She just wished it didn't leave her feeling as if he didn't trust her. 'So are we visiting Steve and Lucy?'

'No.' Adam continued smiling as he reached for his helmet. 'Feed him a couple of beers and you'll get information about my life I *definitely* don't want you knowing.'

'Like stories about women.'

'Among others…'

Great, and now she was jealous of unseen women who had absolutely nothing to do with her. But they knew him in his new life—which meant they knew him better than she did. Roane hated them for that.

A thought made her shudder. 'Have you ever been married?'

'Hell, no.' He frowned at her. 'Where did that come from?'

Roane ignored the frown. 'Kids? Don't say not that you know of…'

'If there was even the remotest chance of me having a child I'd know about it—' the frown darkened '—and I'd be there. Want to tell me where you're going with this?'

'Am I allowed to know anything about you or are secrets part of the deal?'

'What damn deal?'

She knew she was starting an argument but she couldn't seem to stop herself from doing it, an emotional cocktail of frustration, confusion and hurt mixing together and forming anger. 'The "you teach, I learn" deal—the one where you get to fill in a few hours before you leave again.'

The control he exerted over his anger was admirable, but the muscle clenching on his jaw told her just how much it was costing him. 'You knew I'd leave when we started this.'

He was right. She did. By saying what she had she'd just told him how involved she was, hadn't she?

With great effort and the performance of a lifetime she buried how she felt. 'I did. You're right.'

After a long moment of tense silence, Adam shook his head, his profile turned to her as he fought some kind of inner battle before looking her in the eye again. Then the soft rumble of sincerity entered his voice.

'I can't give you more than this. It's not that I don't want to. I can't.'

Roane blinked at him. She knew he meant what he said, she could hear it in his voice, see it in the intensity of his gaze. Ridiculously she felt as if she would know if Adam was lying to her. How could she know that?

But what really got to her was she could feel such a strong sense of *emptiness* in him. It was the most dreadful sensation. She immediately felt the need to make him feel better, to wrap herself around him and stay there until she couldn't feel it in him any more.

Pursing his lips into a thin line, he looked away and then back; even the minutest hint of uncertainty in a man so sure of himself was heartbreaking to behold.

'I can give you now.'

She didn't hesitate. 'I'll take it.'

His eyes softened to a darker brown than she'd ever seen before, then he nodded. 'Good.'

Roane knew she'd take whatever she could get, she was already that addicted to him. She just had to remember not to allow herself to think about the fact that every day had a 'now'.

A genius like Adam should have known that too, shouldn't he?

CHAPTER TEN

IT FELT AS IF Roane was changing something in him.

Adam had no idea why he'd said the things he had in the Haven. Or why it was he'd felt as if he had to tell her the things he knew he couldn't. For a brief moment he'd wanted to tell her *everything*—every last detail. He'd never done that—*with anyone.*

It had been a roller coaster of a day. He'd made love to her in the open air as the sun came up, had let her make love to him and been astonished by just how quick a study she really was.

Then he'd spent the time on his motorcycle excruciatingly aroused by her pressed so tightly to his back. He'd even contemplated keeping driving until they were far away and no one could find them until he'd sated them both.

More surprising than anything else, he'd had fun with her on their shopping expedition, had felt—happy was the right word, he supposed. Yes, that was it. He'd been happy spending time with her doing something completely mundane, brief as it was. He couldn't remember the last time he'd felt that way—if he ever had.

Then they'd met Steve. He couldn't risk meeting someone

rom the city when it was so important Adam hold onto his
nonymity. Of course Roane was curious. How could she not
e? Especially when Adam couldn't tell her about his job—
ot that he wasn't prepared to; he wanted her to know about
ie life he'd made for himself. He was proud of that life, of
ie things he'd achieved. He'd worked hard. But she was too
ed to his family—he wouldn't let her get caught in the
niddle of the battle looming on the horizon.

As it was she didn't think he trusted her, did she? When
: had nothing to do with trust—he trusted her. A somewhat
iiraculous change of personality for someone who trusted
s little as Adam did. By holding back from her he'd hurt
er—and he'd hated that.

He'd found himself holding his breath while he waited for
er to choose what they already had, because he wanted it.
Ie wanted it more than he'd wanted anything in a very long
ıme.

Familiar frustration had bubbled inside him like boiling
cid for a long while afterwards, even when she'd made her
ecision so fast. Until the soothing balm that was Roane
vorked its magic on him and he let himself get lost in a
urreal world where for a brief moment he actually felt—
ontent. She was amazing. All the more so because she had
o idea of the miraculous effect she had on him.

He'd never been content a day in his life.

By the time they got back to the estate he was burning up with
he need to demonstrate how she'd made him feel. He wanted
o make her feel as good as she'd made him feel. In the absence
•f words or emotion it was the only gift he could give her.

But Jake was waiting in the guest house. And Adam barely
ıad time to release the small hand he was holding before a
ıst made contact with his jaw.

'*Jake!*' Roane yelled and stepped forwards. 'What ar
you *doing*?'

Adam lifted an arm and hauled her back to his side, almos
as if he was stating where she belonged. 'Don't.'

He then glared at his little brother. 'First one's free. Nex
one will cost you.'

Roane tried to pull free, her eyes wide as she looked from
Adam's jaw to Jake's face. 'What the hell was that for?'

'Ask *him*.' Jake's face was dark with anger. 'Go on. As
him what he's been doing.'

Her wide-eyed gaze swung to Adam, a million and on
questions silently being asked in the blue depths. 'What's h
talking about?'

Adam knew. Someone *had* been doing some digging
hadn't they? But he wasn't going to let her get caught in th
middle, it was the very reason he hadn't told her himsel
'Leave. *Now*.'

'*No*.' She lifted her chin and defied his firm tone.

'I mean it. Go.'

'No. She stays. She's part of it, after all, isn't she, b
brother?'

Adam felt a wave of anger crashing in on him. 'She ha
nothing to do with it.'

'No?' Jake's tone was laced with sarcasm. 'I saw you tw
in Tisbury. Seducing her is another way of getting at me, isn
it?'

Adam didn't much care for the insinuation, steppin
forwards and pushing Roane behind him. He then fought t
keep his voice cool and his words as clear as possible. 'I didn
do anything to get at you. That wasn't what I was doing.'

'Then what *were* you doing?' Jake stood his ground, hi
hands bunched in readiness at his sides.

Roane got loose, and before Adam could do anything to top it she was standing between them. In the face of bristling anger radiating from the two large males she bravely lifted her chin and glared in warning at each of them in turn. 'Okay. Which one of you wants to tell me what's going on? Because I swear—I'm ready to cause actual bodily harm if one of you doesn't start acting like an adult.'

They both looked down at her, Roane not the least bit fazed by the fact she had to lift her chin higher to continue glaring at them. Under normal circumstances Adam would have smiled, hauled her close and kissed her hard for how beautiful she looked with that much fire in her eyes. She was feisty, his girl.

Instead he frowned at her. 'Leave, Roane. It's the last time I'm gonna say it.'

But again she defied him. 'And let you both pummel each other into a pulp? I think not. You're *brothers*! Tell me what's going on.'

Adam swore under his breath and looked at Jake, repeating his words through clenched teeth. 'I didn't do it to get at you.'

Jake had the guts to laugh sarcastically, which Adam begrudgingly respected him for. They weren't so different, were they? He'd been known to laugh in someone's face mid-argument. In fact, if there was a way to escalate things through sarcasm Adam was pretty much the master.

'Okay, then.' Jake nodded, his eyes narrow and his jaw tight. 'Let's just work our way through the facts, shall we? You knew I was head of the company.'

'Yes.'

'Then tell me how it wasn't to get to me?'

'I'm telling you it wasn't.'

'So what was it, then? To prove you're the better man? Revenge? To step in and take over? If you wanted the job so bad, then all you had to do was stay—it was yours. It was yours by birth, for crying out loud!'

That was an archaic notion, Adam thought. The way he saw it, their father was happier with Jake at the helm, Jake was happy being there, Adam was free to do as he chose. The world was the way it was meant to be.

Roane's voice rose. 'Would *someone* please tell me what's going on?'

When Adam remained impassive Jake jerked his brows in challenge and then looked at her. 'Okay, then. I'll tell you. The company has been fighting off takeover rumours since Dad got sick. Share prices dropped when I took over—I had to prove myself. Then there were whispers someone had been buying, they'd been buying for years. Small numbers, but collectively they added up to a threat. That's why I needed *him*...' he jerked his chin at Adam '...back here to talk about selling his shares to me. Dad signed half the family shares to each of us when he wrapped up his affairs.'

Adam was still staring Jake down when he caught sight of Roane's head turning. He could feel her gaze burning into him but he didn't look at her. He couldn't take the chance—because if there was so much as a flicker of doubt in her eyes he would feel the need to hit something...

He clenched his teeth when realization laced her words with disbelief. 'You were buying the shares?'

Jake cocked his head to the side and studied Adam with malice. 'And along with his family shares he now owns the majority. You're looking at the Bryant who holds the reins. Question is: is he planning on riding the horse—or shooting it?'

Instead of any of the questions Adam had been expecting from Roane she asked, 'How did you afford—?'

Jake smiled at her, but it was anything but warm. Adam silently dared him to say a single thing that would cause her pain. *Go on. Give me a reason not to stand here and let you let it all out in one go...*

'Didn't he mention that part? Turns out my big brother is a bona-fide multibillionaire. He could buy the Bryant Corporation with what would be the equivalent of chump change to him. Right, Adam?'

The room fell into the kind of silence that sat oppressively in the air, Roane's small voice eventually sounding beside him, 'Adam?'

'He prefers A.J. these days. Hates us that much he won't even use the family name, will you—' Jake stepped forwards and practically spat the word in his face '—*Jameson*? What I'd like to know is what we did to you. Leaving wasn't enough? You had to work from the outside to bring us down and then come back to use someone who's more a part of this family than you ever were and hurt her too? What did she ever do to you? Why couldn't you *leave her be*?'

Because it felt *right,* goddammit! For the first time in his life he'd come home and felt as if he *belonged*.

As if he'd come back *to her*!

The truth of it hit him like a blow to the chest. Adam had had enough. He lifted his hands and pushed Jake back a step—not with any degree of force, but with enough controlled strength to move him out of Adam's face. 'You leave her out of this!'

It happened in the blink of an eye. When Jake lifted his arm to swing, Roane reached out. Before Adam could move she was on her rear on the floor, a squeak of surprised outrage leaving her lips. He hadn't hit her, but when he'd swung his arm back from her hold Jake had inadvertently knocked her over.

Adam saw red.

'Son-of-a—' He knelt down and reached for her, frustration rising to boiling point when she shrugged away from his touch.

'Don't touch me, Adam.'

'Are you—?'

'I'm *fine*!'

It only marginally appeased him when she did the same thing with Jake when he reached for her. 'Don't *you* touch me either!'

She struggled ungracefully to her feet and absent mindedly rubbed her behind as she blew a strand of hair out of her eyes and glared at them both. 'I hope you feel awful for knocking me on my ass, Jacob Bryant. You're both *pathetic*!' She folded her arms, her cheeks flushed as she fixed Adam with a furious gaze. 'Is it true? You're some kind of squillionaire?'

Adam fought for some semblance of control. 'Yes.'

'Since when?'

'I inherited some money when I turned twenty-one—from my mother's estate.' Hadn't been much after her lavish lifestyle, but it had given him a start. 'I dabbled in the markets and commodities—invested—I'm good at what I do. There are patterns I can understand.'

Jake began to pace.

But Roane kept looking at Adam as if she was barely aware there was anyone else there. 'And the shares you bought in the Bryant Corporation?'

'I'd heard rumours the old man's touch was slipping, so I bought where I could. When Jake took over the word on the

reet was someone would try a takeover. So I bought enough
) make sure it wouldn't happen unless it was me.'

Her eyes narrowed. 'Why?'

Adam glanced at Jake and saw he'd stopped pacing, his
ooded eyes studying Adam with caution. He wasn't
repared to explain himself to his younger brother. Let Jake
iink what he wanted.

'Well?'

He didn't look at her. 'We're done here.'

There was no way to avoid walking past his brother to get
) the stairs so Adam straightened his spine, staring straight
t him and daring him to make a move.

But Roane wasn't done. 'Go away, Jake.'

'I'm not—'

'Yes, you are. I'll feel safer if I only have one of you to
eal with at a time. But don't think I'm done with you—
cause I'm not.' She took a breath. 'Adam and I need to talk
nd he won't while you're here.'

Under normal circumstances Adam wouldn't have talked
) her either after that kind of insight. But she deserved better.
o he didn't say anything as he kept walking, ignoring Jake
vhen he dropped in a low warning, 'Hurt her and I'll hunt
ou down—got it?'

Said the guy who'd knocked her over? Now there was irony.
3ut Adam shook his head and kept walking. The kid had never
nown when he was out of his league; he had ended up with
lozens of black eyes and bloody noses that had never taught
im a lesson in school or at camp. Gutsy but stupid—that was
ake as a kid, and there'd been a time when Adam had found
t amusing in an almost affectionate, brotherly kind of way.

But those days were gone.

Now he would for evermore associate Jake with the rage

he'd felt at seeing Roane on the floor. If she'd been hurt i
any way—well, Adam didn't like to think what he'd hav
done. Accidental or not—Jake had done it. But then Adar
would never forgive himself for inadvertently putting her i
the middle. He'd *tried* not to. He'd *tried* to protect her. He'
failed.

Now he was going to have to tell her the answers to every
thing she asked as penance instead of because he wanted to
Then they'd be done. No more 'now'. He'd leave and she'
stay and 'they' would be something amazing that happened i
a few days on Martha's Vineyard—in his memories, in th
past…

Adam had no idea why knowing that felt so bad.

Roane waited for Jake to leave, her foot tapping on the floo
while she was torn in different directions. She knew Jak
hadn't pushed her over on purpose but she hated the momen
tary fear she'd felt. Jake had some major grovelling to do an
he knew it.

He was the easy one.

Her gaze rose to the top of the stairs. What to do abou
Adam—that was the more difficult question. Walking awa
would definitely be the easier option, but she couldn't. Sh
didn't want to believe he was the kind of man Jake though
he was. Not the Adam who'd made love to her with so mucl
tenderness. He couldn't be that vengeful. It couldn't be true
If it was her faith in mankind was about to be shattered.

She was already caught between the devil and the dee
blue sea. Jake was like a brother to her—had been her bes
friend for years. Adam was her lover—in the truest sense o
the word she'd ever experienced or probably ever woul
again. She didn't want them at each other's throats.

To her surprise he wasn't packing. Instead he was in the library-cum-office, standing behind a desk staring out a window. His stance was rigid, defensive; sunlight streaming through the windows to illuminate his profile and highlight the blond in his hair. Yes, still beautiful to her, but the loneliness in him was heartbreaking. Was that what she'd felt earlier?

He didn't turn, but he knew she was there, the flat tone of his deep voice striking at a chord inside her. 'You shouldn't have got caught in that.'

'But I did.'

'Ask whatever you want. I'll answer. It's up to you if you choose to believe it.'

Now he was an open book? It was too much of a temptation to resist. The burning need to know everything drew her further into the room.

'Well, we've covered how you make your living, not that you need to do anything…'

'Everyone needs to do something.'

'You left the second you inherited, didn't you?'

'I wasn't that patient; I left before the paperwork was through. I took work where I could find it and thought about what I wanted to do and the kind of man I wanted to be.'

She watched as he lifted his arms and pushed his hands into his pockets. 'I never lived up to the Bryant name here so it made sense not to carry it out there. The old man helped with that decision.'

'How?'

He shrugged, 'He spent a lot of time telling me what a disappointment I was—not that he wasn't pushed. I had attitude back then. Still do some would say…'

Roane's steps faltered when she was able to see his face.

He was so calm. So detached. As if he were talking about someone else's life and none of it mattered. How could he be so cold? It suddenly hit her: *control.* He'd taught himself to exert so much control he was able to appear unfeeling on the surface. Everything he thought and felt was hidden away.

It made her long to know what lay underneath.

She silently cleared her throat and braved another step closer. 'I'm sure he didn't mean it.'

'People have a tendency to state the harsher truths in the heat of the moment.'

'You have to know he's regretted it ever since. He told you he felt he'd let you down.'

'"Every man is guilty of all the good he didn't do."' He glanced sideways at her, warily or with resignation? Roan couldn't decide which one it was as he added, 'Voltaire again.'

When he looked back out the window she stilled, waiting. Eventually he glanced sideways at her again. But he didn't say anything. Meaning he wouldn't volunteer the information unless she asked the questions. Okay. She'd known this wasn't going to be easy.

'So you took your inheritance and invested it and made buckets of money. You have a base of operations?' She remembered something he'd said. 'Do you have offices in New York?'

He looked back out the window. 'I don't have an office. The people who work for me have them. I have places I stay. An apartment in New York overlooking Central Park, another in San Francisco—a house in New Orleans; cities I like— told you that.'

Not all of it, he hadn't. Therein lay the rub as far as Roan was concerned. Why couldn't he have told her these things? Why did he have to make it so darn difficult? He'd given her small pieces of the puzzle, had never lied, but had never told

he truth either. Was he like that with everyone or just the ones
e was determined not to get emotionally involved with?

'The project you told me about in New Orleans—the one
where you made those friends you swapped bracelets with—
was that rebuilding your house after Katrina?'

'No. I donated twenty million dollars to a fund for the rebuilding of schools and low-rent communities. I work the
sites when I get a chance. The friends were from the communities we helped.'

Twenty million dollars, he made it sound as if it were nothing.
Yet he didn't flaunt his money, didn't run around with a chauf-
feur-driven limo—he could have been any guy on the street.
Okay, maybe not *any guy*…but he wasn't like any billionaire
Roane had ever met. The Vineyard had its share of them…

Adam took a breath and turned, sitting down on the edge
of the window seat and lifting his chin to study her with
hooded eyes. 'Next question.'

Roane's breath hitched. 'Don't you dare take that
attitude with me.'

'What attitude? You sent Jake scurrying off so you could
ask questions, so ask them.' Infuriatingly he smiled the lazy
smile that had always sent her pulse skipping. 'You wanted
to know plenty this afternoon—now's your big chance. The
secret's out now.'

A realization hit her so hard she almost rocked back on her
feet with the force of it. 'You didn't trust me not to tell Jake.
You thought I'd pick a side. That's why you wouldn't tell me
anything this afternoon.'

'If that's your opinion of me again—' his eyes narrowed
dangerously '—I think we're done here. I'm obviously
exactly the kind of guy who would spend years plotting his
revenge on his family and who'd bring down his brother just

to prove he's the better man. I should really have dressed i
black from head to toe for the full effect, shouldn't I?'

Pushing to his feet, he removed his hands from his pocke
and stepped around the huge oak desk. 'Of course seducin
you was obviously part of my great plan to wreak havoc too–
just like Jake said. I'm one helluva guy, aren't I?'

But the man he'd described wasn't the man who'd mad
love to her. She knew him. As if by stripping away layers o
clothing he'd bared more than his glorious body to her. A ma
that driven on destruction could never have touched her hea
the way he had. If he thought he was scaring her away, the
he could just think again.

She folded her arms and took a deep breath as he reache
the door. 'Are you done?'

For a second she thought he would keep walking—it wa
what he'd done for most of his life, after all—but after
moment he turned, leaning his shoulder nonchalantly agains
the door jamb. 'More, is there?'

'Tell me why you did it.'

'Plotted against my family, planned Jake's demise o
seduced you? I might need you to narrow it down for me.'

Instinctively Roane knew the only way she was going t
snap him out of the control he was exerting was to goad hir
into anger. It was a risky move; she'd seen him downstairs an
he had one heck of a temper. When he'd seen her on the floor–

He'd been mad as hell she was on the floor. He had bee
concerned she might be hurt, yes, but it was more than tha
She felt a smile blossoming inside her as a flicker of hop
sparked to life. But smiling wouldn't help her cause so sh
damped it down and lifted her chin, 'Throw many of thes
pity parties, do we?'

There was a flash of green in his eyes. It was all the proo

he needed that she was on the right track. His eyes would change colour: emerald-green flashing in the brown when he was angry, brown softening the green to a mossy tone when he was turned on, brown clouding the green out altogether when he was laughing...Roane knew so many of the meanings, *already*.

Right now she was rattling the tiger's cage.

'Get to the point, sweetheart. I have a bag to pack.'

She nodded. 'Yes, 'cause that's what you do best, isn't it? You run away.'

Large hands curled into fists at his sides, fingers uncurling and stretching when he saw she'd noticed. He wasn't even prepared to show that much of a loss of his precious control, was he?

'When did goading me seem like a good idea to you?'

Roane searched the air above his head, moving her head from shoulder to shoulder while she considered her answer. 'Oh, I dunno. Maybe round about the time you started acting like an ass again. In the absence of a rudder to kick a girl has to get creative.'

There was a brief narrowing of his eyes and then he lowered his chin and stalked towards her. It wasn't all that long ago it would have jumped her heart into her throat, but she stood her ground and willed her thundering heart to stay where it was.

'Intimidating me won't work this time either. I'm a new woman. You helped with that some, but being knocked on your ass will do it too, I've discovered. Always wondered where the phrase "knock some sense into you" came from...'

He clenched his jaw, hard, stopping a couple of feet away from her. 'Maybe you should just tell me what it is you want from me.'

'I want you to stop holding back from me. Last night
thought we'd agreed we wouldn't do that.'

'In *bed*. This isn't the same thing.'

'That's a cop-out and you know it is.' She felt anger bil
lowing up inside her, frustration carrying her feet forwards
'Tell me why you did it, Adam—the real reason. Look me in
the eye and I'll know you're telling me the truth.'

The cruel smile bared his teeth. 'You think I can't look you
in the eye and lie? *Still* have a lot to learn, don't you, little
girl?'

'You won't.' She stopped a foot away, shaking inside as
she forced back the tears of frustration threatening behind her
eyes. If she got this wrong and pushed him further away from
her it was going to hurt. She just needed to find a way to reach
him. 'I know you won't.'

'How can you?' The full force of his anger roared the
words into the still room, his eyes flashing sparks of green
fire and the cords of his neck strained. 'You've known me *four
days*!'

Roane faced the storm by summoning every ounce of
strength she had in her. 'You think this makes any sense to
me? It doesn't. I know it's too fast and too soon and at least
a dozen other things that don't make any more sense than the
last. But I just know—*I feel it!* There's no way to explain
that—it's just there. If I didn't trust you I would never have
slept with you!'

When a tear slipped off the edge of her lashes she swiped
angrily at it. 'Even when I didn't like you I trusted you with
my body. Because it *felt right*. I wasn't wrong about that
Adam—I *know* I wasn't…'

Even as her voice lowered to a harsh whisper at the end
the memory of their lovemaking sent a rush of heat tingling

ver her skin. Whatever else he was, Adam was an incredible over; he'd touched her as though she were infinitely fragile, issed her until she could hardly breathe… He'd stolen a part f her in one night. So, yes, she'd been absolutely right to trust er body to him. There wasn't a single doubt in her mind.

He looked as if he was ready to hit something, but Roane ept going, her voice stronger but cracking on some of the words. 'I wasn't wrong to trust you with my body. I'm not rong about this. So look me in the eye and tell me why you id it and I'll believe you—even if it's something I end up ating you for.'

When he turned his face towards the open window she ould feel the deep-seated need for flight in him. Just by ooking where he was looking he was telling her—even if it vas subconsciously—he was ready to leave. And how much nore of an effort it would take to stay.

She silently begged him to make that effort. Because he idn't have to be alone—he had her—didn't he know that? le'd had her from the get-go.

A muscle jumped in his jaw, his impossibly thick lashes lickered as his gaze moved to random points in the room, he ursed his lips into a thin line and then finally—*finally*—he ooked her straight in the eye and the deep rumble of his voice poke the words she'd hoped to hear.

'I did it to keep it safe.'

Her lower lip trembled. 'To protect the company.'

'Yes.'

'Because you could.' She nodded. 'Not because you wanted : for yourself or because you didn't want Jake to have it.'

'Yes.'

The inner shaking had worked its way into her chest so that reathing became difficult. 'You were looking out for the family, weren't you? No matter what you say or do, it still matters to you…'

He looked back out the window.

Roane cleared her throat and blinked to clear her vision. 'If it mattered so much why didn't you come home? You were gone for twelve years.'

When he looked at her the truth sent a chill over her entire body, goose-bumps breaking out on her arms. 'Oh, my God. You did come home, didn't you?' She breathed the question. 'When?'

'I've been on the island at least once a year.' He shrugged. 'I've always liked the Vineyard…'

She stepped closer and could have wept when he stepped out of her reach. 'Why didn't you come *home*? They would never have turned you away. I think your father secretly tried to find you—maybe he did and couldn't face you, I don't know for sure. And Jake—'

Her voice broke. 'Why do you think he was so angry downstairs? He was hurting. He hero-worshipped you when he was a kid—you should have heard the way he talked about you. When you left—it felt like you'd left *him*. He didn't understand why. For a while I think he thought *he'd* done something wrong. That if he'd done something different he could have stopped you…'

Adam frowned at her, his voice rough. 'He didn't do anything wrong. I didn't leave him. I left the ring.'

'What ring?' She shook her head, her gaze dropping to the ring Adam was twisting almost absent-mindedly with a thumb curled into his palm. Her brows wavered. 'That's what the ring is? It's for Jake?'

She'd known that everything he wore had meaning. Friendship, family legacies—the things he valued…

'It's a Celtic symbol for brotherhood. I left him one in that dumb-ass tree house he got me to help build. Who the hell has a tree house at fourteen anyway?' He shook his head. '*Loser*. It was in an envelope with instructions how to find me if he ever needed me.'

Roane remembered the second he said it. She remembered the names they would toss at each other. *Jerk,* Jake would call Adam. *Loser,* Adam would reply. She'd forgotten that. At thirteen she'd thought they were both dorks. They'd spent weeks and weeks building that dumb tree house two years before Adam left. Jake had taken a crowbar to it a month after he'd finally accepted he wasn't coming back. He'd never found the message his brother had left him. He'd have told her if he had.

He'd have been so happy.

A choking sob broke free from her chest when she understood the gravity of the one clue that had been missed. Things could have been so different. 'But when he didn't come find you, you thought…'

She couldn't even finish the sentence.

Adam's brows jerked as realization set in. 'Right.'

That was all he had to say? *Right?* Then his mouth twitched as if he was about to smile. Surely he wasn't seeing it as ironic? She would have to slap him if he did. It wasn't ironic—it was incredibly sad—for both of the brothers she loved.

Before the impact of that hit her she got another word from Adam: 'Okay.'

'Right and okay? Are you *kidding me?*'

'What do you want me to say?' He frowned at her. 'I can't change history. It's just a variable I hadn't considered, that's all.'

A variable he hadn't considered? Blinking in astonishment, Roane shook her head to clear her thoughts.

'But you can build some bridges now. Tell him. I'm not saying he'll make it easy for you—you have a lot in common that way—but tell him. Stay and try.'

The words faded into the silence and Roane watched as he worked the suggestion through his mind a few times. Half his problem was that incredibly large brain of his, she decided. He over-thought things. But just when she was about to say that he looked at her with the intense heat that curled her toes—

She knew his thoughts had turned to her.

A distinct sense of impending doom hit Roane, her heart twisting painfully in anticipation of being told she'd gone too far—it was none of her business—he was leaving anyway...

They were done.

CHAPTER ELEVEN

ADAM MOVED TO the edge of the desk and sat down, his legs wide and his forearms on his thighs so that his large hands angled between his knees. Then he considered her, slowly, silently, until Roane thought she might scream if he didn't say something…

'Even if I try some bridge-building, I'll still leave. You need to understand that.'

Trying to hide the fact the words hurt like hell, Roane nodded. 'I know. You have a life.'

'I do.'

'And responsibilities.' Like the work he did in New Orleans. Roane wondered if he had any idea how impressed he was by that. Or how proud. He really was the most incredible man she'd ever met.

'Yes.'

'I know.' She said the words softly and smiled at him, almost afraid to break contact with his amazing eyes. She loved his eyes.

They narrowed a barely perceptible amount and then his silent study continued where it had left off. Only this time he took a deep breath and lifted a hand to rub his palm over his face, suddenly looking incredibly weary to her. It made her fingers itch to reach for him, to touch and to soothe and, well. .

Touching him had only ever led to the one place.

Except now there was an even greater distance between them than before—and for all her bravado and determination when it came to Adam and his family, when it came to her tentative relationship with him…

Roane was scared silly.

Then he was on his feet, pacing the room like a caged animal with frustration radiating off his large body in waves. He frowned as he looked at her. 'I told you I can't give you more than this.'

'I know you did.'

'Staying wouldn't change that. I can't give you what I don't have to give.'

Roane didn't understand what he was saying. But judging by the way he was pacing, frowning, and searching the air with a completely focused gaze, he was working his way up to something. So she willed herself to stay absolutely still and wait, while her palms went clammy and her heart beat erratically.

'You'd want more. This wasn't supposed to be anything more.'

'I know.' She did. But he was right; she would want more. She was slowly dying without it already.

Adam was flexing his long fingers in and out of fists. 'See, that's what I don't get. Why are you trying to build bridges between me and my family when you know that'll bring me back here more often? You know what'll happen if I do. You're not that dumb.'

Roane had to clear her throat when he turned and looked at her, anger and confusion clouding his eyes. 'What will happen?'

'This will happen.' His deep voice was threaded with frustration. 'Every time. Because I've only to look at you and I want you. You can't tell me some part-time affair is what you want.'

'It's not.' She wouldn't lie to him. Even if she could she wouldn't after his confession of how much he wanted her physically.

'The thing is, you can tell me to leave you be, but even if I say I will I won't stick to it; you fight me off—I'll probably want you more. I know me.'

'I'm not fighting, in case you hadn't noticed.'

'Why *aren't* you?' He leaned forwards to shout the words at her and the force of his frustration was a shocking thing to behold. Not that she thought he would do her any harm, she knew he wouldn't. It was the ferocity of his emotion, the echoing emptiness, the need in him—all mixed into one and let loose as if they'd been held inside for decades that did it.

That was what made her step closer.

To where he stood his ground and kept going. 'What you want from me I *can't give you*. I've told you that. Yet here you are—you chose to side with someone you barely know over someone you've been friends with your whole life.'

'It wasn't about picking a side.' She stopped in front of him and tilted her head back. 'It was about being where I wanted to be most. Where I knew I was needed most. You needed me to believe in you, didn't you?'

He frowned dangerously at her, pulse pounding at the base of his neck, muscle jumping in his square jaw, hooded gaze fixed on hers.

Despite the fact Roane could feel the raging storm being held inside him again, she set her palm on his chest above his thundering heart and told him in a low, firm voice, 'I believe in what's in here.'

The kiss wasn't gentle. He kissed her with desperation hard and fast—demanding her response. Heat immediately shot through her with stunning speed, every thought blown clear out of her mind.

Adam groaned and walked her back until she was trapped between him and the wall; his hands in her hair, her arms tight around his neck as she gave in to the need to give as much as she was receiving. Then one of his hands left her hair, sliding down to cup her breast. No foreplay, no teasing—and Roane's heart soared when she realized he wasn't holding back. It was all of his pent up emotions thrown into one kiss, he was raw and wild and uncontrolled—that was how much he needed her. No man had ever needed her that badly. It equalled how inconceivably much she needed him after so little time, as if she couldn't breathe without him there.

It gave her the courage to show him.

So she moved her hands under his arms, the already tense muscles of his back clenching beneath her fingers as she traced the width of his shoulders. But it wasn't enough. Moaning in frustration she tried to free his shirt from his arms, but even when he moved to help her and it was tossed to one side, it still wasn't enough.

The heat of the smooth male skin on his arms beneath her hands enflamed her—but it still wasn't enough. So she dropped her palms to his stomach and pushed him to make room as she reached for the bottom of his T-shirt.

Adam broke his lips free from hers and grasped the hem of her sweater. 'Off.'

'You too.' She let go of him long enough to tug her sweater over her head, reappearing to discover he'd done as he was told. But it was the look on his face that undid her; the rumble of his voice a low, sexual growl that sent shivers down her spine.

'You're so beautiful.'

He stared at her body with something close to reverence. Seeing how the sight of her affected him Roane had never felt so beautiful. She loved how she looked through his eyes. Any whisper of inhibition she had left fled before the sight of his naked desire. She had to see him, touch him; have him deep inside her.

'You have no idea how much I want you right now.' She let her gaze slide lovingly over the ripples of hard muscle beneath golden skin.

'Show me.'

Leaning forward she kissed her favourite place on his neck, impulsively running her tongue up the strong column of his throat. He groaned something she couldn't hear and then lifted her off her feet and held her high against the wall with one arm around her waist. Her breasts on a level with his mouth, Roane gripped his shoulders as he leaned in and suckled her through her bra, the abrasion of wet lace against her already hard nipple making her gasp out loud and writhe against him.

'Adam!'

Her already dizzy mind whirled as he spun round. Marching determinedly across the room, he lowered her to the desk. Roane didn't resist when he leaned forwards and pressed her down, didn't release her grip on his shoulders; she didn't do anything beyond murmuring words of encouragement before touching him everywhere she could reach.

His hands slid over her ribs and across her belly as he switched his attention to her other breast. So swept away was she by the glorious sense of abandon she felt that it was only when he unfastened her jeans and started to tug them away that she realized she'd lifted her legs and wrapped them around his hips. But then everything with Adam had always seemed so natural to her. Sexually there were surely no two people better matched on the face of the earth than they were.

Somehow he managed to reposition her, dragging denim and lace off as one. Better, but still not enough. She was on fire, so much so that she almost sobbed with impatience during the seconds it took for him to leave her and shed his own jeans. Filled with a violent, possessive drive she'd never felt before, she hauled him back down to her and kissed him hard. Feverish and insane with need, she wanted to bite, scratch, brand him with a visible mark if she had to so that the whole world knew he was *hers*—even if he wasn't. But for *now* he was. She would never forget him as long as she lived.

Adam didn't try to calm her down or slow the frantic pace of what was happening—if anything he seemed to welcome it. Apparently he considered it either too much trouble or too time-consuming to reach round and unhook her bra, so instead he tugged the straps down, freeing her breasts for his hungry mouth.

To Roane's ears the sounds she made as his lips and his tongue worked their magic barely sounded human, let alone as if they were coming from her; it *still wasn't enough*. Would she ever get enough of him? When she reached for him he caught her wrists and pinned them above her head with a growl of warning that reverberated through her body every-where his touched. Roane then shocked even herself by re-taliating with a nip of his shoulder, a sharp intake of breath turning into a deep groan of approval as he covered her body with the full weight of his.

When she lifted her hips and dug her heels into the small of his back he groaned again. When he rocked his pelvis against hers, his hard length sliding only inches from where

he wanted it, she moaned into his ear and arched her spine
ff the desk.

'Please.' Obeying a deep instinct that told her just how to
ntice him most, she rocked her hips up in invitation, coating
is length in her slick heat. 'Please, Adam. I need you.'

Adam lifted his head and looked down at her, flexing his
ngers around hers where their joined hands lay on the desk
ver her head. He looked so deep into her eyes she felt as if
e could see her soul, but Roane didn't try to hide from him.
Vhile joint ragged breathing filled the silence she looked back
t him, her smile trembling on her lips as she silently told him:

I love you.

Adam's brows wavered. Then he dropped his head and
levoured her mouth, made a guttural sound in the base of his
hroat, and rested his forehead on hers as the confession was
vrenched from deep inside him. 'I need you too.'

With one sudden thrust he sank deep into her, releasing her
ands to tangle one hand in her hair and wrap an arm tight
round her waist. The sudden fullness, the hard rhythm he set,
ow tight he held her—it was so overwhelming that he had her
vhimpering against his mouth as he tangled his tongue with
ers.

It was fast and furious and primal and within moments she
vas wrenching her mouth from his to throw her head back
nd cry out with the force of her release. Again and again the
vaves came, making her writhe like a wild thing against
im. She dug her nails into his back as he continued to thrust
nto her, hard and fast. He nipped, then suckled the hollow
etween her throat and her shoulder so hard she was sure he
vould leave the very brand she'd wanted to put on him, but
he didn't care. Because the fire still pounded through her
eins, her writhing was matching his thrusts, she was pushing

against the desk to get her hips higher so he could go deeper. When she honestly thought she might pass out from an excess of pleasure, Adam lifted his head, groaned loudly into her hair and his body went rigid with his own pulsing release.

The feel of it inside her sent Roane over the edge again, leaving her limp as Adam collapsed on top of her, holding his weight on one elbow while they both struggled for breath.

'I'm sorry.' He mumbled the rough words into her hair. 'I'm so sorry.'

Roane felt her throat closing over at the shuddering breath he took after he said the words. She smoothed her hands over his back in circles, turned her head to kiss his throat. 'You have nothing to be sorry for.'

'I can't give you more than this.'

Roane choked out the words she wished with all her heart weren't true. 'You can't give me something that's not there. I know that.'

His head lifted and he looked down at her with the most tortured eyes she'd ever seen. 'It's not there. It never has been.'

She was still fighting the piercing agony of being told it wasn't there when she felt it so deeply for him when a sudden thought stole her breath away and twisted her battered heart. 'You don't think you can feel love?'

His gaze shifted to her hair as he brushed a strand of it off her heated cheek. 'I don't have it in me. That's what I've been telling you. That's why I'm sorry.'

'Who told you you couldn't?'

He shot her a brief frown. 'No one told me. I know. If I had it in me I'd have felt it by now. In case you hadn't noticed from what just happened—me and emotions? We don't get on so good.'

Roane blinked up at him in stunned amazement as he continued in a low, deep rumble that made it difficult for her to
think. 'I get angry. A lot. It's better as I've got older 'cause
I'm better at controlling it now, but being back here has
reminded me of how it used to feel. Emotions are a variable—
that's the problem. I like things with patterns and rhythms.
Those I get.'

Somewhat miraculously it made complete sense to Roane.
She'd been right—he did think entirely too much. He was the
most intelligent man she'd ever known, he'd made a fortune
from the fact he could figure out stocks and shares as easily as
breathing in and out, but he hadn't a clue how to deal with
emotions.

He looked into her eyes again. 'I can't lie to you. I've been
economical with the truth the last few days but I can't lie. Not
to you. Don't ask me why.'

Roane smiled at him, not caring if how she felt showed in
her eyes. 'I know why.'

His brows lifted.

She wrapped her arms around him and lifted her chin. 'So
the only reason you're not prepared to give this a try is because
you think you're incapable of loving me, that's what you're
saying?'

'That's what I'm saying. I want you, you know that. And
I need you, God only knows how much. If I could feel more
for anyone I'd feel it for you. But I can't.'

'Do you want to leave?'

It took a moment, then she got a low, 'No.'

'Do you want to see me with someone else?' His coarse
answer made her flinch. 'That'd be a no then.'

'Damn right it would.' He frowned.

Moving a hand to frame his beautiful face, she brushed

her lips over his and asked, 'Do you want to make love wit
me every day and every night for the foreseeable future?'

The answering smile was so devilishly sexy it sent a shive
up her spine. 'Hell, yes.'

Smoothing her thumb back and forth against his cheek sh
continued smiling as she nodded. 'Me too.'

He studied her eyes for a long while. 'I'll still have to go a
some point. You're saying you'll come with me, aren't you?'

'Yes. And you'll stay with me here too, won't you?'

'Yes. It might take a while to figure that out though…'

Roane's smile grew, the world suddenly brighter than
had ever been before. 'Yes, but it's a place to start. We coul
take it from there. See what happens. Consider me your fixe
mark from the compass poem from here on in and I'll rel
on you to make me soar on terra firma…'

'Now *that* I can do…' His smile faded a little.

But when he opened his mouth she set her finger over
to stop him, her voice soft with sincerity. 'Adam, I don'
believe for a single second you're incapable of love. No on
who makes love with the passion and the tenderness you d
is incapable of love.' She tried to keep the smile on her fac
for the next part, but it wasn't easy. 'It might not be me yo
fall in love with. But I hope it is. I really do. Because…'

The words sat on the tip of her tongue, but when she sav
the silent question in his sensational eyes she knew she wasn'
going to stop them being said. No matter how soon it was o
how far they had to go before she knew if she was having he
heart broken…

She smiled tremulously. '*I* love *you*.'

Adam stared at her for what felt like for ever, then h
moved his head enough to dislodge her thumb from his lips
his voice husky. 'You don't know me well enough to love me

She lifted her shoulders, her smile becoming shy. 'My heart says it knows you enough.'

His throat convulsed as he swallowed and Roane held her breath as she waited to see if he would argue with her or try and convince her she was wrong or laugh or—

'What does it feel like?' he asked.

Tears formed in her eyes. And just like that Roane knew they were going to be okay. They had time. And for as long as he wanted her they had a chance. One day at a time. She would love him with all her heart and pray every day that one day he'd feel the same about her.

She had to.

With a deep breath made difficult by the swell of her heart, she framed his face in both hands and nodded as she told him in a firmer voice, 'I still have a lot to teach you.'

Adam laughed. She loved it when he laughed. She loved him, period. Always would. End of story. If waiting for ever meant he'd love her one day, then she'd wait for him. He was worth it. And she had a sneaking suspicion a girl only got one naked Adonis on a beach per lifetime…

'We'll teach each other.'

'We will.'

Adam scooped her off the desk. 'I'm gonna teach you about joint showers now, sweetheart…so pay attention…'

EPILOGUE

Eighteen Months Later

THERE WERE CERTAIN days in a man's life, Adam decided, tha
stuck in his mind; a special day in a long chain of events
There was a pattern to that. He should have known if he
looked hard he'd eventually find one.

The day he'd decided to go home, for example. That ha
been momentous. Life changing. More for the moment he'
got off his motorcycle dusty and sweaty and decided on
impulse to take a swim in the ocean than for the trip itsel
The first link in the chain…

Then there was the day he'd decided to make it plain she
was going to end up in his bed. Okay, her bed. But it had bee
a bed. That was all that mattered. Another link in the
chain…and he'd felt the same way she had regardless of the
lie he'd told himself about her being a distraction—it was in
evitable, was *right;* it made perfect sense when viewed with
the rest of the chain.

The first time they'd made love would stay in his memory
until the day he died. He didn't doubt that. Not just for how
amazing it had been or how perfect or how seriously hot, bu

because he'd never wanted to see her cry like that again. That was the day she'd touched him in a way no other woman ever had—or ever would. Two links in the chain in one day. They'd maybe done things a little fast according to tradition—but then Adam had always been a bit of a rebel.

The next links—there were a ton of them all in the one day. But the one that had stuck most clearly in his mind now was when she'd said she would be his fixed mark. She was. No matter how many trips he took away from home or how many flights she made or how often they went to places together—she was a fixed mark in his life. A touchstone. A sounding board. A voice of reason when he wouldn't listen to anyone else. The one woman who could turn him on with a glance and soothe his soul with a touch…

Adam couldn't remember what his life had been like without her in it. He didn't want to. She loved him. She knew him better than anyone ever had and she said she loved him more each day. Yelled at him when she was mad; yes. But she loved how they'd make up…

The next day in the chain had been one neither of them had planned but they'd been overjoyed. Okay so Roane had been nervous about it at first but Adam had been ready to shout it from the hills. It had put a seal on the sense of everything somehow being meant to be. With time Adam's opinions on fairy tales like that were becoming more relaxed. Yes, she had that much influence over him.

He couldn't have said when he fell in love with Roane. But he knew the day he recognized it for what it was. And once he understood what it was he knew it had been there for a long time. Hints of it were scattered throughout, from the night she'd found him on the beach to the day he'd watched her walk across a crowded room to him and he'd just known—

he'd looked at her and she'd been everything there was to him. He'd known he would rather die than live without her.

So there, in the middle of the crowd, he'd framed her face with his hands and looked deep into her eyes so she knew he was telling the truth. He'd said the words for the first time.

'I love you.'

Her eyes had shimmered and she'd wrapped her arms around his waist. Then she'd simply lifted her mouth to his and told him in that soft voice of hers, 'I know you do. And I love you. I'll love you for ever.'

Adam was grateful for that every single day.

'So when are we getting hitched?' he'd teased her with a completely deadpan expression not long after.

'Oh, well, that's romantic—one for the grandkids right there. I can see their little eyes shining as Grandpa says the word "hitched" and everyone goes awww.' She shivered with mock delight and crinkled her nose before lifting her chin and cocking a brow at him the way only she could. 'Try again, Romeo. And when you get it right…I'll think about it.'

So he'd taken her to bed and made her say yes—again and again and again. Somehow he had a feeling the grandkids might get a watered-down version of the story.

Jake nudged his shoulder. 'She's here.'

Adam felt his breathing change, his heart swelling in his chest as he turned and watched her walking towards him. He knew he'd never forget how beautiful she was then, how calm and serene and *certain* that giving herself to him was right. How she looked straight into his eyes and smiled the smile that made him want to sweep her off her feet and carry her away…

He'd never got round to sating them both. He doubted very much he ever would.

Sunshine glinted off the pendant at the hollow of her neck: her something old from the list—his wedding gift to her. It had been passed back and forth for over a year, every time one of them took a trip away from the other, but it was hers now—the way she'd be his in a few minutes. But then she'd always been his, hadn't she?

They even had their own quote. One that was as apt for them as the one the compass had had before: 'I carry your heart with me (I carry it in my heart).'—by E.E. Cummings. Because he did—and she did—it was that simple.

Part of it was engraved inside the rings Jake had in his pocket. Or had better have. He'd forgotten where he'd left the box twice in the last week—hence the fidgeting he'd been doing while they'd waited for her to make the walk onto the beach.

Roane's fine-boned fingers tangled firmly with Adam's as he stepped up beside him. Then she angled her head and hit him with an impish smile, her voice low. 'You know this is a private beach, right?'

'Ocean belongs to everyone, sweetheart.' He smiled back. Man, but he loved her.

She mouthed she loved him too, then leaned around him to ask, 'Got the rings, Jake?'

Adam dropped his chin and stifled a chuckle. But when there wasn't an answer he pursed his lips, jerked his brows at Roane and swung his head round to glare at his brother. 'You're kidding me, right?'

Jake held up the ring box with a grin.

'Loser,' Adam whispered.

'Jerk,' Jake whispered in reply.

Then Adam looked back at Roane and found her luminous eyes dancing at him. So he winked and squeezed her fingers.

'Ready, woman?'

'More than ready.' She turned her head and smiled th
most beautiful of smiles. 'Come on, honey. Your dad ca
hold you while we say the words.'

Adam released Roane just long enough to reach out larg
hands as two chubby arms stretched his way. 'Hello, little gir
remember me?'

That was the most memorable of his memorable days
He'd never forget the day he held their child for the firs
time. It'd been the most overwhelming thing he'd ever experi
enced. And for a man who'd once thought he was incapabl
of love, somewhat ironically he'd almost burst with hov
much of it he'd felt as he'd placed her in her mother's arm
and looked at them both.

He'd even forgiven Roane's insistence she wouldn't marr
him till she was pre-baby weight for a dress.

Yes, she'd taught him a lot, this woman of his. He planne
on spending every day of the rest of his life thanking her fo
that. He loved her with all he was. And he didn't need to knov
how or why. Roane Elliott-soon-to-be-Bryant had taught hin
that too.

'Do you, Adam, take Roane…?'

Hell, yes, he'd take her. It had been her fantasy after all
And whatever made her happy…

* * * * *

Merry Christmas

& A Happy New Year!

Thank you for a wonderful 2013...

A sneaky peek at next month...

By Request

RELIVE THE ROMANCE WITH THE BEST OF THE BEST

My wish list for next month's titles...

In stores from 20th December 2013:

❑ The Snow Bride – Jennie Lucas, Helen Brooks & Anne McAllister

❑ Bedroom Seductions – Nicola Marsh, Anne Oliver & Lucy King

3 stories in each book - only £5.99!

In stores from 3rd January 2014:

❑ Boardroom Kings – Catherine Mann, Emilie Rose & Maya Banks

❑ Playboy Bachelors – Marie Ferrarella

Available at WHSmith, Tesco, Asda, Eason, Amazon and Apple

Just can't wait?

Visit us Online

You can buy our books online a month before they hit the shops! **www.millsandboon.co.uk**

Special Offers

very month we put together collections and
nger reads written by your favourite authors.

ere are some of next month's highlights—
nd don't miss our fabulous discount online!

 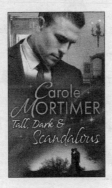 

On sale 3rd January   On sale 3rd January   On sale 20th December

Come in from the cold this Christmas with two of our favourite authors. Whether you're jetting off to Vermont with Sarah Morgan or settling down for Christmas dinner with Fiona Harper, the smiles won't stop this festive season.

Visit:
www.millsandboon.co.uk